Witnes
Wendy

By

M K Turner

This edition published 2018 by 127 Publishing

Edited by Sharon Kelly

Cover by ebook-designs.co.uk

ISBN 978-0-9927529-9-6

Acknowledgements

A brief note of thanks to everyone who helped and encouraged me in the creation of this and other stories. Sometimes I think I'll never get there, and then one or more of you will say or do something, that keeps me going.

THANK YOU!

To: My family for putting up with the distant looks and peculiar questions as I worked on the plot, and of course to my editor Sharon Kelly, proofreader Jill Buss, and my wonderful Advanced Reader Team and Beta Readers, who (in no particular order) are: John Clegg, Angela Heron, Jenny Emmet, Richard Bavin, Susan Haughton, Jan Meredith, Wendy Pace, Mag Mclachlon, Sheena Exton & Susan Pace.

By M K Turner

Meredith & Hodge Series
The Making of Meredith
Misplaced Loyalty
Ill Conceived
The Wrong Shoes
Tin Soldiers
One Secret Too Many
Mistaken Beliefs

Bearing Witness Series
Witness for Wendy
An Unexpected Gift

Others
The Cuban Conundrum
Murderous Mishaps
The Recruitment of Lucy James

~1~

She knew without a doubt she was going to die, yet still she struggled to survive. If only she could get her arms forward and loosen the tape around her wrists, she could be ready to take whatever opportunity presented itself. There had to be a chance she could catch him off guard. There was always a chance. If you were willing to take it, if you were ready to take it.

She hadn't been ready when he'd taken her. There had been a chance, but she simply wasn't ready.

Twenty Minutes Earlier

Tess, the golden retriever, had been towelled dry following their romp across the fields at the rear of the supermarket, and as the dog settled, head resting on the wheel arch, she made herself a little more presentable. Windcheater replaced with a jacket, muddy boots abandoned as she removed the waterproof trousers which had protected her jeans, and her slightly damp socks were laced into her sensible shoes.

Using the wing mirror, she rubbed a smudge of mud from her cheek. Now she was ready for a quick sprint around the supermarket. The rear windows were locked open, and the biting spring wind flowed through the car, hopefully reducing the smell of wet dog. She stooped and collected the first boot, slinging it into the footwell on the passenger side, before bending to find the second, which she had managed to kick behind the front tyre. Barely glancing at the car reversing into the next space but one, she retrieved the other boot. This corner was a favoured spot for dog walkers to park, and she hoped the dog in the red car wasn't a barker who would disturb Tess.

At that moment, at that crucial moment, all her concern was focused on Tess. Had she considered her own safety, had she been ready, perhaps things might have been different.

Her car was parked in the far corner of the carpark as usual. The best place for accessing the gap in the fence and the fields beyond, and the quietest place to leave Tess if she needed to dash into the shop. It was less likely Tess would be disturbed there.

It was a large area, and as was the norm in any supermarket carpark, sensible shoppers parked as close to the entrance as possible. Not too far to walk to return the trolley, not so likely to get soaked in an unexpected shower, and not so likely to be abducted.

Other than the red car, and a couple of dozen cars parked immediately in front of the supermarket over five hundred yards away, she was alone. Exposed. With Tess shut in the rear behind the dog guard, she was ripe for the taking - because she wasn't ready.

She missed her chance, which she would have willingly taken, when he came marching towards her. And he was marching. In total control of his body, each step, every movement considered, and he willingly took his chance.

Increasing the speed of his approach with each step, he threw his weight against the open driver's door, slamming it into her body, her head colliding with the window, her shins trapped. As he pulled the door open, she should have clambered inside, flattened her hand on the horn, filled her lungs with air and shouted for help.

But she wasn't ready.

Having slung the second boot to join the first, she pulled her bag from under the seat and was turning to exit the car. When the door hit her, she hadn't realised he'd caused the pain, she thought a gust of wind had caught it, so when he pulled the door back she believed he was helping her. She stopped cussing and forced a smile.

"That hurt! I wasn't expecting . . ."

His fist found her face in a precise, calculated movement, and she fell silent as her head snapped backwards with the force of the blow. Tess lifted her head, but settled again when the car door was slammed shut. This was what happened every few days. This was nothing out of the ordinary for Tess.

Having pulled her to the ground, he'd been quick in his actions. As she fought for consciousness she knew he'd done this before. He was practised and he was efficient. Every movement calculated and necessary. For him. He taped her ankles together, then flipped her onto her front, the gravel scraping the skin of her cheek and her exposed belly. Kneeling on the small of her back, he grabbed her hair, yanked up her face, and wound the tape around her head, covering her mouth as the first scream reached the air.

Why hadn't she screamed earlier and drawn some attention to her plight?

He punched her again, and let go of her hair, her eyebrow split as it hit the ground. Stooping, he pressed his lips against her ear, and she closed her eyes.

"Don't fight me, bitch. You can't win."

A searing pain, which pulsed from each muscle in her upper body, brought her back to her senses. He was lifting her by her arms, her body a dead weight unable to resist. Her hands had been taped behind her back, her ankles were bound together, and he was dragging her towards the red hatchback. She knew she should look for the make and model of the car. She'd watched enough episodes of Crimewatch to know it would be useful, but all she could think about was the pain.

The rear door was open, the small compartment behind the rear seat was lined with thick polythene - ready for her.

When had he opened that?

Lifting her higher, he pushed her body against his car. She screamed her agony into the sticky tape which kept her pain from filling the near-empty carpark. Almost upright now, the pain lessened, and her eyes scanned the interior of his car. She needed to remember this. If she survived, she had to give the police clues to help catch him.

She started the inventory. Black cloth upholstery, dark grey carpet, cracked knob on the gearstick, extra strong mints sticking out the ashtray, traffic light air freshener, and . . .

Her body flew forward as he shoved her in the back, and manhandled her until she was lying face down. Her body was too long for the void, so her knees were bent, and her taped ankles forced to one side. She didn't bother vocalising the pain, knowing it was pointless and she needed to conserve energy. From the corner of her eye she saw him lean into the car, his arm outstretched towards the back seat, collecting the green and black tartan picnic blanket which was to be added to her inventory. Before he covered her, he had a warning to deliver, and she flinched as his lips touched her ear.

"If you move I'll be angry. If I have to change my plans because of you, your death will be painful. Lie still, be patient and do as you're told, and everything will be just fine." He laughed. "You might even enjoy it."

Then there was darkness. Suffocating, plastic-smelling, darkness. He tucked in the edges of the picnic blanket and she thought she might die before he'd even driven away.

Doors banged shut, the engine started, and the car was on the move. She needed to breathe. The blanket was tucked so tightly around her body its plastic backing was suffocating her. He hadn't considered that. Her nostrils flared as she pulled in the foul-smelling air surrounding her. Lifting her shoulders as best she could she rocked her head back and forth, loosening the grip of the blanket. A voice reached her and she stilled, listening intently. There had been no one else in the car, was he speaking to her? A jingle for a local furniture store filled the car. He was listening to the radio. Her pulse quickened, if the bastard was that relaxed, she'd be able to take her chance, she was willing, she had to make herself ready.

With small, jerky movements, she forced her body onto its side, and the blanket moved, the top of her head was now exposed, the air was cooler, the music louder. She blinked away the droplets of sweat stinging her eyes, and tried to move her jaw. The effort was futile. The tape too thick, and her jaw too weak. She froze as the car slowed. Not now. Don't stop now, her mind shouted silently. She wasn't ready yet. Her shoulders relaxed, when seconds later, the car's speed increased. He must have slowed for traffic.

This scare brought a new awareness. She needed to see where they were, work out where they were going. No longer caring about what noise she might be making, she forced her knees along the back of the rear seat. If she did escape, she'd need to know where she was. She had to move the blanket enough to be able to see, and she had to get her hands to the front of her body. Then there would be a chance.

Now in a foetal position, with little space to move, she rocked her body back and forth as best she could. Stretching her arms as far as possible, all the while pulling her wrists apart she tried to force her hands around her backside. The effort was exhausting, and after five minutes she allowed her body to relax. The first tear escaped.

"NO!" she screamed into the tape.

Crying wasn't new to her. When she was with him, the man who should have protected her, he'd always made her cry, and when she was finally alone in the cottage, free of him, she'd done plenty of crying. She knew if she cried her nose would run and then it would get blocked, she could barely get enough air now. Crying had never done her any good in the past and now it might be fatal. Rolling back, she tried again. The tape was stretching, but not enough to allow her to free her hands or bring them to the front of her body. The blanket had moved though, and she lay still looking at grey, nondescript sky. A large signpost flew past, and she felt sick as she realised that unless she could sit, she would only see the back of any signpost. No help at all. She had to move her hands. She tried again.

The car slowed a little and she paused in her efforts and her heart soared, as buildings came into view. Only the roofs or chimneys, but they were near civilisation. Then there were trees, then the sky and a church steeple. The clock told her it was almost four o'clock. Her ordeal had lasted fewer than twenty minutes. So far. How far could you travel in twenty minutes? Her abductor grumbled at the radio, and it fell silent for a moment. She listened to him rummaging and mumbling to himself, it seemed as though he'd forgotten about her, taped up in the back of his car. Almost at the second the thought occurred to her, he called out.

"Hey, listen to this. It should have made number one!"

A male voice suddenly boomed out of the speakers making her press her knees closer to her chest. The tune was vaguely familiar, it wasn't her type of music, perhaps he had played it before she was rid of him. She listened to the opening lyrics of Meatloaf singing about *'Paradise by the Dashboard Light'*. Was he taking her to a lake? The volume increased as her eyes caught the sign directing walkers to a public footpath and bridleway. It had pointed across the road. She closed her eyes for a second. A church, a bridleway. Church on the right, bridleway to the left. Storing the information, she tried again to force the loop of her arms around to the front of her body. To her amazement, with the curl of her body being so tight, her wrists skimmed across the back pockets of her jeans. She tried to smile into the tape.

With her hands now resting on the back of her thighs she wondered how to get her feet through her arms. If her ankles hadn't been taped it would have been easy, but they were and it wasn't. She rolled onto her side as Meatloaf promised endless love to his teenage lover, and she drew up her knees until her chin rested on them . . .

~2~

"Angie . . . Angie." Ryan Clark shook his wife gently by the shoulder and bent to kiss her neck. His eyes flicked to the screen in front of her.

Angie flinched at the unexpected contact. Instinctively her hands clasped her ever-increasing bump. With a half-smile for Ryan, she contracted her pelvic muscles until baby Clark protested with a kick, or perhaps it was an elbow. Whatever it was, it was a welcome connection with her child. Her shoulders relaxed and she closed her eyes.

"What are you working on?" Ryan adjusted the screen of the laptop. "The Village doesn't usually take you away with the fairies, and that doesn't look like a script."

"Sorry, I didn't hear you," she shut the lid on her laptop and tapped it. "New idea I'm playing around with. Got a bit involved, and with you snoring and baby doing somersaults, I couldn't sleep. I didn't hear you get up. What time is it?"

"Seven-thirty. No need to rush but you should get moving if I'm driving you in today." He blew on the back of her neck.

Angie grunted and pushed herself upright. "I need to pee. Again." She stretched and smiled at him. "As you're up, and as I'm parched, I'm sure it's your turn to do the breakfast."

She laughed as Ryan turned away and groaned. He hated marmite, and he hated sardines, but it was what she'd had on toast for breakfast every day for the last two weeks. Before, it had been cheese on toast, which he liked, and now he kept coming up with suggestions of weird concoctions which wouldn't make him gag as she ate it. He'd not yet found a suitable alternative.

"I might go back up, I had a disturbed night too. How big is your bladder? You must have been back and forth five times."

"About the size of a cow's I reckon. Wait until junior arrives, then you'll know all about disturbed nights." She tousled his hair as she walked past him. "Have a coffee before you get breakfast. It might help. I'll have a bath first."

Angie started the bath running before positioning herself carefully on the loose toilet seat. From that position, she poured a healthy measure of bubble bath under the running water. As she watched the water change colour and the foam grow to hide it, she thought about her writing. Ryan had interrupted at the wrong moment, and she hoped she could get back into it quickly. The story had come from nowhere and it had been a while since that had happened. With any luck, Harry Grayson wouldn't be a diva today, and the meeting would be over by lunch-time so she could get home and get back to it.

Sinking into the bubbles, Angie closed her eyes and thought about the back of the car. Had the girl managed to escape? Had she taken a chance and been successful? Angie reminded herself to keep her notebook with her at all times. She hadn't tried to write anything, other than scripts for The Village, for too long. Looking back, it seemed odd how thrilled she'd been when she got the job with the popular soap. Regular money, and prime time TV. The world would become her oyster.

It hadn't, although, she conceded, piling foam on the bump of her pregnancy, the money was good, and when baby Clark arrived she could carry on earning from home most of the time. She blew the foam away, and an idea occurred to her. What if . . .

"This being pregnant is making you deaf." Ryan appeared in the doorway. He held out a glass of orange juice. "I've been calling you for five minutes. Are you prune-like?"

Angie inspected the tips of her fingers, "I am a little. How long have I been here?"

"Almost half an hour, I know your meeting doesn't start until ten, but we need to get a move on. Get dry, I'll make your breakfast. I've had mine, I enjoyed it without having to watch you eat yours. Do you need a hand getting out?" He grinned as he held out his hand.

Angie loved his eyes. One was a paler blue than the other, but they suited him, and drew attention away from his Grecian nose, a gift from his Cypriot mother. A simple glance from him could send shivers down her spine.

She smiled. "No, thank you very much. Although, give it another month and you may need to invest in a crane." She took his hand. "I could do without this today. It's hard enough trying to write a believable storyline with the suits demanding every new craze gets a mention, however crazy, without the ssstarsss wanting to make stuff up." She exaggerated the hissing noise. "I wouldn't mind if he could act, wait until you see his speaking to camera bit. Bloody ridiculous."

Ryan appraised his naked wife. Despite the growing pregnancy, she was stunning. Her skin flawless, her movements graceful. He wondered how her slender hips would cope with childbirth.

He grinned. "For a past pop star, I don't think he's bad. You're being too hard on him." He ducked as the towel flew across the room. Hanging it on the radiator as he left the room, he warned, "No more daydreaming. The toast is going in now."

When she came down, the table had been laid to include a pansy in an egg cup. There was only one place setting.

"You were serious, you're not eating with me?" She turned the pansy to face her. "This is sweet though."

"I'd have starved to death if I waited for you, dolly daydream, and anyway I can't eat with you until you start eating something sensible. Sorry it's not a rose. The garden was limited."

"It's the thought that counts. Do you know where the little recorder dictating thingy is? Have we unpacked it?"

"Not seen it yet. It should be in the box labelled office stuff. I can have a look, what do you want it for?"

"Well, I was going to record Harry making unreasonable, prima-donna demands, and sell it to the tabloids." She cut into the toast and Ryan turned away.

"And the real reason is, what? I'll look for it while you eat."

"I want it handy in case something occurs to me, or I have a plot query. I want to record notes so I don't forget what pops into my mind."

"Generally, or notes for The Village?"

"I don't think notes would help The Village, it's doomed now megamouth is allowed to have a say. No, it's for this new thing I'm working on."

Ryan paused in the doorway. "I'll find it, grab a shower, and you can tell me about it on the way into town."

Angie bit into her toast. How could she tell him about it, when she didn't know what *it* was? She had thought it would become a novel, but then in the bath she considered it would become a screenplay. Friday Night Thrillers loved this sort of thing; if she knew where she was going with it, she could have asked if they were keeping the series running while she was at the studio later. She needed to get more of it written, and then she'd ask Ryan for his opinion. For the moment, she'd stick with it being a novel, then he'd not want to look at it too soon.

~ ~ ~

Ryan pulled over at the bus stop outside of the BBC headquarters on Whiteladies Road in Bristol.

He placed a hand on her bump, and blew a kiss in the direction of her face. "Play nicely you two. If he is becoming as influential as you believe he is, you don't want to wind him up."

"I'll do my best. What time are you likely to be home tonight?"

"No idea. We were supposed to be filming a few staff interviews, but James messaged me this morning, head keeper says one of the orangutans is about to give birth, if she's popped it out by the time we get there, should be early evening, if she has a long labour, definitely not. James won't want to miss getting it on camera. I'll call once I get there and see how the land lies."

"Pop it out? I hope I *pop* this one out. At least it will give you some idea of what I'm in for. Although I'm . . ." She turned as a bus driver blared his horn. "Better go. Love you."

Ryan was pulling away as she slammed the door. Clasping her bump in both hands she turned to face the bus driver and mouthed 'sorry'. He gave her the thumbs up. Turning away, she smiled at how easy this acting lark was, or at least it was for most; Harry Grayson was clearly the exception that proved the rule. She shook the thought away, she was being mean and she didn't like it, the man brought out the worst in her.

Stepping into the main lobby she fixed a smile on her face as she showed her ID and signed in. Harry Grayson appeared from nowhere. Both his skin and his hair were a deeper shade of brown today, it was spring, and nowhere in the script did his character use a sunbed. She bit her tongue and wondered if it would be mentioned by one of the others.

"You look happy today, Angie. Nice to see you smiling for a change." He gave the receptionist a conspiratorial wink and a flash of his perfect smile which lit up what some would consider a perfect face, and she grinned at him. He turned his attention back to Angie. "What did you think of my proposal?"

Attempting to keep her voice light, she walked towards the lifts. "I don't know enough to form an opinion. When Alan suggested we meet, all he said was that it was something about a talent competition." This wasn't strictly true, he'd been fairly descriptive, probably to temper her response to the proposal when delivered by Grayson. She pushed the button. "We'll have to talk it through, I know we have some talented singers in the cast, but we have to ask ourselves what the point would be? What would it bring to The Village, which as you know is supposed to be about real people dealing with real issues. I don't think many *real* people hold little talent shows on the high street, do they?" She stepped into the lift, her smile bright. "That said, Natalie has a fabulous voice, perhaps we could do something with her and Britain's Got Talent, or the other one Cowell is involved in. He loves the limelight, and a cameo role in a soap may be attractive to him. We're on three, aren't we?"

It was Harry's turn to force a smile, and he gave a curt nod in answer to her question. He'd known the bitch was going to be awkward, but he wasn't going to give her the satisfaction of an argument. Not yet. He needed Alan to back him up.

Harry all but pushed Angie out of the way to get to the meeting room ahead of her. Pushing open the door, he strode in, and with his shoulders back, and his arm outstretched, he greeted Alan Ferris, the producer, with a confidence he didn't feel.

Alan Ferris was a good-looking man. His soft brown eyes, framed by long blonde lashes, seemed to twinkle when he smiled, and despite being a tall, well-built man, there was always a hesitancy when he needed to assert himself. It was almost as though he doubted his own words. This morning he looked worried, despite his wide smile.

"Alan. Thanks for calling a meeting, it will be good to talk things through, although I'm sure Angie would have chosen to do this via email, or perhaps a conference call." He turned to smile at Angie, "You must be feeling tired now, what with the baby about to come." He pulled out the nearest chair. "Here, rest your wearies."

Angie ignored the chair and walked to a table holding a selection of drinks where she selected a fruity teabag. "I'm not weary, it's only nine-thirty in the morning, and the baby is not due for almost three months. I am pregnant, not ill. My brain and body are functioning perfectly normally."

Dropping the teabag into a mug, she turned to smile at him. "But thanks for the thought, I don't know what type of women you're used to, but I come from sturdy stock." She turned back to her tea. "Can I get either of you anything? Who else is coming?"

Alan Ferris pointed to a bottle of water on the conference table, "Got one thanks, Colin is on his way, and Karen's here somewhere. That's the lot until we know where we're going with this."

Harry was on the way to the fridge to collect his own water. "What's it got to do with Karen?" he demanded.

Angie's head snapped towards him. "You're serious, aren't you?"

"Of course. I know she's Colin's favourite, but this storyline wouldn't affect her. I don't see the point in her being here." He looked at the producer. "Help me out here, Alan."

Alan lifted his hand to halt Angie's response. He resisted the urge to close his eyes and sigh. "Let's discuss it when everyone is here, but for the record, Harry, Karen started life in The Village as a scriptwriter. She co-wrote the first six episodes, and when they were let down at the last minute, she had to step into the role of Fran. The Village was then written around Fran's character, and they didn't have time to find another actress who would have to learn her lines, etcetera, etcetera. They were on a limited budget in those days, the show stopped for no one. Since then she has been involved in the writing as and when needed."

"That was twenty-odd years ago. History. Totally irrelevant, and it's not all about Fran now, is it? How —"

"Let down?" Angie exclaimed. "For the record," she plonked her bag on the table and pulled out a chair, "when Alan says let down, he means the key actress disappeared. No note, no anything, never seen again." She clicked her fingers like a magician completing an illusion. "Gone. Karen told me about it when . . ." She stopped speaking and stared at the drink in her hand.

That was where her latest idea had come from. The unusual circumstances in which Wendy Knight had disappeared. She closed her eyes and tried to remember the conversation with Karen. It had been weeks ago, but Karen hadn't given much detail, there was none to give. Although she did mention that Wendy's car was found in a supermarket carpark. Had she mentioned a dog?

Angie looked up as someone called her name. Alan was standing next to her, and Harry Grayson was smirking at her from across the table.

She looked at Alan. "What? Why are you looking at me?"

"You're flushed. You stopped speaking midway through a sentence my lovely. Are you feeling all right?"

"I'm fine, I was . . ."

"Are you sure you don't want to go home?" Harry was still smirking. "I'm sure the rest of us will manage without you."

"I'm bloody fine, okay!" Angie's eyes dared him to continue smirking. "I'm pregnant not ill. *They* could manage without me, but you, you need reining in. Big time. A great storyline came to me, and I was processing it, and guess what? No room for egos, and absolutely no bloody talent contests." She looked at the door as it opened. "At last, someone who doesn't see me as an invalid. Karen, how are you? Come in, quickly."

Harry's smirk had gone, his stare was cold. "Pre-judged before you even got here. I thought you didn't have the detail? Liar!"

Alan took a step closer to the table and rapped it with his knuckles. "Let's not have a to-do, children. We're all grownups here." He sought Harry's eyes and gave a silencing stare.

"What fun. What have I missed?" Karen Ellery looked around the table. "Have I interrupted a lover's tiff?" Winking, she bent and kissed Angie's cheek.

Angie noticed that Karen looked tired. Dark shadows underneath her eyes had accentuated her laughter lines, and her curly hair seemed to have lost its normal bounce. Angie guessed Karen was aged somewhere between forty-five and fifty, but she looked much older today. She looked back at Harry as he snorted.

"I wouldn't poke her with a stick." It was a lie. Angie was a good-looking girl, he was particularly taken with the light sprinkling of freckles across her nose, if she wasn't pregnant he might have tried harder. But she was pregnant, and she was a pain in the arse, always arguing with him when he suggested a change to the script. He was determined to put her in her place.

"I heard you poked anything with a pulse," Angie retorted, and realising she was being drawn in to something unsavoury, added, "but that's tabloid gossip for you. I'm sorry, I lost concentration, where were . . ." She smiled as the door opened. "Colin. Come in and let's get going."

Colin Anderson smoothed flat the few wisps of pure white hair he had left on the top of his head, before running his fingers across the top of each ear until they met at the nape of his neck. A useless exercise as he kept the rest of his hair short. He looked around the room. He was fast approaching his sixtieth birthday and he was tired. Tired of The Village, tired of the people he had to be civil to on a daily basis, tired of pretending to be interested in things which bored him rigid, tired of not living the life he wanted. It was almost laughable when he remembered how hard he'd fought to keep his place on The Village, but having been the key director for more than twenty years, he'd had enough.

His financial advisor had told him to string it out for another few years, something to do with pension premiums, but he didn't have the stomach for it. He was ready to go. This new girl Angie would look after Karen. He wanted to sell up, buy a little villa in the sun somewhere picturesque, drink red wine, and read books. He wanted some peace.

Colin wasn't stupid, he knew at the first sign of ill health he'd panic and come back to the grey miserable winters which lasted six months, just to be sure he could access decent affordable healthcare. That was if the current lot didn't break the NHS, and it still existed. He'd promised Karen he'd stick around until Christmas, but he wasn't convinced he'd keep his promise if they were going to have a drama off set every five minutes.

"What's happened now?" He looked at Alan. He liked Alan, he'd not yet tired of him, and he wondered how long that would last. Alan had joined the show four years earlier. Alan understood what the show should be, he'd been watching it since the first episode, and he'd been clever enough to recruit Angie, who was also trying to get back to the real Village. It was those idiots upstairs, who wanted to jump on the latest fad bandwagon each time the *Sun* changed its headlines, who peeved him. Like the idiot grinning at him from across the table. Crap actor, but a big celeb who made headlines. True, his arrival had boosted the ratings for a few weeks, but Colin guessed even Grayson's aging fans couldn't stomach more of his erratic arm movements. Alan though, poor old ever hopeful Alan, had a soft spot for the man. He certainly needed some luck, Colin hadn't known him have a partner since he joined the show. But Harry wasn't the man. As if on cue, Alan flapped his hand.

"Misunderstanding. Come on in, Colin, sit yourself down, there's lots to talk about."

As everyone settled themselves at the table, Angie frowned. "Am I the only scriptwriter here? Where are the other two?" she looked at Karen, "Are you writing this one too?"

"Not invited." Alan crossed his arms and leaned forward. "This is a need to know storyline. It will blow the other soaps out of the water. Karen is here only for her thoughts on how to best make this work."

Angie glanced at Harry, who was grinning. "This is your idea?"

"It is. Even you'll like it."

"Really? Let's hear it then." Angie leaned back in the chair and rested her arms across her bump, telling herself to bite her tongue even if it were the most ridiculous plot line ever.

"Not yet, not yet." Alan grabbed Harry's arm to stop him speaking.

Colin cocked his head. He'd been right. The grasp had lasted a little too long. Alan was smitten. He watched the look of horror flit across Harry's face and stifled a groan. On top of everything else he had to put up with, there was going to be unrequited love on the set. He'd seen Grayson with his hand up the skirt of the latest runner. Grayson wasn't interested in Alan, he was leading him on.

Colin wanted to go home, he glanced at the time. "Why wait? I understand you want it to be hush hush, but you have the director, the producer, key scriptwriter, lead actress . . ." He looked Harry in the eye. "And the latest celeb to grace our cast. What exactly are we waiting for?"

"I need you to sign one of these." Alan pulled a pile of documents closer, and handed three out.

Colin skimmed it quickly. "But the whole production team have already signed a confidentiality agreement." He lifted the document and waved it at Alan. "Why?"

"Several reasons, it's a belt and's braces measure. A reminder if you will."

"No, I bloody won't!" Karen slid her form back towards Alan. "Not without a good reason. Are we suddenly less than trustworthy? What next, blindfold the cameramen?"

"Of course not. To be honest, I don't know what your problem is, Karen," Alan said, a slight edge to his voice. He'd told Harry it wouldn't go down well, but the bloody man wouldn't listen. He glanced at him over his glasses, before turning to Angie. "Angie, I take it you have no problem with it?"

Angie had now read the document twice. "I'll sign anything you want me to. My lips are always sealed, it's those seeking the limelight we have to worry about, those who would benefit most from having their faces in the newspapers." She managed to resist a glance at Harry. "However, what losses are we talking about? This is the BBC, there are no advertisers to placate if it all goes tits up." Tapping the document, she looked at Karen. "Has this ever happened before, with, or without an explanation."

"It has not." Karen drummed her fingers, tilted her chin and stared at Alan. "What now? We won't sign because we don't know why we're being asked to, and you won't tell us what the hell we were called in for. It is tedious, I have things to do, I'm on set first thing tomorrow, this was my first day off in two weeks. So many retakes." She didn't need to look at Harry, everyone knew who was eating up the time.

"Hang on a minute." Angie snatched up the document, her eyes searching for the appropriate line. "Here we go, blah, blah, blah, *agrees to take personal responsibility for any perceived losses caused.* What does that mean?" She looked Harry straight in the eye. "What do you *perceive* you might lose?"

Harry's already tanned cheeks coloured. He opened his mouth, but Alan spoke first.

"If this gets out, so it doesn't have the impact we'd like it to, then it may affect ongoing, or indeed any contracts which come up for renewal, therefore . . ."

Colin had put his hand over his face and laughed into it. Angie and Karen exchanged glances as Alan bristled. Colin allowed his hand to drop, it thumped the table causing Angie's cup to rattle in its saucer.

"I've been directing The Village for more years than I care to remember, some might say too long, me included. But never in the history of guest appearances, celebrity casting, and the odd regular getting too big for their boots, have I come across an ego so enormous." He looked from Angie to Karen. "Ladies, do you give your word, irrespective of the outcome of this meeting, whether we run with it or dash it into the nearest bin, you won't discuss it with anyone outside this room, even your nearest and dearest?"

"Of course, can we get on with it?" Karen glanced at her watch and tutted. "You have me for one more hour, unless it gets interesting of course."

Angie agreed, and Colin linked his fingers behind his head and settled back in his chair.

"The nays have it. No one will sign, and no one will speak of it outside this room. Can we proceed?"

Harry Grayson's lips were now a thin line. He didn't speak, he wasn't sure if he could remain civil. His head bobbed agreement, and Alan flipped open his note pad, and spoke without looking up.

"We can fill in the detail later, but this is the rough outline." Alan tapped his pad. "The Village has something to celebrate, a centenary of something or other, and decide to hold a show in the hall." He flipped his hand back and forth. "There's some toing and froing as to what, and a talent contest is agreed. Annie Barnes will have a cousin who is a music producer and agrees to be the judge, along with some others, the vicar, possibly the head teacher, but here's the thing - someone wants to kill Kelvin,"

Kelvin was the character played by Harry. Alan ignored the movement around him as the others looked at Harry.

"What we need to decide is whether he finds out about it, you know, shall we have some threats before the event etcetera, etcetera, or shall we only see the plotting and Kelvin remains oblivious?

Anyway, it all goes wrong. There will be a struggle, there will be a shot, there will be blood, but it won't be Kelvin who dies." Alan looked over his glasses and grinned. "He'll be injured, but the show will—"

"Go on!" Angie finished the sentence, "And Kelvin will win, and be a hero, I can bet who gets killed." She shook her head. "Jealousy is a terrible affliction."

Alan clapped his hands together, he knew full well what she meant, but tried to deflect it. "Exactly. It will all be about jealousy. You are quick, Angie."

Karen rolled her eyes. "She wasn't talking about the plot. But that aside, what is the cause of this jealousy?"

"We were thinking Kelvin's talent would do it, but as I pointed out to Harry, it's not enough to kill someone, especially as we haven't had any history of animosity, if anything we've had the opposite."

"Too right." Angie tutted. "Think about it, Alan. What does it take to hate someone enough to kill them?" She held out her hand and started counting the reasons on her fingers. "Crime of passion, blackmail of some sort, hatred for whatever reason. We have had none of those things, not even a hint. Are we going to write something in and plan this as a winter storyline? Because if that's what you're suggesting, we won't need to have an unnecessary talent contest."

She looked around the table. "Am I wrong? And the other thing that is simply not right, is killing off Natalie's character. Natalie is popular with our audience across the board. She's brought so many new viewers, it would be folly." A frown creased her brow. "Unless of course Natalie wants to leave. Does she?"

"How did you know it was Natalie?" Alan sighed inwardly, he knew this wasn't going to go well, he was going to have to drum up some patience from somewhere. "Do you think it should be someone else?"

Angie looked at Harry. "I believe there are better candidates, if we agree The Village needs another murder. It was only last month that we bumped off the post mistress."

"Which is why it will hook the viewers." Harry's tone implied she was missing the point. "They will be on the edge of their seats. They won't want to miss an episode."

"True," Colin agreed. "But Angie is right. We don't want to lose Natalie. She's everyone's favourite. The girl next door, sweet, intelligent, hardworking . . . do you know, we should have something horrible happen to her. We'd be pushing our luck with another rape, it would seem desperate. But perhaps an unwanted pregnancy - she'd have to lose it of course, or maybe an accident. What about putting her in a wheelchair for a couple of months? We could use the disability angle to show how difficult life is, and what a fight it is to get help."

His mind was racing with the possibilities. "In fact, if we do run with the talent show thing, she wouldn't be able to go on stage in a wheelchair. Not without it being carried, so she'd have to sing in her chair, in the audience." He inclined his head. "That would work."

"And, I suppose, win with the sympathy vote." Harry didn't even attempt to hide his anger. "Where does that leave me? I was offered this role and accepted it on the basis I'd have a key storyline throughout the first year."

Angie's lips twitched. "You could try and kill her. That way you get someone plotting a murder around a talent show, but we don't lose Natalie."

Harry's shoulders relaxed. "Yes, it's possible. Although I'm not sure Kelvin would be jealous of Natalie. He's not the type."

"Oh, I think he is." Karen interjected. "I think the arrogance you give him, would allow for that."

"You could be on to something." Alan wanted to laugh. He'd warned Harry, but now the bugger could squirm for a while. "It would, of course, mean we lose Kelvin, but as you say, the viewers would be on the edge of their seats."

"Why would you lose Kelvin?" Harry had raised his voice. Panic was setting in. If they wouldn't sign the bloody agreement, he needed to keep working. He was drowning in debt and had intended to leak the plot himself so he could sell a few stories and bring in some extra cash, not work himself out of a job. "That would be stupid, I'm as much a draw as Natalie. We'll have to have someone else try and bump her off, or Kelvin. He could thwart the plan."

Angie doubted that he could pull it off. "Who and why?"

"I don't know! I did my bit, you didn't like it, you lot are the writers," he made speech marks with his fingers, "write something that works. What would make any of you kill someone?" He looked around the table. "Let's see what would push us over the edge." He turned to Alan. "Alan, what about you."

"I haven't got it in me. It would have to be me or them." Alan shuddered, "But that would be self-defence not murder."

"Colin?" Harry looked at his director. "What would be the reason you wanted to bump someone off?"

Colin closed his eyes and rubbed his temples with his fingers. "Because I could." His stare was menacing before he grinned. "And I could cheerfully kill all of you at this moment." He pushed his chair out. "This was a meeting about nothing which couldn't be handled in the normal way. Unless anyone has anything pertinent to say I'm off." He waited a beat. "I thought so. I'll see you the day after tomorrow as scheduled. I'll give a murder some consideration, but as Harry pointed out, it's best left to the scriptwriters." He lifted his hand in salute. "Bye for now."

Karen waited for the door to close. "He's pissed off, and quite frankly I don't blame him." She got to her feet. "I'll see you tomorrow on set." She looked at Alan, opened her mouth, but decided not to speak her mind and shut it again. Standing she walked towards the door. With her hand on the door handle, she turned and added, "We all need to go away and think about not letting our feelings get in the way of what's best for the show. After all, it is what pays the wages."

Angie was on her feet and frowned, wondering if that was aimed at her. She knew she wasn't alone in her feelings about Harry, but it did make her wonder if she would have reacted in the same way if anyone else had made a similar suggestion. She called goodbye and thanked Karen who had held the door for her.

"Alan has blinkers on. I think Harry is leading him on." Karen spoke quietly as they waited for the lift. "Silly man. If nothing else, Harry is undoubtedly straight. I might have a word with Alan if the opportunity arises."

"Ah, so that comment wasn't directed at me then? Unfortunately, I find it difficult to mask my dislike of Harry." Angie pushed the button again. "This is taking a long time."

"My dear girl, if it were you I would have said so. Ah, here we go." Karen stepped back to allow a couple of passengers out of the lift. "Homeward bound."

"I might go shopping actually, I've got a few bits I need to pick up, and I've started writing . . . Oh, I meant to ask . . ." Angie paused as the lift stopped and four suited men squashed in with them.

The doors opened to the ground floor and they followed the men into the foyer.

Angie turned to Karen. "I've started writing something this morning, it came to me from nowhere, or so I thought, but I think it was because—"

"He must have run down the stairs. Oh Lord, he's coming this way." Karen interrupted, and Angie turned to look.

"Angie, a word if I may." Harry's shoes slapped the tiled floor as he hurried over to them.

"I can't do this. Call me." Karen blew a kiss in Angie's direction and hurried towards the exit.

"I wanted to speak to you about Wendy Knight, I have some questions." Angie called and Karen paused.

"Ah, with Wendy there are always more questions than answers. Even though I didn't know her that long. Call me." Harry stepped up behind Angie, and Karen waved her hand. "Got to go, Harry. Bye"

Harry waited until she was out of earshot. He placed his hand on Angie's elbow. "Let me buy you coffee. That didn't go well, Alan didn't explain it as well as he could have."

"Harry, can I be honest with you?" Angie saw his shoulders stiffen.

"Of course." he said. But his eyes asked what now?

"I know it must be hard for you getting settled in this new career, but just relax into the role and you will become the star. Forcing certain things will only make life more difficult. Trust the writers to do the best for the show, and it will be the best for you, you'll find it all becomes a lot easier."

She looked into his eyes, her smile genuine. There, she'd done it. She'd offered an olive branch in the interest of on set harmony. Her smile was short lived as his finger was jabbed towards her.

"You arrogant bitch," he snarled. "Who are you? My mother? I'm sorry you are jealous of me, I have no idea why. Is it because I didn't pay you enough attention when I arrived? It wasn't intentional, but I'm not going to suffer because your ego is hurt. I won't have you making life difficult because you are miffed."

Angie slapped his finger away and stepped closer so she didn't have to raise her voice. "You are older than me, Harry, and if I were your mother, I might have taught you a little common sense. You aren't a natural actor, you need to work on it, and I'm afraid no hope for a BAFTA, however good the storyline. As to wanting attention from you? Behave! I think Natalie's refusal was on behalf of all the women working on this production, and by the way, you are old enough to be her father. Come to that you're old enough to be my father, so she could call you grandad! Don't try and kill her off because you didn't get your leg over. And while on the sub—"

Harry grabbed her wrist and yanked her forward. "Don't mess with me, Angie. Others have tried and failed."

His nose was almost touching her cheek, to an onlooker they looked as though they were being intimate. She flinched when his lips touched her ear.

"Be careful, Angie. I can be dangerous. You worry about the baby, I'll worry about me."

Pulling her wrist from his grasp, and pushing his chest away with her other hand, she took several steps away from him.

There was so much she should have said, but her brain failed her, and to her mind, her response was pitiful. She sounded like a schoolgirl. "Fuck off, Harry. You are picking on the wrong girl."

Angie could hear him laughing as she walked towards the exit. It sent a chill down her spine. Once outside she hurried to the taxi rank, she was going to go home and she was going to write. She knew she wrote better when she was angry or worried, the shopping could wait until another day.

The taxi driver turned to look as she pulled open the rear door. "Good morning, love. Where are we going?" he leaned closer. "Are you okay? You look a bit flushed, tell me we're not on a dash to the hospital."

"I'm fine, thank you. Hallen Road, please. On the left before you get to Dog Lane."

"No problem, have . . . excuse me, I'd better speak to her."

The driver slid the hatch closed and answered a call from his dispatcher. Angie settled back against the seat. She'd call Karen later, it would be interesting to find out more about Wendy, her subconscious clearly found her interesting. At least she had a name for her character now, she could always change it later if necessary. *She* would now become Wendy.

Angie glanced at her watch, she'd be able to get back to work on the story with no interruptions for the rest of the day. She was itching to write about the two characters who had flown from her fingers, hoping they would reveal more about themselves as soon as she hit the keyboard. It always worked that way when Angie wrote, a nub of an idea, sit at the laptop and let the rest come. No plotting, no outlines, just words. Sometimes it was easy, and little cutting and chopping was needed, and sometimes she wanted to smash her laptop in frustration when she knew the words weren't good enough, but she still had the story, it just needed polishing. Right now, she had to know Wendy, polished or not.

The driver interrupted her musings. "I'm going to go along The Portway, love. We'll avoid the road works on the Downs that way."

Angie nodded at his eyes in the rear-view mirror. The road works hadn't caused any problems earlier, but she couldn't be bothered to discuss it, she wanted to return to her thoughts. She rested her head back against the seat and stared at the stained roof of the taxi. Would her Wendy have a family or a husband? She felt a pang of guilt as she didn't know if the real Wendy had been married or had children. Why had she not cared enough to ask? How awful. She patted her bump, married or not, Wendy would have had family of some sort, and they would have cared.

~3~

Edward Knight smiled at Wendy before looking at the guests who had gathered in the lobby hoping to celebrate his only daughter's wedding. She held her chin high and gave his hand a squeeze, and he wished he was young enough to take the little shit on.

"Bad news I'm afraid. The groom hasn't turned up, can't get him on the phone, and his mum's none the wiser, either." He wanted to turn his head to look at the bastard's mother. It was all right snivelling into her handkerchief, but it was he who had to stand and face them. "The registrar is aware of the situation, and is happy to slot them in for three-thirty . . . assuming he's been delayed," It was clear to the guests he didn't believe that to be true. "So we have an hour and a half to waste. I'd . . ."

He paused as Wendy took his hand, and standing on tiptoe, whispered into his ear. He pecked her forehead. "Good girl." He looked back at the guests. "My beautiful daughter suggests we make our way across the road to the hotel. The food will be ready to be served about now, and there's no point in letting it go to waste." His smile was unconvincing.

A murmur of surprise rippled around the guests. How could they do that? How could they go and stuff their faces when poor Wendy's life had imploded? Wendy watched their neighbour shake her head and dab away a tear, and an anger took hold. She'd not been expecting this, she wasn't ready to deal with the sympathy, but she was damn sure she wouldn't crumble. Not now, not yet.

Squeezing her father's hand, she took a little step forward. "Please come to the hotel. I don't know why he's not here, but the world has not ended, and I don't know about you lot, but I need a drink. It will help me knowing that all the money didn't go to waste." She attempted a joke. "But let me ask if they will give me a refund first."

A few of the guests smiled.

Her uncle, Tom, stepped forward and held his hand towards the door. "If our Wendy wants to get drunk, then the least we can do is join her. They charged a bloody fortune for the food, so we should try and make a dent in it, and what we don't eat we'll take to the homeless shelter around the corner, and some good will come of today." He threw Wendy a smile. With one hand still held towards the exit, he waved the other back and forth. "Come on, move it. Give the girl a moment."

Wendy's nails dug deep into her palm as she watched the guests snake out onto the terrace, and head for the hotel across the road. She was glad she'd opted for the registry office, it would have been awful for her father if he'd had to walk up and down the aisle to find out what was happening. The best man approached, and she felt her father stiffen.

"It's not his fault, Dad. Stay calm." She whispered as she nodded a greeting, a smile was impossible.

"Wendy, I'm so sorry, I . . . that is . . . Shit, Wend, I don't know what to say. He was fine last night, in fact, he went home early. Left us lot at eleven. When he wasn't at his flat, I thought he'd come straight here. I thought I'd messed up." He put his hand in his pockets, and shrugged, his fingers clasping the box holding the wedding band. "If I find him I'll have him back here by three-thirty." He looked at her father. "I'll call you at the hotel if I hear anything, Mr Knight."

They stood in silence and watched him leave, taking the opposite direction to the other guests, as he headed towards the carpark. Mr Knight sniffed and pulled his hand from hers, flexing his fingers to help the blood flow. He pulled her into his arms and rested his chin on her head.

"You don't have to do this you know. They're gone now, we can just slip away." He felt the first sob jerk her body. "I know," he whispered. But he didn't. How could he? Edward Knight had proposed, got married, had Wendy, and lived a normal happy life. His wife had died too young, breast cancer had taken her when Wendy was only fourteen, but he'd never been let down by someone he loved, not like this. Murderous thoughts entered his head again. "If he's not unconscious in a hospital somewhere, I'm going—"

"Dad, don't say that." Wendy's tear-streaked face pulled away from his chest and she looked at him. "Don't. It would be better if he'd just changed his mind than know something awful has happened to him."

"And that's why I love you. You are beautiful inside and out. My beautiful girl." Edward blinked back his own tears. "Am I taking you home? We'll chuck some things into a suitcase and head for Cornwall. You've always loved Cornwall, then we'll sort out everything else once we're back. Let's take a couple of days to catch our breath."

"No. Not yet. I meant it when I said I needed a drink. Although I won't join Uncle Tom in getting drunk." She ran her fingertips along her bottom eyelid. "Am I smudged?"

Pulling a handkerchief from his pocket, her father sucked one corner, then gently wiped away the smudges. He handed it to her. "Blow your nose."

By the time they arrived at the hotel, the staff had been told the wedding hadn't taken place, and the waitress, holding a tray of drinks and standing in the doorway of the banqueting room, watched Wendy's off-white, lace dress approach, unable to look her in the face. Wendy took a champagne flute and thanked her. The waitress's chin trembled. She wanted to tell Wendy how beautiful she looked, and how the bloke who had jilted her was a scumbag, but she couldn't, she was a crier. She'd have cried because she was happy for them, and now she might cry because she felt sorry for them. So she didn't speak but blinked furiously as Wendy walked away.

Uncle Tom hurried over with a brandy bowl in each hand, the brandy sloshing back and forth. He held out his arms presenting them. "This is what's needed, you can have a girlie drink later."

Wendy now stood with a drink in each hand, she sipped the brandy as she looked over her uncle's shoulder. It seemed like the whole room was looking at her. A few waved, a few looked away, and most just looked sad. She didn't want their sympathy, not yet anyway. She emptied the champagne into the brandy and knocked it back.

"I'm on cocktails, Uncle Tom. Another please."

"That's my girl. Fuck the lot of them." Uncle Tom rolled his eyes at his brother, "Don't look at me like that, Ed, she's heard swearing before." He looked at the glass in his brother's hand. "Knock it back, being sober won't help today end any quicker." He watched his brother obey, before taking back their empty glasses. "My round. You grab the champers, I'll get the brandy."

An hour and several drinks later, Wendy got to her feet. It was three-fifty. He wasn't going to show. The best man hadn't reappeared either, but why would he?

She pointed at her father. "Now you may escort me home. I need to cry and here is not the place." She swallowed back the bile threatening to spew forth. "Uncle Tom, you have been wonderful, but I now task you with feeding the homeless and trying to return the gifts to the right people."

Her uncle heaved himself to his feet. "Done and done. Come here." He pulled her into a hug. "Don't cry too long. He's not worth it."

"Let me go, you're making it happen too soon." Wendy pushed him away. "Thanks though." She took her father's arm. "Come on, Dad, no goodbyes. Let's go." She patted her uncle's rotund stomach. "Let me make a clean escape. Head them off at the pass if they try and follow." She gave a quick glance around the guests, most of whom had stopped staring, and taking her father's hand, made for the exit.

Her father held the heavy door open for her, and she drew in the fresh air. Her resolve not to cry almost failed as she watched another bride and groom being positioned for photographs outside of the registry office. Her tears were halted only by the angry eyes now fixed on her own, as he made his way around the edge of the wedding party. Her father hadn't seen him, and was surprised when she barked at him to stay where he was, and lifted her skirt to hurry down the steps. The ferocity of his anger shocked her.

"Why didn't you wait?" His fingers dug into the top of her arm as he grabbed her roughly. "You should have waited! You've made me look a right fool."

"I made you look . . . Where the hell were you?" Wendy tried to shake her arm free, but his grip tightened and she winced at the pain. "You're hurting me."

"No more than you deserve. I was expecting to get married, not have some snivelling clerk offer her apologies. Come on." He pulled her a few steps along the street.

"To get married? Now?" Wendy managed to free her arm, and looking at the angry red marks his fingers had left there, she massaged it.

"Home. Don't be awkward, Wendy, I'm only just keeping my temper."

"That's not home. We haven't had the wedding. I've done nothing wrong. I was here at twelve-thirty as I should have been. I waited until two o'clock and had to keep stepping outside to allow the next bride in." Her anger bubbled and she poked him in the chest. "I sat with our guests, and waited until half three, the last chance for us to marry today." She poked him again, "Don't you dare tell me you're keeping your temper. I even had to comfort your bloody mother."

The slap came from nowhere. One minute his hand was by his side, the next it whipped back behind him, and then flew at her face. It knocked her off balance, and she sat at his feet in her wedding dress, as passers-by slowed down, wide-eyed, and open- mouthed. Only one middle-aged woman hurried forward to help.

She pushed him out the way. "You bastard." Holding out her hand, she helped Wendy to her feet as her father rushed past and threw himself forward.

"Dad, NO!" Wendy screamed at the top of her voice, but it was too late. The bodies of the two men she loved, crashed to the floor. She was relieved her father had landed on top. She looked at the stranger who wrapped an arm around her shoulders. "This isn't how it should be."

"I know my love. But you mark my words, as you haven't already done it, don't marry him. Dump him, and do it now. He'll apologise and give you a million reasons why it was your fault, and tell you he didn't mean to, then the next time it will be harder. Men either use their fists or they don't." She looked at the two men wrestling on the floor, her eyes found his and she screwed her nose up at him, her eyes never leaving his. "That bastard does. You've had a lucky escape." She pulled Wendy to one side. "Stand back, here come the cavalry."

Two of the hotel staff, followed by Uncle Tom, came hurrying down the steps and separated the struggling men. Uncle Tom managed to get a kick in, before he led her father over to the wall and sat him down.

Wendy watched with her hands covering her mouth, she couldn't believe this was happening, not today.

"Whatever else you say, say no to going anywhere with him." The woman pulled her closer.

"What?"

Wendy looked back as he stepped in front of them, and she grimaced as he coughed phlegm into his mouth and spat it into the woman's face. He raised his hand and his finger stopped inches away from Wendy's nose. She cowered into the woman's embrace.

"I'll be in touch," he snapped. Then he turned calmly, and walked away without a backward glance. Not bothering to wipe the blood from his injured nose.

The woman rummaged in her coat pocket to find a tissue, and wiped her face.

"I'm so sorry." Wendy was aware the tears were flowing now, but she didn't care, things couldn't get any worse. "How did you know I'd not married him yet?"

"No ring. Don't marry him, whatever he says, don't do it. They don't change. They can't."

"Did your husband hit you?"

"Does, love, does. I listened and I believed, then I hoped. Now it's me or the kids, so I stay for it to be me."

"Why don't you leave him? There must be something you can do."

"No. I tried, several times. He always finds us. Not too late for you though." She looked at her watch. "I need to go and get the dinner on." She opened her handbag and pulled out a notebook. Secreted in the lining of the back cover was a card. She handed it to Wendy. "I keep this in case I can't cope any more. I know the number, you'll need this if you take him back." She pecked Wendy on the cheek. "Bye, love, go and find a new life. Anything will be better than him."

"Thank you for helping my daughter." Wendy's father had walked over to them, he held out a trembling hand, which the woman patted.

"Look after her." She pushed Wendy into his arms and hurried away, hoping she'd have dinner ready on time.

That was the first time Wendy cried so much her nose blocked and she had to gulp air in through her mouth to fill her lungs.

~4~

"No, no, NO! Take five everyone. It's not working." Colin Anderson clapped his hands and walked across the set to Angie.

"I don't like it. We can't have the confrontation in the pub, or, if we do, someone else has to become involved, there's no way the others would sit and watch." He glanced at his watch. "You get it sorted and I'll press on with scene six. How long do you reckon?"

Angie pushed the script to one side and pulled forward her laptop. "Get it sorted how? It was originally in the carpark, but I was told by Alan to write indoor scenes until the building works are complete across the road. There would be too much background noise to shoot outside. If we take it anywhere else you'll need to get the crew mobile, etcetera. What do you want me to do, or will you speak to Alan first?"

"That's not a reason. Bribe the workmen, flash your . . ." He looked at her belly and laughed. "On second thoughts, we need someone to go and have a word. I'll find someone, perhaps we'll let them amble past in the background as a bribe. We can get set up, and then it will be ten, maybe fifteen minutes to shoot it."

"You do know Harry is in this scene, don't you?"

"I do. He's a bit quiet today. I think the knock back yesterday might have subdued him."

"So, what's happening?" As always, Harry managed to appear from nowhere, and he slapped Colin on the shoulder.

"It's like he knows when someone is talking about him." Colin started to walk away. "I need to find someone to chat up some builders. Angie will explain."

Harry waited until Colin was out of earshot. His gleaming smile disappeared and his nose wrinkled. "Talking about what?" he demanded.

“The scene. Colin wants it outside, but the building works are too noisy.” Angie looked back at her laptop, and searched for the scene she'd removed. “I have it here—”

“What else?” Harry craned his neck forward, forcing her to look at him and not the screen. “Have I done something to offend you? Because you seem to be causing me grief at every turn.”

“Harry, behave.” Angie let her hands rest on her pregnancy and leaned back in the chair. “Surprising though it may seem, not every conversation revolves around you. We have a large cast.”

“He said you were talking about me. What about?” He pushed the screen flat. “It's a simple question.”

Angie held back her temper and slowly pushed the screen back into position. “And a simple answer. Colin wants the scene outside, he says he'll make it happen, so we're moving to six first.” She lifted the script from the table. “Have you learned it yet?”

Harry knocked the proffered scene away. “I don't need your help. I know what I'm doing, and I know what you're up to. What I don't know, is why.” He straightened his back and pointed at her. “You be careful lady. Pregnant or not, you don't want to make me an enemy.” He heard his name being called and glanced over his shoulder before looking back at her. “That was a warning, be careful.”

“I beg your—”

“Shut up.” Harry turned away. “Who wants me?” he called jovially, “Don't rush, form an orderly queue.” He sauntered away as a few of the others laughed.

Angie watched him go, a little wave here, a smile there. He could act when it suited him. Why didn't he apply that skill when the cameras rolled? Deciding he wasn't worth further consideration, she went back to finding the scene. As her eyes skimmed the list of documents, she paused on the document she had now named 'Wendy'. She looked around and searched the set for Karen, she'd not bothered to call, as the writing had taken hold of her. Perhaps now would be a good time to speak to her. Karen had only one more scene to film this morning, although that may change if Colin altered the schedule. Karen was nowhere to be seen, and Angie decided to finish what she was doing before going to search for her.

“Sorry, Wendy. I'll be back soon though, we need to decide what you're going to do now.” She muttered as she continued to scroll.

Having found what she wanted, she emailed it to herself, and then made her way to the rest room. A large bright room, it was filled with a selection of comfy sofas, a refreshment area, and several bistro tables to allow the production team to take a break when not needed. A large television was suspended from one wall, and was always tuned into the sports or news channels.

Today it was news, and Angie glanced up as the weather man apologised to Scottish viewers for the predicted gale force winds approaching from the North Sea. Waving at Natalie Stone, who was curled up at one end of a sofa, engaged on a phone call, she walked to the desk in the far corner and put the memory stick into the adjacent laptop. A few minutes later, the printer clunked into life, and spewed out the required copies.

Natalie finished her call and walked to the water cooler. "Do you want anything, Angie?" she asked as Angie stapled the sheets together.

"No thanks." Angie walked towards her. "I don't suppose you've seen Karen, have you?"

"Not for a while, but she did say she was going out for a ciggy." Natalie sipped her water before topping the cup back up. "I hear we're going to have a talent contest."

Angie stopped walking. "Who told you that?" She asked although she already knew the answer.

"Harry. He seemed chuffed." She lowered her voice. "He gives me the creeps. I know he's important around here, but . . ." She rubbed her arms. "I can't explain it, he just seems menacing. I try and avoid him." She moved closer to Angie. "To make it worse, he's pissed off with me. He asked me out and I thought he was joking, and I laughed." Her cheeks coloured as she spoke and she fanned her face with her hand. "Oh God, it makes me hot just thinking about it."

"I hope you said no." Angie had already received this gossip and smiled at her. "He's not right for you, in any way."

"Of course I did. Apart from the fact I'm with Kieran now, he's only a year younger than my dad."

Angie laughed. "Did you say that?"

"Yep, not as an insult, just an explanation, and I told him about Kieran. If looks could kill I'd be long gone."

There it was. The reason Harry had concocted the talent show, and a murder. It was the way to get rid of Natalie, Angie concluded. Angie had believed it was a way to take the limelight, but it was more likely because his ego was bruised. She wondered why she was surprised, but decided to keep her opinion to herself. Why upset the girl unnecessarily? She'd work with Colin, and get the idea binned.

She waved the scripts at Natalie. "Don't worry about it. Too big an ego. I have to go and dish these out, if you see Karen, tell her I'm looking for her."

Wandering back onto the set, she spotted Karen talking to one of the cameramen. In the far corner Colin was directing a scene being filmed in the bar. He threw his arms into the air, clearly frustrated, and she walked over to see what was going on. When she got there, she found it wasn't the scene causing the problem. Colin stormed towards the exit before she could catch him.

One of the runners, stood red-faced watching him go. Angie placed her hand on his arm. "What's the problem?"

"The foreman said they couldn't hold up the job this morning. I pleaded with him, but he said maybe at three. Colin doesn't think I tried hard enough. He's got a bloody temper on him. I've never seen him fly off the handle like that before."

"It's not just this, there's a lot else going on. You were in the wrong place at the wrong time. I'll see if I can calm him down." She hurried away to catch Colin. As she entered the carpark of the pub for The Village, she spotted him. "Colin wait for me. I'll come with you."

He spun to face her, throwing his arms into the air. "How fucking difficult can it be to give us ten or fifteen minutes' peace. I thought builders liked tea breaks. Well I'll take his mug and shove it where the sun don't shine!" He turned back towards the gate, the security guard raised a hand in greeting. "Not got time to talk," he said as he marched out into the street.

Angie caught him as he waited for a car to pass, then crossed the road with him. "Calm down, Colin. Use your charm."

"I'm flattered you think I have any." Colin marched to the nearest worker.

"Who's in charge here?"

"I'll have to stop you there, sir, you can't come on site, health and safety. Who do you want?"

"As I said, the man in charge." Colin took a step forward. "I'll take my chances."

The workman stepped in front of him. "More than my job's worth. Wait here." He pointed at Angie. "And you can definitely stay there."

Once he'd secured their promises, he disappeared around the side of a large concrete mixer, returning minutes later with a similarly dressed man whose hard hat was labelled 'Manager'.

The man held out his hand. "Phil Jones, I'm the site manager. What can I do for you?"

"Stop work for fifteen minutes or so." It was more of an instruction than a request, and Colin forced a smile.

"What he means is, is there any possibility you can time your next tea break with us filming outside?" Angie also smiled at the man. "I know it's a pain but, we're on a tight schedule and you are particularly noisy today. There's no building work going on in The Village." She offered a second smile as she pointed back across the road.

"Us too. We're already three days behind due to the rain flooding the footings last week. I've got a concrete pour starting any minute, which I need to get done to allow the next one in." He jerked his thumb at the truck.

Angie looked at the huge rotating drum. "How long will it take?"

"Just finishing the prep now, then about half an hour, maybe more. Then the next one will be here."

"So maybe an hour and a half then, assuming it's just the two?" Angie put her hand on Colin's arm. He'd opened his mouth, and she didn't want him aggravating the situation.

"Yes, but then the deliveries of materials will start." He lifted his hat and scratched his head. "Look, love, we'll be done by half four, five at the latest. You'll have to wait until then."

"We can't. The light will be wrong." Colin clenched his fists in frustration.

Looking at her watch, Angie suggested, "Shall we agree that you can stop at one o'clock for half an hour, I'm sure your chaps need to eat, and if any of them want passes to come and watch what's caused all the fuss, I'm sure we can get something organised. There may even be cake."

The site manager looked at his watch. "They eat on the go most of the time, all on price, and time is money when it's your money." He laughed and pulled out his phone. "Give me your number, I'll see what I can do and give you a call."

Walking back to the set, Angie looped her arm through Colin's. "There, job done, and no fisticuffs. We can get set up and ready to roll at one, and you'll still get a couple more scenes done inside."

"We'll see. Thanks, Angie. Did you sort out the new scene?"

"Yep. All printed and ready to go, the main event hasn't changed, just how they end up out here, and how we get them back in the pub. It shouldn't cause any problems, Karen's now involved but she's a pro."

"Meaning our Harry isn't." Colin laughed for the first time that day. "He'd better not cock this up, or I'll make sure he's our next murder victim."

Angie followed him on set, and handed out the new script to the relevant actors as he described what was happening. He explained with such conviction, she hoped the builders would play ball, or there could be fireworks. Colin gave the task of setting up to one of the cameramen, and although he addressed the group as a whole, he looked at Harry when speaking.

"It's a minor change, and shouldn't cause any problems. But read it, learn it, and get it right first time, because if they start work and we're not done, whoever cocks it up will end up in the effing mixer. Understood?" With a curt nod, he turned away. "Let's have everyone needed for the shop scene in position in five."

Five of the workmen came over to watch the filming, which went without a hitch, and they applauded when Colin said he was satisfied and everyone could take a break. He went over and shook hands with them before disappearing on set.

Harry could see they were impressed and sauntered over, his smile bright, his hand held forward. "Well done, lads. Much appreciated, I might have had to stay late if we hadn't got that done, and I've a girl with my name on lined up for tonight."

The men laughed and two of them shook his hand, before they turned away to get back to work.

"Do you want an autograph before you go?" Harry fell into step towards the gate with them.

"Nah, you're all right, mate. We're not star struck," The last in line shook his head. "Now, if you can get Natalie out here, that would be a different story."

Harry forced a laugh as the security guard took back the passes. He was glad everyone but the cameraman had disappeared when he turned back to the set. He gave a shrug, you couldn't please all of the people, and they were men. His thoughts strayed to Alan and he shuddered. He was still unable to believe the man thought he was interested in him, he wasn't sure how long he could carry on stringing him along. Alan had taken to touching him. Nothing too overt, a squeeze of the arm here, and an arm across the shoulders there, it took all Harry's will power not to pull away. And the bitch script-writer thought he couldn't act.

~5~

Wendy went into the small en-suite bathroom and splashed water on her face. Her father had called the ward and the nurse had told her he was on the way to see her. He'd seen her shed enough tears, although these had been the most bitter yet. The woman who helped her on the day they should have married came into her mind. If only she'd taken her advice, come to that, if only she'd listened to anyone but him.

After he'd left her waiting at the registry office, her father had refused to let him in the house, he wasn't even allowed to open the gate. On his third visit, her father had actually whacked his hand with a spade. So he'd followed her, and eventually she'd agreed to meet him for coffee. She chose a busy café. She had treated it like a blind date with a stranger she was unsure of. He'd arrived with the most embarrassingly large bouquet, and despite their bustling surroundings, he'd dropped to his knees, head bent and asked her forgiveness. Wendy couldn't remember whether she'd given it due to the embarrassment or because she'd wanted to. He placed the flowers on the chair and squeezed onto the small bench seat next to her.

"I know why you hate me. I hate me too. I've forgiven your father for all he's said and called me, even for hitting me with the spade." He flexed his fingers at the memory. "But if you'd let me explain, I always intended to be there, but I had to sort something out, something that could have caused us great unhappiness. I was hoping I'd never have to tell you."

"Tell me what?" Wendy continued to stir her coffee relentlessly.

"Why I was late. I thought I'd just said that."

Wendy was staring at the ever-decreasing foam, and missed the look of irritation. "Tell me now."

"I will my darling, but we need to be in a less public place." He glanced around. "I have to say I was surprised at your choice of venue, given the nature of our meeting."

"It was close, and I like the coffee."

He placed his hand on hers to stop the stirring. "Well drink it, and we can go home."

"My father would never—"

"Not his home, our home. It's still half yours you know. I've made everything perfect for you."

"It's not my home. I've never even slept there." She allowed herself a smile. "Not in the true sense." Shaking the memory away she lifted her cup. "Tell me here."

Inside she congratulated herself. She'd rehearsed this meeting over and over again in her mind, and the only constant was that she made the rules.

"No." He got to his feet. "I can see you don't care. I'm sorry to have bothered you. You may keep the flowers."

She knew he wanted to march off, but having squeezed himself in behind the table, there were a few awkward seconds as he manoeuvred himself out into the gangway. They were enough for his resolve to weaken. Picking up the flowers he placed them on the floor and dropped onto the chair.

"Wendy, please. What I have to tell you is personal, very personal. I don't want some busybody eavesdropping." To make his point he gave a manic smile to the woman on the next table, who, flustered, looked away and made a pretence of reading the menu. "You see."

Wendy smiled. "I do. Okay, let's go and sit on a bench under the trees." She checked through the window, "There's no one else there."

This time she saw the irritation, and how he controlled his response.

"Okay, I'm willing to give it a try, but I'm leaving if even a pigeon comes near."

He got to his feet and headed to the door. Wendy scooped up the flowers and walked after him. She sniffed them. This was new, in the past he'd always claimed flowers were a waste of money as they died too quickly. Such gifts in the past had been chocolates, or books, or on one occasion a teddy bear.

Placing the flowers next to him on the bench, she took a seat on the other side of them. "What did you have to do that was more important than turning up on time for our wedding?"

His hands grasped his knees. "Blunt! What happened to beat around the bush Wendy?"

"She's long gone." Wendy tilted her chin. She was actually bloody doing it. She was standing up for herself. "You were right about that, it wastes too much time."

His fingers loosened their grip a little. Wendy looked at them. Was that because they were getting somewhere, or because she'd told him he was right?

"So, tell me," she prompted again.

"I will. It's where to start I'm having difficulty with."

"Spit it out." She pulled back as his body twisted towards her. "Is what you used to say to me," she added quickly.

"You're right. I will. I should have told you before but I was worried about losing you."

"Tell me now." Picking a petal from one of the flowers, she smiled at him. "We've been a while making it to this point, might as well say what you want. There's nothing to lose."

"I was married before I met you." His eyes found hers. "There. I've told you."

Wendy closed her eyes and processed his words. When she opened them, she looked at a man she didn't know. Again. His surprises were never pleasant. "To whom?"

"Spoken like an actress. You sounded very proper then. More like a teacher, or some posh finishing school bird, than my Wendy." His eyes narrowed. "Don't put an act on for me, Wendy. It's not the time, nor the place, and if I'm brutal, more than a tad irritating."

Wendy could see that. The whites of his knuckles stood out against the blue of his jeans, and a tic twitched away in his cheek.

~6~

Angie's hands lifted off the keyboard, and she held them suspended while she read the scene again. Was she going to make Wendy an actress? Should she do that? They say you should write about what you know, but surely that would be wrong. It felt as though she were encroaching on someone's grief.

"What are you stuck on?" Ryan muted the television and got to his feet. "I'm going to open a bottle of red. We don't start filming until mid-morning, so a drink on a school night is permissible. Can I get you anything?"

"Yes, cranberry juice." Angie was still staring at the screen.

"Go on, tell me, I may be able to help." Ryan put his hands on her shoulders and squinted at the screen. "You've been going like the clappers. Not even paused for the half hourly pee. Then suddenly the clicking stops and you're looking at the laptop like it answered you back. "What did she do that irritated him?"

Hitting the save button, Angie dropped back against the chair and closed the laptop.

"She asked him who he had been married to, he didn't like the question, or rather the question was expected but he didn't like the way she delivered it. And now you've mentioned it, I do need a pee. Ouch!" She grabbed Ryan's hand and pressed it on the side of her pregnancy. "Junior thinks so too." She returned his grin. "Get out of the way, because now I'm desperate."

When she returned, her cranberry juice sat next to the laptop. She collected it and joined Ryan on the couch.

"I've still got another forty minutes, the All Blacks, are a try away from a world record." Ryan glanced at the laptop. "Don't you want him to tell her who it was?"

"No. I'm confused. You carry on watching, I'll sit here and sniff your wine while I drink my juice."

"Was the correct answer." Ryan held his glass under her nose and she inhaled. He pointed the remote at the television. "And we're off."

The commentator's voice filled the room. The volume was far too loud, but Angie hadn't noticed it when she was writing. She watched for fifteen minutes before she got bored. She placed her glass in Ryan's hand while she heaved herself off the couch.

"Are you going back to it?" Ryan didn't look away from the television.

"Nope, I'm going to run naked around the garden." She took her glass from his hand which hadn't moved.

"Good girl, I'll get us some supper when this is over."

Angie dipped her fingers into her glass and flicked juice at him. "I'm going to make a phone call."

"What did I do?" His glance was momentary, but his smile remained. As she walked away he called, "Will the recipient know you're naked?"

Angie laughed as she collected her phone and notebook from the table. Taking them to the bedroom, she piled all the pillows on her side of the bed and squashed her body into them. Now comfortable, she was ready for a gossip. She dialled Karen Ellery.

Karen sounded flustered when she answered. "Angie, darling, now is not a good time, I'm dishing up dinner. Can it wait an hour or so? I invited Colin round and he's ravenous."

"I'm sorry to interrupt, don't worry, I'll catch up with you tomorrow. What are you having?"

"A new concoction I picked up on a supermarket recipe card. Smells divine, but I think I overcooked the meat. Are you sure it's not urgent?"

"No, I was going to ask you about Wendy, but it will keep. Say hi to Colin for me."

"Will do, see you in a couple of days. I hear you're not back on set until Thursday."

"No. But I am working. Bye then . . . actually, one quick question. Did Wendy have a dog?"

"A dog?" Karen paused. "Do you know I believe she did um . . . her name was Jessie, I think. What an odd question."

"I know, Ryan, calls it baby brain. Right, get back to the cooking. Bye."

Angie rested the phone on her bump. Wendy did have a dog. Karen hadn't told her about it, as she'd had to think about whether or not Wendy had had a dog. It was her imagination that had given her character the dog. She smiled, at least she was still capable of creating such stuff. She had been worried for a while that she was cribbing it. Although, she mused, the dog was called Jessie, or perhaps Jess for short, that was close to being Tess. Yawning she snuggled further into the mountain of pillows, and was asleep within minutes.

Ryan woke her an hour later. "Come on, sleepy head, get up and pee, then come and eat supper or you won't sleep tonight."

"What's for supper?"

"Lasagne. Jeepers baby brain, you made it. I only heated it and dished it up. I hope your memory improves once junior arrives or we'll have to fit him with a tracker."

"Or her." Angie stood and stretched her back. "It could be a her, keep reminding yourself of that. I don't want a groan when the midwife slaps her backside and announces she's a girl."

"Do they still slap babies? Surely not. Mind you, Freda picked off the sac and dangled little Bernie by the arm to get him in the right position to suckle. I suppose they are resilient."

With a quick unexpected movement, Angie pushed him onto the bed. "Because I love you, I'm not going to lie on you and crush you. But please, please remember we aren't orangutans, and there will be no dangling by the arm, whatever sex junior is. Now feed me."

An hour later, Ryan had his third glass of wine and was flipping through the television channels. He found a film he wanted to watch. He called to Angie who was loading the dishwasher. "Do you want to watch *Saving Private Ryan*?"

Angie appeared in the doorway. "I've seen it twice. You must have seen it at least five times, and it's about twelve hours long."

"Don't exaggerate. It's a classic and I didn't fancy any of the others."

"You carry on. If you fall asleep I'm leaving you there. I'll get back to my writing."

"Have I told you how much I love you?"

"Not in the last hour, no."

~7~

Wendy flipped his comment away. "I always irritate you. It's why I'm not sure why you want me back. But, back to the question, who were you married to and when?"

"Who it was doesn't matter. It's over, she's gone." He looked at his hands and Wendy wondered if he was embarrassed. "It was about five years ago. A wild fling which ended with a never-should-have-been marriage."

"What did you need to do, on our, never-actually-made-it, wedding day?" Her own eyes widened, she was being sarcastic. "And who she was might be important to me."

His head shot up. "You've changed."

"It's what happens when someone smashes your world apart." Wendy's face remained impassive but inside she was punching the air at her bravery. Perhaps she had changed. "Are you actually going to answer any of my questions? If we are to move forward in any shape or form, I need to know what stopped you getting there on time."

"Okay, I'll give you the highlights, or low lights would be more accurate. But I'm not going into detail, it's in the past."

His tone was measured, he wasn't angry, and Wendy relaxed a little, relaxed enough to push a little harder.

"For you maybe, but from where I'm sitting it's very much part of the present. Tell me."

"I went on a stag party to Vegas. There was a hen party from England staying on the same floor of our hotel, we hooked up. I became close to one of the girls, and in a moment of drunken madness we decided to get married. This was on day three, we went to the Graceland Wedding Chapel with some chap from the hotel who said he could make it happen. We completed the paperwork, and two days later, still drunk and in lust, Elvis married us."

He shook his head at the memory. "I got back to the UK first, she still had a couple of days left. I met her stone cold sober at Manchester airport, and realised what an awful mistake we'd made.

She didn't at first and we gave it a go. That lasted two weeks, we went to see the solicitor together, and I went home." He paused and scuffed his shoe in dirt at the base of the bench. "It wasn't my finest moment."

"No. But what I don't understand is why you didn't tell me all this, and what you had to do on our wedding day."

"I had to make sure I was free to marry you of course." He looked at her as though she were simple. "I've already said that."

"No, you haven't. If you're going to get angry there's no point in us talking." Wendy got to her feet and he stretched across the flowers grabbing her wrist. "Let me go!" She yanked her wrist from his grasp.

"I'm sorry, I'm sorry. Please let me explain."

"Okay, but remember, I've done nothing wrong. Nothing. All I did was love you. Trust you. Forgive you."

"Forgive me for what?" He rubbed his forehead. "It doesn't matter, sit, please." He waited until she had done so.

"We made initial declarations at the solicitor, and he sent some other forms which had to be completed before it was over. I completed them and sent them off. I didn't hear anything else so I assumed all was well. About two weeks before we were due to get married it occurred to me that I'd never had a final . . . anything. No letter, no certificate or what have you. But I'd moved twice since then. Anyway, I wrote to the solicitor and asked for confirmation."

Wendy's heart sank. "Which confirmed you were still married."

"No, not quite. It said it was all done bar the shouting, but Bernice hadn't sent the final form back. Once that was in, and it went off to be registered. Done."

"I still don't get why you weren't there. Especially as you went to so much trouble to see everything was in order."

"The letter arrived the day before we were due to get married, but it must have been put into the wrong postbox in the hall, and into the correct one too late for me to find. When I got in from my stag do with the boys it was there, waiting for me. I was so mad at that moment, you wouldn't believe."

Wendy said nothing, but she would believe it. She'd seen his temper before. Not focused on her of course, not if you excluded their wedding day. He had a short fuse. "What did you do?"

"The solicitor had sent a copy of what was needed, so, I found her address and took off. I left at about two in the morning. It only took me three hours to get there."

"But you'd been drinking. How could you drive?"

"Illegally. What a stupid bloody question. It had to be sorted or I'd be a bigamist. Would that have been better?" His knuckles were white again.

"I'd rather have known what was going on."

He laughed. "What, tell Daddy his princess was going to marry a bigamist? Give me a break. He'd have called the whole thing off and talked you out of it."

"I doubt that."

"Oh Wendy, Wendy, Wendy. How little you know men. He thinks I'm after his money for some reason. He's as good as told me."

"What! When?" Wendy's father had indeed done his best to sour her thoughts about him after the never-to-be wedding, but before then he'd not said a word. "He's not that rich."

"He's loaded by most standards. You're simply used to it." His eyes betrayed his disbelief at her naivety. "It's why I insisted on a registry office do, I didn't want him spending a penny more on the wedding than was absolutely necessary."

"I believed it was because you wanted it to happen quickly. Not because you were making a point."

"Well now you know. It was because of him. The sun doesn't always shine out of his rear end."

"I never for one moment . . . this is wasting time." She checked the time. "What happened when you got there?"

"I'm sorry, is us sorting out the rest of our lives holding you up? Do you need to be somewhere?"

Ignoring the sarcastic tone, Wendy's response was calm. "I have an audition. It's only an advert, but from little acorns . . . I have to be there at three. Are you working?"

"That's irrelevant." He looked at his watch. "I'm on borrowed time it appears." He kicked a stone towards a nearby pigeon. "I had to wait. It was too early to knock, I didn't know if she was with someone, and if so, I wasn't about to stir up a hornet's nest, I had a wedding to get to."

"Oh, was she . . . hang on a minute. If you found out this paper hadn't been signed, even if she did it there and then it wouldn't have been immediate. Technically, you would still have been married."

"No. Simply waiting for the red tape to be severed." He held his hand towards her, wanting her to take it. She didn't, and he allowed it to drop into his lap. "You must see I was doing my best to make it right."

"Yes, I suppose so. Did she sign it?"

"Eventually, yes."

"What does that mean? Was she awkward about it or something?"

"Her boyfriend was . . ." He closed his eyes and huffed. "Look, it doesn't matter, it's done. She's gone. Can we please get back to us?"

Wendy got to her feet. "Not now. I need to think about this. It's come as quite a shock. But thank you for telling me." She took a step back as he got to his feet and grabbed her elbow.

He let her go. "You flinched then. Are you scared of me?" His voice sounded concerned, but his eyes showed his amusement.

"You have a temper. You knocked me to the floor on what should have been my wedding day, so yes, I'm a little scared of you. I'm sorry . . ."

Her words were lost in his kiss. He pulled her to him and reminded her of what she'd felt for him before. When he released her he collected the flowers, and holding them in one hand, he took hers in the other and led her back to the main street.

"Can I give you a lift somewhere? I've nothing on for the rest of the day?"

"How do you know I'm not driving?"

"Because you have sensible shoes on, that says you're walking."

Wendy looked at her feet. "I'm too predictable."

"Only because I love you. And I do love you." Pulling her to one side until she bumped into him, he slung his arm around her shoulder. "I will have you back."

She wanted to say yes, but she had to think it through, so instead she replied, "The auditions are in the Marriott, are you okay to drive me there?"

"Of course." He checked the time. "I have some things I need to do, I'll come back when I'm done and I'll take you home too. If it's only an advert you shouldn't be much more than an hour."

Wendy wasn't sure, so she smiled at him. She wondered what her father would say if he saw his car outside. It would be best to speak to her father before he had that shock. If it were the following week, she'd already be in the cottage. She wondered if that would have made a difference, if she would have agreed.

Removing his arm, he pulled a ticket from his shirt pocket and walked towards the pay station. "I forgot to do this first the other day, bloody mayhem when I got to the barrier, I had six cars behind me." He laughed.

Wendy raised her eyebrows, in the past he'd have become angry simply talking about it. She wandered along the first row of cars while he sorted through his loose change.

"Here we are. Where are you going?"

Turning back, she looked at him pointing the ticket towards the second car in the row. "I was looking for your car. Have you got a new one?" She looked at the almost new car.

He waved the keys at her. "I have. Only twenty k on the clock. It was a bargain."

"When did this happen, you loved your old car?"

"When you left me, when you wouldn't return my calls, I thought, sod it. I deserve something nice to happen and I traded the old one in." He held the door for her. "Your carriage awaits."

~ ~ ~

Audition over, Wendy stood in the busy foyer and looked around. She couldn't see him, perhaps it would be best if she went home alone. She hadn't had time to think about what he'd said, and she should definitely warn her father. Making her decision, she headed for the exit, wondering how angry he would be when he realised she'd not waited. Stepping into the revolving door she lifted her chin. It didn't matter. She was in control, not him.

The wind had picked up, and her hair blew into her face as she stepped outside. Rummaging in her pocket, she found a band and secured her hair.

"You weren't leaving without me, were you?"

Her heart skipped a beat and her cheeks coloured. She turned to face him. "No, I was hot, I wanted some fresh air."

Tucking a piece of hair she'd missed behind her ear, he smiled. "You do look flushed. Come on, let's get you home."

They'd been driving a few minutes before Wendy realised they were heading in the wrong direction.

"Where are we going?"

"Home."

He was taking her to the flat they were going to move into once they had been married. Wendy didn't know what she should feel. She wanted to protest, to maintain her newly found confidence, but she was curious. "Oh," was all she could manage.

"I hope you like what I've done with it. Still has our furniture of course, but I've collected some pieces you might like." He looked at her and smiled. "I thought you'd refuse."

"We're half way there. I'd like to see it."

He smiled the rest of the way. The air was cool in the underground carpark, and he held her hand as they waited for the lift.

"It's the only thing which irritates. It takes so long for the lift to come."

"It's minutes. Better than climbing all those stairs. I could hardly breathe when we came to see it the first time." Stepping forward she squeezed his hand. "You see it's here."

When they reached the entrance to the two penthouse apartments, he handed her the key.

"I can't carry you over the threshold . . . yet. But I can let you do the honours." He pushed her forward. "Go on. I'll wait here."

And he did. Leaning on the door jamb, he watched her wander along the spacious hall disappearing into different rooms. Her smile grew wider the more she saw. Then there was only one room left. The master bedroom. He wandered in to join her, and placed his hand on the door knob.

"May I?" He smiled at the flush, and how she was unable to meet his eye. "You're going to like this."

The large brass bedstead they had chosen wasn't against the far wall as she'd expected, but was positioned off centre, the pillows facing the panoramic window overlooking the river. Her eyes darted around the room as he walked to the window. It was pretty much how she would have furnished it. Simple, solid, warm and welcoming. He slid open the windows and the breeze caused the voile curtains to billow a little.

"It's lovely, I'm not sure about the bed though." She hesitated as he held out his hand.

"Come," he commanded and she walked forward. "Sit here." She sat on the bed and he slipped the sensible shoes from her feet, gently lifting her legs and turning her body to face the river.

"Wow!" Wendy looked out at the view. The road below had disappeared, and all she could see was the river and the trees on the far bank. True she could also see a couple of rooftops, but even so, it was magnificent.

"I knew you'd like it. You'd hardly ever see this if the bed was against the wall." Moving quickly, he went to the other side of the bed and kicked his shoes off. He lay propped on one elbow looking at her. "What do we do now?"

"Talk?"

"I wasn't thinking about talking."

His eyes twinkled and she was lost. She pulled off her blouse as she moved closer.

"That's more like it." He kissed her, pulled her onto the bed, and removed her remaining clothes, throwing them on the floor. As he sat to remove his shirt, she placed her hand on his arm to stop him.

"Have you got something? I'm not on the pill anymore, there was no point."

He continued to pull off his shirt. "I haven't. We'll be fine."

"You don't know that."

His trousers hit the floor. "I'll be careful."

Pulling her to him, his lips caressed her neck as he whispered, "I promise."

As she knew would be the case, he wasn't careful, but at the time she didn't care. She loved him, she'd always love him. They sat propped on the pillows, her head nestled against his chest watching the noisy gulls swoop by. Eventually she pulled herself away. "I need a drink."

"Good idea. There's wine in the fridge, unless you want red or something stronger. I'm peckish. Shall we eat? We should be able to rustle up something edible."

Wendy paused. She'd promised her father they would go for a meal at the local pub that evening. She glanced at her watch. A snack wouldn't hurt.

"Okay, but I'll have to go in the next hour."

"Somewhere important to be?"

She could sense his irritation. "Only dinner with Dad. It's been planned for ages, I don't want to let him down. He's not been well lately." The latter was true, but the meal had only been agreed that morning.

"I'm sorry, nothing serious I hope." He retrieved his boxers and stepped into them.

He sounded genuine and she smiled at him. "He had a chest infection, he's getting over it now, but he hasn't been out and about much.

Walking up behind her, he wrapped his arms around her and kissed the back of her neck. "And I bet you've been waiting on him like the devoted daughter you are. He'll be sorry to lose you."

Wendy knew he meant when she came to live in the flat. He didn't know about the cottage, she'd have to tell him. But was now the moment? She decided it wasn't.

"I've been busy, I had a small part in a production at the Old Vic, but it's come to an end now." Stepping out of his embrace, she collected her blouse and pulled it on. "He was a good patient actually, did what he was told by the doctor. To be honest he didn't have the energy to do much else. But he's on the mend." She fastened her skirt. "Shall I make a start?" Collecting her sensible shoes, she walked into the hall and left them by the table which held her bag.

"We can do it together. What would he say if I joined you for dinner?" He had no intention of doing any such thing, but her reaction would be interesting.

She spun to face him. "It would probably finish him off. I'm sorry, you can't come. I'll have to talk to him, explain. Explain what, I don't know. I don't know what's happening here myself . . . yet." She hoped her smile looked genuine. "Slowly, slowly, I think is the best course of action." Turning back, she headed for the kitchen.

"Well I wouldn't want him dead, so I'll agree," he said as he followed her into the kitchen.

He watched her prepare their slight meal with pleasure. She looked comfortable, she was relaxed, and she was smiling. Compliments flowed as he ate the food and sipped the wine. When they had finished he gave no complaint when she said she had to go.

"Give me five minutes to get dressed. I have to go into town, so I'll give you a lift and we can discuss when I can next see you."

"Thanks, did you not get what you wanted earlier?"

"No, I wandered aimlessly thinking about you." Flashing the smile which caused her heart to skip a beat, he went back to the bedroom.

Wendy put the crockery in the dishwasher and wandered into the hall. Catching sight of herself in the mirror she went to collect her bag, and rummaged for her hair brush. She looked a mess, a happy mess, but a mess all the same. Smiling at her reflection as she pulled the brush through her hair, she knew she wanted to give him another chance. That meant telling him about the cottage, and telling her father about him. Her smile disappeared. Dropping the brush in her bag, she lifted it and slung the straps over her shoulder. As she did so something fluttered to the floor and she picked it up. It was the receipt from the carpark earlier, if he'd been wandering aimlessly, how did it end up under her handbag? Why didn't he say he'd come back to the apartment? The thought disappeared as he returned to the hall, and she placed it back on the table.

"Are you ready?"

The journey to the corner of her street was pleasant. Wendy agreed to meet him the next day for lunch, and he was agreeable, charming, and sincere. Despite her trepidation about the conversation she needed to have with her father, Wendy was happy as she slammed the door and blew him a kiss.

He returned the gesture and waited until she'd disappeared up the driveway. Pulling away he drove a hundred yards down the road and parked on the drive of a house almost opposite the Knight's residence. Far enough forward so he could watch the house, far enough back to be shielded from view by the shrubs. She wouldn't see him unless she was looking.

Fingers drumming the steering wheel, he sat waiting to follow her. If she was going for a meal with her father rather than stay with him, he'd have to accept it . . . for now, but he wanted to make sure. He was a patient man. He'd been following her for months on and off, and he knew the owners of the drive he'd chosen were on holiday. They'd left two days ago, he'd watched their luggage being loaded into the boot of the taxi. It was the last time he'd park anywhere other than on her father's drive. The old man would have to lump it. If only the chest infection had been more serious.

~8~

Angie's fingers drummed the sides of her keyboard in time with his drumming on the steering wheel. Should she let him kill the father in some way? Was Wendy going to go back to him, or would she stand her ground and move into the cottage? Lifting her pencil to jot down the questions, she stared out at the garden, if only she knew where she was going with the storyline. It was all well and good letting it develop as you go, but she didn't want to write thousands of words which would end up being deleted. She didn't want to waste the time. Smiling at the sense of urgency to get back to Wendy, still trussed up in the back of the car, she replaced the pencil. If the story was telling itself, she'd go with the flow for a few more chapters.

"What are you stuck on?" Ryan placed a mug of tea beside the mouse mat.

"I'm not. I was wondering if I should plan this a little better. I'm making it up as I go along."

Ryan laughed. "It's what you do isn't it? Make stuff up. How else would you do it? Would you like me to have a read? I've got half an hour or so before I need to shoot off if you want a second opinion."

"No, it's fine. While I would agree making stuff up is what I do, I usually have half an idea of what's going on before I start work on it, then once into it, I decide where it's going to go. With this, it's different, I begin to write and it unfolds in my mind. I simply write what I see. It's weird but bloody wonderful in some ways. The problem I have, is not knowing what happens in the end. I don't know where this is taking me. Right now, my female protagonist has been left tied up in the back of a car while I wander through her past, and I want to go back to the car and find out what happens, but I can't because I don't know yet."

She sipped her tea. "And don't start me on him. He's . . . just there, I can't get to grips with him. Other than the fact he's a typical bully-cum-controlling type, I haven't got a feel for him. Yet there he is, on every page." Placing her elbows on the table she cupped her face in her hands. "Come to that, she's coming across as weak, yet I know she's not. I like her, but I don't know why. I've . . . Forget it, I'm rambling. Let me get another couple of chapters done and you can have a read."

"No problem. It's nice to see you fired up like this. I've usually got to listen to you swear at the screen. If you're working from home all day, do you want me to pick anything up? What's for dinner?"

"It's nine in the morning, I haven't thought about dinner. I'll go out if we need anything. I've been thinking about popping into the garden centre, I might buy something for the garden. Something to focus on when I'm sitting here, looking out there for inspiration. I might buy a new bird bath. It's a shame the one we found behind the shed was broken. My little robin might like that."

"Your little what?" Ryan stepped forward and placed his hand on Angie's forehead. "Nope, you're not running a temperature."

"Get off." Angie knocked his hand away. "Robbie comes every day and hops around on the patio, sometimes he has a sing on the back of the chair. His girlfriend came with him last week."

"And Robbie is the best you could come up with? What was the girlfriend like?"

"Small and sweet."

"Colour?"

"Brown, no red breast so I knew she was a she." Angie sounded triumphant.

"Wrong! Females have a red breast too. Males have a brighter beak, eye ring and—"

"Okay, okay. I'll check next time. What time do you have to leave?".

"Now it seems." He placed a kiss on the top of her head, and placed his hand on her bump. "Have a good day you two, and call me if you change your mind. If you're a good girl, I'll get a couple of cameras set up so you can see what happens in our garden."

"Sounds perfect. Bye."

"And so, the man of the house was dismissed. He walked slowly, not wanting to leave the bosom of his family, but cast aside . . ." Ryan rounded his shoulders and slouched away, his legs dragging his feet across the floor.

"Very dramatic. You should give up this filming lark and get on the other side of the camera. There's hope for you yet. Oh." She pressed her hand against her side. "Junior waved. Have a good one."

Sipping her tea, she stared at the screen pondering whether to carry on with the storyline involving Wendy's father, or concentrate on Wendy. Unable to decide she thought she should get out and grab some fresh air. A wander around the garden centre was in order, and she'd find a shop and get something nice for dinner. They'd lived a little outside Bristol for two months, and although she knew the city well, she didn't know what was where in her immediate area, other than the pubs, and of course the garden centre on the main drag into the city. Today she might go wild and find out.

Deciding to get the garden centre purchases completed first, Angie drove straight there. She wandered round the various buildings and greenhouses selecting a variety of plants, before heading off to the area signposted 'Garden furniture & more'. After spending over half an hour checking out the prices of attractive patio furniture, she made her way to the stone ornaments and chose a birdbath of a similar style to the one lying broken behind the shed. She was assisted in loading it into her trolley by a helpful young man named Jamie, with arms plastered in tattoos, and piercings all over his face. He'd have been handsome without all the metal, and she wondered why he'd done it.

"I'll push this through to the checkout for you, I can help you load it then. Do you need anything else?"

"Bird food. I have a pet robin. I say pet, it comes into the garden and I thought it would be nice to watch them feed."

"And bathe." Jamie pointed at the birdbath.

"Of course. One has to be spruced up for dinner.".

They collected a variety of bird feed and some dispensers on the way to the checkout, and then Angie stood back and watched him load her purchases into the car. She wondered if she should tip him, and decided she should, and pulled a note from her purse as he slammed the door shut.

"Thank you, Jamie." She held out her hand, the note now neatly folded.

"I don't need a tip. Thank for the thought though."

"Please. You've been very helpful."

"It's in my nature to be helpful. It's also my job."

Angie insisted again, and he reluctantly took the money and told her he'd put it in the charity box.

"If that's what you want." She pulled open the driver's door. "Oh, one more thing. Can you point me in the direction of some local shops?"

"What do you want to buy?"

"Something nice for dinner and a few bits for the cupboard."

"Supermarket, not corner shop then."

"I was hoping for a High Street, with a butcher, and greengrocers, you know the sort of thing." Angie raised her eyebrows as he started to laugh.

"Not round here. What could be mistaken for a High Street now has two pubs, one at each end, never drink in the White Swan." Jamie shuddered dramatically. "One charity shop, one betting shop, one funeral directors, a greasy spoon which only opens if the owner feels like it, and last but not least the aforementioned corner shop, although to be fair it's in the middle of the rank. They only sell overpriced tinned goods and the like, so unless you're after a tin of corned beef and some frozen chips, I'd recommend the supermarket. It's not far."

"It's not distance I'm worried about, I was hoping for quaint, friendly, support your local businesses."

Jamie turned the trolley to face the other direction. "Ah, that long forgotten gem. You're about ten years too late." He gave her directions to the supermarket. "Then you'll see the signpost." He concluded, "Happy shopping."

"Thanks, Jamie. Can't remember the last time I received such helpful, courteous service."

"You're welcome, see you again I hope." With a tight salute, he sauntered off towards the trolley park.

Angie set off to find the supermarket. She followed his directions until the crossroads, she slowed on the approach, trying to remember if she had to take a right or left turn. Tossing a mental coin, she opted for left, and allowed herself a self-satisfied smile when a hundred yards down the road she saw the sign for the supermarket. She pulled into the first space, collected a trolley, and grimaced as a large raindrop hit the middle of her forehead.

Forty minutes later, she had a trolley full with overstuffed carrier bags, each containing many items which were not needed but impulse buys because her tummy had rumbled all the way around. She blamed it on the smell of freshly baked bread coming from the in-house bakery. As she exited she smiled and sniffed the fresh air. Everything around her glistened from the heavy shower she'd managed to miss, and the sun, now released from the clouds which had moved on, was warm and welcoming. She patted her bump as she arrived at the car.

"Today is going to be a good day little one. I can feel it." She opened the rear of the car, and groaned. While throwing goodies into her basket with gay abandon, she'd completely forgotten her earlier purchases. She slammed the door and lifting one of the bags squeezed herself between her own car and the one next to her. She half slung the bag onto the middle of the back seat. Repeating this on both sides, she emptied and returned the trolley.

"Home." She stroked the steering wheel, and started the engine. Pulling out of the space, she followed the arrows indicating the exit. The route took her around the main bulk of the carpark, and looped back round to where she had come in. She tutted. She'd know better next time she came. Checking her mirrors, she brought the car to a halt. Rummaging around in the glove compartment she found her trusty satnav, placed it on the dash, and hit the home button. She needed to pee, and needed to take the direct route, not one which might eventually get her there. The screen told her it was finding her location, and she relaxed back in her seat while it did so. She thanked the satnav when it told her to exit current location and turn left.

Angie put the car in gear, checked her mirrors and pulled away only to brake violently. Her hand flew to her mouth. That was the fence, there was the gap Wendy and Tess had gone through. Without checking anything she headed for the fence. The driver who had been about to overtake her, slammed their hand on the horn, and Angie stopped again. She waved an apology as a red-faced man shook his head at her as he drove past. Angie waited until he had travelled some distance, before slowly and carefully heading for the fence. She reversed into a space to the left of the gap, just as Wendy had done.

With her heart thumping wildly in her chest she got out. Drawing in a breath she looked around. This was Wendy's supermarket. Turning quickly, she looked to where the red car had been parked, and gave a laugh as there had been no car there when she'd arrived seconds before, so what the hell was she doing. The only other vehicle in the area was a battered old Honda parked in the corner. She noticed the dog guard, and the dog snot all over the rear windows. There was no dog, they must be walking in the fields behind. Walking briskly to the gap, she stepped through, there was hedgerow on either side of a well beaten track which ran for a hundred yards or so. She then discovered fenced fields with a few cows on the horizon to the left, and open fields to the right. There were no dog walkers.

Angie turned back to the carpark. "Well it doesn't mean . . ." She stopped muttering. What had she thought it meant? What was it she thought was going on? The baby did a somersault. "I know, I know, Mummy's going mad."

Hurrying back towards the carpark she paused at the gap and surveyed the scene. It was identical to the one Wendy had seen. Her heart raced, and she practiced the breathing exercises she had been taught to use when in labour. Her scream was loud and shrill, when, without any warning she was knocked sideways. She grabbed at the fence to stop herself falling, and snarled at the owner of the hand that had taken hold of her elbow.

"I'm so sorry, he has no sense . . ." The petite woman took a step back. "Oh dear. He could have knocked you over, and in your condition. I'm going to have to put him on the lead before we get to the lane. Jackson, you naughty boy." She called to the large German Shepherd sitting patiently at the rear of the Honda, before turning her attention back to Angie. "Can I help you? Have you lost your dog?"

Angie's snarl had become a forced smile while her brain shouted at her to get a grip.

"No, no, thank you. I don't have a dog, but I'm thinking of getting one, and I heard this was a good spot to walk them."

"A new baby and a new dog, you must be mad." The woman suggested. "This is a great spot. Nice class of dogs here. I've been walking here for years." Jackson barked and she looked over at him. "I'd better let him in, he's after water. Are you sure you're okay?"

"Absolutely fine. Thank you." Angie tried to smile reassuringly, and walked back to her car. She was anything but fine. Freaked out is what she was, but it wasn't open for discussion with strangers. She needed to get home, to think calmly, and if she had the courage, to discuss it with Ryan.

Once home she scanned the first chapter. Everything she had written was exactly the same as she had seen in the carpark at the supermarket. Except the abducted woman of course.

'HOW CAN THAT BE?'

Angie typed the phrase numerous times at the end of the chapter, and resolved to speak to Ryan as soon as he got home. In the meantime, as she was back in Wendy's world, she might as well try and get some more written. She scanned the last page of the manuscript. Ah, yes. He was watching the family home.

~9~

It was only ten minutes later that Wendy reappeared with her father. They were both grinning as though sharing an amusing secret. Wendy clearly hadn't told her dad about him, perhaps she was waiting until after dinner. He watched them climb into Wendy's car and started the engine.

"What is it you want me to see? What are you up to?" Wendy grinned at her father as she pointed the car in the direction of the cottage.

"It wouldn't be a surprise if I told you. Keep your eyes on the road." Mr Knight pointed ahead and fell silent, but only for a few seconds. "But you're going to love it."

Wendy laughed. "Dad! You're teasing me. Shall I have a guess?"

"Nope, my lips are sealed." He settled into the seat. "You only have to wait ten minutes or so."

"Yes, but I'm excited now. What could you have done? You've hardly left the house in the last few weeks."

"I'm an intelligent man, I have many talents. You'll see soon enough. Tell me about the audition. Do you think you got it?"

"No idea. I hate auditioning for adverts. They want you to be all Shakespearian when all you have to do is hold a mop and smile."

"An advert for mops?"

"No, floor cleaner." She slapped his knee. "Don't laugh, it pays the bills, or it will do once I move in."

Their laughter died away, and the silence was deafening for a few moments.

"I'll miss you." He turned to look at her. "You could always stay, we'll let the cottage to someone who will look after it."

"Dad. We've had this conversation so many times. I have to move on. I have to have my own place and feel like I'm achieving something."

They'd arrived at the cottage and she reversed onto the small drive. Neither of them noticed his car drive past.

Wendy took her father's hand. "I know you paid for this, but it's not the where, so much as the how. I want to be stronger than I was. I want to make my own decisions and do what I want, when I want. I want to be independent." She squeezed his hand. "Every Sunday for lunch, which I'll cook, and dinner at least once a week. Unless of course I'm filming in some exotic location with Brad Pitt or Tom Cruise."

"You can be independent at home. You already do what you want and when. But if you want this, then I won't stand in your way." His hand flew to his stomach. "Did you hear that? I'm starving, can we get a move on?"

Slamming her car door, Wendy turned towards the cottage, she saw it immediately and ran around the car to join her father.

"It's wonderful. Perfect. How did you manage this?" She threw her arms around his neck, pulling his head down to enable her to kiss his forehead. She didn't see him park in the pub across the road so he could watch them.

"I called a man. He collected the keys while you were out, prepared some drawings, and got it done. You like it then?"

Wendy hurried along the path and stood before the new hardwood door. She studied the colours in the stained glass, her head bobbing approval. "I love it. Look there's a sheep, and a dog and a cat." She grinned at him. "I could get a cat. It will be company for me."

"So, you think you'll be lonely. I knew it."

"No. No, I didn't say that did I? Don't make stuff up." Turning back to the door she ran her hand over the image. "Perfect." Turning away she looked at the pub across the road. "Let's eat there to celebrate. We might be able to get a window seat and I can gaze across at my new home."

"Oh, okay. You didn't want to see the rest then?"

Wendy spun back towards her father. "Rest? There's more? What have you done?" She snatched the keys from her father's outstretched hand and hurried back to the door. "I'm so excited now, I need to pee."

"In which case, I think you'll be pleased," he muttered as he followed her into the house.

Taking the stairs two at a time, Wendy headed for the bathroom, and squealed with delight before slamming the door shut. She sat on the toilet and looked at the roll top bath. The shower curtain hadn't been hung properly on the circular rail, but she'd soon fix that. She pulled the flush, washed her hands, drying them on her jeans, before making the necessary adjustment. She stood back to admire her handiwork. The bath now looked like a large cradle, comforting, and inviting.

Her father knocked on the door. "I take it you like it?" he called.

"I love it!" Wendy pulled open the door. "It's perfect, it's the one I wanted. How did you get them to finish the tiling so quickly and get this sorted?"

"I can be very persuasive you know. Right, the surprises are done, let's eat."

"I have to look in every room first."

"Again? You've had all the surprises." Mr Knight started back down the stairs.

"I know. Because. Just because."

She was still smiling when she locked the door and went to where he waited at the gate. She held his hand, jabbering away happily as they crossed the road and entered the pub without so much as a glance at the carpark. As Wendy had hoped, they managed to get a window seat, and she glanced out at her new home occasionally as her father tried to convince her why he needed the pie and chips as carbohydrates were essential to a man of his age.

Ducking down in the seat when they looked across the road, he was surprised to find he was nervous. He didn't know who they were visiting, but someone they knew well enough to allow them to park on the drive. After a few seconds, he raised his head a little. Wendy was opening the door of the cottage, he wondered if her father was moving to somewhere a little smaller. They disappeared inside and he settled himself, knowing he may be there for some time. He took several photographs to occupy himself, and was surprised to see them leaving less than fifteen minutes later.

They crossed the road towards him, and he leaned towards the passenger seat. It would appear to a passer-by he was looking for something in the footwell. He gave them enough time to go past before sitting up straight. It crossed his mind to go in and suggest he joined them, but decided it would be too much. After all, it was only day one. He contented himself with adjusting the rear-view mirror so he could monitor the front of the pub. He was delighted when they took a seat in the window. It was bright enough inside to illuminate them perfectly, allowing him to be ready to follow when they left.

Steaming plates were carried to their table and he realised he hadn't eaten properly all day. Wendy's arrangement with her father had been more important than eating with him. His anger increased at the same rate as his hunger. Edward Knight raised his hand to his mouth and kissed his fingertips. The food was pleasing him. With a grunt, he slung open the car door and slammed it behind him. Why should they enjoy themselves while he sat, starving in the car? Marching to the bar he snatched up the menu.

"Sorry, sir, the dining room is full at the moment, a table should be free in about twenty minutes. Unless you want a bar snack. I can clear a space at the end there." An attractive barmaid, pointed to the far end of the bar.

He glanced towards the restaurant area and back again. Perfect. "A snack will suffice." He opened the menu and scanned the snack section. "Chicken and bacon club, please, and a small plate of chips." He looked at the pumps. "Half a pint of bitter too." He waited while she jotted his order on to a pad, and then walked to the end of the bar. Pulling out a stool, he watched as she removed the dirty glasses and gave the bar a cursory wipe with a disgustingly dirty-looking cloth.

"It'll be ten minutes. I'll bring your beer."

True to her word she returned minutes later with his drink, and some cutlery rolled in a napkin. No thanks were forthcoming as she placed them in front of him, as he could see them from this new vantage point and ignored her.

Edward Knight's bald patch was getting bigger, and Wendy looked happy. She was chattering away non-stop pausing only to fork the odd morsel of food into her mouth. Inclining his head, he studied her. Her eyes were bright, and she looked both innocent and sophisticated at the same time, but it was the aura of happiness that was mesmerising. That's how she would look when they eventually got married, only her smiles would be for him. His thoughts were interrupted by the arrival of his food. He shook his head at the offer of condiments.

"If it's been prepared properly, it shouldn't need anything extra," he told the barmaid.

"Not even salt for your chips?" She seemed amazed at his refusal. "This isn't a five-star hotel you know, it's only pub grub." Lifting the wooden box containing a variety of sauces, she stowed it beneath the bar. "Enjoy your food."

"I'll try." He smiled before popping a chip in his mouth. The barmaid walked away, and he looked away from Wendy only to lift more food from his plate.

The barmaid came to collect his empty plate. "How was it? Seasoned enough for you?"

He was watching Edward Knight wander off out of sight. "Perfect." Should he go and speak to Wendy? That would force her to tell her father they were back together. "Where is the gents'?" he asked the barmaid.

"Around by the games room. You got the wrong end of the bar, the ladies' is behind you. Can I get you another half?"

"Shandy. I'm driving. Thanks." He flashed a dazzling smile. With any luck, Wendy would need to walk right past him.

His luck was in. He'd only taken the first sip of his drink when she left the table, and walked towards him. She hadn't seen him yet, so he pulled a newspaper from the stack behind him, and pretended to read. Seeing her approach from the corner of his eye, he raised his hands above his head, stretching his back and yawning. He fixed a startled expression on his face and left his mouth open for a little too long.

"Wendy!" he exclaimed as she stopped dead in her tracks. "What are you doing here? Who are you with?"

"Dad." Wendy resisted the urge to turn and make sure her father wasn't watching. "Why are you here?"

"I pop in from time to time, a friend recommended it."

"Have you eaten?"

"Yes, unfortunately or I'd offer to join you." He smirked, knowing how uncomfortable she was. "Or was that not an invitation?"

"No, no. We've finished. We'll be leaving in a moment. Dad gets tired."

"Well then I'd better not hold you up. How come you were here?"

"I'm moving in across the road in a couple of weeks." Wendy explained, and immediately wondered if she should have told him.

"What the cottage? Small world." The smile was warm enough, but inside he was seething. She didn't need a cottage however attractive it might seem. She needed to move in with him, to make love in front of the open window, to thank him for choosing only furnishings he knew she would like. They could never fit the bed in the cottage.

"Isn't it. Anyway, I need to . . ." Wendy pointed behind him.

Sliding from his stool he held his hand towards the door of the toilets. "Of course, sorry. I'll pop over and say hello to your father. Is he in the restaurant?"

"No." She grabbed his arm.

"He's not in the restaurant? The carpark then?"

"I meant, no, don't go and see him. I've not spoken to him yet."

"But you've had so much time. Why haven't you told him about us?"

"Is there an us? I'm not sure what's happening at the moment, and I don't want him to get all het up." Wendy tilted her chin a little. She was strong, she was independent, she wouldn't be intimidated by him.

"Did you love me when you said you would marry me? Did you love me when you arrived at the registry office? Did you love me this afternoon when I showed you how much I loved you?" He stepped closer.

She could smell his aftershave and she wavered.

"I think you did, otherwise why agree?" He touched her arm and smiled at the goose bumps which appeared. "And other than try to put things right, I did nothing wrong. I've done nothing but declare my love for you these past nine months." His hand rose to her shoulder. "On that basis, I can see no reason, no reason at all, why you won't come back to me, or let me marry you. Tell your dad tonight, I'm going to come and see him tomorrow whether you do or not." Finally, he paused.

Wendy faltered. "I . . . that is, you . . ." She pushed the memory of their afternoon together out of her mind, and remembered the woman rushing home to cook dinner and protect her children. "You hit me to the ground." She stepped back a little. "It might have been the first time you actually hit me, but you always intimidated me. I don't want a life like that."

"I think we can agree there were extenuating circumstances. I'm sorry if I ever intimidated you, that was never my intention. I wanted . . . want everything to be perfect. I love you. I loved you then, I love you now, I'll love you forever. Please, I beg you, tell your father about us." He dropped to his knees. "Do I have to beg? I will."

Behind him he heard the barmaid hush a customer. "Hush, look, he's proposing."

Wendy grabbed his shirt and pulled him to his feet. "Stop it," she hissed. "It's embarrassing, you don't need to beg."

He pulled her to him, his lips brushing her cheek as he spoke. "So, you'll tell your father tonight?"

"I don't know about tell, but I might speak to him, yes."

"Thank you. Now, I believe you were on your way somewhere?" Stepping to one side he allowed her access to the toilets, and she hurried away.

The minute Wendy had gone his smile disappeared. How dare she accuse him of hitting her, it was more of a shove, and what provocation he'd had. Her father must have put that in her head. He climbed back on his stool and stared at his drink. The barmaid bustled over on the pretence of wiping the bar.

"I'm sorry, love. Can I get you something stronger? On the house."

Frowning, he held out his hands for an explanation. "Why are you apologising?"

"I'm not. I was commiserating, showing sympathy. Sorry, I shouldn't have disturbed you." She turned her back, mumbling.

"Why?" he called after her. "Please, explain yourself."

Reluctantly she turned back, hoping the girl wouldn't appear before their conversation was over. "I thought she'd said no."

"I'm obviously being extremely dense tonight." The hairs on his neck rose and he pressed his hands flat on the bar to stop them forming fists. "No?"

Sighing the barmaid stepped closer and lowered her voice. "You were on your knees. I thought you proposed, and when she disappeared you looked evil. It looked like she'd said no. I'll leave you in peace." Feeling uncomfortable under his gaze she made to turn away, but he grabbed her arm.

"Barmaids are supposed to be chatty. Deliver cheery banter. Not go nosing into other people's business, making incorrect assumptions and broadcasting them. It's how rumours start and trouble is caused." He controlled his facial expression, but his eyes told a different story. "With a mouth like yours, you'll get yourself into trouble." He stared at her mouth for a second. It looked inviting, and he licked his lips.

Yanking her arm away, she stepped away from him. "Sod off. I was trying to be nice. Get out, you're barred."

Sliding off the stool he shook his head. "I don't think so. This is going to be my local. I'm going now, but I'll see you very soon."

The barmaid watched him turn away, a shiver running up her spine and she rubbed her arms as though they were cold.

"Are you okay, Jenny?" A customer who had caught the animosity got to his feet and looked from one to the other.

"She's fine, aren't you, Jenny?" With a broad smile and a wave, he left the bar.

Jenny opened her mouth to share the exchange, but Wendy appeared and she shut it again. She had enough on her plate without looking for more trouble.

Wendy's eyes shot to the dining area, and she relaxed when she saw her father was alone.

"Don't worry, love. He's gone." The barmaid snatched his glass and threw the dregs into the sink. Her smile was sympathetic and Wendy was confused. Having no idea how to respond she went back to her father.

~10~

Angie heard the front door open and stopped typing. Hitting the save button she switched on the printer.

"Hello. Are there any fat women in here waiting to show me some love?" Ryan called from the hall.

"In here. Less of the fat if you want to eat tonight."

Ryan walked in and looked at the printer churning out paper. "You shopped *and* worked? What a talented large woman you are. What is it? I'm starving."

Angie's hands flew to her mouth. "Shit, shit, shit. It's still in the car." She glanced at the time. "It's not been in there long. Come on, I need some muscle. I went to the garden centre too."

Twenty minutes later the lamb was roasting in the oven, and Angie was supervising the placement of the birdbath. They positioned it on the lawn a little off centre so it would be in shade for part of the day.

Satisfied, she handed Ryan the first of the feeders. "I thought we could have two on this tree, and one over in the corner."

"Am I also tasked with setting up the webcam? It would be interesting to see what comes and goes when we're not watching. It won't take long, what time will dinner be ready?" Having hung the first two feeders, he walked to the tree next to the shed in the far corner of the garden.

"An hour or so, but I want you to read something first."

"Your novel? Wow. I thought it would be months before you were happy to show me. But I can do the webcam tomorrow." Feeder fixed, he walked behind the shed. "The new bird bath is identical to this one. Did you do that on purpose? Minus the moss and the damage of course."

"No, I chose the one I thought would look nicest. I suppose it could have been in the back of my mind though. Talking of which, come and read this for me, it won't take long."

Ryan settled himself on the couch with a beer, the manuscript, and a red pen.

"Do your usual, comment, question, and general overview. I'll get the veg on, and we'll discuss it over dinner."

"You mean you're not going to sit chewing your nails while I do it?" Ryan smiled. "You must be very sure of this one."

"Not at all. You're reading it because I don't know what the hell is going on."

An hour later, Ryan called from the sitting room as Angie spooned the vegetables onto the plates.

"I've finished. How long to dinner? It smells fabulous and I could eat a scabby horse."

"Ready. Bring the manuscript."

Angie skimmed through the notes Ryan had made while he tucked into his dinner. She forked the odd morsel into her mouth. Ryan became aware she wasn't eating as she normally would.

"Are you feeling okay? This is fabulous, and you're barely touching it."

"I'm fine." Angie turned the manuscript to face the table. "I'm distracted. Look I'm eating." She loaded her fork and shoved it into her mouth.

"Good girl. Now, do you want to discuss that?" His knife pointed at the manuscript. "I'm surprised you haven't already challenged me. I liked it by the way, although it's not your usual style."

"Not yet. Let's finish dinner."

"But you told me to bring it with me."

"Because I wanted to see your comments. Eat."

When they had finished eating, Angie piled the plates to one side and pulled forward the manuscript.

"I was surprised you didn't make more comments actually, I've not edited it at all." She found the first comment. "Where you've written, description with a question mark, do you mean the characters, or is that a general comment?"

"The characters mainly. Short, tall, fat, thin, blonde etcetera. You usually go overboard, and I've got zilch. Why are you frowning? I don't want to do this if you're going to be emotional. This is constructive, I don't want a divorce on my hands."

Angie shook her head, and after several false starts she held her hands up to stop him speaking. "I'm going to tell you why I'm frowning, and it's nothing to do with you. But it's weird, so you must hear me out. Don't interrupt me. You can laugh when I've finished."

"But—"

"Seriously, bite your tongue or something, because I might lose the courage."

"The courage? What are you—"

"Ryan! Please will you listen or not. I don't mind, if I'm freaking you out we can forget it."

Ryan looked at his wife. Her cheeks were flushed as though embarrassed, and her hands fiddled with everything within reach. That told him she was nervous. It was his turn to frown, she hadn't been freaking him out, until she told him she thought she was.

His smile was warm. "Talk. I won't interrupt."

Angie tapped the manuscript. "This wasn't planned. Not in any sense of the word. I woke up, couldn't get back to sleep and came to get a drink. I sat at the table, opened the laptop and wrote about the abduction. I didn't plan it, I didn't think about the characters, who they were, how they would develop, why he'd taken her, I simply wrote what I saw. The best way I can describe it, is that it was like putting a dream down in writing."

"Well it would explain the lack of character description, if—"

"Please, you promised." She nodded as Ryan clamped his lips together and pulled his finger across them.

"Even now I don't know what happened to her. You got up, I stopped writing, so she's still in the back of the car, and I need to know if she escapes, but I can't get there, all the other stuff is happening. You see?"

"Sort of." Ryan scratched his head. "Perhaps it's because you need to know her first? You're obviously writing some sort of thriller, you've not done that before, perhaps you don't want to write something too bloodcurdling."

"No, it's not that. When I think about it, all I have are a million questions, no ideas, no plot, just an urge to write."

"That's good. Spontaneity. You can always edit out anything you don't like . . . was that the correct thing to say? What?" he asked as Angie huffed.

"Hush. I'm going to speak quickly to get it said. There is no correct thing to say by the way." She pushed her hair away from her face and leaned back in the chair, her hands resting on her pregnancy. "Are you ready?"

"I am. Concerned, but ready."

"I haven't described the characters because I don't know what they look like, if I try to bring them to mind, or even create them - nothing. I know Wendy has blonde hair, I know her father was balding, I know the woman who helped her when he knocked her to the ground needed to get her roots done, and I know he has muscular arms, and neat fingernails. But they don't have faces."

Ryan didn't speak, even if he were allowed to, he wouldn't know what to say. He nodded acceptance.

Relieved, Angie continued, "So, I accepted that, as you said I could always go back and put something in. It was the emotions of the characters which were important, and I experience her fear and confusion, almost as if it's happening to me. But it's not me. I'm a bystander, watching it all unfold. I feel proud when she stands up to him, and I sense his anger brewing. I know what I've written so far doesn't even touch what he's capable of, but I could deal with all that. I thought perhaps being pregnant was making me more in tune with the emotional side of the story. Then I went shopping."

Angie stopped speaking and Ryan sat patiently for a few seconds, she was clearly thinking about something which had happened. Eventually, he prompted her. "And . . . what happened in the supermarket, or was it the garden centre?"

"Nothing. It was the location. I have never been to that supermarket, I only found it because Jamie told me how to get there."

"Who's Jamie?"

"The guy at the garden centre, but he's not important, what *is* important, is that it was *the* carpark. The one in the story. Right down to the last detail. The trolley park, the broken kerbstone by the fence, the . . . the everything. How can that be? As you pointed out, I didn't actually write half of that, but I knew it was there. I expected to see it. I can't tell you how freaked out I was." She was becoming animated and she jabbed her finger at him. "And Wendy had a dog called Jess . . . I think. What do you think's going on?"

Ryan considered his words carefully. He had no idea what Angie's problem was. "Wendy's dog was called Tess, I believe, and I'm sorry if I've missed something, but why is the dog's name relevant? You've haven't given the villain a name."

"No, not this Wendy." She tapped the manuscript. "Wendy who disappeared, Wendy. The lead character in The Village."

"Is there a Wendy in The Village who disappeared? Angie, I love you, you are beautiful and intelligent, but for the life of me, I don't know what you're talking about. You're not making much sense."

Angie ran her fingers through her hair. "No, I'm not. Sorry. So, from the beginning. Wendy Knight was an actress. She was going to play the character of Fran, and—"

"Karen's Fran? Hasn't Karen had always been Fran?"

"She has, but only because Wendy disappeared. Karen was a scriptwriter, she stepped in at the last minute as they had to continue filming and couldn't change the schedule. The original plan was that they would get rid of her quickly, only six episodes had been written, so it could be sorted, but she was, and is, perfect for the role, so she's still there. You see?"

"Almost. So, this Wendy went missing twenty-odd years ago, and you've decided to - what? Dramatise it. What happened to her? I . . . oh, I see. No one knows what actually happened, which is why you can't get there, it's why she's still in the back of the car."

Ryan scratched his head. "You know, Ange, I'm not sure those who know the real Wendy will be keen on you making up a story about her disappearance. Isn't that a bit . . . I don't know, off? A little insensitive, especially given the fact you work on the show. I'm not sure what you are planning on doing with that," he pointed to the manuscript, "but, it might be thought you are cashing in. Even after all this time." He shrugged. "Sorry . . . not what you want to hear."

Angie waved the comment away. "It's not a problem. I agree, or I would if that's what I was doing." Banging the table in frustration she groaned. "Okay, as you can't read between the lines of what I can't say . . . I'm not making this up, it comes to me. I write what I see. I saw the carpark in great detail, but I've never been there before. I had a passing conversation with Karen who explained how she went from scriptwriter to soap star. Yes, that might have got me thinking, but we didn't discuss any detail. For instance, she didn't tell me Wendy had a dog, she didn't tell me her name was Tess." Angie's eyes widened. "That's what we need to do." She got to her feet. "We need to find out more about her disappearance. I'll get my laptop, perhaps we'll find something online."

Ryan opened and shut his mouth. He'd been humouring Angie, but now he was worried. Did she think she was having visions of some sort? He watched her disappear. Perhaps if he continued to humour her it would help, he could inject some logic if she got overexcited. This couldn't be good for her, and therefore it couldn't be good for the baby. He smiled at her as she hurried back to the table and opened the laptop.

"Tell me about the carpark. A carpark is a carpark. There will be some logical explanation, Ange. You are writing a good story, and it's about a horrible subject, and it's clearly got you gripped, you might be seeing things as you want to see them. Making the fact fit with the fiction . . . or do I mean vice versa? But you get my drift?"

"I do. And I'd agree. It sounds like I'm going mad, but I've never been in that carpark before, yet I knew it in minute detail."

"Where is this carpark? Is it local?"

"Yes, and that's the point. I've not shopped locally since we moved in. I've always done the shopping while I was in town. It's the first time I've ever been there, I . . . Here we go, there's something here. Oh. . ."

"What?" Ryan dragged his chair round to join her.

"There's a reference to Wendy here. But it's because Harry was joining the cast."

Ryan read the report from the local newspaper, "*Ageing pop star, Harry Grayson* - Ha! I bet he loved that, he's not that old, former pop star would have been kinder - *has signed a contract to join the cast of popular soap, The Village. His character, Kelvin Brown, makes his appearance in the Easter double bill, when disgraced actress Julie Wayne departs the show after two years. Wayne's conviction for drink-driving was unacceptable to the producers. The Village, filmed on the purpose-built set in Whitchurch, and in the studio on Whiteladies Road in Bristol, is currently the number one soap in the UK. Asked about Wayne's departure, Grayson commented, 'While I admire Julie's acting talent, I understand why she has to go. We actors are here to set an example, the public expect it of us.' The Village is—*"

"What a hypocritical bastard. He's been trying to seduce girls young enough to be his daughter." She patted Ryan's hand. "Sorry, carry on."

"*The Village is no stranger to hitting the headlines for the wrong reason, in two thousand and seven, fire ripped through the mainly wooden set, causing major damage, and it took over two months to rebuild it. Arson was suspected, although no one was charged for the offence. By far the show's most disturbing claim to fame, was the unexplained disappearance of actress, Wendy Knight. Miss Knight disappeared shortly before the show hit our screens and had recorded several episodes. Actress Karen Ellery stepped into the shoes of lead character Fran, and has been in the show since the first episode. Miss Knight is presumed dead, although her body has never been found.*" Ryan shrugged. "It doesn't tell us anything you didn't already know. What else is there?"

Angie went back to the original search. "Nothing I can see. Surprisingly common name. Hang on, I'll change the query." This time Angie added, missing actress, into the search before the name. "This is more like it."

Scrolling through the results she clicked on one that caught her eye. *The funeral of Edward Knight, father of missing actress Wendy Knight, was held today at Canford Crematorium. Mr Knight's daughter, Wendy, went missing in nineteen-ninety-four. Despite an extensive investigation, Wendy, who was twenty-five when she disappeared, has never been found, and must be presumed dead. The case remains open. Mr Knight was a successful local business man, and his brother, Tom Knight, gave a touching reading, and ended by saying Edward had never recovered from the shock of his daughter's disappearance, and died of a broken heart. Mr Knight left the bulk of his estate to two charities he had supported for many years, and a substantial sum to an undisclosed beneficiary. There are rumours it was an officer involved in investigating the case, although this has not been confirmed."*

Angie screwed her nose up. "Still no detail. Let's have another go." She went back to the search results and mumbled as she read through the headlines.

"Newspaper archives," Ryan announced. "We can check the archives. Not sure how much will be online, the internet hadn't really got started in nineteen-ninety-four. Not as we know it today anyway."

Angie turned the laptop to face him. "I need to pee. Do your stuff."

When she returned, the laptop was shut and Ryan was on his phone. He was speaking to someone about their quest. The conversation wandered and Angie left him to it. Going back upstairs, she sat on the bath and watched the water rising. Perhaps she should let the Wendy thing go. It was after all ancient history, and Ryan was right, she could be imagining things or making connections where there were none.

Climbing into the bath, she resolved to change the name of her character. She would be Susan, or Jane, anything but Wendy. That would help.

Five minutes later, Ryan shouted up the stairs, he mentioned something about a library, and asked if she wanted anything. Angie shouted no, as it was easier than having a disjointed conversation. Later, dressed in her most comfortable pyjamas, she went to join him. The television was on, but Ryan was fast asleep. She shook her head. She thought it was the mother who was supposed to become increasingly tired in pregnancy, this napping was becoming a habit.

Opening the laptop, she sat at the table. She wasn't going to write, she was only going to do a find and replace. She couldn't even remember where she'd left the story.

~11~

"Over my dead body!" Edward Knight bellowed, slapping the newspaper on the breakfast table. "I thought you'd moved on. You've had all these auditions, something will happen for you soon, and the cottage. YOUR home, your lovely new home. No horrible memories of him."

"Dad, it was a chance meeting. He wants to explain. He's always wanted to explain, you know that. It was me who said no. Now I'm thinking I should hear what he has to say."

Although brave enough to tell her father she'd spoken to him, Wendy wasn't brave enough to tell him she'd gone to the flat with him. She jumped to her feet when her father developed a coughing fit, and she filled a glass with water, and patted him on the back until he'd recovered.

"You see. He's bloody killing me, and he's not even wormed his way back into your life yet. Bastard!"

Wendy forced a laugh. "If you remember, you've had this infection for several weeks. I only bumped into him yesterday."

"And that's another thing. Why didn't you tell me yesterday?" Mr Knight banged the newspaper again. "I'll tell you why, because you were too ashamed to admit you were considering going out with him. Don't do it. He'll manipulate you. You give your uncle Tom a ring, he'll tell you what's what."

"Dad, calm down, in fact sit down. I'm twenty-five years of age, I'm old enough to make my own decisions without consulting you and uncle Tom."

"Then why tell me? You knew I'd not like it, why not just get on with it? Because you wanted me to talk you out of it. Deep down you know it's the wrong thing to do." Mr Knight answered his own question, but he did sit down.

"It was conversational. What if he has a really, really good reason? We don't know he doesn't." Wendy lifted her empty bowl from the table and took it to the sink.

"Good reason? Good reason? What bloody reason can there be for knocking my baby to the ground when she was in her wedding dress. There is no reason in the world for that, my girl, and don't you forget it."

"He was stressed out because he was late, I was horrible to him, he wouldn't have meant to do it. It was more of a push anyway."

"Oh, that's all right then. Marry the bastard. Then spend the rest of your life not being horrible to him, and hoping to God he doesn't get stressed out. You can call it what you like, but men do not lay hands on a woman in anger. Not a punch, not a slap, and not even a push. He's a bastard, and he will never, and I mean NEVER, come under my roof again. Am I making myself clear?"

"Crystal. I'll meet him in a café. Are you going to eat that?" Wendy pointed at the half-eaten bowl of porridge.

"For some reason which escapes me, I have no appetite, throw it away."

Wendy watched her father wander out into the back garden. Hands behind his back he walked slowly around the perimeter, a general inspecting his troops. Wendy knew he was troubled, any form of bad news sent him heading for the garden.

Lifting the phone from the wall, she dialled his number. It rang several times before the answer machine cut in. Wendy hung up. She hadn't planned what she was going to say, and she wasn't going to be recorded mumbling and talking gibberish. She filled the sink and started to do the washing up. She'd barely got started when the phone rang. She knew it would be him.

"Hello, I wasn't expecting to hear from you so early. I was in the shower. I was wishing you were with me, but I suppose a phone call was the next best thing."

Wendy's cheeks flushed, she was glad her father wasn't in the room. Suddenly tongue tied, she racked her brains for a witty retort. Unable to come up with anything, she settled for a lunch invitation. "I'm not sure what you have on today, but I'm free at lunchtime if you'd like to join me."

"I have something on this morning, but should be back in Bristol by two o'clock, where shall we meet? I take it you've told your father about us?"

"I've told him I bumped into you yesterday, yes. As you can imagine it was a bit of a shock for him."

"He'll live. Do you want to come here, I'll cook, and then you can bump into me again?" There was laughter in his voice.

Wendy closed her eyes remembering the man she'd fallen in love with. She had been a pain to have a relationship with, always dashing here and there at the drop of a hat to get to the next audition. If he'd turned up on their wedding day she would have married him. One misunderstanding, however huge, and it was all over? She opened her eyes, she would give him another chance. He deserved that, she deserved that. Her father would come around.

"I can't come there for the afternoon, I have to be at the cottage. There's a delivery of furniture coming between three and five o'clock." She hesitated for a second. "Why don't you come there. I've got basic crockery and stuff there, I'll grab some groceries, or we can eat at the pub first and keep an eye out for the delivery. What do you think?"

He could hear the excitement in her voice and it made him smile, he almost forgot his irritation that she was continuing with this cottage nonsense. When push came to shove they would live in the flat, but he'd deal with that problem another day, there was no rush. At the moment, he simply needed to have her back.

"Perfect." His voice was husky. "I'm already ready for you." And he was. "I'll be there as soon as I can. What is it you're having delivered?"

"Oh, a few bits, kitchen table and chairs, a bed, and—"

"Stop right there. Perfect. I'll be thinking of you every second until I get there. Regards to your father."

And he was gone. Wendy smiled as she replaced the hand set. She was still smiling when her father returned to the kitchen.

"Look, I've been thinking, if you must see the bastard then do so on your terms. Meet him somewhere neutral, find out what his excuse is. Don't go jumping back in there . . . Why are you smiling? Am I amusing you?" Huffing he turned away grabbing the kettle. "I'll make my own tea. Would you like one?"

"Don't be grumpy. I was smiling because you are being reasonable. I have arranged to meet him for lunch, in a pub. Is that suitable?"

"Shall I come, or at least take you. I can wait in the car if you want."

"No thank you. I'm a big girl I can look after myself."

"I hope you're right. What time will you be home? What pub are you going to?"

"Dad! This is unnecessary. Not long ago you were planning on giving me away to him. I hate that expression - women shouldn't be owned. But you know what I mean."

"That was then, this is now. Tea?" Mr Knight gave no further explanation, none was needed.

"No thanks, I'm going to have a shower, my hair needs washing."

"Looks perfectly fine to me. You don't need to make an effort for him, because I doubt he'll make one for you."

"It's not for him, it's for me. I have standards."

Mr Knight mumbled into his mug of tea.

"I'm sorry I didn't hear you."

He shooed her away knowing full well she'd heard him tell her that her standards weren't high enough. But he wasn't in the mood for an argument. When it all went pear-shaped again, and it would, she'd need him, and he didn't want her to hesitate in coming to him. He was still in the kitchen half an hour later when she came back downstairs.

"Dad, I'm off now. Not sure what time I'll be back, you carry on and have dinner without me," she called from the hall as she slipped her feet into her not so sensible shoes. Hearing her father moving, she grabbed the bag she'd packed from the stairs. "Bye," The door banged shut behind her before he could get into the hall.

Wendy drove to the supermarket she'd noticed on her last trip to the cottage and bought a selection of food, so providing different options for lunch. She also stocked up on the basic larder necessities, milk, tea, sugar and the like, and finally a small case of his favourite beer and a bottle of cheap but adequate champagne. Satisfied she'd thought of everything he might want, should he not want to go to the pub, she steered the trolley back to her car. The supermarket was busy, and she'd had to park a fair distance from the entrance, and she cursed the wonky wheel all the way back to the car. She'd almost finished loading the shopping into the boot, when there was a shout and something knocked into the trolley causing it to bump against the car.

"Charlie, you bugger. Come here, it's this way." A harassed looking middle-aged woman slammed the door of her car. "Grab his collar if you can," she called to Wendy. "He won't mind. Don't let him jump up on you though. Trying to get him out of that."

The puppy had stopped running, the crash of the trolley against the car had frightened him, and he cowered at her feet.

"Hello, puppy. You have to be careful in carparks. You're too small to be noticed." She picked him up, and cradling him in her arms she walked to meet the woman. "He's okay, luckily none of the cars were on the move."

"Too excited. Now he's allowed out for a walk, he knows when I open the back door he gets some freedom. Normally he would run straight into the field," the woman waved her arm in the direction of the corner of the carpark, "but it's so busy here today, I had to park further away. Come here. I'm going to leave your lead on in future so I can grab you." She relieved Wendy of the puppy. "Thank you."

"You're welcome. He's a handsome boy."

"I got him from the rescue centre up the road. Mum was found wandering, and had nine puppies. They think it's a Retriever, German Shepherd cross. Going to be massive if these paws are anything to go by. Two girls left if you want one." She laughed as she turned away. "Thanks again."

Wendy smiled as she collected the last bag and loaded it into the car. A puppy would be great company in the cottage, she'd always wanted her own dog, and if by any chance they did get back together, it would mean they'd have to live in the cottage. You couldn't keep a dog in a flat, especially not *that* flat. But perhaps today was too soon, she needed to sort the rest of her life out first.

She drove to the cottage and unloaded the groceries, before unpacking the bag she had brought from home. It was mainly household linen and towels, but she had also packed a change of clothes. Checking the time, she realised she had at least an hour before he arrived, time enough to make the cottage look more lived in. She collected the box of assorted knickknacks from under the stairs, and added the things she'd acquired at the supermarket. Lugging the box from room to room, she found homes for everything. The bathroom was the last port of call, and her eclectic collection of candle holders, complete with new candles was arranged on the windowsill, deep purple towels were set to hang casually on the towel rings, and a porcelain soap dish complete with new soap was balanced on the edge of the bath.

Wendy stepped back to admire her handiwork. Perfect. Would he think so? She didn't care, she told herself. Although as she went back downstairs she knew it was a lie. She wanted it to be perfect, she wanted him to think it was perfect. She shook the possibility that he wouldn't from her mind, and collecting some scissors went to cut some fresh flowers to put in the kitchen window. They would be the first thing he saw, as the kitchen was at the front of the cottage. As she wandered to the rose bushes at the bottom of the garden she was unaware he was parking in the same place as he had the night before.

Jenny Croft was collecting empties from the picnic tables immediately in front of the pub. He gave her a cursory glance and locked his car. As he strode out towards the road, she spotted him and called to him.

"This is for patrons only." She walked towards him and pointed at his car.

"So the sign says. I believe I have and will be attempting to enjoy what this establishment has to offer." Looking her in the eye, he added, "Go and be useful, Jenny. Don't be rude to the clientele, barmaids have been sacked for less.".

Jenny simmered. "Well don't come crying to me if it gets damaged." She added a whine to her voice. "As the sign says, you park here at your own risk." Laughing, she turned back towards the pub. He grabbed her arm and yanked her around to face him, and she gasped in shock.

"Listen, you interfering bitch, I've now run out of patience. When I come back, and I will, you had better show some respect." His lips were almost touching her ear and she shivered as his warm breath found her skin.

"Or else what?" Despite her pounding heart she couldn't let him have the last word.

"Or else you might not live to regret it." His laugh was brief and cruel.

Jenny pulled her arm away. "What the hell does that mean?"

"Exactly what it says. Now go about your business, I haven't got time to sort you out now." From the corner of his eye he saw someone appear in the doorway and he smiled warmly at her. Lifting his hand, he squeezed her shoulder, and spoke louder. "Thank you so much Jenny, you are a star. I'll buy you a drink later." Giving her a quick wink, he turned and walked away.

Jenny stood open-mouthed. She'd not seen the arrival of Old Bill in the doorway, or minutes later turning away believing he'd misread the situation., She watched him walk along the path to the cottage wondering whether he was right in the head. Deciding he wasn't, and she would give him a wide berth in future, she carried the empties into the pub.

Glancing over his shoulder, he was pleased to see the barmaid had gone. Nice looking girl, she'd be good sport, but too close to mess about with. He studied the stained-glass door before knocking, expecting it to be thrown open, and tapped his toe in disappointment when he had to knock again. Still she didn't come and he tried the handle. The door appeared to be locked. Tutting, he walked to the side of the house and around into the rear garden. It was empty, but the patio doors stood open, and he walked in.

Finding himself in a decent-sized sitting room he looked around. It was acceptable in a girly way. The comfortable looking brown leather sofa and chair were draped with colourful throws and an array of cushions. Above the mantle was a mirror with a sturdy wooden frame, and various ornaments were dotted on the shelves in the alcove. Hearing a tap running he continued his journey into the hall. Rough plastered walls were painted white, and the beams newly stained. The sun on the stained glass gave it a warm glow.

He heard her movement and turned towards the kitchen. "I knocked, twice. Where were you?"

Wendy yelped and dropped the scissors in her hand, which clattered on the tiled floor. "Oh my goodness. You scared me to death." Wendy's smile was warm. "I was collecting those, I thought they would cheer the kitchen up."

"Very nice. It is a little bare in here." He cast an eye around. "It's clear you haven't moved in yet."

Wendy was a little hurt. She'd purposely put everything away in cupboards knowing he hated clutter. She opened her mouth to say so, but decided to change tack. "I can't believe I missed your arrival. I wanted to answer the door with a bottle of bubbly in my hand." She was relieved to see his smile and opened the fridge to collect the champagne. "I wanted to welcome you properly."

His smile disappeared. He had assumed she meant to celebrate them being together, but apparently it was to welcome him to her home.

"What would we be celebrating?" He remained on the threshold of the kitchen.

Catching the edge to his voice, she turned to him. She didn't know what his problem was, but she wasn't going to let him ruin her good mood. She'd been happy about today, right up until his arrival.

"Everything. It's a glorious day, we're here together, when the furniture arrives this place will seem more like a home, the sun is shining," she held up the bottle, "and I have bubbles. Isn't that enough?"

The smile returned and he stepped into the kitchen. Taking the bottle, he put it next to the sink and pulled her into his arms, kissing her passionately.

"It will do for a start." His voice was husky as he released her. "What time is the delivery due? Do we have enough time to bump into each other?"

"Probably, possibly, I don't know. It was a two-hour slot."

"Then you'd better show me the rest of the house. Let's start upstairs." He gave her a push towards the hall, and grinning she took his hand and pulled him up the narrow staircase.

Pushing open the first door, she revealed an empty room. "Spare bedroom, or possible study, I'm not sure." She walked into the bathroom. "Perfect bath. Big enough for two." Her eyes twinkled at him. "And although the view isn't as spectacular as the flat, I think you'll like the bedroom. Come." She hurried along the landing to the bedroom. "I think it's wonderful."

Stepping into the room he looked around. Hefty beams lined the ceiling which sloped around the edges. Everything gleamed with fresh white paint, and a stubby oak wardrobe stood in one corner. The stained floorboards were partially covered by a Persian rug, and deep red damask curtains hung from a wooden pole above the diamond-leaded window.

"Very nice," he walked to the window. The narrow road was obscured by hedges, and the pub looked picturesque surrounded as it was by trees. "Very tranquil." He looked towards the pub. "It looks like a scene from a biscuit tin."

"You like it then?" Wendy was relieved. It shouldn't matter what he thought. But it did.

"It's feminine, but yes, I can imagine having some fun in here once the bed arrives . . . on second thoughts . . ." He turned away from the window, unbuttoning his shirt as he did so. "Take your knickers off."

Wendy's body responded to the passion in his voice and the lust in his eyes. But she protested even as his shirt dropped to the floor and his trousers were unzipped, leaving her in no doubt of his intentions.

"Shouldn't we wait? What if they arrive?"

Kicking off his shoes, he stepped out of his trousers and removed his socks. Her heart skipped a beat. She wanted him. Now. Hiking her skirt, she removed her kickers, he pulled her against him and unzipped her skirt which fell to the floor. His hands exploring her, his teeth grazing her neck as she pushed against him. He groaned with pleasure when he found she was ready for him.

"I knew you couldn't wait." His mouth found hers and she was lost for a moment.

Freeing her lips, she whispered, "Let's close the curtains."

"We can't, you won't know if the delivery arrives." Taking hold of her shoulders, he spun her round to face the window. Pressing himself against her he nudged her forward. "Hold the sill," he commanded, his foot slipping between hers and spreading her legs.

"We can't. What if . . ."

With an urgent thrust he penetrated her, her words were lost.

"There's no one to see us. Look." His hand grabbed her hair and pulled it gently to lift her head.

Wendy looked out at the pub. There were three cars in the carpark but not a soul to be seen. He thrust again and she gasped.

"Would you like me to stop?" Another thrust, and pulling her hair harder, her head tilted and she looked up at the curtain pole as his lips caressed her throat.

Closing her eyes her body responded to the rhythm of his. This was right. It had always been right. Her body moved faster.

"Don't rush, there's no hurry," he murmured into her neck and stopped moving.

She squirmed against him. "Please." Her voice cracked.

He looked out and saw Jenny reappear from the side of the pub. When he'd seen her wander around to the rear of the pub moments before, he'd been worried she would use a back door. "Are you sure?" His eyes were on Jenny willing her to look up at him. He pulled at Wendy's top, "Lift your arms. Quickly, I must have all of you." Wendy did as she was told, and her top and bra hit the floor. Eyes still on Jenny, he fondled her breasts. "I asked if you were sure?"

"Oh yes."

"Then hold on." His thrusting became more urgent, but as Wendy's groans of pleasure increased, his eyes never left Jenny. When Jenny looked up she came to a halt and he grinned at her, thrusting harder.

Jenny squinted up at the window. Were they . . . She watched as Wendy's head jerked backwards, causing her shoulders to rise and her naked breasts to thrust forward. She watched the rhythmic movement of his shoulders, and then she looked at his face. The bastard was smiling at her. She wanted to turn away, but it seemed impossible. Wendy's head fell forward and revealed his muscular upper torso, the movement more urgent now. He smiled at Jenny, before his mouth opened in a roar of pleasure, and his head fell forward and rested on Wendy's back.

Released, Jenny turned and hurried back into the pub.

“Are you all right, Jen?” The landlord paused in the polishing of a glass.

“Yep. I'm going to take my break now if it's all right with you. I've been all the way round, all the glasses are in.”

“You look pale. Are you sure you're feeling okay?”

“I do feel a bit odd. But nothing to worry about.” Jenny lifted the hatch and disappeared into the rear of the pub. If truth were told she didn't know how she felt. Spooked, angry . . . aroused? She shook the thought away and hit the switch on the kettle.

~ ~ ~

Wendy zipped her skirt and walked to the window. “Oh my God. It's here. The furniture.”

“No time to see if the bath is big enough then.” He slipped his shoes back on. “I'll go and let them in.”

Half an hour later they sat at the new kitchen table while the delivery men completed putting the bed together.

“Do you like it?” Wendy ran her hand over the table. “We can eat in a civilised manner now. I'll give you your choices as soon as . . . and there they are.” She tilted her head and listened to the footfall on the stairs. She made to stand.

“Stay there, I'll see them out.”

Wendy smiled as she listened to his casual banter with the delivery men. She heard one thank him, which told her he must have tipped them. He must be happy.

When he returned she opened the fridge and listed the options available for their meal. He walked to her and gently pushed the door shut.

“I'm taking you to the pub. That way you can conserve your energy, relax, and when we get back the bed will need testing.” He kissed her grin. “Not to mention the bath.” He took her hand and pulled her forward. “And when we've done all that, you may prepare my supper.”

Jenny was shocked to find them sitting at the bar when she returned from her break. She glanced around. Other than Old Bill, reading the newspaper in the window, the bar was empty. No sign of Gary, the landlord. She looked everywhere but at them. Bill called to her.

“I'll have another half, Jen, then I'll be on my way before the evening lot start arriving. Those bridge workers are noisy buggers.”

Jenny lifted a half-pint mug from the shelf and walked to the pumps, studiously ignoring them. He shook his head. That wasn't right. She should at least be polite.

"Bridge workers? What bridge workers?" he asked. Bill had gone back to his paper, so Jenny had no choice but to answer him.

"The second Severn crossing. Lots of the men working on the bridge, lodge in the area. Some of them come here for their evening meal." Her lips twitched a brief smile before she went back to pouring the drink.

"That must provide a nice steady trade. How long before the bridge opens?"

Jenny sighed inwardly. The bastard was determined to talk to her. "No idea." She turned away lifted the hatch and carried the beer to Bill. Not wanting to go back behind the bar, she tried to engage Bill in conversation, but he wasn't interested, so she wandered around the bar, straightening chairs and tidying tables.

"What time do you get busy? I'll make a note to avoid coming."

"All bloody day if that's the case," she muttered under her breath, and then more loudly, "Starts around six as a rule."

"In which case we have a good hour of peace. I'll have another pint."

Jenny walked slowly back behind the bar and he held out his glass. Refusing to look at his face, she shook her head and lifted a clean glass from the shelf.

"Leave it there. I'll use a fresh one." She looked directly at Wendy though. "Anything for you?"

"No thanks." Wendy slipped off the stool. "I'd better spend a penny before our food arrives."

Jenny placed the beer in front of him, and he held out a note.

"I'd say keep the change. But it's not that that you want, is it?"

Jenny was genuinely confused and finally she looked at him. "What?" She regretted it instantly. He was smirking, and his eyes travelled to her cleavage and back.

"Or do you prefer to watch? Some people do, although I like the action myself. Which is it?"

Jenny snatched at note, but he had a tight grip. "I wasn't bloody watching. I looked up and there you were. Shameless."

"But you didn't look away." He leaned closer. "You watched as I took her. Waited for me to come. Did you wish it was you?"

Jenny tugged at the note. "No, I didn't. It was unintentional, perhaps next time you'll draw the curtains."

His hand released the note, and darted forward, catching Jenny's wrist in a firm grip.

"It could be you. Not in the window necessarily, but in here perhaps. What about up against the bar, or bent over the pool table. Can you imagine it?" His voice was throaty, he watched the colour rise to her cheeks. "Can you imagine me thrusting into you?"

Jenny's stomach did a somersault. She was ashamed to realise she was becoming aroused, and she wondered what would happen if they were alone. With a final effort, she pulled her hand free. "There's something wrong with you," she snapped, turning away to the till.

Amused, he watched as shaking hands sorted his change, and held out an open palm when she returned. "When you're ready, and you will be, let me know."

"What about your girlfriend?" Jenny shook her head in disgust.

"I don't think she'd do a threesome. Could be arranged though." The smirk was back.

"That's not what I meant."

"Oh, you'd like to watch again." He leaned forward and rested his chin on his hands. "Interesting. Very interesting."

"What is?" Wendy climbed on her stool.

"Jenny here was telling me she likes to watch men at work. Apparently, seeing them in action, and watching the methods they use to finish the job turns her on."

Wendy gave a laugh. "Ha! I'm sorry but that sounded sexual."

He turned to look at her. The spark was there. "That's because you have been satisfied today. Do you need more? We can always cancel the food." Clapping his hands together he laughed. "Oh, I see what you mean." He turned back to Jenny. "You wouldn't watch us make love, would you? Would it turn you on?"

Wendy slapped his arm. "Stop it. You are embarrassing me, and as for poor Jenny . . ." She looked at Jenny. "He has an odd sense of humour. Please ignore him."

"I'd call it warped, and I'm trying to." Jenny put the change on the bar. "Thank God for that." She muttered as the landlord appeared carrying two plates.

"At the bar, or do you want a table?"

"Oh, I think a table. This one will do." He lifted the drinks and walked to the table opposite the bar.

The landlord placed the plates on the chipped table mats and called to Jenny to provide cutlery and condiments.

"He won't need them. He told me if it's prepared properly additional seasoning wouldn't be necessary." Jenny looked at him triumphantly.

He beamed at her. "Well remembered. She's a good one, sir. You want to keep hold of her."

Mumbling his thanks, the landlord wandered back to the bar, calling goodbye to Bill who had decided to leave. "Cheers, Bill. See you tomorrow." He turned his attention to Jenny. "I'm going to put my feet up for five minutes. There's only this lovely couple for you to watch. Give me a shout if I'm not back by half past."

"Did you hear that, Wendy? Alone, with only Jenny to watch us. Keep a close eye on us, Jenny, you don't want to miss anything."

Wendy joined in with his laughter. "She knows we're not going to run off with the cutlery. How boring would it be, watching someone eat?"

Jenny tried her best to give Wendy a warm smile as she placed the cutlery down. Poor girl, she didn't know what he was really like.

"Thank you, Jenny." He winked at Wendy as Jenny turned away. "Keep watching, you never know what we'll get up to."

"Behave." Wendy slapped him playfully. "This looks delicious."

"You did work up an appetite," he nudged her arm.

Without moving his head, he watched Jenny return to the bar. As he ate his meal he watched as she wiped the bar, before turning her attention to the optics. He put down his cutlery as she stopped in front of the mirror. His hand slipped under the table and he placed it on Wendy's knee. She turned to smile at him. Stroking his hand along her thigh in a slow calculated motion, he slowly pulled up her skirt until he was stroking her skin.

"Stop it," she whispered harshly, squirming in her seat.

"Hush. We're alone. She's busy, look. Let's have some fun." He leaned closer and blew on her neck as he forced his hand between her legs. "Good girl. No knickers, you can follow instructions. Now, carry on eating or at least looking at your food, and enjoy this. You deserve it."

"But—"

"Relax. Do as you're told." He opened his fingers, and she shifted so her legs were parted slightly. "Good girl, if anyone looks over, you're simply enjoying your food. Look at the lovely food."

Wendy looked at her plate. This was new. They'd made love in a field, in the back of his car, but never had he been so brazen before. She wasn't sure she could do it. His fingers found their target and she gasped.

"Look at the plate," he insisted as Jenny's head shot up and she looked at their reflection in the mirror. He held Jenny's eyes, while quietly instructing Wendy. "Open a little wider . . . good girl. Is that good, or is this better?"

Jenny dropped her eyes from his and they travelled down. The girl's skirt was around her thighs and she'd opened her legs wider. She blinked, but she didn't look away until one of Wendy's feet lifted from the floor. She looked him in the eye, as almost unable to contain herself, Wendy gripped the table, her nose almost touching her food. Jenny watched her rock back and forth with the rhythm of his fingers. She wanted it to be her. He ran his tongue along his lips and jerked his head towards the restaurant.

Jenny's nod was almost imperceptible. She lifted a bottle and clinked it against its neighbour. He pulled his hand free.

"Oops, she's on the move. I'd better let you finish your dinner."

"Oh my God. What are you doing to me. I can't eat." Wendy watched Jenny move further up the bar, and pulled her skirt back down to her knees.

"I have a bit of a predicament here." He glanced into his lap with a smile. "I'd better go and sort myself out. May I?" Making a pretence of hiding his modesty with her napkin, he walked to the far end of the bar, through the restaurant and towards the gents'.

Jenny watched him go. "Do you need anything?" she called to Wendy. "I need to make sure the restaurant's ready.

Wendy smiled. "No, thank you." She watched Jenny disappear into the restaurant.

When Jenny pushed open the door to the gents' toilet he smiled at her.

"I told you you liked watching"

He sounded smug, and Jenny bristled, but she wanted him. To save face she tilted her chin. "I like doing better."

"Oh, then come and show me."

"Not here. Not in the bogs for God's sake."

"Please. Spare me the protestations. You came out here to what? Tell me you liked doing, but not do anything, come here."

He yanked her to him and the door closed behind her. Shoving her roughly he backed her up against the sink, and pulled down the zip on her jeans, he spared her no thought as he shoved his hand between her legs. She winced.

"Don't be a baby. Pull them down."

"But—"

"Now. We don't have much time."

Fumbling she pulled her jeans and panties to her knees, and flushed as he stepped back to look at her.

"Turn around."

When Jenny turned around she gazed at her reflection in the mirror. Her cheeks were red, her eyes kind of wild and she looked at him as he pushed her forward. His eyes laughed at her but she didn't care.

"Would you like me to fuck you, because let's make no pretence, this isn't love making not in any sense of the word."

"Just get on with it," she snapped, she'd already made herself look stupid, she wasn't going to beg. She gasped in pain as he grabbed her hair and shoved her face against the cold mirror.

"Then I shall."

She heard him pull the zip on his trousers, and was suddenly frightened. She'd never done anything like this before. She gave the punters a wide berth as a rule, he could do anything and it would all be her fault. She'd come to him willingly. His arm went around her waist he pulled her back towards him.

"Hold on, Jenny, we're going for a ride."

Gripping the taps, she pushed back onto him, and gasped, her arousal and fear was such that her orgasm came as he thrust into her. She yelped as wave after wave took hold, and then he was gone. The cubicle door slammed shut and the lock slid into place. Suddenly embarrassed, she yanked up her jeans and stared at her reflection in the mirror. She was ashamed, but her eyes were bright. Then she heard the shout.

"Jenny! Where are you?"

Gary was coming. Running her fingers through her hair, and wiping the back of her hand across her mouth, she called back.

"In here. Come and help. This gentleman has got stuck in the toilet."

Inside the cubicle he smiled. Clever girl. He heard the main door open and for good measure, he rattled the cubicle door.

"Hang on, I think it moved." He rattled the door again before sliding back the bolt. He tried to look shamefaced. "I'm sorry. What a bother. I thought I was going to be stuck in here for hours." He looked at her, his eyes laughing.

She forced a smile unable to speak to him.

"Thank you, Jenny. I'd better get back to Wendy. She'll think I've run off with you."

Gary laughed as he stepped into the cubicle and slid the bolt back and forth. "Seems fine. Must have been one of those things."

Back behind the bar, Jenny watched them preparing to leave, and hoped he wouldn't try and speak to her. She'd humiliated herself enough for one day. Her hopes were dashed as he approached the bar. Wendy went to wait at the door.

"Thank you again, Jenny." He held out his hand and she shook it. "Much appreciated." He lowered his voice. "What time do you finish?"

"Eleven-fifteen. I have a taxi booked."

"Cancel it, I'll come back and give you a lift home. We should finish what we started."

"No. I can't, my housemate . . . I . . . no. Sorry."

He threw his head back and laughed as though she'd told a joke. Still smiling broadly, he wagged a finger at her. "Don't be silly. I'll be back for you." Abruptly he turned away and walked to Wendy shaking his head. "She's funny. I like her."

"What did she say that made you laugh?" Wendy slipped her arm through his.

"I can't remember exactly, something about locking me up. I won't be using that cubicle again."

Wendy bumped her shoulder against his. "You shouldn't get yourself so excited."

"Oh I should have." He turned and kissed her. "I haven't enjoyed an outing to the pub so much in ages."

Wendy squeezed his hand. "I'm so glad you like it here. I've been thinking about getting a dog. Do you think I should?"

"No!" His answer was clipped and absolute. He felt her stiffen and he softened his voice. "What if you get offered a long-running job which keeps you away from home? You know what it's like in this business. If you have to go into a hotel or digs, even rent somewhere, you'll be stuffed."

"I thought I'd speak to Dad about it."

"Hmmm, I suppose. But how old is he now? Dogs live for ten years or more, would he cope? I'd offer to help, but I'm in the same boat, and quite honestly don't want that sort of responsibility."

Wendy sighed. "You're probably right." She unlocked the front door. "It's a beautiful evening. Shall we sit in the garden?"

"I think not. We have unfinished business." He tilted her head, his kiss gentle. "Upstairs now. Bed then bath."

His lovemaking was tender, and as Wendy brushed through her damp hair she decided she could make it work. He still loved her, he even liked the cottage and the pub. Perhaps their new life could be here. It was already a happy place to be. The flat would always hold memories of what should have been. She wouldn't say anything yet, she'd wait a while to see how things worked out. Pulling her damp hair into a bun she went to the kitchen to join him. She grinned at what she found.

He was still naked except for her butcher's apron, and was busy chopping onions. A glass of wine stood on the table awaiting her arrival, and an open bottle of beer sat amongst various ingredients dotted along the work surface.

"What a sight for sore eyes. You have a magnificent backside. What are we having?"

"True. You can't argue with the truth. And we're having a stir-fry. You need to stock up on more spices, but we'll manage." He blew her a kiss. "Take a seat madam, this won't take long."

The meal was delicious, and they chatted happily about nothing much while they ate. When they'd finished they cuddled on the sofa in the sitting room.

"Sorry about the lack of a TV. I have one coming at the end of the week. The phone goes in tomorrow. But I'm not holding my breath, it's the third date I've been given."

"I'm fine without tonight. Happy just to relax with you before I make my weary way home. You've worn me out."

Wendy pulled away from him. "You're not staying the night?"

"No. Are you? I didn't think you'd moved in yet?"

"I haven't, but I . . . well, apart from anything else I've had too much to drink to drive home. You have too."

"Nope. Two pints in the pub and that was hours ago, and one small beer here. I'm fine to drive. I have to go home, no change of clothes, a meeting tomorrow morning, and not enough time to be buggering about with the commuter traffic." He glanced at his watch. It was ten-forty-five. "If you don't want to stay here, or drive home, I could give you a lift. But now would be best."

Wendy considered this for a moment. "No, I'll stay here. I would prefer you did too, but I understand why not."

He huffed. "Now you've made me feel guilty."

"No, no . . . I didn't mean that."

"Too late, you did. I'll tell you what, I'll go home and get some clothes and a razor and stuff, then I'll come back. Only because it's you though."

Wendy grabbed his face and dotted it with kisses. "I love you."

He held her at arm's length. "I know, but you had forgotten. I love you too. Always have, always will." And he meant it. He loved her. He didn't want to, but he did. He had to have her, she had to be his. She was sweet, she had been innocent, and she would make an excellent wife. Any side interests he might have were of no consequence, he had needs she wouldn't want to fulfil. Not yet anyway.

"Let me show you how much I love you." Wendy nibbled on his bottom lip.

"Again? When did you become insatiable?"

"I have a lot of catching up to do." Wendy giggled.

"Do you?" He tried to keep his voice low and calm. "Are you telling me you've not had sex since our wedding day?"

"Nope. Not so much as a date. Never met anyone who took my fancy."

At this moment he loved her even more. He checked the time, it was now eleven o'clock.

"Hold that thought. You can indeed show me how much, but I need to get some stamina back first. I'll go now, and be back in an hour or so."

"Okay, I'll walk to your car with you, I need to phone Dad or he'll worry."

He jumped to his feet. "Come on then let's do this now."

He hurried her along and insisted on waiting outside the phone box on the corner while she made her call and walked her back to the cottage. While he waited he watched the few final customers leave the pub. His car was the only one left in the carpark. He saw the lights go out in the restaurant area, and as he walked Wendy back to the cottage, he saw the landlord wave his arm and then heave the heavy wooden doors shut. He couldn't see Jenny, the bitch. He'd show her next time. Kissing Wendy on the cheek he pushed her through the door and told her to lock it behind her, then sprinted over to the carpark. There was no one around. He checked the time - eleven-twenty. How did he miss her leave? He pulled his car keys from his pocket and almost dropped them in shock when she spoke.

"You're late." Jenny stepped out of the shadow at the side of the pub.

"Get in the back." He grinned at her.

"I'm not shagging you in a car."

"No, you're not. It would ruin the upholstery, but I don't want . . ." he looked at the cottage and Wendy completed closing the curtains. "No problem, get in the front. Where do you live?"

"Patchway. But I was telling the truth about having a housemate. We can't go there. Too complicated."

"Ah so you have a bloke."

"Yes." She looked at her hands, ashamed of what she was going to do.

"No problem, I know just the place."

Halfway to her home he pulled into a layby.

"I don't want to do this in a car."

"You're not going to. Get out." He slammed the door behind him, went to the boot, and collected a picnic blanket and roll of duct tape.

"What's the tape for?" Jenny eyed him nervously. "I don't want anything kinky."

"Have you ever been restrained before?"

"No, but—"

"Then you don't know. If you don't like it, we'll stop." He climbed over the stile and held out his hand to help her.

"Promise?"

"Of course."

Taking her hand, he walked her a few yards along the hedgerow and placed the blanket on the grass. "Strip off. Everything."

Jenny found herself unable to resist. She was terrified, but the fear was heightening her arousal. She dropped her knickers on to the top of the pile. He took her hand and a jolt of electricity soared through her body. She cursed herself for finding the situation erotic.

"Pardon?" He made her sit on the blanket. "What did you say?"

"I cursed."

"Ahh. I like a woman who curses. They seem more responsive."

Trying to sound less innocent than she was, Jenny asked. "So, this is a regular thing then?"

"Not as regular as I'd like. Not all woman like it. But you do." He pulled a length of tape from the roll and snapped it with his teeth.

"How do you know? I've never—"

She was silenced, as with one swift movement he fixed the tape across her mouth. Jenny scooted away from him, her hands grabbing at the tape.

"Oh no you don't" Lunging forward he pushed her shoulders violently, losing her balance, her head hit the ground with a thud, and she lifted her feet to kick him as he grabbed her arms. He dropped his body on top of her. She lay under him, feeling his arousal pressed against her stomach, his hands pinning her arms above her head. "Now, you were willing to give this a try. If you struggle you will get hurt. Your fault. Now, will you do as you are told?"

She grunted into the tape. How could she tell him if she wanted him to stop, how could she tell him if it hurt? He was a liar. She didn't want to be hurt. Eventually she nodded.

"Good. I'm going to release your arms for a moment. You lie still." He knelt between her legs and picked up the tape. "Clasp your hands together and give them to me." She shook her head and he smiled. "Oh, you do want it rough, you do want to be hurt. That's okay by me."

Pulling back his arm he slapped her face. It wasn't too hard, and she pulled her arms up to protect herself from the next blow. She had no idea how he managed it, but in a few swift movements he'd managed to flip her onto her stomach, pin her arms with his knee and tape her wrists together, before flipping her back again. It was awkward and uncomfortable. He took her breasts in his hands and caressed them. He pinched her nipples until tears formed in her eyes.

"Lovely. Now lie still. I'm going to give you instructions, and you will follow them." He smiled at her frown. "You'll be amazed at what you can achieve when bound." He got to his feet and removed his own clothes, before kneeling between her legs. "Lift your hips off the ground."

Jenny did her best, he grabbed her buttocks and pulled her forwards until they rested on his thighs.

He smiled at her. "Now let's see how much you can take. I'm going to play with you for a little while, you will keep your eyes open and watch me enjoy myself. When you can take no more and you want me more than you've ever wanted a man before, you may close your eyes and I'll give you what you want."

Having no idea what he was about to do, although she made several correct guesses, Jenny wondered whether to shut her eyes immediately, but instinct kicked in and she knew she had to endure a little longer.

For what seemed like hours, but was probably no more than twenty minutes, he did things to her that she didn't know were possible, but stopped every time she neared an orgasm. She closed her eyes several times, and each time he'd slap or punch her for telling lies. The third time she'd closed them, he'd bitten her nipple until it bled. She was exhausted. Keeping her eyes open she turned her head away. It was the way he looked at her which aroused her, or that's what she told herself, if she couldn't see his eyes then it couldn't happen. He sensed he'd gone on long enough and he stroked her body gently.

"Look at me." When she didn't, he took hold of her chin and turned her to face him. "Look at me." She blinked and he smiled. "Have I pleasured you?"

She nodded.

"But you feel I've been unfair?" He brushed a strand of hair away from her forehead. "Now you want me to release you, so I will." His fingers stroked her cheek before grabbing the tape and yanking it off her mouth.

Jenny yelped and moved her jaw up and down. She wondered how he knew she wouldn't scream, not that there was anyone to hear. "Why didn't you let me speak? How could I tell you to stop when I was gagged? You lied."

"I told you you would like it." His fingers skimmed her stomach and she lifted her hips. "Oh no. Now you have to tell me what to do. Now you have to curse like the whore you are, and tell me."

"Will you untie my hands?"

"Of course. Roll over." He moved to one side to give her room, and removed the tape. "Now what?" He smirked as she rolled back and got to her knees.

"Will you take me home?"

"Of course. Have you had enough?"

"Yes."

"Then I shall take you home." He stood, and looked down at her. "That's twice you've not satisfied me. Are you sure you want to owe me?"

"I owe you nothing." Jenny was mesmerised by the man.

"Stand up." He helped her to her feet. "Kiss me." When Jenny didn't move, he smiled. "Shall I kiss you?" He stepped closer and she lifted her face to his. He kissed her passionately and she clung to him, her body needing a final release. Without warning he stopped kissing her, and punched her hard in the stomach. "You'll have to learn to do as you're told. I told you to kiss me. Never disobey me again."

"Now tell me what you want."

"I want you to stop fucking hitting me, is what I want." Jenny wrapped her arms around her torso.

"Will you obey me?"

Jenny's eyes were defiant, but she nodded.

"Speak!" he shouted.

"Yes, I'll obey you. You said I could tell you what to do. Is that still on?"

"Of course. Shall I get dressed and take you home?"

"No. Get on the blanket and do it again. This time finish what you started."

When she clambered out of the car, Jenny could barely walk straight. She'd made him stop at the bottom of the road, in case he was seen. She'd decided to tell her boyfriend she'd fallen down the cellar steps, it would explain the bruising which she knew would be there. What she wouldn't tell him, is that she'd be late again the next night.

~12~

Angie closed the lid of the laptop slowly, and sat perfectly still with her hands resting on it. Sex. She'd written about sex. She'd never done that before. Why? How was it relevant? She hated gratuitous sex scenes and wondered if it was necessary, and realised it was rubbish to boot, but she was too tired to read it through tonight, and she didn't want Ryan reading it. God, how embarrassing would that be? Tomorrow she'd be brighter, less tired, and would look at it all with fresh eyes. If nothing else, wherever these ideas were coming from, it wasn't Wendy. Wendy couldn't possibly have known what happened with Jenny. Naughty Jenny.

Angie smirked. "I wonder what happens with you?" Yawning, she got to her feet and went to wake Ryan.

"Wakey, wakey. Time for bed." She shook his shoulder gently and bent to kiss his cheek.

"I did it again." Ryan stretched and swung his legs off the sofa. "It must be the fresh air." He looked at his watch. "Blimey look at the time, did you fall asleep too?"

"No, I was writing. You lock up, I'll get the water." Angie walked towards the kitchen. "What time do you have to be in tomorrow?"

"Early. I'll be gone by seven. By the way, I know you weren't listening, but you can view newspaper archives at the Central Library if you're a member. Then you'll know for certain this thing you're writing has no connection with the real Wendy. No messages from the grave, or paranormal psychic stuff going on. And on that note, why don't you change her name? That would help."

"Yes, I've already decided to do that. I think now my brain is working on something other than The Village again, it got a little overexcited." She filled the glasses and watched him bolt the back door "I've got to work on The Village tomorrow, but I'm working from home. I doubt I'll bother with the library."

"Glad to hear it. I don't want the mother of my child to be flipping tarot cards or gazing into crystal balls. While I will, of course, support your every endeavour, I don't want people to think I'm mad too."

"You're all heart. Turn the light off."

~ ~ ~

The next morning alone at the table with her laptop, her mouse hovered over the file named 'Wendy', but tutting at herself, she opened the latest script for The Village and worked on it for several hours. Having completed the first five scenes, she frowned at the notes on the opening of the sixth.

The vicar was to have a difference of opinion with the pub landlord over what time the village fete should end. Standing outside the post office they are oblivious to the car rapidly approaching, its driver slumped over the wheel. They are saved only by the quick action of Harry Grayson's character, Kelvin, who pulls open the door of the rolling car and manages to apply the handbrake before disaster strikes. It was the next part which concerned Angie. Not only does Kelvin stop the car, but he also pulls the driver out and performs CPR while they await an ambulance, and is the hero of the moment. In a previous episode, Kelvin went to meet a woman when he should have been attending a first aid course funded by his boss and got caught. She closed her eyes and let her chin hit her chest.

She remained in that position for five minutes, pondering whether to raise the problem, or bury her own disbelief and do as suggested. Harry was bound to say she was purposely trying to reduce his screen time, or worse, make him look stupid. Deciding to have some lunch before she made her final decision she left her laptop, and ambled back into the kitchen. Her mind inevitably moving back to Wendy.

She cradled her stomach. "Come on, Junior. Give me a new name, I must change it. Inspire me."

Receiving no such inspiration, she opened the fridge and removed a jar of pickle and pondered what to have with it. It didn't matter what, the pickle was her latest craving. Deciding to be predictable, Angie had a chunk of the extra mature cheese she had bought the previous day. She carried her plate back to the laptop, knowing she would ignore The Village and go back to her own work.

She was wrong. Her mobile vibrated next to the plate. It was Karen.

"Hello, poppet. Can you speak? Hope I'm not interrupting."

"No, I'm only having lunch. What can I do for you?"

"I can't get hold of Colin or, I'm guessing more appropriately, Alan."

"Not heard from either of them, but they'll be at the meeting on Monday, what's the problem?"

"I received the outline of the next few months' scripts. You're probably working on them now, and I'm confused."

"By Kelvin the first aider by any chance?"

"The what? No, nothing to do with Kelvin, it's this thing about the vicar having an affair with Fran."

"What?"

"I know, ridiculous. There will be a hellish backlash from public opinion, quite apart from the fact it was intimated he was gay last year, and Fran is courting the attention of Fergus Cook. What do you think?"

"I don't. I haven't got that far yet. What week? I've been working through methodically, and I haven't had any input on it as a storyline. What's the outcome? I mean what's the point of it?"

"I have no idea, I stopped reading and called Alan immediately. Got his answer service, left a message over an hour ago. Week thirty-six it's still at plotting stage, which is why I have it. I always get the proposals for my opinion. And, well, poppet, my opinion is - bloody pack it in."

"But who was involved in writing it? Does it say?" Angie waited while Karen leafed through the papers in front of her.

"Ah here we go . . . no. Nothing. Can't tell you who's been putting it together. What was that about Kelvin?"

"Hang on a minute, I've found it. You're way ahead of me." Angie fell silent as she skimmed through the outline of weeks thirty-six to forty. "Bloody Harry!"

"What about him?"

"Go forward to week thirty-nine. Vicar gets drunk and confesses all to Kelvin, who talks him out of asking Fran to marry him. Week thirty-nine is a two man show, one of them being Harry."

"Oh dear, he does like to hog the limelight. I've not got a problem with that, but the vicar is fifteen years younger than Fran, neither of them would . . . well even if they would, it won't go down well. It wouldn't bother me, but I want to leave the show sooner rather than later, I'm thinking early next year, and I want to go out with a bang. Oh, bugger I've told you too now."

"You're going? Why?" Angie was truly dismayed. Karen was one of the few people who made working on The Village bearable. "Sorry, Karen. Don't answer if you don't want to. I'm being nosey, I'll be sad to see you go. In fact, I might join you."

"I want to write. I don't know what. Anything and everything. I've got notebooks full of ideas. Don't even care if they don't get published, I've simply had enough of this acting lark. Don't get me wrong, I am grateful. Steady salary, nice little savings pot, good pension. But it's not what I want to do. If The Village was decommissioned now I'd never set foot on a set again."

"So why do you care about the storyline? I agree it's ridiculous, but why worry?"

"The same as Colin I suppose. Been there, done that, now I'm off wearing the t-shirt, but I want to leave a successful show, and not have the press hounding me because I leapt from a sinking ship."

"The same as Colin? Don't tell me he's off too."

"Oh dear, I've said too much. Poppet, you mustn't say anything, particularly about Colin, not even to him. He wouldn't like it, we don't want him angry."

"Are you both resigning at the same time? Is this some form of pact? Are you two an item?" Angie listened to Karen laugh heartily. "Why is that so funny?" Angie was now smiling herself.

"You have no idea, do you?"

"About what? Colin? Noooo, he's not gay! I've seen the way he looks at some of the girls, I used to be one of them before I got pregnant."

"No, not Colin, me. It's not a secret, but it was in the terms of my contract not to broadcast, discuss or . . . I don't know, be proud of it I suppose. There was a flurry of speculation around the millennium, but it died down soon enough."

"I'm sorry, Karen, I didn't know. I thought as you were so close to Colin you might have something going on, either now or in the past."

"Colin helped me . . ." Karen cleared her throat. "I'll tell you all about it, but I still get a bit emotional, so not over the phone, over a bottle of wine would be preferable. I'll tell you what, you wanted to talk to me didn't you, what are you doing for lunch? We can have a long chat, and then pull together a plan of action to deal with these ridiculous plots."

Angie eyed her cheese and pickle and pushed it away. "Meeting you?"

"Splendid. Shall I come to you, you to me, or shall we go somewhere expensive?"

The women arranged to meet in town, and a little over an hour later Angie walked into the latest restaurant to open on the riverside. Karen arrived a few minutes later. They exchanged air kisses before being shown to a table on the balcony overlooking the river.

"The fish dishes here are to die for apparently, I hope they didn't catch them in there." Karen pointed into the murky sludge-coloured water of the Avon. She lifted the menu and scanned it quickly. "Shall we share a bottle of something . . . oh bugger. You're not drinking, are you?"

"No," laughed Angie, "but you can always take home what you don't finish."

"Good idea. Let's order and then we can put the world to rights, and hopefully this damn bloody nonsense."

Karen waited until the waiter had poured their drinks before starting the conversation. "You first. What was it you wanted to speak to me about?"

"Ah, that. I'm not sure I do anymore." Angie saw the frown appear on Karen's forehead. "I was spooked about something I thought was connected to Wendy Knight, but I've since realised I was wrong. I was—"

"Oh yes, I remember. Poor old Wendy. Nineteen-ninety-four was a bad year all round. If it wasn't for the show, and Colin, I think I'd have gone under."

"Do you want to talk about it?"

Karen blew out a breath which caused her lips to vibrate. "I don't mind, it helps, I get a bit emotional though, so don't panic. I don't need hugs or cuddles if I do. It's just the way it is."

"Look, let's stick to the scripts. I don't want to upset you."

"No, no, I'll be fine. Not sure where to begin. I suppose when I met Colin. He was so vital back then. Possibly over-confident. Good-looking, the network's latest find, and he took charge of the meetings. Firm but fair, no room for idiots. That was his introduction when new people joined the team. I didn't think we would get on at first, he made a pass at me in a club we'd gone to after one of the initial meetings and I rejected it. He wasn't happy, so the next day I took a huge risk and explained why."

"You told him you were gay?"

"Yes. I flattered him, and told him how wonderful he was, etcetera, but also that he had too much equipment for me to deal with." Karen snorted a laugh. "He thought that was hysterical, and we became friends. I say friends, close at work, but he pretty much kept his private life well away from work."

"Did he have a partner?"

"Not serious, at least I hope not. He put himself about a bit. We socialised regularly in those days, and he was always disappearing or leaving with some pretty . . ." Her face screwed up in thought. "Actually, they weren't always pretty. They were all a little . . . I was going to say common, but that's not it either, some of them were perfectly respectable girls, just unrefined, rough around the edges." She pursed her lips. "Yes, he had a type, but difficult to put a label on it. Never stuck with any of them, I don't know why."

"But he kept your secret?"

"He did, he came to dinner with us occasionally. When poor Wendy disappeared, it was he who convinced everyone to leave me in the show. But then he'd propped me up for weeks, helped me in so many ways. Bless him."

"How do you mean propped you up? Were you having difficulty with the work? I've read those first scripts they were excellent, the bedrock which allowed the show to run this long."

"No, they were all done by the time it happened." Karen looked out at the water and blinked several times. When she looked back her eyes glistened. "I was in love with, living with, living for, a wonderful young writer called Louise. She was perfect, perfect in every way, and it's my fault she was there."

"I know you said not to fuss, but this is clearly upsetting you. We can talk about something else." Angie was becoming concerned. Karen's voice croaked with emotion as she spoke, and Angie was worried she'd break down completely.

"I'm fine. We'd had a drink after work, and Louise came. To everyone but Colin she was my flatmate. It was a horrible, grey, miserable February evening, and freezing to boot. I remember there were warnings on the news about ice patches forming overnight. We all went to the pub after filming and were having a good laugh. Everyone slowly dispersed, and I sent her on an errand before we got a taxi. She never came back. When I went to find out what was taking her so long, I saw the flashing light, heard the murmur of voices and knew something had happened, something horrible. I pushed my way through the crowd and there she was. Unconscious on the cold road. A huge gash on her forehead, an obvious broken leg, and a paramedic, asking if she could hear him, and she should stay still."

Karen looked into her lap for a moment. "She never moved again. Only her eyes, but they never focused, the doctors doubted she could see. They kept her alive for six months, and then her parents agreed to switch off the life support system."

Angie handed Karen a napkin.

Karen dabbed the tears from her cheeks. "Colin was a dream. He gave me lifts back and forth, regularly took me out for dinner, and when poor old Wendy disappeared he talked me into standing in, and then later to stay on." She smiled at Angie. "I had no family to mention, Louise's family believed I was just a flatmate, so Colin was my only support. We used to joke the show was our baby, and it kept us going."

"I'm so sorry, Karen. Do you have a partner now?" Angie's hands flew to her mouth. "I'm so sorry, there I go again being nosey."

"I've had a few." Karen's smile was cheeky. "And yes, I'm with someone now. We don't live together, we visit each other, and she doesn't like showbiz types so steers well clear of any social events." Karen shrugged. "I haven't lived with anyone since Louise, I can't bring myself to."

"I'm glad you have someone, and I'm sure Louise would want you to be happy. Tell me about Wendy's disappearance. What do you remember?"

"Wendy was cast in the role of Fran about a month before the show went out. She was a lovely girl, seemed a little aloof on occasion, but I think she had things on her mind. Once you managed to chat to her for any length of time, she was bright and witty, and dotty over her dog. She'd disappear frequently in the middle of the day to let the dog out, used to drive Colin mad, but she was perfect for the role. Worked hard, never fluffed her lines, always prompted others when they might have forgotten theirs." Karen stopped speaking and pointed at Angie. "I knew I'd remember eventually."

"Remember what?" Angie glanced over Karen's shoulder at the approaching waiter. "I think our food has arrived."

"Where I first met Harry. I say met, but . . ." She paused as her lunch was placed in front of her, and thanked the waiter. "He was starting to make it into the charts and there was *An Audience With* filmed at the studio. That fabulous looking chap from Wet Wet

Wet was on, as was a singer from the girl band Eternal." Karen tapped her head. "But, to the point. A bunch of tickets was given to our production and I went with Louise, a couple of cameramen, and . . . do you know, I can't remember? There were about ten of us, Wendy included."

"This was when Wendy was still around then, did Wendy meet Harry? Is that what prompted your memory?"

"You're right. She did but it was brief as I remember it. We were all milling around afterwards, mainly taking advantage of the free booze and canapés, and the then producer brought him over and introduced him. He wasn't quite so . . . desperate then, but Louise, who is a people watcher, said he made sure he was never in the same place as the Wet Wet Wet guy. He took no notice of me at all, made eyes at Louise, which was of course a waste of time, and asked Wendy if she'd like a drink. But she had to go, and he looked most put out I'm told. When he joined the cast, I knew I'd met him years ago, but couldn't remember where."

"How old is he? I was a mere child when he was popular, so I'm guessing fifty or thereabouts?"

"Yes, it will be somewhere around there, he wasn't thirty in ninety-four. I only remember because I saw some photographs in the newspaper of him misbehaving in a nightclub on his thirtieth sometime after, and thought he looked younger than when I'd met him a few years before. He still looks remarkably good for his age. I'm guessing Botox."

"Probably, but some men do have a babyface prettiness. I do wish he wasn't such a pain in the backside. I was getting jaded . . . bored with The Village, which is madness because we bought the cottage because it promised longevity of the wage slip, but he makes it so much worse. I have no idea what his problem is."

"Not used to people saying no." Karen forked some food into her mouth. "This is wonderful." She closed her mouth and swayed. "Melts in the mouth. Let's eat before it gets cold and then you can tell me about your interest in Wendy."

They finished their meal, and Karen half the bottle of wine and relaxed back into their seats to contemplate whether to have a dessert.

"I promised myself no more pudding." Angie put the menu down. "I'm never going to lose this weight otherwise. And don't tell me I'm eating for two, it's rubbish apparently."

"At least you have an excuse." Karen laughed and patted her stomach. "But you're right, too indulgent, we'll make do with a coffee." Lifting her bag from the floor she pulled out a crumpled bundle of papers, Angie noted the green ink notes.

"You use green instead of red. Interesting, I'm sure that says something about you."

"That I don't want to feel like a school teacher I expect." Karen made room for the papers and placed her hand on them.

"Before we tackle this, you ask me what you want to know or we might never get to it."

Angie considered this for a few moments while Karen ordered the coffee. "It's difficult to know where to start, so from the top." Her smile showed she was nervous. She'd have to word this carefully or Karen, like Ryan, would think she was a fruitcake.

"The beginning always works," Karen encouraged, intrigued as to what Angie might say.

"I've always written, rubbish mainly, but making stuff up is what I did best. In my mind, I became a famous novelist with people queuing to buy my latest offering, but the reality was I thought I'd won the lottery when I got the job with The Village, and found regular paid work."

She fluttered her hand, "Anyway, I digress. Unable to sleep, I got up at some ungodly hour and started to write. It opens with a girl being abducted from a carpark. The idea came from nowhere, but I could see the action as clear as day for the best part. It flowed as though I were writing about a film I'd seen the night before."

"But you weren't." Karen topped up her wine glass.

"No. I was a little flummoxed by it to be honest. Then we had the meeting and Wendy was mentioned. I remember you and I had had a brief conversation about her, and I guessed that's what put the thought into my head. So, what I wanted to know, was whether you could remember how much you told me . . . it sounds ridiculous now I've said it out loud to you."

Karen smiled kindly. "Not at all. All ideas come from somewhere, in the case of The Village, most of them from the tabloids it seems." She frowned. "I doubt it was our conversation, as you say it was brief. I simply told you how I came to be an actress. I don't have any detail, I was so wrapped up with losing Louise, I wasn't socialising much. I attended the odd meeting when the rehearsals needed a scriptwriter and it had to be me. If it wasn't for Colin, I doubt I'd have even managed that."

"That's what I thought. But couldn't decide if I'd simply forgotten. So, you didn't tell me Wendy had a dog?"

"I don't think so. Why would it have been relevant to our conversation?" Her smile was kind, but Angie could see the same disbelief in her eyes as she'd seen in Ryan's.

"I know you think I'm mad. I won't even ask if you told me it was a supermarket carpark." Angie rolled her eyes and pulled the bundle of paper across the table. "Let's get stuck into these."

"It was a supermarket. Her car was found with the dog in the back." Karen gave a gasp. "Is that why you asked about a dog the other day?" She clapped her hands together. "Of course it is. Oh my God." She sipped her wine. "You know it is all probably coincidence though, don't you? Although, I am a believer in being able to . . . contact the other side."

"It's a coincidence. I called my dog, Tess. You told me Wendy's was called Jessie." Angie wasn't sure, but it looked like Karen flinched, but she said nothing, so Angie opened the top document. "Right, so what shall we do with this Vicar nonsense?"

They spent the next hour putting both the world and the script proposals to rights. They came up with alternative ideas, or more appropriate outcomes.

Karen banged her green biro down. "Right, we've done as much as we can. Now we're going to be naughty and have something worth at least a thousand calories. I enjoyed that, and now I'm celebrating."

Angie beckoned the waiter, and once they'd ordered, she slumped back in the chair. "That was the easy bit. Now we have to get Colin and Alan to agree to our proposals. When I get home, I'll give the other scriptwriters a courtesy call, I don't think either of them are involved in this, but better not to step on too many toes without warning." She smiled at Karen. "You look . . ." She stopped speaking as Karen's phone rang.

Karen pulled her phone from the side pocket of her bag and glanced at the screen. She hesitated for a minute, mouthed sorry, and took the call glancing around the now near-empty restaurant before hitting the speaker button.

"Hi, Colin, you're on loud speaker so don't shout."

"No problem. What's the emergency I've had three missed calls from you."

"Not an emergency as such, I was hopping mad and needed someone to shout at. I settled for Angie."

"Shout about what?"

"Have you read the latest script proposals?"

"No, why, what's the problem? Are we going to have a plane crash or an earthquake?"

"Hush, don't give them ideas!" Karen laughed. "You don't know about Kelvin the paramedic or Fran having an affair with the vicar then, I assume?"

"Oh bollocks. The sooner I'm out of here the better. I'm going to speak to someone tomorrow. I know we have a heavy schedule, but I've got to resign. I have to have a light at the end of this tunnel."

"They'll offer you more money, then what will you do?"

"Tell them to shove it. Do you want to meet today, or can we deal with it tomorrow?"

"Tomorrow will be fine. Angie and I have reworked it already. Will Alan be around tomorrow?"

"He will if Harry is filming. Smitten. Stupid bugger."

"Good. Then we'll sort it then. I'm not having Fran retired because she shagged the vicar. Thanks for calling back, darling. See you. Oh, one more thing before you go. Can you remember the name of Wendy's dog?" She waited for an answer before prompting. "Colin are you still there?"

"I was thinking. Tess, I believe. Why? I can't for the life of me imagine where that question came from."

Karen glanced at Angie who sat wide eyed staring at the phone. "Angie was asking. Well I'd better dash. Thanks again, see you to —"

"Why was she asking? She called you about Wendy before, what's her interest in raking all that back up?"

"Just conversational darling, it was a one thing leads to another conversation."

"Then you have strange conversations. See you tomorrow. Bye."

Karen tapped the screen to terminate the call and looked at Angie. "Well, I don't know what to say."

"Me neither. Thanks for not telling him though. I don't want everyone to think I'm losing my marbles, you and Ryan are enough to be going on with."

"Coincidence, that's all." Karen shivered. "I hope this isn't what you think, unless you want it to be of course."

"I don't know what I think, Karen. All I know is that it's weird." She saw the waiter approaching. "I'm going to enjoy this pudding and then go for some retail therapy, and forget all about Wendy and her dog. I am not psychic, I am not having visions, it's all one creepy coincidence and we shall never speak of it again. That's what I think."

"Probably a good idea, poppet. You don't want to be stressed not in your condition."

"Exactly. Oh my goodness, a pot of cream too."

~ ~ ~

Angie spent the rest of the afternoon shopping. She spent far more than she should have, but was chuffed she had finally bought the last of the items on the pre-baby list. Once home she prepared a chicken casserole for dinner and collapsed onto the sofa with a cup of tea. She had dozed off, and slept for about thirty minutes when Ryan called. They'd had a glitch in filming, and wanted to work on, as the vet they were working with wasn't available the next day.

"Don't worry. I've made a casserole. Call me when you're on your way and I'll put it in the oven." Hanging up, she settled back down, but unable to sleep went to her laptop. She spent some time on social media, but eventually gave in and opened the Wendy folder. "Oh, Wendy, what are you doing to me. I don't want to read it again."

She skimmed the last two pages, and her fingers took seconds to get to work.

~13~

Wendy woke to the sound of running water, she could hear him singing as he showered. She smiled contentedly. She'd been living at the cottage for three weeks now, and although he regularly stayed the night, it wasn't all the time, he was busy with his own work, and that suited her. She had the space to think and be her, without any pressure. Their sex life was wonderful, better than before, and she hadn't thought that possible. Her father had accepted he was back in her life, but he refused to eat with them, although he would call round and be civil. All in all, things were going well. She'd also been cast in a decent role for a television play which was being filmed in Somerset, so for the best part she was able to commute. Wendy was happy. The water stopped running and seconds later he appeared in the doorway, a towel wrapped around his waist.

"I thought I'd wake to find you in the kitchen preparing a hearty breakfast," he pulled away the towel, using it rub his hair.

"Only just woken up." Wendy threw back the quilt and swung her legs off the side of the bed. "Let me clean my teeth and I'll see what I can rustle up."

"Don't bother. I won't have time to wait. I have to be in Manchester by mid-morning. I did tell you."

There was the accusation. It didn't happen as often as it used to, but his temper could still flare at the drop of a hat. Wendy knew she had to pacify him, she didn't want him leaving after they had argued. She made a sad face.

"I wish you'd woken me." She walked towards him. "I look forward to eating breakfast with you, I feel cheated now." Wrapping her arms around his still damp body, she snuggled into his chest. "I wish I could come with you, but I have another rehearsal this afternoon."

"Perhaps you should set an alarm." There it was again.

She ran her hands from his shoulders down to his buttocks. "What's this?" Letting go of him, she leaned around his torso. "You've damaged yourself." She gently ran her fingers along the eight-inch weal on his back.

He glanced over his shoulder. Unable to see anything, he shrugged. "The bush." Walking away from her, he collected his clean clothes which had been stacked neatly on the dressing table. Placing them on the bed he began to dress.

"What bush. It looks sore, does it hurt?"

"Do you know, sometimes I don't think you listen to a word I say. I told you I had to park in a tiny space because some idiot in a four-by-four decided he needed more than the allocated parking slot, and I had to squeeze out of the door. The bush won the battle."

He buttoned his shirt, hiding the sign of his infidelity. His mind shot back to Jenny the afternoon before. Having picked her up from the bus stop, they'd taken a detour on the way to the pub. Parking in a little used layby, large overgrown bushes shielding them from the road beyond, he'd taken her across the bonnet of his car. As always, he'd tormented her first, and when finally he'd entered her, she'd dug her nails into his back, hence the wound Wendy had inspected. Jenny had received a slap for that, crushing her lip into her teeth. He smiled when he saw the blood appear in the corner of her mouth.

"Shall we grab ten minutes before you go."

He stared at Wendy as she giggled. "What?" His tone was sharp, and he looked down as Wendy pointed at his boxer shorts.

"You look like you have something on your mind."

"Come here," he grabbed her wrist.

The sex was rough, but not painful for Wendy, he was careful not to hurt her while he took his pleasure. Wendy was different, Wendy wasn't one of those girls. Eyes closed he pictured the bruising on Jenny's thighs, and the blood on her mouth. It was over in minutes.

Pecking Wendy on the forehead, he apologised. "Hardly romantic, but I've got to go. I'll make up for it tomorrow."

"You won't be back tonight?"

"No. Hopefully tomorrow, but if this goes well perhaps not. I'll call you to let you know."

He'd not even buttoned his shirt as he ran down the stairs. The door slammed soon after.

Wendy went to the window and watched him hurry to the car, parked in its familiar place in the carpark. He didn't look back and she smiled as she walked into the bathroom. Peace and tranquillity for a while.

It was gone eight by the time she got back from Somerset and not wanting to cook she changed and went across to the pub. She was almost a local now, and Gary waved as she entered.

"You on your own?" he called.

"Yes. Lonely pub meal for one." She climbed onto a stool and lifted one of the menus. "I'll have—"

"Hang on. The barrel's gone." Gary called for Jenny. She appeared in the entrance to the dining room a stack of dirty plates in her hands. "Dump those and serve. I need to go down to the cellar. Wendy wants to order some food."

Jenny placed the plates at the far end of the bar, lifted the hatch, and walked to Wendy. "What can I get you?" She forced a smile.

"Lasagne please, some garlic bread and a lemonade."

"No wine tonight?"

"No, thanks."

Wendy watched Jenny walk away, her heart pounding a little faster in her chest. Her period was over two weeks late. It could be nothing, but if she was pregnant she wanted to be sensible. She had no idea what she would do, half of her screamed keep the baby, even if he wouldn't stick around, the other half told her not to be stupid. That it was ridiculous. She was getting an increasing number of offers of work, her career was heading in the right direction, and she didn't know what she wanted to do about him. She knew she loved him, but she also knew the relief she felt when he was away for a few days.

Jenny returned with Wendy's drink. "Anything else?"

Wendy noticed the swelling on her lip and decided not to ask. "No, this is perfect, it's been a long day. When I've had something to eat, it's home, bath and bed for me."

"You're an actress, aren't you? What are you doing at the moment?"

Jenny had had enough of being roughed up, good though the sex was. Her bloke, Brian, was getting fed up with her excuses not to have sex, suspicious even, and she loved Brian, despite her betrayal. If Wendy wasn't around, then he wouldn't be either which suited just fine.

"A period drama, a poor man's Pride and Prejudice." She saw the slight frown and decided it wasn't her place to educate Jenny.

"Sounds nice." Jenny's smile was lopsided due to the swelling. "Where's your boyfriend tonight? We don't often see you here alone."

"Manchester. Keep your fingers crossed he's hoping to sign a great deal today."

"What does he do?" Jenny often wondered, and if whatever he did kept him away from here, it would be good news.

Gary appeared behind her. "One lasagne. Jenny stop gassing there's a queue up the other end." He placed Wendy's meal on the bar.

Jenny looked. There were two people there, and one still had half a pint. She rolled her eyes at Wendy, who smiled. "Right. Form an orderly queue. Who wants what?" she called as she approached.

"Nice to see her smile." Gary confided in Wendy. "I reckon her bloke has been hitting her about." Realising he might have broken an unspoken confidence he added. "Please don't say anything, she'd hate it. But be nice to her, I reckon she could do with a friend right now."

"Oh no. How awful, I noticed the swollen lip but didn't like to say anything."

"I think that's the least of it. She could barely stretch to reach the optics last week." Shaking his head, Gary walked away.

When Jenny came to collect the now empty plate, Wendy attempted to engage her in conversation.

"I like your skirt. Is it new?"

Jenny looked at the flowing red jersey skirt. It was new, as were her other two skirts. She knew it was only a matter of time before his choice of venue caused them to be discovered, and she could hide her modesty much easier in a skirt. She'd also found they were more comfortable and didn't rub any damaged areas. She looked back at Wendy and knew he wasn't like it with her. She moved too easily, and smiled too readily. A week or so ago she would have given anything for him to take her to a proper bed and do the glorious things he did without the violence. It was the violence he got off on, and it was getting more frequent. Wendy was welcome to him, Jenny had already applied for new jobs elsewhere, then she could be rid of him.

She smiled her lopsided smile. "Yes. I thought I'd give feminine a go. I got fed up with jeans."

"I know what you mean, but they are so practical. I've been in a corset and bonnet all day, so these are a luxury now. I don't know how women coped in those days. Must have been stifled in the summer, and dragging it through the mud in the winter."

"Yes. If I had to choose, I'd go for the fifties. Big skirts and bobby socks, flat shoes, and those cropped trousers." Jenny turned as Old Bill called to her. "Can I get you another?" She lifted the empty glass.

"No, thanks. I'll make a move. What time do you finish?"

Jenny's heart stopped. She never knew if he'd appear at closing time. He must lie about his whereabouts to Wendy a lot. He'd be pissy if he even knew they were having a real conversation.

"Not sure tonight. Hopefully before eleven, then I get to see my boyfriend before he goes to bed. This job is crap for your sex life." Jenny was impressed with herself. That would throw Wendy off the scent.

"I didn't realise you were living with someone. We'll have to exchange notes on our men." Wendy smiled but caught the look of horror which flashed across Jenny's face.

Jenny couldn't believe her ears. Brian was a million times better than him. How could she tell her that? Shame burned into her conscience as she thought about the betrayal. "Yes, maybe. I doubt they have anything in common."

Wendy pointed at the ugly bruise a little above her wrist. "That looks nasty. You look like you've been in the wars."

"Bloody cellar steps, missed the bottom one the other day. We need more light down there." The lie tripped easily from her lips, she'd already used it for Brian. "Oh, he's getting mad." She grinned. "Better get him a half, or we might have the third world war on our hands."

Wendy knew she was lying, but only because Gary would have mentioned a fall in the cellar. She sighed and decided to make more effort to be friends with the poor girl. Perhaps she could help. The wind was howling with an icy chill when she stepped outside the pub, and she ran along the path to the cottage. What happened to pleasant autumnal evenings? It seemed they'd gone from summer straight into winter. As she pulled her keys from her pocket she heard the phone ringing and left the door as she darted forward.

There was no pleasant greeting. "Where the hell have you been? This is the third time I've called. I've got better things to do with my time than stand in phone boxes."

"I got back late, I went to the pub for dinner and got talking to Jenny. You didn't say you would be phoning. How did it go?"

Wendy bristled. He had no right to be angry with her. Did he expect her to sit by the phone in case he called?

"Jenny! Who's Jenny?"

"The bloody barmaid you tease every time we go in there. How did it go?" She wondered if he'd been drinking. How could he not remember Jenny? "Have you been drinking?"

"Celebrating! I've only got the bloody contract. I did it, Wendy. I did it. Are you proud of me?"

"Very. Well done you clever, handsome, lovely man." Wendy's anger was forgotten, she was genuinely pleased for him. "Shall we celebrate tomorrow? I've heard there's a nice—"

"Can't, I'm afraid. I'm likely to be here for a few days, maybe a week. They want to run through some stuff, and it's who's available when. I'll know more tomorrow."

"I'll miss you, but I'm delighted for you. Let me know as soon as you know, I'm off tomorrow, so should be around most of the day. Although I might go and buy one of those answer machines so I don't miss any of your calls."

They listened to the beeping telling them his money was running out.

"Give me the number I'll call back . . . or not." The flat tone indicated the call had been terminated and she replaced the receiver. She managed to stay awake for another hour before giving up and going to bed.

The next day when he called, she was reading through the script for the next day's filming, and she snatched it up on the second ring.

"Blimey, were you sat on the phone? How are you today?" He sounded far cheerier than the night before.

"I'm fine, thank you. Script reading. Before you carry on, give me your number in case we get cut off again."

"We won't I'm calling from the studio. I've had coffee and croissants with the producer, don't you know."

"How wonderful. Did you have anyone to celebrate with last night. I felt awful for you up there alone."

The dark-haired girl he'd picked up on the corner by the Hacienda entered his mind. She'd actually thought he was going to pay her. "Yes, I found someone to entertain me. For a while at least. Oh, they're on their way back. Got to go. I'll try and call later."

Wendy checked the time. She'd go to the pub for lunch, only a sandwich, but at least it was company for an hour. She was pleased when she saw Jenny behind the bar.

"Don't you ever go home?" She asked as Jenny approached.

"Doesn't feel like it sometimes, but I'm not working tonight, so didn't mind coming in. What'll it be?"

"Chicken salad sandwich and a diet coke please."

Jenny eyed her suspiciously. "Still no wine? You're not pregnant, are you?"

"Ha! Not that I know of." Wendy laughed. She didn't know because she didn't know if a pregnancy test would work this soon. "Just off the booze for a while, less calories, and, more importantly, less headaches when I'm filming. I've got to be on set at six in the morning. So, my choice is up at the crack of dawn, or drive down tonight and stay in some lonely hotel. I lead a glamorous life, one that can't cope with hangovers."

"Beats working here."

"Probably." Wendy grinned. "We're British, we wouldn't be happy if we didn't have something to moan about. Work, the weather, politics."

"I know. What is the thing with the weather. I bet three out of four conversations in here refer to the weather, what it was, what it's like, what it's changing to." Jenny shook her head as she placed a straw into Wendy's glass. "I'm twenty-four. I should be talking about the latest band, where I'm going tonight, and how much I paid for my shoes."

Wendy laughed with her. "What are you doing tonight?"

"What?" Jenny looked confused.

"I'm asking you to act like a twenty-four-year-old. You're not working tonight, so what are you doing?"

"Oh, right. I thought you were asking me out for a minute. I thought hang on lady, I'm not, you know . . . gay."

"Did you? Did that sound like an invite to a date?" Wendy blushed. "I'm sorry. It wasn't."

The two women dissolved into giggles and Old Bill grinned at them from his slot in the window.

When the giggles faded, Wendy tried again. "I'm on my own tonight, if you have nothing else planned we could go to the cinema or grab a pizza. I can't be late because of the early start tomorrow. That's what I was trying to say."

"I'm having a night in with my Brian. I've been neglecting him, but thanks for asking, although it still sounded like an offer of a date, but thanks for the offer." Jenny's eyes twinkled as she turned and walked away.

Wendy stayed in the bar for a couple of hours, the banter with Jenny came naturally, and she was happy and relaxed when she headed for home. Jenny wasn't happy. Wendy was a nice girl and didn't deserve to be cheated on, particularly if she was the other woman. She resolved never to see him again, and decided she needed to step up her efforts to get another job.

~ ~ ~

Four days later, Wendy reversed onto the drive and looked across at the carpark. His car wasn't there, she'd not heard from him for two days, and had no idea how to get hold of him. She wondered whether to go to the pub, Jenny always cheered her up. Deciding against it, she'd had far too long a day already, she hurried along the path.

Stepping into the hall, she dropped her bag, and without stopping to take her coat off, hurried to the bathroom. Stiff and irritable from her journey, Wendy decided to read in the bath. Pouring some bubble bath into the gushing water, she watched it change to a deep purple, and the scent of lavender filled the room. Within twenty minutes of being home, she was in the bath, hot chocolate steamed in the mug next to the soap dish and her book lay unopened on the floor. The hot water soothed away the tensions of the day, and Wendy looked forward to her bed. The phone rang, and she opened her eyes momentarily and closed them again. It was either him or her father, they'd call back. She agitated the water so it sloshed over her shoulders. The phone rang again. Cursing silently, she sat up, and had just grabbed a towel when it stopped. Stepping back into the bath, she made a mental note to invest in an answer machine, a task she'd been putting off. She closed her eyes and drifted off to sleep.

Waking with a start as the bathroom door flew open and banged against the towel rail, Wendy screamed and sat up, water slopping onto the floor. With her heart hammering in her chest, she watched as he paced into the bathroom.

"Too important to take calls now you have a mainstream drama role?" He shouted, fists clenched at his side.

"No . . . I . . . Sorry, where were you? What did you want? What time is it?"

"I was in the pub. I was inviting you to eat with me? But no, Wendy is too important to get out of the bath."

"I didn't see your car."

"Because I have a new one. Anyway, what difference does that make?"

“A new car? Why? What was wrong with the old one?”

“Are we really going to have a conversation which has no bearing on why I'm here?”

“I'm sorry. I don't know why you're so mad.” Wendy stood and grabbed a towel. Her nakedness made her feel vulnerable and she wrapped it tight around her body. “If you were only across the road, why didn't you just come over?”

“I've already told you, because I wanted to eat with you.” He rolled his eyes at her stupidity.

“I've eaten. Sandwich on the motorway when I stopped for petrol. I still don't understand . . .”

“You bloody ignored me. It was too much trouble to get your arse out of that bath and—”

Having had a long and tiring day, for the first time in their relationship, before and after their non-existent wedding, Wendy lost her temper. “Go back to the pub! I've had a long and shitty day, and I have no patience to deal with you in a strop over nothing.”

She flung her arm towards the door. “Go on. I'm not arguing with you tonight. I didn't bloody ignore you, I ignored the phone. It could have been anyone, and I thought it was Dad. You were supposed to be in the studio in Manchester.” She stomped out of the bathroom towards her bedroom. “You and your temper can just bugger off.”

She went into her bedroom and slammed the door. It didn't stay shut long. He opened it and stood there staring at her as she hurriedly pulled on her pyjamas. Although the look on his face told her not to push him, she didn't care. She'd had enough, but unable to meet his eye she turned away and grabbed her hairbrush before speaking.

“I mean it. I'm not having a row. Please go back and have your meal. I'll speak to you tomorrow.”

Two steps and he stood behind her. His hands gripped her shoulders, his fingers digging into her flesh.

“I've been gone days. I thought you would be pleased to see me.”

“And I would have been had you been in a better mood.” She shrugged one shoulder free. “You're hurting me,” she yelped as he grabbed her, managed to twist her round and throw her onto the bed.

“I'm sorry. I've had a long day too. I was hoping for a warmer welcome.” He was unzipping his jeans.

Wendy looked at his hands. "No. Don't. Seriously, let's leave this until tomorrow."

"I don't want to. I want you now." He caught hold of her trousers and attempted to pull them down.

Wendy broke a nail in holding them in place. "No. I'm serious. Stop."

He dropped his body weight on top of her and she could feel his erection. "You don't mean that." He bit her neck.

"Ouch. I do. Get off me." Try as she might, she was unable to roll free, she could sense his enjoyment and stilled. He smiled at her as though he'd won a victory of some sort, and she shook her head. "No. I'm deadly serious. I don't want this."

He pressed his hips forward. "Are you sure?"

"Yes. Now unless you intend to rape me, please let me go."

His body went rigid and a frown appeared, his smile forgotten. "What?"

"That's what it's called when someone says no and you ignore them. You're not a rapist, are you? I mean no!"

Placing his hand on her chest he pushed his weight up, his other hand raised ready to slap her. The pain was incredible and Wendy was frightened, almost wishing she'd let him do as he pleased. She gave a cry of relief, when his hand fell to the bed, and he got to his feet.

"I can't believe you said that. I can't even look at you." Turning away, he rearranged himself and zipped his jeans. "I'm going back to the pub, don't bother coming over."

Wendy had no intention of doing any such thing, and she lay there until the front door slammed shut. Then jumping to her feet, she hurried to the window, opening the curtains slightly to watch his progress. He didn't look back. Once he was safely inside the pub she ran downstairs and slid the bolts in place on the front and back doors, and set the alarm. She didn't want him anywhere near her, especially with more alcohol on board. She didn't want to be frightened like that again.

Wendy needn't have worried, he had no intention of coming back.

Jenny's heart sank as she saw him march back into the bar. He demanded rather than ordered his drink. Gary attempted conversation, but soon realised that he wasn't receptive.

"Give him a wide berth, love. They must have had a row, he's not in a talkative mood."

"I will. Gary, I'm not feeling too good, do you mind if I leave early?"

"What sort of not well, you've been all right so far."

Jenny sighed. "Lady's issues, do you want details?"

"No." Gary held his hands up. "When do you want to go?"

"Can I call a taxi, they usually take at least twenty minutes to get here?"

"Go on then." Gary agreed. He was disappointed she was going. He was hoping to get a break, he'd been on his own most of the day. He watched her disappear to make her call shaking his head. Women's problems were the bane of his life when he was married, he'd thought those days were over.

"Another when you're ready."

Gary turned around and looked at the empty glass being waved at him, wondering if Wendy was having women's problems too. He pulled a fresh pint, and feeling miserable asked the question he should have avoided.

"Is Wendy not joining you?"

"No."

"Ah, I won't ask. Bloody women." Gary took the note offered.

"Why are you complaining? I thought you were divorced."

"I am, but I still have to deal with the excuse of *women's problems*." He whined the words.

"Who? Jenny?"

"Yes, booking her taxi as we speak."

"Poor old Jenny. I'm off in a moment, tell her not to worry I'll give her a lift." Jenny appeared in the door way and he called her over. "Jenny, come here. Gary tells me you're not well, I'm leaving now I'll give you a lift."

"No!" Jenny answered quickly, and leaning against the bar added. "I think I might throw up, I've got a bag ready in case, but if I do, I'd prefer I was in a taxi not a customer's car. Thanks anyway." She forced the smile.

He eyed her for a moment, knowing she was lying. He was hoping she'd have welcomed his return, but it seemed no one wanted him tonight. Clenching his glass tighter he emptied it in two swigs.

"Okay, please yourself. I'm off." With a brief salute to Gary, he turned and left the pub.

Jenny was worried he might wait outside for her, so she didn't wait for the taxi by the door as she would normally, she waited until the driver came looking for her. She hurried to the taxi, scanning the carpark as she did so, only relaxing when she couldn't see his car. She was wrong to relax. As the taxi pulled out of the carpark, he started the engine of his new car and turned on the lights, pulling out a little while later. He knew where she was going so no need to alert the taxi driver he might be being followed. He turned on the radio, and Meatloaf sang to him.

"She might be barely dressed, but not by the dashboard light. This upholstery is still clean my friend." He joined in the singing as he drove the familiar route.

~14~

Angie found Karen waiting for the lift as she turned the corner.

"Morning, poppet. How are things, nothing new to report I hope?"

"Never even thought about it," Angie lied.

The lift opened and they stepped in.

"I spoke to Colin, eventually, these storylines are nothing to do with him. He seemed a little put out by it all, if I'm honest. Alan didn't come back to me, but he's here this morning so at least we have Colin on side."

"Gemma is here too, so hopefully he'll be persuaded."

"Wonderful. Two script-writers, the director and lead actress can't all be wrong."

"I hope you're right." Angie stopped and pushed open a door. "We're in here today, the larger room is in use. Oh . . ." Seeing Harry sitting at the head of the table, in conversation with Gemma, her fellow scriptwriter, she stopped dead causing Karen to bump into her. She attempted to keep her face neutral. "Hello all, are we late?"

"Not at all." Alan looked past her. "We were early. Is Colin not with you?"

"No." Karen dropped her bag on the table and lifted out the heavily marked document they had worked on the day before. "Harry. What a surprise."

"Why?" Harry became defensive. Pulling his shoulders back he cocked his head awaiting her response.

"Because you aren't usually part of the creative team, yet here you are, two meetings in a row." Karen looked at Alan. "Is this a permanent thing now?"

"No, well, possibly. Harry and I had dinner together yesterday, and one drink led to another. He was over the limit so had to stay at mine."

Harry saw the rise in Angie's eyebrows although she didn't speak, and he tapped the table. "In the spare room, before any of you jump to conclusions." What he didn't add, was that it wasn't for want of a drunken invitation from Alan. But he'd managed to avoid that by acting more drunk than he actually was.

"Quite," Alan agreed. "He was with me when I got your message this morning, so I invited him along. The extra input might be useful."

The door opened and Colin blustered in. He glanced around the room, and Angie noticed he looked angry and wondered if that was because Harry was there. Pulling out a chair, Colin dropped onto it with a huff. He glanced at the pile of paper in front of Karen.

"Is that all ready to go?" He jabbed a finger at it, and when she nodded, snapped, "Good, then let's get on with it."

"Are we not going to run through the usual business first?" Alan wasn't impressed. He liked more order at these meetings.

"Nope," Colin pulled a pad from his briefcase which he slapped on the table.

Angie glanced from one to the other. Technically, this was Alan's meeting, but Colin was taking no prisoners, and Alan was allowing it.

"The other stuff can wait. We need to sort this bloody rubbish out so the girls can get on and give us something to work with."

"What rubbish would that be?" Harry pretended he was unaware of the objections which had been raised.

"Shut up," Colin snapped. "We'll be here all bloody day if you get involved. Karen, item one please."

Karen grimaced at Angie and lifted the top document. "The near miss with the vicar and—"

"Two seconds, Karen." Alan waved his finger. "Colin, not sure if it was the wrong side of the bed this morning, but a bit of civility wouldn't go amiss."

"Then you may be disappointed. We have two and a half hours before we're due to be on set. So short sharp and no fannying about is in order. If Harry wants to sit and listen, that's fine by me, but we don't need another opinion holding us up. Truth be told, we shouldn't even be discussing this," he jabbed his thumb at Karen, "it never should have been sent out in the first place."

"That's your opinion, before we've even discussed the pros and cons?" Alan was irritated, and his normal affable attitude had disappeared.

"From what I hear, yes."

"You mean you haven't even looked at it?" Harry challenged.

"No, didn't need to. I trust Karen's instincts. But as you haven't either, you won't have an opinion."

Angie bit her bottom lip to hold back the smile. This was looking like it would be the most interesting meeting they'd had all year.

"But I have." Harry smiled at Gemma. "Gemma was kind enough to run through it with me this morning while we awaited your arrival."

"Harry stayed with Alan last night." Angie told Colin by way of explanation.

"Fucking hell, that's all we need." Colin threw his arms wide and arched his back, his head dropping back as he stared at the ceiling. He was tense already. Angie was impressed with the muscle definition visible through his shirt. He certainly kept in shape.

"Meaning what exactly?" Alan demanded, placing his fists on the table and leaning forward in challenge.

It put Angie in mind of the silverback gorilla Ryan had been filming.

"Meaning we don't bring our love interests to meetings. It doesn't work."

"I'm not having—" Harry was interrupted by Karen.

"Can we keep all this testosterone under wraps until we break? We'll never get started let alone finished if this chest beating continues." She held up the document. "Issue one. The runaway car. Angie and I have discussed this in some depth. Kelvin didn't attend the first aid course, and we made quite a meal of that, so he shouldn't be the one to save the driver. We think it should be Terry or perhaps even the vicar himself."

"When did they do a first aid course?" Harry demanded, ignoring the look from Colin.

"That's the point, it doesn't matter because the viewers haven't been told he hasn't, and, we can possibly have Harry giving it a go and getting it wrong, making the salient point that we should learn how to perform effective CPR."

"Perfect." Colin slapped the table. "Gemma write that in. Bloody perfect. A lesson in helping others, the top floor will love it. We can even get an *if you would like* announcement at the end of the show."

"Yes, you may be right," Alan agreed, but catching the glance from Harry, added, "Let the girls write it, and we can talk again. And the next, Karen."

Karen lifted the second document down. This one was a full scene to be played out in the pub. "Terry would not be able to pick up the table with his bad back, and is there a need to? What does it add? If we are trying to expose his short fuse again then perhaps throwing a glass to the floor is enough."

The meeting carried on in this vein for the next fifty minutes. Various objections were raised and dismissed or agreed, but, Angie reflected, at least it was getting things sorted, even if she dreaded having to write some of the scenes. One thing that was perfectly clear, was that Harry and Colin had a mutual dislike for each other, which although amusing could prove troublesome. Harry was trying to charm Gemma, much to the irritation of Alan, and everyone in the room appeared to be hostile to one degree or another to both Karen and herself, but more so her, despite the fact she'd attempted to be as tactful as possible. They finally got to the last issue. Karen pushed all the other papers to one side, and pulled the single sheet forward.

"Having gone through all this, which I believe is for the good of the show, I have an announcement to make." Karen glanced at Colin, she hadn't told him yet. She had intended on mentioning it the day before, but he became so irate over the storyline issues she hadn't got around to it.

Colin frowned. "Is this going to be what I think it is?" He huffed as she confirmed it was. "I thought so, get on with it then." He stared at the scribbles he'd made on his pad. If Karen was leaving, then the sooner the better. He had plans to make.

Karen cleared her throat as a stillness fell over the room. Twiddling the corner of the sheet, she looked at Alan. "I know this isn't the proper channel, and I will, of course, deal with that. But I'm going to retire, and . . ." She paused as Alan slapped the table, Gemma gasped and Harry grinned. "And, I'm not sure when. But as soon as. So, the final notes I have are on possible exits for Fran. I know I don't need to say how wonderful it's been working on this show. But there comes a time when it's time." She shrugged and lifted her notes. "So, possibility number one—"

"Hang on, wait one moment. Karen, I'm devastated. Is there anything that will change your mind?" Alan was shocked.

"She's already planned her exit, so it doesn't look that way." Harry failed to hide his pleasure at the announcement.

"Thank you, Harry. He's right I'm afraid. It wasn't an easy, I . . ." Karen cleared her throat again as tears threatened. Getting to her feet she handed the paper to Alan. "I need to take five minutes, perhaps you'd be good enough to run through these for me. I shall return shortly."

Alan was still shocked and after he accepted the sheet, his arm remained outstretched as she left the room. He only placed it in front of him as the door clicked shut.

"I'm stunned. But I'm sure that much is obvious." He looked at Colin who was still studying his hands. "You're close to Karen, is there any point in not doing this? Can she be persuaded do you think?"

Slowly, Colin shook his head. "Nope. What is she suggesting as her exit, big bang, or quietly into the distance?"

"But . . ." Alan ran his fingers through his hair and looked at Angie. "Angie, did she say anything to you, you've obviously been spending time with her."

"Not in any detail. She wants to write and she's had enough. She gave me no indication it would be this soon." Angie lifted helpless hands. "Everyone moves on eventually, Colin is right. We may as well get started on this now, we might be able to tie it in with one of the other storylines we've discussed."

"Okay, but I'll give it a try." Alan picked up the sheet and skimmed it, a frown appeared. "She's not given much detail."

"She wouldn't, would she, not until you've decided which way you're jumping." Angie turned to Colin. "Are you okay, Colin. I'm sure she intended no insult in not speaking to you first."

Colin looked her up and down as though he'd only just realised she was in the room. "I'm a big boy. Can we get on with it, or we'll be asked for overtime from the crew." He looked at his watch.

Alan tutted, and stared at him for a second. The man was being particularly irritating today. "Okay, I'll read all the ideas she's noted down. Then we can discuss them, let's not do this one by one. As Colin correctly points out, time is not on our side." He drew in a breath. "Take notes please."

His voice took on an authoritative tone, he waited until everyone had a pen poised, and ignoring the snort from Colin, he proceeded to read through Karen's list.

". . . Number five. Karen disappears, several suspects for her abduction or murder, although she doesn't suggest who. Then she says, it can either be an open-ended storyline, where her body never turns up, or when ratings are low it can be discovered in the least likely place - for example, church cellar." He was nodding as he read that one, Angie could see it appealed to him.

"Finally." He pushed his glasses onto his forehead and peered closer. He realised everyone was waiting for him and waved his hand "Sorry, handwriting is a bit wonky. Ah, I have it, although I don't understand it." He looked at Angie. "Perhaps you could help, Angie. It says, body not found, is Wendy in touch with Angie? Then I believe something to do with a dog."

Allowing his glasses to drop back into position he looked back at Angie and held out his hands.

"Oh, nothing to do with it. It was a separate conversation." Angie brushed the question away, not wishing to discuss what it meant. She found it difficult to believe Karen hadn't at least crossed through the note.

"About what?" Gemma asked innocently. "Another storyline, because I don't think we have room."

"No, we don't. Can we get on?" Harry's foot could be heard tapping the leg of his chair.

"You may leave if we're boring you." Angie threw back. "There is no reason for you to be here. But we were talking about something only vaguely related to the show."

"Wendy Knight again?" Alan grunted. "She came up last time too." He glanced back at the note, and his hand flew to the top of his head. "Are you in touch with her?"

"Oh, dear God." Colin uttered through clenched teeth, "History, bloody history. Can we deal with the here and now, please?"

"Agreed," chipped in Harry. "If Angie thinks she has super powers, well bravo, but it doesn't get us out of this room."

Karen opened the door. She was beaming from ear to ear. Having finally confirmed her intentions it was like a weight had been lifted from her shoulders. Her smile dimmed a little when she saw the faces of her colleagues.

"Have I chosen the wrong moment to return? Please don't tell me you're now arguing over which way to get rid of Fran." She pulled out her chair and sat down.

"You'd made a note about Angie and Wendy, we got sidetracked," Alan explained.

"Did I write it down? Sorry, I was doodling. It's a project Angie is working on, and I was thinking about it. Cross it through," she ordered. "No point in wasting time."

"Project?" Harry asked. "Haven't you got enough on your plate with the show and the baby, without starting something else rolling?"

"It's nothing, but thank you so much for your concern." Wishing to change the subject she looked to Alan. "I'm in favour of the what-happened-to-her plot. Gives us more leeway. I think you preferred that too, didn't you?"

"I did yes. Anyone have any objections?" There was a shaking of heads around the table. "Good, then I suggest Gemma and Angie sketch some outlines for the meeting on Friday. Is that possible?"

"Yes, but as I said earlier, I'm going to stay with my mum for a couple of days, I can work from there. Is it possible to get together with you tomorrow, Angie?" Gemma turned to face her.

"Ah, having a delivery in the morning, and we'll probably need all day, any chance you could come to me?" Angie kept her fingers crossed. It was the baby's cot, and she didn't want to miss the delivery.

"Sure, no problem. Give me your address." Gemma located a fresh page in her notebook.

"Applegate Cottage, Hallen Road, BS . . ." Angie turned to look at Karen who had gasped. "What?"

Karen shook her head. "Nothing, carry on. I had a moment, that's all."

Angie looked her in the eye. She was lying, but clearly didn't want to discuss it. She finished giving her address to Gemma.

"Okay, let's grab a quick lunch before filming starts. I saw the canteen had Spanish chicken on today, it's to die for. Thank you all. We got there in the end. Ladies, I look forward to seeing your initial outlines." Alan collected his papers.

Angie slipped her belongings into her tote bag and placed it on the desk.

"Thank heavens for that. I'm bursting, I'll catch you up." Leaving her bag, she headed for the toilet opposite the meeting room.

"We're all leaving for the canteen. I'll take your bag with me," Gemma called to her.

When Angie arrived at the canteen Karen and Colin were sitting at the end of a row of tables, heads close together. Colin got to his feet as she approached, and headed towards the queue. Angie slipped into his chair. "What did you gasp for. Are you okay? What happened in there?"

Karen took Angie's hand and patted it. "Brace yourself, poppet." She breathed deeply before blurting out the explanation. "Wendy Knight used to live in Applegate cottage. It was her home when she disappeared." She continued to pat Angie's hand as she spoke. "Which means nothing, of course. As Colin pointed out we are intelligent people, and you probably already knew that. Hence your interest." She grasped her hand tightly. "If you didn't know, don't tell Colin I told you. He said not to as he doesn't want you worrying about anything other than the show. He thinks you're becoming distracted."

Angie was lost for words, her mind racing so fast she couldn't process coherent speech.

Karen placed her hand on Angie's arm. "He's coming back. Mum's the word, go and get yourself some food." She watched Angie get to her feet. "Angie, don't overwork this. It's a coincidence." She watched Colin carrying his tray back to the table. "And even if it's not, keep it to yourself. You don't want people to think you're going crazy. I don't by the way."

Angie lifted the first meal in the display and was quiet as the others chatted through the lunch break. When they were ready to leave she realised she didn't have her bag. "Gemma, you had my bag, where is it?"

Gemma's hands flew to her mouth. "I thought we were sitting . . . Oh, it's okay, it's still there." Gemma went to the table near the entrance and collected Angie's bag which sat in the centre of the table.

With everyone ready to go, they made their exit.

Colin called to a couple of camera men who were sitting in the corner. "Come on, I want to get to the gym at a decent hour. I hope you're set up."

A couple of the actors who had also been in the canteen joined them, and the unwieldy group walked through the building and out to the warehouse at the rear where several of the sets were housed.

Colin was in luck. Filming went smoothly with only a few problems, which were resolved. Gemma and Angie were barely needed and they'd been discussing Fran's exit from the show. Although Angie's mind kept wandering, and she wanted nothing more than to get home and speak to Ryan.

With one final scene to record she stepped up behind Colin who was watching the set being prepared. "Do you mind if I leave now? Gemma's sticking around."

"No." He turned to look at her, and his eyes searched her face for a reaction as he spoke. "Enough with this Wendy crap, Angie. This is not the place to have distractions. You have enough with the baby on the way, I don't want sloppy work because you're chasing fairy tales." He held in the sigh of frustration as she first flushed, then frowned stepping forward.

"I have never produced sloppy work. Ever. You know that, and I don't intend starting now. For the record, Wendy Knight was a real person. She lived, she loved and she disappeared with no trace. She is not a figment of my imagination, and I don't know why it bothers you." She stepped back wondering if she'd gone too far. "That said, it was just a passing interest, it won't affect my work."

Colin knew she was lying, but the set was ready and he wanted to get away promptly as much as Angie, so he agreed and turned away, calling to the actor to take his position. Angie collected her things, and left without speaking to anyone. She'd already arranged her meeting with Gemma the next day.

Ryan was in the kitchen when she arrived home, and she took a moment before going to join him. Standing in the hall she looked around, was this the home she'd written about? The walls had been white and not grey, the floorboards had been stained a deep brown and were now carpeted, but yes, she decided, this could be it. Her musings were brought to an end when Ryan appeared in the doorway.

"What's wrong? Are you okay?" He looked concerned and Angie went to kiss him.

"I'm fine, don't be silly."

"I watched you come in, you looked like you had the weight of the world on your shoulders, then the door opens and there's no, 'Hi, Honey, I'm home.' Not even a grunt of recognition that I'm slaving over a hot stove to make you a roast."

Angie grinned at him. "Is it lamb?"

"But of course. My speciality because it's your favourite. Now, you go and slip into something more comfortable and I'll check the roast potatoes." He blew her a kiss. "And I don't think you were born in a barn, so shut the door." Whistling, he went back to the kitchen.

Angie pushed the door shut and then stepped back. It was the wrong door. Wendy's door had been solid at the bottom with the large stained-glass panel above. Angie closed her eyes and could see the sheep in the stained glass. This door had two strips of glass on each side of a centre strut. It wasn't the same door. As she went upstairs she thought what a shame that was.

When she came back down, Ryan informed her dinner would be at least an hour.

"No problem. I've got some notes to type up. Gemma is coming around tomorrow to work on Fran's exit. Oh, I didn't tell you, did I? Karen is retiring."

Ryan appeared in the doorway as she opened her laptop. "Blimey, I bet that set the cat amongst the pigeons. Anything else momentous happen?"

Angie had already decided not to mention their home once belonged to Wendy and she shook her head. "The usual posturing from Harry, although it's clear Colin doesn't like him. He put him in his place at every opportunity. While it was amusing, it's also worrying, this job is difficult enough at the best of times, without those two running at each other thumping their chests. Talking of which, Alan did this—"

Ryan held his hand up. "Hold that thought. I need to tend to my masterpiece. You can tell me all about it over dinner." He blew her a kiss and left her to it.

Angie opened the Wendy document and typed - THIS BLOODY COTTAGE! Then inserted a page break and continued the story.

~15~

Wendy stared at the pub carpark and watched him lock his car. It was his birthday, but she didn't feel like celebrating. She would have to use all her acting skills to pull this one off. She'd only seen him once for a few minutes, since he stormed off five days before, and she missed him. He looked up at the window and she waved before going to let him in.

"Happy Birthday." She threw her arms around him and kissed him. "Your present is in here, come on." Taking him by the hand she led him through to the sitting room. She lifted a brightly wrapped gift box from the table and placed it in his hands. "I hope I got it right."

He could see the concern in her eyes and he smiled. "I'm sure whatever it is will be perfect. If I were a guessing man I'd say it was the watch I admired a couple of weeks ago."

She grinned at him. "Open it and find out."

It was the watch. He was delighted and immediately removed his old watch and buckled the new one on his wrist. "Perfect, and it's the right time. Too early for dinner, shall we go for a drink?"

"I've booked a restaurant in town. We could walk along the waterfront and have a drink there."

"What's wrong with going across the road? Not that I mind."

"I won't be able to drink as I need to drive us to town." Her period had still not arrived, and unsure whether or not she'd keep the child, Wendy knew she shouldn't be drinking. Driving was an easy excuse to use.

"We can get a taxi. It's my birthday, we're allowed to be extravagant."

"I know, I was trying to be practical. Let's be extravagant once we get there."

He took hold of her chin and looked into her eyes. "I would like to pop in for a quick one. We don't need to stay long."

"I don't want to. It depresses me." She tutted. "You don't know do you?"

"Apparently not. Know what?"

"Jenny has gone. Disappeared. Gary is so mad with her, but I'm worried. She's not the type to do that. The new barman is okay, but he's not Jenny."

He released her chin, his hand falling to his side, and looked incredulous. "She might have been sick of working in a backwater. She's a young woman, probably landed herself a better job. Anyway," turning abruptly he walked back into the hall, "what's it got to do with me? Come on, grab your stuff, let's celebrate *my* birthday."

Knowing better than to argue, Wendy followed him across the road, hoping it would be just the one drink. The pub had lost its charm for her, and she didn't want alcohol. She forced a smile as she climbed onto the bar stool.

"What'll it be?" Gary slung the grey tea towel over his shoulder. "I hope you're not thinking of eating here, the new bloke's called in sick. Already. Three bloody days into a new job too, and he's sick. He won't last long. I'm going to lose a fortune not being able to get into the kitchen. I've only had a couple of packs of crisps myself. I'm starving."

"Oh dear. Lemonade for me. Any news on Jenny?" Wendy grimaced as he shook his head. "I'm worried, do you think you should call the police?"

"And say what, my barmaid is missing?" Gary rolled his eyes. "I've spoken to her boyfriend, and he says she's gone. Probably run off with someone and didn't have the guts to tell him."

"That doesn't sound like Jenny, does it?"

"How would you know?" He climbed off his barstool and walked towards the table in the bay window. "You've only known her two minutes."

"I know." Sliding off the stool she followed him. "But we talked for hours when I was here on my own."

"And she came to the cottage? You went to the cinema, or out for a pizza together?" He tutted as Wendy shook her head. "No. She wasn't a friend but a barmaid doing her job and talking to the customers. Forget about her." He held up his finger as Wendy opened her mouth to speak. "No buts, unless we're not celebrating my birthday, and we're here so you can pretend some trollop was your friend."

"Don't say that. She wasn't a trollop, I liked her. And I did say I didn't want to come here, it makes me sad. But it is your birthday, so tell me what other gifts you had, and how your day has been."

He talked about himself nonstop for twenty minutes. Mainly complaining about things which weren't going right. Wendy murmured sympathies in the right places. She knew they shouldn't have come to the pub, the way things were going, it was sure to be a depressing night. She focused on his words to stop her mind was drifting off.

". . . and then a lighting rig crashed to the floor, and the whole bloody thing was ruined. I was so mad I had to leave before I hit someone." He stopped speaking as Gary approached their table and asked if they wanted a refill. "No thanks, we have to make a move. Wendy has booked us a table in town."

"I must spend a penny before we go." Wendy got to her feet. "Gary, I don't suppose it's possible to have Jenny's address, is it? I'd like to go and see for myself."

"Well, it's not the done thing, but—" Gary took a step back.

"Don't be bloody stupid," he snapped. "You don't know these people, you are interfering. Now go and pee and let's get out of here." He watched her scurry away, embarrassed he'd shouted at her in front of Gary. Getting to his feet, he held out his hand. "Sorry about that, but she does like to interfere." He was surprised when Gary grinned at him.

"I know why you don't want them speaking. I'm not stupid, I saw the way Jenny watched you when you were in here. Saw her get into your car one night too." He pulled his finger across his lips. "Don't worry. They're sealed."

"I have no idea what you're talking about." His face was deadly serious. "I'd thank you not to speculate on anything to do with me. It could get you into serious trouble, and I'd ask you not to give her the address. Jenny's bloke could have her body hidden beneath the floorboards for all you know. Don't put Wendy in danger."

"I hear you, no address. As to the other, I'll keep my mouth shut." Gary walked away with a nasty taste in his mouth. That had sounded like a threat, and in his own pub too. He wasn't having that. Back behind the bar he wrote Jenny's address on the order book. Tearing off the sheet, he folded it and held it in his hand ready for Wendy's return. Gary didn't realise he was being watched and his actions anticipated.

Wendy smiled at Gary as she closed the door behind her, she turned towards the window as he began to speak to her, and was surprised when her bag was shoved into her hands.

"We'd better make a move. Don't want to be late for dinner." With his most charming smile, he turned to Gary. "Hope you have some luck finding a good replacement. I'd miss the food here if you stop cooking. Have a good night." Taking Wendy by the arm he steered her out of the pub.

"What an abrupt exit," she looked at him in surprise. "Is this the new car, are we taking yours into town?"

"Yes, well it's new to me. Too good a bargain to miss. I feel a bit queasy, not sure if the beer was off? More than likely. Gary doesn't seem to be coping."

"Oh no, are you sure you want to go for a meal?"

"Yes, of course. I wouldn't want to spoil your surprise."

He was charming, witty, and full of compliments during their meal. Wendy enjoyed the meal, the company, and a little too much wine. Having ordered a bottle, he'd decided not to drink and insisted she do so. Unable to think of a reasonable explanation for refusing she went along with his wishes, reasoning that many women would have had a drink before they realised they were pregnant, and it all turned out fine.

As the wine took affect she wished it was like this more often. He'd made a show of attempting to pay the bill, but in the end conceded as it was his birthday.

She linked her arm through his as they walked back to the car. "That was lovely." Resting her head on his shoulder, she gazed at him. "I hope you enjoyed it too."

"I did. But now you're drunk and we need to get you home to bed."

"I am not."

"Wendy, it's two steps forward and one to the side, if I didn't have hold of you, there would be one to the back too."

"Perhaps a little." She giggled. "Are we going to have birthday sex?"

"Of course."

Back at the cottage, he didn't park in the carpark as was his habit, but bumped up on the little verge outside.

"Why are you parking here?" she demanded her voice a little too loud.

"Because you are drunk and it's not too far for you to walk."

"I might be a bit . . . Ouch." Wendy tripped over her own feet. "Point taken." She giggled.

"You are laughing a lot tonight." He opened the front door and held out his hand to help her. "You don't usually laugh this much."

"One has to have something to laugh about."

Pushing her in the direction of the stairs, he replied, "Get in the bedroom and I'll put a smile on your face that will last for days."

They didn't draw the curtains, they barely took the time to undress, and he was right, she *was* smiling.,

"That was wonderful."

"I know." He swung his legs off the bed.

"Where are you going?"

"To close the curtains. You get to sleep."

Wendy watched him pull on his trousers before closing the curtains. "Are you not staying?"

"No. I still feel odd and I'll be restless and disturb you." He collected his shirt and sat next to her as he fastened the buttons. Forcing his feet into his shoes, he stood and looked down on her. "I do love you. Truly love you." Bending, he kissed her tenderly.

"I know, I love you too."

Wendy was barely awake when she heard the front door shut, and asleep as he pulled away. When she woke three hours later, she didn't know what day of the week it was. She lay on her back staring at the ceiling. Something was wrong. It was the noise. The noise and the movement of light flickering above the curtains. Rubbing her face in an effort to wake fully, she ambled over to the window, and froze in horror at the sight which greeted her.

The pub was on fire, flames everywhere, jumping through the windows and curling along the roof, there didn't seem to be an area which wasn't ablaze. Two fire engines blocked the road, and the crews shouted to each other as they fought to bring it under control. A policeman in a bright yellow jacket leaned back against his car speaking into his radio as he watched.

"Oh no, Gary." Fumbling for something to put on, she settled for her pyjama trousers and a sweatshirt. Ignoring her bare feet, she ran out into the street. A fireman grabbed her arm.

"No closer, please miss. The building is becoming unstable."

"What about Gary, the landlord, is he okay?" Wendy scanned the scene, she recognised a few faces huddled behind one of the engines. She didn't know her neighbours by name, their properties were positioned so a wave as you passed was all she had managed.

Having received no reply, she tried again. "Is Gary the owner of the pub safe?"

"I don't know. We were second on the scene, I don't even know who called it in."

"Can I go and wait with my neighbours?" Wendy hurried to join them when the fireman stepped aside. "Does anyone know if Gary is safe?" she called on her approach. A woman she didn't recognise stepped forward.

"We don't know. It doesn't look good though, we called the fire brigade, and they didn't know about it. We've just got back from Corfu. Night flight. The ground floor was well underway, now look at it."

Wendy did look, and she knew no one could survive that. Gary must have escaped. She was too numb to consider the alternative. She jumped when the woman tapped her arm.

"We might find out a bit more now."

Wendy followed the direction of her gaze and saw the policeman approaching.

"Did one of you call this in?" he jerked his thumb behind him.

The woman and her husband stepped forward and explained why they were out and about in the early hours. The officer made a note of their names and address.

"Does anyone know how many people lived there?" He established Gary lived alone since the collapse of his marriage some years before. "And you've not seen him?"

"What now or generally today? I was in the pub earlier with my boyfriend. He was on his own, his barman had called in sick?"

"What time was that?"

"Oh, I suppose we left around eight. There were a couple of other customers in there, but I don't know who they were, I think some of them were the bridge workmen having a drink after . . . Oh, they couldn't eat because Gary couldn't get to the kitchen with no staff."

Wendy knew from the look on his face he was wondering why she considered that relevant. He looked around the others. "Were any of you in there later than that, do you have any idea what time he closed?"

"We got back from town about eleven, it was all closed up then. At least downstairs there were no lights on. It must have been a quiet night." Wendy looked at the others who were shaking their heads.

"Where is your boyfriend, not gone over there I hope." Again, the jerk of the thumb.

"No, he went home, I'd had too much to drink and he wasn't feeling well. But he didn't drink," she added quickly.

"Time?" The policeman held his pencil poised.

Wendy grabbed her wrist. "I don't have a watch on." She heard a snort from the woman.

"He means what time did your boyfriend leave."

"Oh, I see. A little later. Not long, twenty minutes or so."

"Well, I'm sure he didn't notice anything."

"Of course he didn't. He would have woken me and called them. What a stupid thing to say. Shall I phone him?"

"I'm sorry, I didn't mean to be stupid," came his sarcastic retort.

Wendy blinked back tears. "I'm sorry. I didn't mean to be rude. It's just if Gary . . . well, if he . . ." She dissolved into tears and the policeman put his arm around her.

"I know. Which one is yours? You'd be better off at home." He sighed as he realised she lived immediately opposite the pub. He walked her up the path. "I think you should call him. Perhaps he can come and be with you." He smiled kindly as he pulled the door closed on the view.

Wendy took his advice and stood looking out of the kitchen window until he arrived. Despite the number of hoses pumping water into the flames, they didn't seem to be doing any good, and the fire raged on. When he appeared at the gate she was relieved to see him and rushed out to him.

"I think Gary was in there." She buried her face in her hands, then pushed him away and vomited into the flower border.

"Oh, you poor girl. What a shock, I should have stayed." Placing his arm around her shoulders, he led her into the kitchen and gave her a glass of water. "Have they told you Gary was in there?" he brushed away her tears and kissed her forehead gently.

"No, but—"

"Then let's try and be positive." Taking the glass, he pushed her towards the door. "Come on, bed."

For one awful moment she thought he wanted sex and relaxed when he added.

"You look awful, you won't sleep I'm sure, but at least you can be snug."

Wendy pulled the quilt around her shoulders and he sat watching her for a while, when it appeared she had gone to sleep he went to the window and stood watching the spectacle across the road. Wendy did sleep for several hours, when she woke he was still standing there.

She checked the time. "Have you been there all this time?"

"Of course not, I made tea. Yours is probably cold." He pointed across the road. "I'm afraid you might be right. The fire is out, there's still one engine, but more police are here, and men in white overalls have gone in with a couple of firemen."

Wendy went to join him at the window. The familiar building of the Rose and Crown, was no more than a blackened carcass. Most of the brick structure remained, but the roof was gone, the glass had shattered in the heat, and you could see the trees behind the pub through the front window. She watched two uniformed police men hammer metal rods around the carpark before tying tape around them, warning people not to enter.

She turned away. "I'm going to shower. I can't watch, I can't."

"Good idea, I'll go and get some breakfast on the go. Any requests?" He too turned away. "I can only stay a couple of hours. I have appointments today."

Wendy groaned. "I'm supposed to be filming later this morning, it's only one scene, I wonder if they'll let me cry off?" She caught the jerk of his head and paused. "Do you think I'm wrong?"

"Yes, of course." He tutted and pushed her towards the bathroom. "This could help you get more television work, even perhaps a film. Why would you risk that for . . . what? A burning pub? I know you lost a few hours' sleep, but shit happens, Wendy. We have to get on with it."

"I know, but if Gary was in there, well that's so awful. We were only speaking to him last night."

"So what? If you went to work and one of the runners who brought you coffee had died, you think the filming should grind to a halt?"

"That's not what I'm saying, I—"

"Then what is it? You've known the man as landlord of the local pub for a couple of months. If you added up all the hours you'd known him, how long would that be? A day? Two?" His tone was clipped and she could hear the anger bubbling below the surface, although she didn't know why. "Unless of course there's something you haven't told me."

"Like what? What are you suggesting." Her heart raced. Surely he didn't think that, he couldn't think that. "He was the landlord of the pub, yes, but he was still a nice person. I feel sorry for him."

"Shock. Not sorry. If he was in there he's feeling nothing now. Have your shower, let's get breakfast inside you, you'll feel better then."

Wendy's stomach somersaulted at the thought, but remaining silent she went into the bathroom. "Just toast for me. I'm not that hungry."

Two fried eggs sat on the toast he placed in front of her and she stared at them and swallowed as her stomach griped. She turned away without a word, drawing in air in the hope she wouldn't throw up.

"Where are you going, this will get cold, nothing worse than a cold fried egg," he called when he realised she'd walked out.

Hand over her mouth, she flew back upstairs and vomited into the toilet bowl.

He walked into the hall two mugs of tea still in his hands, and frowned. "Are you okay?" he called. When she didn't reply he turned back to the kitchen, "I'll throw my efforts in the bin then."

Wendy waited long enough for him to do so, before venturing downstairs. "I'm sorry," she apologised. "Perhaps I have the same thing you did, mine's a little more violent though."

"The same . . ." He'd forgotten about his excuse the night before, and held out his hand. "Cup of tea at least. You look nice in that blouse."

Glancing at the floral shirt she'd worn many times before, a surprised Wendy thanked him.

He smiled. "What time are you due on set?"

"Midday. I'll need to leave soon, I never know how busy the motorway will be."

"No problem, I'll stay here I think, I've nothing to do now. I called the producer when you were in the shower and filming has been cancelled."

"Why?"

"Why has it been cancelled?" He racked his brain for a reason.

"No, why did you call in?" Wendy lifted the mug to her lips but barely sipped the lukewarm tea.

"Because of the disaster yesterday. He was going to call round with a time once the rig has been repaired." He tutted. "I did tell you about this, but you clearly weren't listening."

"I'd forgotten. Sorry. Yes, I remember you said you had to start again. I should only be three or four hours, if of course everything goes to plan. I . . . Oh, something's happening."

Wendy had caught a movement through the kitchen window, and hurried over to look. She wished she hadn't. Two men in overalls were carrying a stretcher holding a zipped-up bag towards a blue van. Her hands covered her mouth as she watched them slam the door. She flinched when he touched her shoulder.

"Poor old Gary." He gave her shoulder a squeeze. "Like I said, it's lucky we didn't really know him." Checking the time, he held his hand towards the door, "I'll see you out to the car, grab your coat.

He ushered her to the car and waved her off the drive as though he were a traffic policeman. Once he was sure she had turned the corner, he shoved his hands in his pockets and walked over to the two policemen standing inside the tape, talking to Old Bill.

"Please tell me that wasn't the landlord." He glanced at the van.

"Sorry, sir, can't help you there."

"Because you don't know, or can't tell?" He wrinkled his nose.

"Because it's an ongoing investigation, and I'm sure an announcement will be made sooner rather than later. Did you know the landlord well?"

"No, my girlfriend moved in," he jerked his head towards the cottage, "a few months ago, so he's served me the odd meal and a couple of pints. Nice chap. Is foul play suspected?"

The second policeman turned to face him square on, his eyes searching for signs of knowledge. "Why would you say that, sir, is there something you should be telling us?"

"I wish I could, but I wasn't here, I went home last night, dodgy stomach. No, I asked only because this officer said it was an investigation."

"An investigation as to the cause," the second policeman explained, "Mind you, depending on what they find, it might be a criminal one come the end. One of the local residents said they heard a bang, problem is they didn't get out of bed, or look at the time. It could have been the cause or the result. Whatever it was, there wasn't much left of that poor bugger."

"Enough said, Jim." The first policeman nudged his colleague.

"Ah, a gas explosion, he mentioned he had trouble in the kitchen. Poor old Gary." He stared at his feet for a few moments, then tutted and gave the policemen a grim smile. "I'll leave you to it, although I'm not much in the mood to do anything. It seems wrong carrying on as normal."

When he got back to the cottage he went to the kitchen and put the radio on, Cyndi Lauper was telling her father that girls just wanted fun, and he laughed. “They do, Cyndi, they do.” He whistled along as he made a coffee, and when Bon Jovi belted out *Always*, he sang along with gusto.

~16~

Angie pushed the laptop away and ran upstairs. She hurried to the bedroom window and looked across the road. A rank of five townhouses looked back at her.

"I never checked out the pub. Because there is no pub!" she announced conclusively to herself, only to grimace minutes later. "But those houses do look fairly new." She gasped as Ryan spoke to her.

"Are you talking to yourself now? Seriously, Ange, a seer, and talking to what? Ghosts?" He was laughing, but there was a hint of concern there.

"Just muttering. I looked out of the window, and thought those houses don't look that old, I bet there was a fabulous view before they squashed those onto the plot."

"Better than those anyway, and more convenient." Ryan started back along the landing. "Come on, I'm dishing up."

Angie followed him. "What was more convenient?"

"There used to be a pub there. It was destroyed by fire, so the land was bought by developers and *voila*, our view."

Angie's pace faltered and she leaned on the jamb of the bathroom door. "How on earth do you know that?"

"Because I talk to the neighbours. I went for a walk the other day, and an old chap called Bill told me."

"Old Bill?"

Ryan stopped his hand on the banister. "You've met him too? You didn't say."

"No, I was checking what you said his name was. Why are you looking at me like that?"

"Because you've gone white." He walked back to her. "Are you okay?"

Angie pushed him away. "I'm fine, make my dinner, slave, I need a pee."

Ryan placed his hand on her forehead. "You are clammy. I hope you're not going down with anything."

"Only starvation. Go on, I'll be two minutes."

Plonking herself on the edge of the bath, Angie listened to Ryan go back to the kitchen. Her mind was a whirl. The dog, the cottage, and now the pub. She pondered whether to broach the subject with Ryan, but decided against it. She'd do some poking about first, and see if there was anything to tell. Standing, she walked to the toilet and pulled the flush. "Wendy if you are communicating with me. Give me some sort of sign I can work with, because to be honest, at the moment, everyone thinks I'm mad. Which given I'm talking to you, is probably not far off the mark."

"Are you coming down?" Ryan called.

"On my way."

The couple enjoyed their meal, with Angie keeping all conversation on Ryan's work, and not what she was working on. When they'd cleared the table, rather than go back to her laptop, Angie snuggled into Ryan on the couch.

"This is new. You know there's rugby on, don't you?"

"I do. I'm tired, I might try this nodding off in front of the television with you."

"No snoring then." Ryan kissed her head. "I'm stuffed, but I fancy a bar of chocolate. Have we got any?"

"Have you bought some?" When he shook his head, she laughed. "Well, there's your answer." She closed her eyes and groaned.

"What's wrong?"

"I need to pee. But don't complain about the fidgeting, I've remembered I've got chocolate in my bag."

He slapped her backside as she heaved herself up. "Good girl, I knew you'd come in useful for something."

Angie went to the bathroom and collected her bag from the hall table. She took it to the dining table and pushed her hand to the bottom, in search of the chocolate. Unable to find it, she unloaded the documents, several pages fluttered to the floor. Ignoring them, she located the chocolate and took it to Ryan.

"Knock yourself out. I'm going to run through these notes. Gemma will be here early."

"I thought you were tired. I don't want you over doing it."

"Twenty minutes. Promise."

Leaving him to his rugby, Angie went back to the table and sorted the papers into relevant piles. Stooping, she collected the sheets that had escaped. One was folded and she frowned. She couldn't remember folding it. She opened it and her hand flew to her mouth to hold in the gasp, her eyes shot to Ryan to make sure he hadn't noticed, but he was oblivious to her shock. She read the note again.

Back off bitch. Leave well alone. Don't make me come and find you. Be careful.

The note was handwritten in block capitals. It looked childlike, which had clearly been the writer's intention as the letters were of different sizes and styles. It would only have been more threatening if they had been cut and pasted from a newspaper. Angie sat at the table and stared at it, wondering who had written it and when.

"How are you doing, it's been twenty minutes," Ryan called from the sofa.

"Fine, not long." Angie had already decided not to tell Ryan yet. She believed the note to be from Harry. He was irritated by her lack of co-operation, and probably thought it would frighten her. Well, he could think again. If she told Ryan he'd come on set and get it sorted. Angie didn't need his protection. Tearing a blank sheet from her notebook and folding it in half, she refolded the note and placed it inside the sheet she had prepared. She then slipped it under the elastic which held the pages in place. Who knew, she may need it as evidence at some stage.

Opening her computer, she typed 'Bristol Pubs - Hallen Road'. She had much better results than when she searched for Wendy. She opened the first link. It was an article for a real ale magazine on old pubs in the Bristol area.

"*The Rose & Crown was originally built in 1798. It was not a lucky pub for its various landlords. In 1858 a fire in the stables claimed the life of landlord, Giles Hill, when the roof collapsed on him as he tried to rescue a customer's horse, and in 1907 the landlord's wife, Victoria Piggott, was hanged for poisoning her husband, who it was claimed beat her on a regular basis, but in doing so, she also managed to kill her sister, who was unaware of her plans. In 1994, the Rose and Crown was totally destroyed by fire following a gas leak, and the landlord, Gary Williamson, died trying to fight the flames. Such was the damage, the Rose and Crown was never rebuilt.*"

Above the text was a grainy black and white photograph, circa 1959. Angie closed her eyes unable to comprehend what she was seeing. When her heartrate had dropped a little, she pulled down the screen of her laptop.

"Wendy, oh Wendy. What are you doing to me?" she mumbled, and realising her hands were shaking, she clasped them together, and wondered how to deal with what to her, was conclusive proof she was writing a true story. The pub was the same as the one she saw when she wrote the landlord who had died there was called Gary. Her scream was shrill as Ryan touched her shoulder. He gave a yell himself.

"Fuck me, Angie." He clasped his hand to his chest. "Were you asleep?" Feeling the frantic beating of his own heart, he grabbed her hands. "Are you okay? I'm so sorry, I didn't mean to scare you."

Angie blew out a breath. "I think so. Oh my God, Ryan, don't creep up on me." The baby kicked her, and she rubbed the spot with the heel of her hand. "You even woke junior up."

"Creep up! I was speaking to you all the way over. I can't believe you fell asleep sitting at the table. Bedtime for you."

"I wasn't sleeping, I was thinking."

"About what?"

Angie looked at him for a minute, wondering if she should tell him, attempting to second guess how the conversation would go.

"What? Ange, I think you need to go to the doctor's, you're away with the fairies again. All joking aside, it's beginning to worry me."

"I was trying to work out how to weave Fran's departure into an existing storyline," she lifted her arms above her head and stretched, "but it's too complicated, not believable." She smiled. "But you're right. Time for bed."

"What a relief. For a moment I thought you were going to tell me you were having one of your visions." Ryan laughed. "You go on up, I'll sort everything down here."

"I have never claimed to have visions," Angie snapped. "Ever."

"You know what I meant." Ryan was now in the kitchen and she heard the bolt slide on the back door.

"I don't," she muttered as she started up the stairs.

Once Ryan was asleep, Angie went to the window and looked out at the town houses. If the pub had not burned down she would have known sooner. Ryan muttered something and she went through to the bathroom as an excuse for being out of bed. Sitting on the toilet she looked at the bath. It was Wendy's bath. The tiling, basin and toilet bowl were all different, but it was Wendy's roll top bath.

"I have to find out more." Looking at the ceiling she blew out a frustrated breath. "Bloody hell, Wendy, I'm talking to myself now too."

Ryan was snoring when she came out, so she tiptoed downstairs and powered up her laptop.

~17~

Wendy watched the bulldozer knock down what remained of the pub. It was over a week since the fire. Various vans and lorries had been and gone. Men in coveralls and safety helmets had visited, and having collected all the evidence they could, they decided the remaining structure was too far gone to save. Earlier, alone in her cosy living room, she'd curled her feet under her, and watched the local news as they confirmed Gary's death. The newsreader had been matter-of-fact in his delivery, no sombre tone they usually used for such announcements.

"And finally, the Rose and Crown pub in Hallen is to be pulled down after fire destroyed it a little over a week ago. It is believed a gas leak was responsible. The body of the landlord, Gary Williamson, was discovered in the remains, and whilst forensic investigations are ongoing, the police won't speculate on the cause of death. Our reporter has been referred the coroner's office, and we have been advised that the inquest into Mr Williamson's death will open at the end of the month."

Wendy switched off the television and stared at the blank screen. She needed a cuddle, and she considered going to see her father, but didn't want to explain why. A pet was what was needed, whatever he thought, this was her house and she lived in it on her terms - most of the time. Deciding to go for a walk, she slipped on her sensible shoes and collected her coat. Having nowhere in particular to go, she turned left and decided to walk for twenty minutes and then turn back. Checking her watch, she shoved her hands in her pockets and walked. Trying not to think about the pub, she ran over her lines for the next day.

"You all right, miss?"

Wendy came to an abrupt halt and looked towards the voice. The man she knew as Old Bill was walking on the other side of the road, a dog at the end of lead.

"Yes, thank you. Sorry was I talking aloud?"

"Quite loud, yes. Off for a walk?" He placed his hand on the dog's head. "No jumping," he warned as Wendy crossed the road to join him.

Wendy checked the time. "Yes, going back now though. I needed some air. I've just seen the news confirming it was Gary in the fire. I know we all knew, but it made me sad."

"Yep. He was a decent . . . I said no jumping."

Wendy bent and ruffled the dog's ears. "No problem. She's beautiful. How old?"

"Fourteen weeks. Only her second walk. I'm fostering her." Bill found a piece of sausage in his pocket and fed it to the dog. "She's a good girl, aren't you, Tess? Only one little accident so far, touch wood." He tapped the side of his head.

"I didn't know people fostered dogs." Wendy straightened up. "I'll walk back with you if that's all right."

"Fine by me. Here hold on to her, I can light up then." Bill pulled a pack of cigarettes from his pocket and lit up. "I often foster puppies, loads of different reasons, this one had a new home to go to, but her new owner had a car crash. In hospital, so I get her until she's well. We were doing some loose lead training." He smiled as the puppy dashed forward yanking Wendy's arm. "Here." He handed Wendy half a sausage. "Talk to her as you walk, anything will do, get her to look at you, and give her a treat every now and then."

Wendy did as instructed, and after only a few yards, Tess trotted happily by her side, looking for the next treat every few steps.

"She's beautiful. I was thinking about getting a dog. I needed a cuddle after seeing the pub on the news and thought it was time I sorted it out. I've been promising myself for a while."

"I'll keep an ear out for you. Bad business the fire. I don't reckon it was an accident. Why would the gas be on? He had no staff, he wasn't cooking. I told the police as much."

"What did they say?"

"Told me they were still investigating and thanked me. They did mention he might have been cooking for himself, but like I said to them. Too convenient. First young Jen goes missing, then this." He took the final drag on his cigarette and dropped it into a drain. "I don't believe it was an accident. Not for one minute."

"I'd forgotten about Jenny, I'd only known her a little while but I missed her when she'd gone."

"Disappeared. Not gone. Gary spoke to her bloke, and he said she'd just disappeared. Gary thought he sounded tearful. I'd put money on it being foul play. But the police wouldn't listen." He held out his hand. "I'll have her back now. This is me."

He stopped by the gate of a mid-terraced house. The three little houses were identical, except for the flicker of a television in the front room of Bill's house. A row of cards lined the window sill.

"Someone's birthday?"

"Mine. Yesterday. Bloody sixty. I told the wife, I didn't need to celebrate, but she insisted, and with no pub to go to we went into town. Missed the last bus back, cost me a fortune for a taxi, and on my birthday too."

"I didn't think you were that old. You're younger than my dad, why do they call you Old Bill?"

"Named my eldest after me, so he became young Bill, and me old. I was only forty by the time it had stuck." He took the lead. "Come on, Tess, let's see what's for supper."

Wendy watched him go, the dog wagging its tail as he told her what she was going to get to eat, and she decided she would start looking for her own puppy. Shoving her hands back into her pockets she continued her journey, crossing back to the other side of the road before she got to the pub, or what was left of it.

Once home, she stood in the doorway and glanced across. What Bill had said made sense. Why did Jenny disappear, who had caused those bruises, and why wasn't her boyfriend making a fuss? You'd have thought he'd have demanded the police look into her disappearance. It was ridiculous that they hadn't. Hearing the phone ring she rushed inside.

She snatched up the receiver. "Hello."

"Hi. Only a quick call to make sure all is well. We've run into a snag, I'll be tied up the rest of the day."

"Oh dear. Another long day. Did you find somewhere nice to eat last night?"

"Yes, nice little club, I had chicken in the basket and a nice pint." He smiled at the thought of what else he had had. "What about you?"

"Just moped about. They're knocking down what's left of the pub, and they confirmed it was Gary on the news this morning, although police aren't ruling out foul play." It wasn't quite what was said, but Bill's words were still at the forefront of her mind.

"You're going to have to move into the flat you know. I can't have you miserable and moping all the time because of the view."

"It's not all the time, it's only been a little while. Anyway, I've decided—"

"Tell me later, got to go. Love you."

Wendy hung up. How could he be so heartless, so indifferent? How could she love him, yet be so different to him? Pulling back her shoulders she lifted the receiver again. She cared, she really did, and if nothing else she would find out what happened to Jenny. She dialled 999.

Having been told off by the operator as her call wasn't an emergency, she was given a number of the local police station. Apologising, she redialled. She was put through to a young female detective who took her details and told her she would call back once she'd checked if they already had the information. Twenty minutes later she received the call.

"Miss Knight? DC Clarke. It wasn't only you who thought she was missing. We did have a file open but it's been closed now. She's been found."

"Oh good . . . wait, she is all right, isn't she?"

"I didn't speak to her, but as I've said we closed the file so she must be."

"Can you tell me where she is?"

"I'm afraid not."

"But I'm very worried, so was Gary and now he's dead, so . . ."

"Are you suggesting the two things are connected?"

"No. That is, I don't know, but I'd like to speak to her. She was being beaten we think, had bruises on her arms, couldn't stretch, and she lied to me about how they had happened."

"That's a shame, but if she doesn't report it there's little we can do. I'm sorry. Now unless there's anything else . . ."

"Can you at least ask her to call me? You have my details, tell her I'm worried about her and I won't give up until she speaks to me." Wendy heard the sigh. "Please. It won't take long, she might be happy to have a friend to talk to."

The detective relented. "On one condition."

"Anything." Wendy grinned into the receiver.

"If she is the victim of abuse, try and get her to come forward and speak to us. Me if necessary, DS Clarke. Sarah Clarke, with an E. Will you do that?"

"Of course, thank you, Sarah, I mean DS Clarke. Shall I give her this number?"

"Yes. I'll try her now, and if I don't get hold of her, I'll call her again before I clock off at lunch-time. If I'm not lucky, I'll try tomorrow, but don't hold your breath she was obviously running away from something so she might not want to get in touch."

"Thank you so much. Please don't ask her about the abuse yourself, she might not call me if you do."

Wendy relaxed for the first time in days, and headed for the bathroom, she had an hour before she needed to leave for work. Leaving the door open in case the phone rang she ran a bath. She'd barely sunk into the bubbles when it did. Grabbing a towel and leaving perfect wet footprints on the floorboards, she flew down the stairs.

"Why are you breathless?"

"Oh, it's you. I was in the bath."

"Were you expecting someone else?" his tone was menacing.

Remembering his comments on Jenny not being a friend, she reassured him, "Of course not, but you got so angry last time I was in the bath and didn't get to the phone." Her irritation matched his own.

"Are you angry with me?" He sounded incredulous. "I've made a special effort to give you the news and . . . Oh sod you." And he was gone.

"Hello, hello? Right!"

Wendy hung up and then took the phone off the hook in case he called back. She was half way up the stairs when she realised she would miss Jenny if she called, and grunting her frustration, she turned back and replaced the receiver.

Checking her hair in the hall mirror, she was ready to head out for the studio and the phone rang again. Assuming it would be him, and still angry she snapped, "Hello."

"Wendy? Is that you?"

"Jenny! Thank God! How are you? Where are you? Oh, and sorry about that I thought it was him, I'm cheesed off with him."

"Good. He isn't there I take it?"

"No. Why?"

"No reason, I won't keep you. The police woman said you were worried, and I've heard about the fire, so thought I should let you know I'm okay."

"But why did you leave like that? Gary was worried, I was worried, even Old Bill, who by the way is only sixty, was worried."

"Ha! Well is nice to know someone loves me. My bloke is barely speaking to me at the moment."

"Oh. You're back with him then."

"You make it sound like that's a bad thing."

"Look, Jenny, I have to get to the studio. Can we meet somewhere later? I haven't got time to talk at the moment."

"That's okay, I've got somewhere I need to be too. Bye, Wendy, take care."

"No, no. Don't go, please, Jenny, I'd like to speak to you."

Jenny considered this for a moment. What if he'd started on Wendy now she wasn't around? Perhaps she needed someone to confide in, and if that was the case, she would make her go to the police. "Okay, meet me in town. Do you know the little café on the corner of St Nicholas market?"

"I do. I'll be finished by mid-afternoon. Can we meet later today?" Wendy's mind was racing. He wasn't due home until the weekend, but if he came home early she'd never find an excuse to go off, and she didn't want him with her. Jenny wouldn't want to open up in front of him. If they could meet today, he'd never need to know. She crossed her fingers.

"Okay. I should be able to be there by four-thirty."

~18~

Angie got to her feet yawning, her shoulders ached and she needed to sleep. Ryan merely grunted as she climbed into bed, and she fell asleep wondering how the meeting with the two women would go. Not well enough, or Wendy wouldn't have ended up in the back of his car.

The next morning, Gemma arrived promptly at nine-thirty, Ryan had already left, and they discussed various options for an hour or so before settling on a way to build Fran's disappearance into the plots which had already been written. They worked solidly until mid-day.

"I need a break," Angie stretched her back. "Can I make you a sandwich or something?"

"No thanks. I'm going to pick up my sister, she said she'd have something ready." Gemma scribbled another note in her pad. "We've done enough for me to get on with this while I'm away. I'll send you over each episode as I finish it. You are happy with getting on with the new stuff, aren't you? I'm happy to do it the other way, but I think . . ."

Angie laughed. "Gemma, I'm happy with that. It's why I suggested it. All we have to do now is hope Alan and the others like it, so we don't waste too much time, and have endless, pointless, bloody meetings. Cup of tea before you go?"

"Go on then. Can I ask you something?"

"Of course." Angie was now in the kitchen filling the kettle.

"Have you fallen out with Alan?"

Angie appeared in the doorway. "Alan? No, of course not, why do you ask?"

"I didn't think so, but Harry said—-

"Let me stop you there. Harry is a shit stirrer, and it's best to take anything he says with a pinch of salt. He is probably attempting mind games to get you to side with him and not me if the occasion requires it."

"I have my own mind." Gemma was insulted Angie would think she wouldn't simply use her own judgement.

"I know, but Harry seems to think we women always need to be steered in the right direction. We are renegades if we think for ourselves." Angie went back to the kettle. "Alan and I get on well, we always have."

"That's what I thought. Harry is funny, but he can be a pain." Gemma collected her things together.

"Funny?" Angie shook her head. "Nope, I never get funny. What I get is . . ." The doorbell rang, Angie grinned. "My delivery."

The delivery men carried the boxes up to the spare bedroom, and put the cot together. When they had gone, Angie and Gemma went to look.

"Ah, it's lovely, Angie. When are you due?" Gemma ran her hand along the rail.

"Ten weeks. Starting to feel real now, I bought a steriliser, bottles and a nappy changer the other day." Angie opened the top drawer in the chest. "And a ton of newborn baby clothes." She lifted out a tiny vest. "How sweet is this?"

"It's . . ." Gemma's phone rang and she pulled it from her pocket. "My sister, excuse me." The call was short. "I have to go. My sister needs me to do an errand on the way. If you think of anything else, please shout."

Angie followed her back downstairs and showed her out. The vest was still in her hand and she laid it over the back of the chair before sitting in front of her laptop. She wasn't in the mood for more of The Village, she'd get to it later, and she thought about going back to Wendy. She re-read the section she'd written the night before. What were the chances of Old Bill still being alive? She smiled as she closed the laptop.

She walked at a steady pace until she came to the row of three houses, knowing Bill lived in the centre of the small terrace. Looking at it from across the street, she knew she was going to knock, but needed a reason first. Deciding to stick as close to the truth as possible, she crossed the road, and was surprised when the door opened before she'd raised her hand. An elderly woman smiled at her.

"I thought you were the new nurse, but you haven't got a bag. Are you lost?"

"No, I was wondering if I might have a word, I'm writing about something which happened in the area, and I'm told you've lived here for a while."

"We have, thirty-five years. Writing about us? Why?"

Angie looked past the woman as the television suddenly blared out.

The woman rolled her eyes. "He's going deaf, won't have a hearing aid so the rest of us have to suffer. Oh dear, I should ask you in." She stepped back to allow Angie room. "Shall I put the kettle on?"

"That would be lovely, thank you." Angie followed the woman towards the sound of the television. She went into the sitting room, and grabbing the remote control switched off the television, her husband banged the arm of his chair.

"Why did you do that? Cash in the Attic is about to start."

"Don't worry about the telly, we've got a visitor. Be nice, I'm going to make tea." Turning to Angie, she instructed, "Go and sit there. Ask him anything you like. He knows most things and has a good memory."

Angie sat on the sofa and smiled at Bill. "Hello."

"Hello. Who are you?" Bill looked her up and down.

"My name is Angie Bear . . . Clark, I've come to ask you some questions, if that's okay?"

"How did you nearly get your name wrong?" Bill's eyes narrowed, "and what questions?"

"My married name is Clark, but for ridiculous reasons, my professional name is Bearing. The questions are about the pub that burned down, and about Wendy Knight."

"What's a professional name? You're not the copper who came, she'd be much older. She was a Clark."

A crease appeared on Angie's brow. It appeared Bill might be a little senile. "What copper?" she humoured him, deciding that at least it had got her out of the house.

"The one who came about Wendy. Lovely, lovely girl she was. Old Tess pined for months after she went."

Angie hoped she didn't look as surprised as she felt. She pictured the words she had typed, DS Clarke, with an E. Was this, absolutely, definitely, proof she was writing a true story? No one could imagine this many coincidences. She blinked as Bill tapped her hand.

"Are you all right, love? You look a bit funny."

"To be honest, Bill I feel a bit funny. But I won't bore you with that, you'll think I've gone mad. It's Wendy I've come to ask about."

"Why mad? I'm very open-minded," a smile broke through his wrinkles, "and I like a good laugh."

Angie returned his smile. She had to tell someone or she would go crazy. She drew in a breath. "Then brace yourself, because I can't believe what I'm going to say either. I'm a writer and I've recently moved into—"

"Applegate. Yes, I know, I've seen you. She lived there, Wendy did."

"Yes, I found out yesterday. I've been writing about her."

"I hope it's nice, because she was a lovely girl. Old Tess loved her."

"Tess, the dog you were fostering because her owner was in hospital?"

Bill's eyes narrowed as he tried to work out how she could know that. "Yes."

"You want to know how I know don't you?"

"I did wonder, yes." Bill was now eyeing her suspiciously.

"I think she is communicating with me in some way." She returned Bill's grin.

"Get on with you." He tapped his temple. "I might be old but I've still got all my marbles."

"I can see that, and yes, I do think I'm losing mine sometimes." Angie grimaced. "Let me start from the beginning, I'll tell you what happens, and some of the detail, and then you decide. If you think I'm mad, I'll drink my tea and go, if you don't I'd like to ask you some questions."

Still smiling, Bill agreed. Linking his fingers, he rested his hands on his stomach and leaned back in the chair. "I'm going to enjoy this, better than that rubbish." He glanced at his wife as she came in with the tea tray. "Sit down, Beth, we're going to hear a story."

"I haven't got time for a story. I've got little Bill picking me up any minute, I need to get ready. I'll leave you to it." She smiled at Angie. "Sorry about this, but we weren't expecting you. You'll have to be mother." Closing the door behind her, she left them to it.

Angie knelt next to the coffee table and picked up the teapot. "Do you take sugar?"

"Two. Leave that a minute, it won't have brewed."

Angie replaced it and spooned the sugar into one of the cups while she waited. "Would little Bill be the son of young Bill who made you Old Bill by the time you were forty?" Mentally crossing her fingers, she watched the look of surprise turn to a frown.

Bill leaned forward resting his elbows on his knees, his hands dangling towards his feet. "I don't know who you've been talking to, but you're right. He's taking her shopping for my birthday present. I'm not supposed to know, but it doesn't take a genius to work it out."

Angie did the arithmetic. "So, you'll be eighty-three soon. You don't look it."

Bill shook his head. "Start talking. You have my attention. Pour the tea before it stews." Smiling, Angie poured and gave it a good stir. "Leave it there, it'll be too hot at present."

"The other night I couldn't sleep and I got up to do some work, but I didn't. I started writing a story about a girl who was abducted. I didn't—"

"Wendy. So she is dead." Bill gave a heavy sigh and rubbed his nose. "I always knew it, but without the body there was always hope."

"I think so, yes, but I haven't got that far yet. If she's not then where is all this information coming from?" She could see the disbelief in his eyes, and racked her brain for something to convince him. "Okay, okay, I'll tell you two things only you and Wendy would know." She nodded at him. "Number one, you met Wendy while out walking Tess. She was only fourteen weeks old, and you told Wendy how to train her to walk on a loose lead. There were cards on the sill." Angie pointed at the window. "It had been your sixtieth birthday, and she told you that you were younger than her dad."

"She could have told anyone that. What else?" Bill already believed her, and if he were truthful, being so close to going to meet his maker himself, the thought that there was some kind of afterlife pleased him.

"Do you remember Jenny?" Angie smiled as Bill rolled his eyes. "Of course you do, because you were worried something awful had happened to her too. You told the police that when the pub caught fire."

"I did. But again, anyone could have told you that. Anyway, Wendy found her. She went to meet her." Bill had heard about people who could communicate with the dead, everyone had, but he'd never met anyone who claimed they could. While it would be wonderful if it were the truth, if this girl had been digging around the story, then it was possible someone else gave her the information.

"But they didn't. I only see what I see, I don't think there is anything else which relates to . . . Ha! Do you remember Wendy's boyfriend?"

"Vaguely, they split up not long before she took Tess."

"You see, I haven't got to the part where she had Tess yet, or the meeting with Jenny, but I do think the boyfriend had something to do with it. He wasn't a nice man, and I think you knew that. When he first appeared, he had an argument with Jenny in the carpark, you left your window seat and went to see if she was all right." She grinned as he raised his eyebrows. "You only got as far as the door, as he was being nice to her, and promised her a drink or a tip or something, but you went back in as you believed all was well." Angie put her hands on her hips. "Am I right?"

"Yes." Bill rubbed his hand over his chin. "Gary thought Jenny was sweet on him, he even saw her get into his car one night. But I didn't like the way she looked at him. She looked troubled to me, not like someone with a fancy."

"She was troubled. She was having an affair with him, but he was hitting her about. Bullying was his thing, having power over people." Angie buried her face in her hands for a moment. "And it's one of the things that worries me about this. How can I know what happened between him and Jenny? Jenny's not dead, so how did I get those details?" With a flick of her hair, she shook the details away. There was no way she was sharing what they did with Bill. He'd probably have heart failure.

"Perhaps Jenny told her. She did meet with her, before Jenny got a job abroad." He clicked his fingers as he tried to bring the memory back. "No, it's gone. Can't remember where, but she let Wendy know, and rang her when she got there."

He lifted his cup of tea and slurped noisily, as a car horn sounded outside. "That'll be little Bill. I've bloody told him about doing that." He looked up as his wife's head appeared around the door. "See you later. Don't spend too much." He studied Angie as he listened to his wife leave and wondered what she was doing, sitting on his sofa, telling him this stuff. "So, to the point. What do you want from me?"

"I believe whatever happened to Wendy, her boyfriend did it. He was a bully and a sadist, and I have this feeling it's where this story is leading. I wanted to know if you remembered anything about him, his name, what he looked like, it might help solve what happened to her."

"Are you going to the police?" Bill looked at the pretty young woman sitting opposite, and stared at her pregnancy. "Not sure you'll get anywhere with this story."

"Exactly. It's why I wanted more real detail. If you remember anything at all about him it might help." Sitting silently, she watched Bill close his eyes and force his mind back.

He opened his eyes. "Can't bring him to mind. I only saw him a few times. I'm sure I'd know him if I saw a photo, but . . . He had muscular arms. I remember him sitting at the bar and he stretched like this," Bill lifted his arms to the side with a wince and brought his forearms back in towards his shoulders, "like body builders do, and I remember being impressed with the size of his biceps. He had a chunky neck too. But I'm blowed if I can remember what he looked like." He frowned, "Hang on a minute, I thought you *saw* all this stuff."

"No. Not as such, some of it I do as clear as day, the supermarket carpark, Tess, the pub, but not faces, not clearly. And I don't so much see it, as write it." She wiggled her fingers. "It just all comes out."

Bill looked unconvinced. "How did you know I was me then?"

"Two things. First, you met my husband while he was out walking and he told me your name and said you were a nice chap, and second, I knew the house, I saw the house. But I never properly see faces." Angie shook her head. "It's all too weird I know."

"Don't you know what Wendy looks like? Would you like to see her?"

Angie clasped her hands together. "No, I don't, that was to be my next trip. I was going to the library to look at the archive newspapers. Do you have a photograph?"

"I do. Go over to the sideboard, right hand cupboard, there's a photograph album in there."

Angie lifted out an ancient looking album and took it to Bill. He placed it on his lap and patted the cover.

"All my puppies are in here. Every dog I ever owned or fostered. Tess is in here, took the photo on the day Wendy came to collect her." He smiled. "Every now and then she would sneak out and come and see me. Not so much traffic on this road then, but it was still naughty."

He lifted the blue cover and started to turn pages. Each photograph had a handwritten label with the name of the dog, and the date it was taken. Some of them caught his eye and he'd stop and stroke the photograph as the memories flooded back. It took almost ten minutes to get to the photographs Angie wanted to see. She knelt by the side of Bill's chair and he slid the album across his legs to her.

"She was a lovely girl. Poor old Tess didn't have her long." He coughed to clear his throat.

Smiling for the camera, there were three photographs of Wendy with Tess. In the first, she was standing, holding Tess's lead, in the second, she was kneeling beside her, one arm around Tess, who sat obediently for the photograph. Fair hair held back in a ponytail, her smile wide, she was an attractive young woman. Wearing her jeans tucked into wellington boots, and a chunky cable knit cardigan open over her tee-shirt, she looked as though she didn't have a care in the world. She looked younger than Angie thought she would, more twenty than twenty-five, but she decided it was because Wendy was of slight build and no more than five feet four inches. No match for a muscular man with impressive biceps. Angie smiled at the third photograph, Tess had obviously become excited, and all that was visible of Wendy were her legs from the knee down, and a hand waved to the camera, the rest of her was hidden by the dog sitting on her.

"She looks nice." A wave of sorrow swept over Angie. She knew Wendy would meet her fate at the hands of that brute, and as she swallowed back her emotions, as she made a silent vow she would try and bring him to justice.

Bill was watching her closely. "You think she'll tell you what happened to her?"

Angie got to her feet. "I don't know. She doesn't talk to me, images arrive as I type the words." She raised her shoulders and held them there. "I know you think I'm mad, I'm sure Ryan does, but it's so real, and you've not corrected me on anything I've told you."

"I can't if you're right, can I?" He looked out the window. "Nurse is here. She's a cheeky one."

"Here for you? I'm sorry I didn't realise you were ill."

"Nearly back to normal. Had a stroke a couple of months back, need that bloody thing to walk now." He pointed at a wheeled frame Angie had failed to notice behind his chair. "My left foot won't behave. She reckons putting me through my paces will improve it."

The doorbell rang, and Bill pushed himself up.

"No, stay there. I'll let her in, and I'll go and leave you to it."

"You'll come back though, won't you? I'd like to know the truth."

Angie smiled. "I will if I find out anything else."

Angie let the nurse in, and stood in the doorway to say goodbye. "Even if nothing else happens," she waved her fingers at Bill, "I'll come and see you if that's okay?"

"That would be lovely." Bill beamed and prodded the nurse who was kneeling at his feet to remove his shoes. "See, I can still attract a pretty face. Bye, love."

On the short walk home, Angie's emotions flipped from elation that Bill had verified the scenes she had written, to sadness that she was writing about true events. She might not be going crazy, but she wasn't sure she liked the alternative much. She opened the front door with a sigh, knowing she'd be sitting back at the laptop in minutes. She was wrong.

As the door opened, a foul smell attacked her senses before she saw it. A rotting rat, complete with what she assumed were maggots, had been pushed through the letterbox. Her stomach somersaulted and she turned away and vomited into the flower border.

It took a while before she was able to hop over the carcass and enter the house. Armed with rubber gloves and a black bin liner she removed the doormat, a piece of polythene it must have been wrapped in, and the rat, and placed the bag outside. Getting to work with a bowl of hot soapy water she scrubbed the area clean.

"Who did this?" she muttered. "I was gone less than an hour, how did they know I wouldn't be in?" She sat on the bottom stair to consider this. "Come on, Wendy," she looked around the hall, "divine inspiration is needed. Did they know I was out, or did they knock first? The car is on the drive, so it was a long shot they wouldn't be caught. Was it even meant for me? Was it someone's sick idea of fun and I got the short straw, or was it someone wanting to scare me? I'm not scared. Pissed off, and will be more so if that stains. I'd like to catch the little . . ."

Angie got to her feet and went to the kitchen. "Thank you, Wendy. I'll call the police, I'll also get Ryan to install those bloody cameras, although it's not the wildlife I want to film." She pulled her phone from her bag noticing the slight tremor in her hands.

Remembering Wendy had been told off for calling the emergency number, Angie googled what to do if it was a non-emergency. She found it was to call 101. Shaking her head at this newly found knowledge, she made her call. She was told to keep the evidence safe and an officer would come and see her. When she asked when she wasn't surprised to be told it would be within a week. Frustrated, she finally got to go back to the laptop.

~19~

Wendy's smile was wide, when she saw Jenny had already arrived and she held out her arms as she approached.

"I've been so worried about you," she told an awkward Jenny.

"I'm okay." Jenny extracted herself.

Wendy took her hand and pulled her back on the bench seat which ran along the wall of the café. "Are you?" She peered at Jenny closely. "Are you really?"

"I am now, I wasn't, and I might not be in a minute."

"What does that mean?" Wendy tried to take hold of Jenny's hand again, but it was pulled away and clasped in her lap. Wendy looked away for a moment, when she looked back she seemed more nervous than Jenny. "Can I be honest with you?"

"Yep. Although, I can't begin to guess what you're going to say." She had a pretty good idea though. She believed Wendy was going to tell her she was being abused.

"No easy way, so I'll just spit it out."

Jenny's eyes widened and she smiled encouragement, and watched Wendy's chest rise as she drew in a deep breath.

"I know you were being abused." She heard the croak in her voice. "I know what you said about the cellar steps, and it wasn't only me, Gary thought so to. Poor old Gary."

"I was." Jenny was unable to look her in the face.

"Then you must go to the police." Wendy announced. "Why go back to him? Don't answer that, I know it's never that simple."

"I haven't gone back to anyone. Brian won't have me back. It wasn't Brian."

Puzzled, Wendy's head shot up. When she looked at Jenny she knew who she was going to name. It was like a lightning bolt. Her chest tightened and she braced herself for what was to come.

"Does he hit you too?" Jenny knew Wendy had worked it out.

"Don't be ridiculous. Why would I stay with a man who hit me? Why? Was he hitting you? I don't understand."

"Has he never hit you?" Now it was Jenny who offered a hand to hold in comfort. Wendy allowed her to take it. "I'm going to tell you the truth, or as much of it as you can bear to listen to, but you also have to be honest. I'm your friend, Wendy, I need to be honest with you."

Wendy's smile was brief. The bastard was wrong! Whatever she was about to be told, it didn't matter, Jenny was her friend. "Tell me," she coaxed quietly.

"It was a sexual thing, I can't explain it, he has a way . . . Oh God, this is so hard."

"Tell me. When did this start? He's only known you a few weeks."

"Do you remember the day your furniture was delivered?"

"Of course. But that was the first time he'd been to the cottage." Wendy's brow furrowed. "Although he was in the pub the night before. Was he there to see you?"

"No. That night he arrived a little after you, I'd never seen him before. He had eyes only for you. He positioned himself at the bar so he could watch you. I thought he was proposing, when—"

"Proposing? Why?" Wendy remembered he had gone down on his knees and told her he would beg. "Oh yes, I can understand why you'd think that. Did he chat you up when I'd gone?"

"Ha! No, he called me names when I said I was sorry because I thought you'd said no to his proposal, and told me to stay away from him. That was fine by me, he scared me a bit. The next day, I saw him in the carpark, he was coming to see you, and I told him he couldn't park there. I thought I was being brave, letting him know he didn't intimidate me. But I gave him more reason to try."

"He does have a temper. Not that he's ever hit . . . well just the once, but those were unusual circumstances."

"Were you having sex?"

"What? No! I was asking him why he hadn't turned up for our wedding." Pushing her hair away from her face, Wendy gave a shaky laugh. "Are you telling me he hit you when you had sex with him?" In her heart she knew it must be true, she simply didn't want to believe it. Her hand went to her belly. She might be having his child, she closed her eyes to compose herself. "I know this will sound weird, but I want you to tell me everything. From the day the furniture arrived, to the day you ran away. It's crucial I know the worst."

"Isn't it enough that you—"

"No. Tell me, please."

"Can you remember what you did before the van arrived?" Jenny watched as Wendy realised she was referring to the sex at the bedroom window. She shook her head when Wendy's mouth opened. "Don't speak or I might never tell you. He saw me coming, I don't know why I looked up, but I did. He was smiling at me, his eyes seemed to trap me, and while he was doing it he was still smiling at me. Then he yanked your head up so I could see you too."

Wendy coloured as she remembered him pulling her hair, and she looked into her lap. "Go on."

"I'm ashamed to say it aroused me. He's a good-looking man. He also made me watch later, when you were eating in the bar." She paused to make sure Wendy made the connection, she did. "He made sure I saw that too. When he said he'd been locked in the toilet, he hadn't. He let me know he wanted to see me, and we were having sex in there, but we got interrupted by Gary. I was ashamed, and I tried to ignore him, but before he left he told me he'd be back when I finished work. He was. He took me to a field and he bound me with tape. I don't believe it was a coincidence the tape was in his car. I think it's his thing."

Jenny stopped and blew out a breath, it was difficult to find the words to explain what had happened without giving too much detail. Her hand shook as she lifted her cup.

"Tell me." Wendy squeezed her hand. "I promise I don't blame you." She gave a brief smile as Jenny agreed.

"I tried to fight him at first, but he hit me if I didn't cooperate. So I cooperated. It was the most disgusting, wonderful, hideous thing which ever happened to me. I'd never experienced pleasure like it before. I hated him, and I mean really hated him, but I still wanted more."

She brushed away a tear with the flat of her hand. "After the third time it became less about the sex and more about how much pain he could inflict on me. I avoided him, he followed me. On the day I left, I'd already decided to go, but not when. When I found him in the bar I knew it had to be right then and there so I got a taxi and went home. But before I got to my front door he called to me. He told me if I didn't go with him he'd tell Brian." She blinked the tears from her eyes, allowing them to fall unhindered. "I went with him. He hurt me badly that time. I found out later he had broken my rib, he also damaged me down there." She looked into her lap. "I told him I would tell you when he refused to give me a lift home. He told me he would kill me if I did. I believed him." She sniffed and dabbed her nose with the back of her hand. "Now I'll have to wait and see."

When she had the courage to look at Wendy, she saw not fear or anger, but a grim determination.

Wendy looked at the ceiling. "I won't tell him you told me."

"But you must. I'm getting out of Bristol. I've applied for jobs all over the place."

"Do you really believe he might kill you?"

"I do."

"You could be right. I won't put you in any sort of danger." Placing her elbows either side of her drink, Wendy buried her face in her hands. She remained there for some time. Jenny simply watched her. With a sudden movement, Wendy leaned back against the bench, throwing her arms into the air. "This is my fault. All my bloody fault. If I'd listened to my father, if I'd listened to that poor woman, I wouldn't have let him back in, and you wouldn't be running away from your life, perhaps for your life. We have to go to the police."

"No. What woman? Did you know he'd done this before?" Jenny's tone was accusing.

"I was told he was capable. The day we should have married, he hit me to the ground, and the lady who helped me told me men either hit women or they don't. If they do, they never change. She stayed with her husband so he could hit her and not her children. She told me never to go back to him. I should have listened."

"Well, you have now, and you can get rid of him. Find yourself a nice bloke."

"I intend to, but first we must go to the police." Her eyes widened as Jenny shook her head repeatedly. "Why not? Jenny, he needs to be punished."

"I know, but I'm a coward. Don't forget, at first, I was a willing participant. Later, I never said no because I didn't want him to be angry as well. Even if they prosecuted him, would they find him guilty, my word against his?" She was speaking quickly, one word merged with the next, this was something which had been given serious consideration. "And if found guilty, how long would he get? Two years, six months, a suspended sentence?" She shook her head, "No. Because then he would be so pissed off if he ever found me I don't even want to think . . . I'm sorry, Wendy, no. I only told you all this so you would leave him."

"I will, don't worry, he won't talk me round this time. But I won't tell him I know about you, not if I can help it."

Jenny glanced at her watch. "If it settles it, you should. I'm sorry I have to go. I'm working in a pizza place on Park Street, my shift starts in a minute."

"Can we stay in touch?"

"Of course. I'm sleeping on someone's couch at the moment, but I'll call you. If he answers I'll put on an accent and pretend I'm from the gas board." She didn't smile, she was serious.

"He won't answer, Jenny. He won't be there."

"I hope not, but I'll practice my lines anyway. It's what you actresses do, isn't it?" She laughed. "When you're rich and famous, remember you have a poor friend."

"I will. Keep your fingers crossed, I had an audition for a role in a new soap last week, my agent tells me they're making the final casting decisions tomorrow."

"Of course, and you do the same for me. I'm excited about some of the jobs I've applied for, don't know why I didn't do it before." Jenny got to her feet. "Please be careful."

"I will. Remember keep in touch."

Wendy watched her leave. She felt sick, quite literally, and sat still until the feeling passed. If she was carrying his child he must never know. Glad he was still filming in Manchester, she made her way home. Bolting the doors and closing all the curtains before setting the alarm, she went to her bedroom. If he made a surprise appearance tonight she wouldn't be speaking to him.

It was almost dawn when she found sleep, having made numerous plans on how to remove him from her life. The only one she believed would put an end to it, was telling him she knew about Jenny and she didn't want to do that.

The phone jarred her into consciousness, she ignored it. But looking at the time, she dragged herself into the shower. Half an hour later she headed into town. Before she left, she called her father to make sure it hadn't been him calling. It hadn't been him, and she arranged to have dinner with him the next day. Her first stop in town was a chemist, the second the electrical shop where she finally purchased an answer machine.

Wendy found out she was carrying his child sitting on the toilet in the ladies on the third floor of Debenhams department store. Wendy stared at the two clear lines for a long time, vaguely aware of people coming and going in the cubicles on either side.

"Bastard." She got to her feet, dropped the pregnancy test into the bin, and pulled the flush.

Once home, she wasted no time in setting up the machine. Now she could screen his calls, although she hoped that once she told him what she knew, he'd not bother her like he had before. The machine had only been active for half an hour when he rang the first time. She listened for a while.

"Wendy? Oh. You bought one then. I'm calling to say I'm here for another day or so. I'm changing hotel tonight, they have already booked my room and can't extend." She heard the irritation. "I'll call you later, I hope you're there. Have you heard about the soap yet? Speak later."

Wendy walked to the machine, it was flashing to tell her she had a message, she pushed play and then delete as the sound of his voice filled her hall again. Staring at the machine for a second, she decided she would tell him it was over the next time he called and then why. Shivering at the thought, she pulled her coat from the hook, lifted her key from the table and set off at a brisk pace. As she turned the bend she saw Old Bill walking towards her, Tess by his side. Tess's tail was wagging frantically long before she got to them.

"She likes you." Bill smiled.

"And I like you, don't I." Kneeling, Wendy allowed Tess to put her paws on her shoulders and lick her face.

"Do you still want a dog?"

"I do." Wendy cupped Tess's face and kissed her nose. "I decided I'm going to start looking, so if you hear of a puppy that needs a good home, let me know."

"What about this one?" Bill was grinning, and Wendy wondered if he was teasing.

"If only." Wendy got to her feet.

"I'm serious. Her owner is going to be incapacitated for some time. Even when she's back at home she won't be able to cope with a dog. Especially a puppy. Tess is up for adoption."

"Oh my God. Yes, yes, yes. What do I need to do, is there paperwork? How soon can I have her?"

"Today if you want. I'll give them a ring and sort it all out. You are sure? Would you like to take her for a couple of days, see if it works for you?"

"Yes." Wendy's face fell. "The only problem is work. I'm around most days, but some are long. I was told it wasn't fair." She gave a smile. "But I could ask Dad to come over and walk her."

"And you could ask me. I'm only down the road." Bill smiled. He'd be getting the best of both worlds then. To his utter surprise, Wendy grabbed his cheeks and planted a big kiss on his nose.

"Absolutely perfect. Can I take her now?" Wendy was beaming. Her eyes sparkled, and for a little while she forgot about what Jenny had told her, and what she wanted to do.

"You've got a basket, food and bowls have you." Bill tutted and turned back towards his house. "Come on, we'll go and get you something to borrow."

"I can go to the supermarket. They have a huge pet display. Baskets, toys, doggy treats."

"Good walking there too. You can let her off the lead and give her a good run once you've taught her a recall. You'll need a dog guard too. Can't see her staying in the back at her age. She's not been in a car yet."

Wendy had nothing better to do, and she decided now was as good a time as any. "Will you come with me. Show me how to teach a recall. You can make sure I get all the right stuff then."

Bill agreed, and they took the dog into the fields at the rear of the supermarket before doing their shopping.

"This will tire her and she can sleep while we go and sort you out."

Tess snuggled down in the back of the car. She was a quick learner and Bill had been impressed with her response. Wendy cleaned the mud from her paws as best she could, followed Bill's instructions on leaving the windows in the back open enough to let air in, and took heed of the warnings about never leaving her in the car when the weather was warm.

Having completed their shopping, Bill pushed the trolley laden with everything Wendy and Tess would need back to the car. Wendy was asking every question she could think of about bringing a dog into her home. Tess heard them coming, and jumped at the window of the driver's door.

Bill laughed. "Told you, you'd need it." He lifted the dog guard. "Look at that window."

Two hours later, the dog guard was fitted, the basket installed in the corner of the kitchen, and two shiny stainless-steel bowls sat on a tray by the back door. Wendy was sitting in the armchair with a cup of tea, and Tess was curled up on her lap. It was the first of Bill's instructions she'd ignored. She didn't care if Tess got on the furniture, it was leather and difficult to damage. Wendy stroked the puppy's ears glad to have her there, but she wasn't fully relaxed. She knew the call was coming, but hadn't decided whether or not to answer it.

The call came a little after eight, and she decided to ignore it. He left a curt message saying he was going for a drink with the crew and wouldn't call again that day. For good measure, he reminded her it was the third time he'd tried to call. Wendy hit the delete button.

"Right, young Tess, I need an early night, I must catch up on my sleep. Garden time for you."

Tess bounded out into the garden, and Wendy stood guard at the side of the house so she wouldn't escape. Bill had promised to help her fix a temporary fence while she organised a more permanent solution. Praising Tess for doing her business, Angie took her back to the kitchen, sliding the bolts home on the back door. She lifted Tess into the new basket and ruffled her head. "Sleep tight little one." Closing the door behind her, she double-checked the locks on the front door and went upstairs to bed, leaving the alarm as she couldn't work out how to disarm the kitchen sensor. She lasted fifteen minutes listening to Tess whimper before she went to get her. She put the basket by the side of her bed, and stroked her until she settled. Eventually, Wendy also drifted off to sleep, only to be woken by the ringing of the phone several hours later. She found Tess snuggled into her shoulder. Closing her eyes against his voice she patted her.

"Sod him, Tess. I have you now."

The next morning, Wendy half listened to his angry words while Tess ate her breakfast. She was about to hit the delete button when he shouted: "I don't know what you're playing at, but I'll call again at eight in the morning, and you'd better be there."

She hit the delete button. "Or else what? You'll hit me. I don't think so." She turned to Tess who had come in search of her. "Time for a walk, and I'll be here to take the next call."

She was. "Before you say anything." Wendy interrupted him. "We're over. It's finished, I tried and I was wrong to. Please don't call again." She hung up.

The phone rang again, she picked it up.

"Did you hang up on me? I have—" He didn't get any further as Wendy dropped the receiver back in the cradle.

Wendy smiled and lifted Tess onto her lap. They sat on the bottom stair to see if it would ring again. It did. This time, Wendy answered and spoke first.

"I asked you not to ring again. Next time you'll get the answer machine." Hanging up as he shouted at her she blew out a breath. "One more."

The phone rang as she spoke. She allowed him to rant, not listening to the words. When he demanded to know if she was listening she gave a cruel laugh.

"To what? Your lies or your bullying? I'll never listen to you again. I've spoken to Jenny." Calmly she replaced the receiver and put Tess on the floor. "It will be a while, let's go and find the ball."

Wendy was on her hands and knees trying to get it out from under the sofa when the phone rang again. Grabbing the ball and rolling it across the floor for Tess to chase, she didn't move to answer it until she heard the caller speak. It was her agent. Flying out into the hall she grabbed the phone.

"I'm here, don't go. Did you say you'd heard from the production team?"

Her smile got wider as she was told she'd been cast as Fran in the newly commissioned television series, The Village. It was the role she wanted, although she'd decided to accept the lesser role of Teresa the landlord's daughter if it was offered. She grabbed a pen and wrote the name of the producer who she was to meet with some of the others in the production the next day.

"Well you've brought me luck, Tess." She threw the ball into the kitchen. "That was just the news I needed to cheer me up." As Tess scooted off into the kitchen, Wendy called her father. "Hello, Dad, two things, our dinner this evening is going to be a celebration. I got the role I wanted in The Village." She laughed as her father hooted his congratulations. "The second is I need you to come to me. I'll cook us something spectacular."

"I'm not coming to dinner if he's there." Her father's tone was flat.

"He's not. It's over. I told him this morning."

"Splendid news. May I ask why?"

"It wasn't working. Let's leave it there. I do have a surprise for you though, someone for you to meet."

"You've replaced him? Isn't it a bit soon?"

"You'll see soon enough. Bring your PJs, then we can open a bottle of something. Unless of course you'd like me to pick you up."

"I'll have a think about it, I'm not drinking much these days. What time do you want me?"

"Anytime you like. I'm popping out for an hour or so after lunch, but then I'll be home."

"You did the right thing you know." Her father's voice was gentle.

"I know. Onwards and upwards again, aye Dad?"

"That's my girl."

"Dad, I have to go, there's someone at the door."

"Make sure it's not him before you open it. You know what he was like last time."

"I will." Hanging up, Wendy leaned back, through the stained-glass panel she could see it wasn't him, so she opened the door. "Hello," she greeted the woman who held out her police identity card.

"Hello, are you Wendy? I'm DS Sarah Clarke."

"Oh, yes. Come on in. Is everything okay?"

"That's what I came to see you about. I was in the area, so thought I'd pop in. Did your friend call you?"

"Yes, she did. We met up, she's living in Bristol and applying for new jobs."

"Did you discover if she was being abused? I'd like to help her if she is."

Wendy nodded. "She was, but she won't speak to you." Wendy looked away. "I can understand why, he's history now though."

"And you?" It was almost a whisper.

"Me? I'm fine."

"Are you sure? Even if you don't want to take it any further, I'm willing to listen. I won't try and force you into anything."

"I have no idea why you're saying that, I'm fine." Wendy forced a smile.

"Most abused women have a look. A sadness around the eyes, a smile which never quite reaches the rest of their face. But, if you're sure." Dipping into her bag, she pulled out a card. "In case you ever need it. I work there on a voluntary basis, but hope to sort something more permanent." She turned to walk away and suddenly turned back. "One last thing . . ."

"What?" Wendy looked up from the card.

"Do you know who was beating her?" DS Clarke studied Wendy's reaction carefully.

"Yes, or I thought I did. Oh, and by the way it wasn't her boyfriend. Jenny was having an affair."

DS Clarke knew Wendy could give his name, but decided not to push, planning instead to revisit her. "That's a surprise, I thought affairs were supposed to be about the thrill. Just goes to show." She opened the front door. "Thanks for your time, Wendy, and don't forget, don't hesitate to call me or them." She pointed at the card. "Bye."

Closing the door behind her, Wendy slid the bolts across before looking at the card again. It was a card for the same organisation as the lady on her wedding day had given her.

~20~

Angie slumped into the kitchen and put the kettle on. With any other story, the reader, or writer, would be glad Wendy had dumped him. Glad Wendy was about to embark on a new chapter in her life. But Angie already knew how the story ended, not because she'd planned it, but because she'd been shown it. It wouldn't matter what words she wrote to give Wendy a fresh start, they would be wrong. The ending was the ending.

Angie wanted to scream, she wanted to cry, she felt the grief of what was to come as keenly as though it were the death of someone she knew. A bloody waste of a lovely life, and for what? Power?

Pouring the boiling water on the teabag she jumped when her phone rang, disturbing her thoughts. She glanced at the screen, it was a local Bristol number.

"Hello." She waited a second or two. "Hello, can you hear me?" Tilting the screen so she could see the strength of signal. It was fine. "Hello, if you are speaking I can't hear you, I'm hanging up. Try again if you need me."

"Ha!"

"Did you laugh?" Angie listened a while longer, nothing. She replaced the receiver and went to collect the milk for her tea. It rang again. This time when she answered she didn't speak.

A deep voice seemed to breathe the one word into her ear. "Biiiiich."

Angie put down her mug. "Fuck off you cretin." Her words were crisp and clear. Sitting at the kitchen table she rubbed her ever enlarging stomach. "Someone is cross with Mummy, Junior. First the note from that idiot, then the . . . Shit! Could he be responsible for all three?" She wouldn't admit it even to herself, she was now worried. If it was Harry trying to provoke her, he was clearly obsessive. She patted her bump. "They were filming today, I wonder if he was there? Let's check, shall we?"

Knowing Karen was due on set today, Angie decided calling her would be the quickest way to find out. Angie was about to hang up when Karen answered.

"Sorry, poppet, phone's on silent. I'm on set."

"Yes, I thought you might be, is Harry there?"

"You want to speak to Harry? Are you sure?" Karen laughed.

"No, I want to know if he's there."

"Yes, having a bit of a discussion with Colin at the moment. I have to ask why, you know that."

"And I'll tell you. Has he been there all afternoon, specifically between about twelve-thirty and two o'clock?"

"Yes. We're on take sixteen. We're going to be here all night at this rate. How did you and Gemma get on this morning?"

"Great. I think you'll like it. Needs more polish, but we'll get there. Did you—"

"Oh my goodness. Colin has just shoved Harry. I'd better go. I'll call later."

"He did what?" Angie couldn't help but grin, but Karen had gone. "Damn. I needed some light relief." Collecting her tea, she went back to the laptop and opened a new document. She typed the title, Harassment, and started her list.

At lunchtime on the 12th my bag was unsupervised from approx. 1.30 until 2. A note telling me to 'back off' was put in there, a vague threat made. I found it later that evening. (Probably Harry)

On the 13th a decaying rat was pushed through my door between 12.30 - 2.00. I notified the police and am awaiting a visit. (Who? Why? Harry on set)

At five-fifteen I received two calls from a Bristol number. The first was silent, the second time he called me a bitch. His voice was disguised. (Could be Harry)

Hitting the save button, Angie closed her laptop. If anything else happened, the police would have to come and see her, or she'd go and see them. She pondered this for a moment. Should she feel scared? Because she didn't. Angry and irritated but not scared, which she concluded was not a good thing.

"Better get started on dinner, Junior. Daddy will be hungry when he gets home. Daddy is always hungry."

Ryan marched back into the hall. "And you called the police?"

"Of course. Calm down, Ryan, no one put a gun to my head." She caught up with him and stood back as he opened the bag she'd placed outside behind a plant pot.

Ryan gagged and quickly retied the knot in the bin liner. He looked at Angie. "And you think this is Harry Grayson?" he snapped, still bemused that she hadn't called him.

"I don't know. He was on set today, I checked, so it's unlikely. It's more than likely kids with a sick sense of humour, or it was intended for the previous occupant. Calm down, Ryan. I've called the police there's nothing else we can do."

"Calm down?" Ryan grabbed her by the shoulders. "I'm worried, okay. I'm away filming for five days soon, and I have to leave my wife and unborn child behind." His smile appeared unexpectedly. "I don't suppose you want to come, do you? Have laptop will travel."

"No. I have to be on set, I have to get the Fran storyline finished, I have meetings to attend. This," she pointed out to the bag, "is unpleasant but not life threatening. Now, close the door. Dinner is almost ready."

Ryan studied her face for a moment, it showed no fear. "Okay, but if anything else happens . . ." He walked towards the kitchen and paused turning back to face her. "Nothing else has happened, has it?"

"Of course not." Angie lied. "Don't go weird on me, that's my job." She blew him a kiss as she passed him. "I met Bill today by the way. Nice old chap. What time do you need to be away in the morning?"

"Early. Very early, I won't have time for a nap tonight, I have to be up at some ungodly hour, so it's an early night for me."

"I'll join you. Oh, that's the other thing I was going to ask. We had an odd-looking bird in the garden this afternoon, I've never seen one before. Any chance you could talk me through setting those cameras up please?"

"I'll do it now if you like, how long have I got?"

"I'll slow it down and help."

Angie watched carefully as Ryan set the cameras. "And I can pick these up on the laptop?" she asked, as Ryan set the second camera. "Do you think we should have one in the front? I did see my robin on the fence today."

"Easy. In fact, it will double us as a security camera, if I'd done this yesterday we'd know who shoved a dead rat through the door. Bugger. So easy to be wise with hindsight. Can we eat first though?"

~21~

Wendy ignored the wolf whistle from the men clearing the debris from the site of the pub. Tess had stopped to look, but she gave a little tug on the lead to encourage her forward.

"Come on, madam. We're having nothing to do with men, remember." She opened the back of the car and Tess jumped in. "We have to grab some bits from the supermarket, and then we'll have some fun."

Tess was whining, her paws rested on the bar of the dog guard, and Wendy talked to her all the way to the supermarket. By the time she'd parked in the top corner of the carpark, Tess had settled, but immediately jumped up again.

Wendy sighed. "You win, we'll walk first, then you have to be a good girl." Grabbing her wellingtons from the passenger footwell, Wendy slipped her shoes off and pulled them on. Shrugging off her jacket she lay it on the seat and pulled her windcheater off the headrest. She walked to the back of the car. "Stay."

Tess was too quick for her, and jumped through the door as soon as the gap was wide enough. She made for the gap in the fence. Slamming the door and leaving the car unlocked, Wendy took off in pursuit. She didn't notice the car slowly approaching. Nor did she see him pull into the space two rows across and sit watching her, a frown creasing his brow.

Despite disgracing herself with the escape from the car, Tess was impeccably behaved on the walk, returning to Wendy for a treat each time she was called. As Wendy towelled her on their return, he remained perfectly still, and watched as she removed her coat and boots. When she sprinted across the carpark heading for the supermarket, he climbed out of the car.

"Hello, mutt." He peered at Tess who had been sleeping, and started wagging her tail when he spoke. "She did it, despite asking my opinion. She ignored me" He scowled at the dog. "When I get her back, you'll be gone." Making a fist he thumped the window, then laughed as Tess bared her teeth and growled at him. He walked away whistling, leaving a frantic Tess barking and clawing at the door. Tess had settled by the time Wendy returned.

~ ~ ~

The phone was ringing before Wendy had shut the door. She stared at it. "We're not answering, are we? Come with me, I bought you a new—" She dropped the shopping bag on the stairs and lifted the phone when she heard Jenny's voice.

"I'm here, I'm here. I was bringing the shopping in."

"That's the top of my list, a bit of shopping." There was a lightness to Jenny's tone which Wendy hadn't heard before. "I have to get some shorts, tee shirts, flipflops . . . I got the job I wanted. The money is crap but—"

"What job? You didn't give me any detail, only that you had applied. What sort of job requires flipflops?"

"A holiday rep in Cyprus. My home for the next six months. Well, I've got some training stuff first but sunshine here I come."

"How fabulous. Congratulations. I love Cyprus, I went there with . . ." Wendy let the sentence drift away.

"Him. Talking of which, what's the latest on that front?"

"It's done, I've told him it's over, and why. But let's forget about him. Tell me everything? When do you go, what do you have to do, everything."

"I leave a week on Friday, but before then I have to go to London and attend training courses. But as to what I have to do, everything. Look after kids, archery, that old favourite, bingo, and I'll be part of the entertainment the reps put on. I think it will be hard work, but I'm up for it."

"Sounds like fun, and all in the sunshine, lucky you. Do you have anything you do?"

"Do?"

"Sing, dance, magic tricks?"

"Oh, my voice isn't bad. I can dance, not ballet or trained or anything, but I know I can follow a routine. I'm looking forward to it so much." Jenny gabbled away happily sharing her plans with Wendy. Finally, she ran out of steam. "I'll call you from London once I get there if possible."

"Jenny, that's wonderful. I do wish you well, if you are ever in the UK you must call me. Promise."

"Of course. I might ask you to put me up for a couple of nights."

"And I'd do it. Good luck with the training, thanks for letting me know, Jenny. I'd have worried if you disappeared again." Smiling, Wendy replaced the receiver and rummaging in the shopping bag found the toy she had promised Tess. "Go fetch." As she released it, a movement at the front door caught her eye. She opened it as he lifted his hand to ring the bell.

"Still feeding you with crap I hear?" He moved quickly, pushing the door wide and stepping over the threshold.

Wendy caught the door and pointed out into the garden. "Get out. You aren't welcome here."

"Without even hearing my side of the st . . ." He jumped to one side as Tess came lolloping out of the sitting room, the toy dangling from her mouth. Seeing the open door, she bolted through it. "Oh dear." He stood and watched the puppy shoot along the path and out of the gate. "I hope there's nothing coming."

"Get out my way." Wendy gave him a hard shove, he staggered against the door frame, as she ran past calling to Tess. Luckily a smell on the pavement outside the house had gained her attention, and toy abandoned she sniffed along the bottom of the hedge. Wendy scooped Tess into her arms and retrieved the toy. "Silly girl, you had me so worried." Nuzzling her face into Tess's neck she retraced her steps.

Standing in the doorway he watched her approach. His face showed no emotion, and a shiver ran up Wendy's spine. She preferred it when he looked angry. Pulling her shoulders back she stopped in front of him.

"I'd like you to leave now. I meant what I said, it's over. I'll write to the solicitor again, and this time I'll make sure they get the apartment put back into your name." He opened his mouth, but she shook her head. "If you don't accept it, I'll go to court and force you to sell. I want nothing from you apart from my freedom."

"I never tried to trap you. I don't know why you would believe the slapper over me." His eyes filled with tears. "I love you, Wendy, I will always love you. I don't want to live without you, I can't let anyone else have you." He stepped forward, his arms open to pull her into an embrace. But Tess growled and snapped at his hand, and he pulled it away.

"I don't think she likes you." Wendy took a step back.

"It's a dog. It doesn't know me. Can you put it somewhere so we can talk?"

"No. I'm not talking about anything. Please leave. Nothing you can do will make me change my mind."

"I'm going nowhere. Not until you explain why you would take her word over mine."

"Because I trust her. Because I saw the bruises, because I know she was scared when she spoke to me. Because you have damaged her so much she is going abroad. Why would she make it up? What would she gain when she's not around to see the result?" Wendy pointed towards the open door. "Go, now."

He didn't move. "How would I know? Perhaps she was jealous of you, perhaps she fancied me? Who knows what goes on in the minds of these people."

"These people? What does that mean?"

"Well she wasn't the brightest button in the tin. Ill-educated, thick even, common. You know the type."

"She might not have had a good education, but she is not thick or common." She watched his lips twitch and wondered if he was about to make reference to some of the things they had done. If so, she would beat him to it. "Or are you talking about being trussed up in a field for sex. For allowing unspeakable acts to be carried out without complaint in public, is that what you mean? Because she was scared. She didn't want any further punishment."

"What? Is that what she said? She's lying! Have I ever hurt you? Do you not know me at all?"

"I don't think I did, I do now. Go."

"But, Wendy, please." He held his hands up. "I admit she made a pass at me. I was taken unawares and I responded, but pushed her away as soon as my brain kicked back in. But yes, I kissed her, I touched her. Instinctively. But I did not do *unspeakable* things to her. I rejected her, and this is payback."

"And the bruises, and broken rib?"

"I don't know about any bruises. What broken rib?"

Wendy had had enough. She could see he was a little nervous, not sure he was going to convince her, she also saw his fists clench and unclench. She stepped towards the door. "Where is your car?"

He jerked his thumb up the road. "Parked back there, why?"

Wendy stepped onto the doorstep and balanced on tiptoes, Tess still cradled in her arms. "The silver one?"

"Yes, but *why*?" He hissed, his temper beginning to emerge. "I'm going nowhere."

"Another new car? That's three in as many months." Wendy stepped back into the hall.

"Two. It cheers me up. Don't make me ask you again. Last time. Why?" He grabbed her upper arm, his fingers digging into her flesh. "Don't play games, Wendy. I always win."

"I'm not. Let go of my arm you're hurting me." She tried to pull away, but he increased the pressure.

"I need to know why you don't love me enough to take my word over hers."

"Because you're a bully. Because you intimidate people. Because you are a control freak. Because everyone, even the woman you spat at after you hit me, could see what you were. Now I can too." She tried to yank her arm away again, yelling at the top of her voice. "FUCK OFF"

With a sudden burst of movement, he barrelled her backwards causing her to fall back onto the stairs, and he dropped his body on top of her, crushing Tess between them. Tess yelped and Wendy let her go, worried he would hurt her. Tess scampered upstairs and hid under the bed. He pressed his nose against Wendy's.

"I asked you why you were asking about the car?" Having Wendy trapped restored his calm demeanour. He was back in control. "I love you. Surely it's not too much to ask you answer my questions?"

"Let me get up and I'll tell you. You are hurting me."

Planting a series of little kisses all over her face, he pushed his hips forward and smiled. "There's a good girl. Once we get this sorted, perhaps we could go for a meal or something."

Pushing himself away, he stood and offered her his hand, she ignored it and resisted the urge to rub her back as she stood to join him.

She held out her hand. "May I have your keys?"

"No. Not until you explain why. What is it about the car." He glanced at hers. "Is yours out of action?"

Wendy wanted him out of the house and knew she had to be smart to achieve that. Shaking her head, she held her hand towards the garden. "It's fine. It's just something Jenny said, you can do it."

He smiled at her. Whatever it was he'd be fine. Jenny hadn't been in this car. He pulled the keys from his pocket and stepped outside. "Okay, I'll play this game, what's the point of it though?"

"I'll tell you as we walk." Wendy stepped out behind him. "This is what Jenny told me to do."

"I'm fed up with Jenny's name. Promise me once we've done this we never have to speak of her again." He carried on walking, a smile flirting with his lips.

Wendy had slowed her pace, there was now a few yards between them. She needed space, space to escape him.

"I promise." She slowed further. "Jenny said, the first time she was with you, you had a roll of tape and a picnic blanket ready to do what she called *your thing*." She stopped walking as his step faltered. "She said she thinks you go prepared." He stopped walking and she took a step back. "If we open the boot of your new silver car will you have a picnic blanket in there, will you have a roll of tape? Because it's November, and there's not a . . ."

Wendy was ready. He spun around to face her, his face red, his eyes wild. She knew she wouldn't make it back to the house, but she could get the attention of the workers clearing the site. She knew the tall one had watched them come out of the house.

"You are fucking kidding me. Jenny said this, Jenny said that," he spat, but he didn't move.

Wendy knew he was extremely wound up, he rarely swore in front of her. "Is it in there or not?"

"No. But even if it was, it would be simply transferring it from one car to the other."

Wendy turned away and took her first shaky step back towards the cottage. She wondered if she would see her heart beating if she looked down.

"Don't ignore me. Why does that prove anything?"

Wendy increased her pace, but instead of heading home she veered across the road towards the workmen. She heard him hurrying after her, and she ran, stopping only when she had reached what had been the wall around the pub. Waving to the tall one who always whistled, she turned to face him.

"What are you playing at? Am I supposed to be frightened of him?"

"No, he's a witness. I need a witness."

"Why? You think I'm going to do something stupid?" His smile was brief. "Well, Wendy, you have your witness." He too raised his arm and waved at the bemused workman who leaned on his shovel watching them.

"So, you're telling me there's nothing in the boot of that car. No blanket, no tape."

"I can't remember. Tell me—"

"I'll tell you this." Wendy blinked, a tear began its course to her chin, and she cursed, she'd promised she would never cry over him again. "If Jenny was lying, making stuff up, or even exaggerating, if all that happened was a momentary thing, how would she know about them?" She held out a shaking hand. "Let me look." The second and third tear joined the first, and she wiped them away with an angry sweep of the other hand.

"This is ridic—"

"Let me look. "Wendy screeched, and the effort caused her head to shake.

The other workmen stopped to look.

She saw the hatred in his eyes, she knew he wouldn't want her now. But had she done enough?

"I'm going to leave you now, Wendy. I want you to calm down, think about the logic of all this, and when I come—"

"You will never come back. I never want to see you again." There was a warble to her voice.

"Don't interrupt me again," he lowered his voice, aware of the audience in amongst the rubble of the pub. "I'll do as I—"

This time her interruption was a fist. She hadn't intended hitting him, and when she looked back later she had no idea where the energy had come from, but her arm flew up and was only fully extended once she'd made contact with his nose. His head snapped back. The blood flowed immediately, and she was reminded of his face on what should have been their wedding day. She heard the shouts from behind her, and someone applauded.

He stepped forward, aware the workman leaning on his shovel had done the same thing.

"You have your witness this time, Wendy, but that won't always be the case. I'll be ready for you next time." Turning away, he walked as calmly as he could back to his car.

Wendy shot a glance behind her and called her thanks to the workmen, before running as fast as she could back to the cottage, and to Tess, where she cried until her nose was blocked and she had to gulp air in through her mouth.

~22~

"What have you done? What could you do? Stay with him, to avoid this?"

Angie slammed the laptop closed and the chair scraped the floor as she got to her feet. She wished there was a way to travel back in time to warn Wendy. To tell her to go abroad with Jenny, anything but stay where she was.

She patted her belly. "I don't want to see anymore, Junior. But I have to. Someone has to be a witness for poor Wendy. Oh, that reminds me. Let's have a look at our witness."

Angie glanced at the clock. It was still only eight o'clock, she still had time before she needed to leave for the set.

Sitting in front of the laptop she clicked on the camera icon, choosing camera one. Following Ryan's instructions, she rewound the footage from the night before and hit the play button speeding up the action while she peered at the screen. A little before three in the morning she stopped the recording and smiled. A fox. She moved the recording on until she was back in real time. She made a note the fox had stayed for three and a half minutes. Checking the other recordings, she found there was nothing to report.

"Ah well, Junior, now we need to leave something out for the fox. I bet Robbie comes to visit today."

Before she closed the laptop, she reopened the Wendy document and renamed it: *Witness for Wendy.*

"What next I wonder?"

~ ~ ~

Arriving on set early, she sorted through some scripts while the cameramen set up. Today was a fairly straightforward agenda. Two scenes in Fran's bedroom, the rest in the bar. She skimmed the first scene and smiled, no Harry. That was a bonus. Hearing her name called, she looked up and waved as Karen approached.

"I can't stop, darling, I'm due in makeup, but can we grab a minute later." Karen barely managed a smile, her mind elsewhere.

"Of course. I'm here all day. Come and find me." Angie watched Karen merely bob her head. "Is everything okay?"

"Yes, I've been . . . can we do this later?" Looking at her watch, Karen shook her head. "I must get a move on." She was already walking away.

Angie was distracted by her phone, so didn't respond. She watched Karen's departure as she answered the call from her mother. Margaret Bearing was speaking immediately the ringing stopped, Angie missed the first few words.

". . . and she's suggested we come and visit. I know Ryan's away, but I told her you might be busy. What do you think? We could be there by teatime."

"Hello, Mum, I'm fine, thanks," Angie laughed. "Now from the beginning, who said what?"

"Your grandmother. Weren't you listening? She's staying with me while her bathroom is done, she said it would be nice to come and see you." Margaret lowered her voice, "Said she might not still be around when the baby comes."

"Oh, right. Today?"

"Will that be okay? Thought you might like the company."

Angie thought about Wendy. "I am quite busy. How long were you thinking of staying?"

"Just one or two nights, whatever suits you." She lowered her voice again. "I could do with some relief."

Angie smiled. She adored her grandmother, she was sweet, shrewd, and always spoke her mind. It was what Angie loved most about her, but it tended to unnerve her mother. Angie's father had been killed in an accident two weeks before her parents' planned wedding, and four days before Margaret even knew she was pregnant. Determined to bring her child up on her own, she'd refused her mother's invitation to go back home, and although she loved her dearly, Margaret had spent much of her life ignoring Bridget's advice.

"Of course. I'm working until about four today so won't be home until at least five."

"Wonderful! I'll drive slowly, it'll give her something else to complain about. See you later, love. Bye."

Angie dropped the phone back into her bag and sighed. It would either be a wonderful light relief from the knowledge of Wendy's impending doom, or it was going to be a nightmare. It was too late to worry, they were probably packing an overnight bag at that very moment, if indeed the bags weren't already sitting by the door.

She got to her feet as Colin called for silence and walked over to take a seat in front of the bar. The three actors were already in position.

"And action." The clapperboard sounded and Colin paced back and forth behind the cameras. He paused in front of her and waved a fourth actor onto the set. Nodding approval as he shouted his line. The scene completed, he dropped into the chair next to Angie.

"That went well, let's hope they're all like that."

"Fingers crossed. Gemma and I have Fran's departure sorted by the way. It will tie in nicely with Cyril finding the drugs."

"So Karen said. I wouldn't mind a summary when you have five." His tone was clipped and Angie wondered if he was angry with her. "I'd like to see her out, and I want it to be perfect. Let me have it as soon as."

"Of course. I'll get it to you tonight, oh, I have my mother coming down."

"Perhaps you could scribble something down during the day then," he snapped.

"I will. Colin, have—"

"Harry, for fuck's sake!" Colin bellowed ignoring her. "Can you please put her down and concentrate on the script. First take today, no more buggering about." He flattened his wisps of hair and got to his feet. "In fact, get off the set, you're not needed until scene five, we'll call you."

Colin was striding across to where Harry had been chatting up the newest actress to join The Village. She would only be around for a month or so, her character was the landlord's young sister who had run away from home and would be packed off after she's caught stealing from the till.

Colin pointed at her. "That goes for you too. Concentrate on your lines, not him."

The girl blushed and moved away, but Harry stepped up to Colin and they stood toe to toe.

"Apologise," Harry demanded.

"For ..." Colin shook his head and attempted to sidestep Harry.

"For being so fucking rude would be a start. All I was—"

"I don't care. I want today to run smoothly. I want you lot to do what you're paid for, first time, and anything else can wait until later."

"You are acting like an arsehole. What's your problem, are you not getting any? I won't be spoken to like this."

"Then fuck off and I won't have to waste my breath. I've got work to do." Colin looked past Harry. "Everyone in position," he shouted. "We go in five." He looked back at Harry. "You're not in the scene."

Angie watched the exchange. Karen had mentioned there was a problem the other day too. She wondered what was fuelling it, glad it wasn't only her Colin had an issue with. She jumped when Alan spoke, not realising he'd come to stand behind her chair.

"Well that's not pretty. That will have to stop."

"Has something happened that I missed?" Angie stood to join him. "I don't think this is the first time."

"I don't know. Have you been winding Colin up again?" he said sharply.

Angie's head jerked to look at him. "Meaning what? Dear God, what is wrong with the men on this set, have they been putting something in your tea?"

"Meaning you are causing waves. I might not say much, but I listen to what's being said. Be careful, Angie, I have no room for troublemakers on this show."

"What? Alan, I've hardly spoken to Colin today. And for the record, he was snapping at me too."

Alan shook his head as Harry walked away from Colin with as much dignity as he could muster. Colin ignored him, calling out directions to one of the actors as they walked over to him. Angie knew they'd asked a question, as Colin was staring at his feet, a trait when he was thinking. When the actor had finished speaking, Colin looked towards Angie.

Without acknowledging Alan, he called over, "Angie, here, now. Ellen wants to drop a line, is there a reason for it? I can't think of one, but no doubt you'll put us right."

"Calm it down, Angie." Alan warned as she collected her script. "As far as I can see there is only one common factor in the upset around here. Be careful." Turning away abruptly, he headed for the rest room.

Angie watched him go. Her resentment at what she considered an unfair judgement, caused her to twist the script into a tight baton. She clamped her teeth together as Colin called again.

"Now, Angie. Today. For Christ's sake, what's wrong with everyone today?"

A couple of hours later, and the morning's schedule was completed ahead of time. Angie had a suspicion a few more takes might have been wise on certain scenes but she kept her mouth shut. Colin wouldn't welcome any such suggestion. The production team drifted off to lunch as Colin shouted that he wanted those necessary for the next scene in the schedule to be back and on set by one-thirty. Angie went in search of Karen, whom she'd not yet spoken to, and found her sitting outside by the set carpark smoking a cigarette.

"Hi, Karen, I'm going to go and grab a sandwich or something, do you want me to get you anything, or perhaps you'd like to join me and we can have that chat."

"I'm not eating but I'll come and find you once I've finished this." Karen waved the cigarette. "I'll have a coffee though. Thanks."

Angie bought her sandwich and the drinks and sat in the canteen waiting for Karen's arrival. When she didn't show, Angie went to find her. There was a small pile of cigarette butts where she had been, but no Karen. She found her in the rest room, sitting at one of the bistro tables.

Angie went to join her, placing the coffee in front of her. "There you go, I hope it's not cold. I was waiting in the canteen."

"I'm sorry. I had to take a call, it took longer than I thought. Now I've got a bloody headache. Ah, well, only two more scenes to shoot and I can escape." She lifted her coffee and took a sip, her nose wrinkled. "Yuck! That will teach me."

"What did you want to see me about? Did you want to run over Fran's exit? Because if you give me twenty minutes, I'll have typed the outline we're going to work with. Colin wants it. While on the subject, what the hell is wrong with him today?"

"I think I made him cross, I told him what . . . Oh, he's coming over. It will keep, probably a silly idea anyway. I don't want to make it worse." She smiled at Colin. "I'm not late again, am I?" It was meant as a joke but Colin wasn't in the mood.

"Not at the moment, but the day is young. Angie are you working on that outline or gassing?"

"I've finished my lunch, thank you, Colin. I was just going to get my laptop from the car. You'll have it within the hour. Is that quick enough for you?"

"It will have to be. Better if you'd brought it in, or sent it via email." He looked at Karen. "Have you done it?" He jerked his head towards Angie who was getting to her feet.

"No. Not yet."

"Then don't, no good will come of it." Returning his attention to Angie, he asked, "Are you still here?" Shoving his hands in his pockets, he turned and strode away.

"I've had enough. I have to find out what's going on." Angie hurried to catch him, ignoring Karen's advice to leave it. "Colin, a word if I may?" she called and he slowed his pace.

"As we walk, I have some things I need to take care of."

"I'm getting the impression I've done something to piss you off. I don't know what, but whatever it was, it wasn't intentional. I apologise."

"Good, keep your head down, get on with your work, and leave everyone else alone."

"I'm sorry? Leave who alone?" Angie caught his shirt sleeve.

"Anyone, everyone. I'm not sure what goes on in your head, but you're causing a lot of upset. Harry, Alan, and now Karen, so as a consequence me." He tapped his lips. "Button those, and do your job please. We don't need any more drama on this set than we already have. Be careful, Angie. Now, was there anything else? I have things to do."

Angie was stunned and had stopped dead in her tracks. Unable to think of anything to say which wouldn't make the situation worse she kept her mouth shut. She half turned to ask Karen how she had upset her, but found she was back on her phone, so she went in search of her laptop. It was best she calmed herself a little before tackling the issue.

The afternoon was uneventful, and Karen left immediately after she finished her scene, and as Colin wanted to discuss something in the outline Angie had dutifully presented to him, she didn't manage to speak to her. Having taken notes on Colin's thoughts, Angie worked at her laptop on a small table to one side of the set. She was called twice for her input on the scenes being filmed, Colin had calmed down, and Harry was word perfect. Everything went as scheduled, and at four-thirty she handed Colin her amended outline.

"I hope this is what you want, if not drop me an email. I'll keep Gemma informed. I'm not in tomorrow, Alex is. I take it he still doesn't know about Fran's exit?"

"No. Let's hope Harry can keep his mouth shut." Colin waved the document at her. "Thank you for this. I'll look tonight, I have a meeting to get to." He sighed. "I was hoping for an early finish."

"I hope it's a brief one. Is it okay if I go now? My mother and grandmother are staying for a few days."

Permission received, Angie set off home. The traffic was kind, and she hoped to get there before her guests arrived. She'd tried calling her mother and each call went through to the answer service which meant she was driving. Margaret always switched off her phone when driving, therefore Angie was surprised when she got home, as not only was her mother's car parked outside the cottage, but so was a police car. Her mother and grandmother had engaged the female officer in conversation. They moved to allow Angie to reverse the car onto the drive.

Angie hadn't even shut the car door when her mother called to her.

"Helen is here about the rat. You didn't tell us about a rat, did she Mother?"

Fixing a wide smile, Angie looked at the two women she loved. As different as chalk and cheese. Her grandmother was tall, slender and always looked glamorous, while her mother was a good head shorter, and looked . . . practical.

Angie kissed each on the cheek and ushered them inside. "You two go and put your things upstairs, you can share our bedroom, I'll go in the spare room as the bed is small in there, and the cot has arrived so not much room to move around." She lifted the kettle. "I'll also make some tea." Smiling at the police officer she pulled out a chair at the kitchen table. "Have a seat, I'll be with you in two minutes." Leaving her sitting at the table, Angie pointed at upstairs. "Go on, I'll join you in the sitting room and tell all later."

Collecting her bag, Angie waited until the two women had started up the stairs before returning to the police officer. "Thank you for coming. I'm not sure what you can do, but I didn't want to let it go."

"No problem. Where is it?"

Angie's hands rested on top of her laptop. She couldn't decide whether to tell the officer about the other incidents. "In a black bag, outside. I warn you it stinks." Angie flipped the screen up. "I'm going to tell you this because although I don't think it's anything to worry about, I guess there should be a record."

"This isn't the first time?" A notepad was pulled from the utility belt around the officer's waist.

"For rats, yes. But I found a note in my bag, which could only have been put there by a colleague, and then I got this weird call and was called a bitch. It all happened within a few days." She gave the dates and the number which were noted.

"I'm not sure if this is someone being mean and trying to frighten you, or if it might be more serious. I'm going to log this officially for you, check out that phone number, although I'm guessing it will be a call box, and if anything else happens you should call immediately." Helen offered her a card. She looked at Angie's swollen belly. "You should be careful, my sister went into premature labour through stress."

"I am careful, but I'm fed up with everyone telling me to be. I promise I'm not stressed. Not the type." She smiled. "What happens next?"

"I'll speak to my sergeant and see what she has to say. If she wants further investigation I'll call you." Angie's grandmother, Bridget, appeared in the doorway. "I'll leave you to your family, but please call, however insignificant you think it may be."

"Will do, I'll show you out. You didn't even have a cup of tea. I'm sorry."

"No problem. I've had enough for one day." As Helen stepped out into the garden, she said again, "Remember, anything at all, call."

"I will. Oh, there is one more thing. You don't know an officer by the name of Sarah Clarke, do you?"

"I do, although she's no longer a police officer. Do you know her?" She held the black bag a little further away from her body. "Not in connection with this is it?"

"What? How?" Angie flapped her hand. "No, it's something I'm working on. Do you know how I can find her?"

"Two minutes." The officer walked out to her car and placed the offending bag in the boot. Pulling a slim leather wallet from her pocket she fanned through some business cards, finally presenting Angie with the one she wanted. "She runs a women's refuge, amongst other things. Give her a call."

"Thank you, I will. Let me know the outcome with the phone number. I should have called it, I can't believe I didn't."

"Don't. Leave it to us."

Pushing the card into her trouser pocket, Angie watched the car pull away wondering how long her mother would interrogate her. Bridget was pouring the tea when she returned. She went over to hug her.

"Hello, Gran. Lovely to have you here."

"Lovely to be here. I love your mother, but she's bloody hard work when you're on your own with her." Bridget chuckled. "I sometimes think she can't be mine. Fussing and bothering all the time. Don't tell her I said that. Now get out the way and let me get dinner."

Angie laughed, knowing her mother would have said exactly the same thing. "I do love you. But no, you can't cook, you're my guests."

"And your guests know you are pregnant, should be pampered, and have been at work all day, whereas we've been sitting on our backsides. Go and have a bath, take a walk, or whatever relaxes you, let me fuss over you. The alternative will be your mother."

"What will?" Margaret appeared in the doorway.

"I was telling Angie she should go and relax while we get dinner for her." Bridget tied on her apron.

"Of course we will." Angie's mother turned her to face the other direction. "Go."

Angie did as she was told, happy to be pampered. She ran a bath, knowing she had some thinking to do, but she hoped it wouldn't give her an urge to get typing. She could do with a night away from Wendy. A feeling of guilt swept over her and she dunked under the water. She'd start by calling Sarah Clarke she decided as she resurfaced gasping for breath. As she came back down the stairs, although she couldn't catch the detail, she heard an angry exchange of words.

Pushing the kitchen door open, she clapped her hands. "Ladies. Please. What's going . . . wow! That smells wonderful, what is it?"

"Risotto, your grandmother's latest signature dish. It is good."

"What were you arguing about?" Angie pulled out a chair. The table was laid ready, and a chopping board had been placed in the centre of the table ready for the pan.

"You, your mother is being over protective. Move back, this is coming through." Bridget lifted the pan into the centre of the table.

They ate in silence for a little while, before Angie asked again, "What were you protecting me from, Mum?"

"Your grandmother's stupidness. Eat up. This is wonderful Mum."

"Don't try and butter me up, you called me stupid. It's lucky I don't take offence." Turning to Angie, Bridget pointed her fork at her. "Your mother doesn't have it, not my fault, but just so you know, this house is haunted."

Angie was so taken aback she choked on her food, and jumped to her feet coughing and spluttering. Her mother patted her on the back while she admonished her grandmother.

"You see. This is where talking nonsense gets you." Margaret took Angie's reddened face in her hands. "Are you okay, my angel? It's not true, there are no such thing as ghosts. Ignore her."

Angie pulled her mother into a hug. "I'm fine, something went down the wrong way." She winked at her grandmother, who grinned. "Tell me about your holiday, that should be a neutral subject."

When they had finished dinner, cleared the dishes, and were settled in the sitting room, the two women were still telling Angie about their trip to Barcelona. It seemed she would be getting an hour by hour account. She was relieved when her phone rang. It was Karen.

"I have to take this, it's work. Watch telly, The Village is on in a minute, I know what happens." She sat on the stairs and answered the phone. "Hi, Karen, sorry I missed you. Hang on a mo."

Her grandmother had appeared, she pointed up the stairs. "I need to go, before I settle down." She smiled her thanks as Angie moved to one side.

"My grandmother is staying for a few days," Angie explained. "What did you want to talk about?"

"Oh, Angie," Karen sighed into the phone, "There's no easy way to say this, so I'm going to rattle it off, ignoring any interruptions from you. Are you ready?"

Angie assumed Karen had a problem with the script. "Do I need a pen?" True to her word, Karen ignored her.

"I believe you are in touch with Wendy in some way. No idea how, but I've done some research, people like you do exist, so you need to be careful, what if you find the murderer? What then? If you do carry on, I don't know, because perhaps you have no choice in the matter, be careful. Tell no one unless you are absolutely sure you can trust them. While doing my research, I read that in America, a clairvoyant was killed when the murderer realised she was getting too close."

"I'm not a clairvoyant, Karen, this isn't what this is."

"It is. I think you need to embrace it. But carefully, and quietly." Angie heard the sharp intake of breath. "And, I want you to help me. Help me contact Louise. I know she tries to communicate with me, sometimes I sense her presence so keenly I look around in case she's there. Oh, Angie, I don't know why they are still here, some say because they have unfinished business, others because they can't rest until justice is done. Who knows, there are many conflicting opinions, but the one thing they have in common, is that they won't rest until whatever it is, is done."

"Karen, I don't know what to say, I don't want to be rude—"

"The other thing is, it's usually necessary for some form of connection. Some people go to where bodies were discovered, others need to hold something personal. I think with Wendy it's the house. It has to be, unless you've found something of hers which was left there. I still have some things which belonged to Louise, it has to be worth a try. Don't you think? What's the worst that can happen? Nothing. In which case *c'est la vie,* we move on, no one gets hurt. Will you do that for me?"

Angie had closed her eyes. It was a most ridiculous suggestion, total madness. She didn't have any sort of gift, if gift was an appropriate word, and she didn't think so. But could she say no to Karen? Her desperation, tinged with hope had brought a tear to Angie's eye, perhaps she should just do it. Karen was right, nothing would come of it, which was surely the best outcome, not the worst.

"Angie have you hung up on me?"

"No, Karen. I was behaving, not interrupting. Have you finished, may I speak?"

"Yes. I'm sorry I was so bossy, but if you'd taken me off in conversation elsewhere, I'd have never said it. Do you think I'm mad?"

"Yep."

"But you'll do it? You will at least try?"

"Oh, Karen, no good will come of it. If you do think Louise is out there in whatever form these things are in then . . ." A scene from the film *Ghost* entered her thoughts, and she watched Patrick Swayze's character trying to kick a can. She shook it away. She was not Whoopi Goldberg! "Look, I'm not the person to speak to. I promise I would know." A thought scratched around at the back of her head. Whoopi Goldberg's character didn't know what she was capable of either.

"Angie, please do this for me. I need to at least try, and I'd rather try with you, knowing what's happening with you and Wendy, than some name I picked off the internet. You might think I'm delusional, but I'm not stupid."

Angie was horrified at Karen throwing money away on some charlatan. "Let me think about it, I'm promising nothing, but I will call you in the morning."

"Thank you so much, you are a poppet. Go and see your grandmother. Bye." Karen hung up, worried she might say something to put Angie off.

Angie stared at her phone. She'd had a lot of odd conversations, but that one topped the lot. Deciding she would refuse when she next spoke to Karen, she got to her feet. A wave of guilt washed over her, she believed Wendy was in touch with her too, so why tell Karen it was rubbish? She tutted, because that would confirm she was mad, that's why. She gasped as her grandmother spoke.

"Was that a friend?"

"Yes, it was."

"Then do whatever she asked. That's what friends do, help each other."

Angie held out her hand, and helped Bridget down the final few stairs. "I said I'd think about it. I'll add your opinion to the other factors."

"Good." Bridget opened the door to the sitting room, "Come on, we've missed the beginning."

Sitting next to her grandmother, Angie watched The Village and the reality TV show which came after it. She hated *Big Brother* with a vengeance, but accepted that her mother liked it. The baby gave her an unexpected kick and she grabbed her grandmother's hand, pressing it on her belly.

"Junior says 'Hello, Great Grandma'."

Her grandmother smiled, as the next generation wriggled into a different position. "Junior is not a good name for a girl. You are having a girl." Her hand flew to her mouth. "Have I ruined it, did you not want to know?"

Angie laughed, but her mother wagged her finger. "Don't start that nonsense again, Mother."

"I speak as I find, and I find this is a girl, and unlike you, she has it." Bridget rolled her eyes as her daughter jumped to her feet.

"Mum, what's the matter?" Angie heaved herself up. "Are you okay?"

"Irritated with your grandmother and her nonsense. I'm going to bed." She paused and looked at her mother, "Enough. No more. Please don't fill her head with your nonsense."

Angie hugged Margaret. "'Night, Mum." She kissed her cheek and whispered, "I'm fine, I'm your daughter, remember?"

"Goodnight, my darling." She looked at Bridget. "Are you coming, Mother?"

"No, of course not, I haven't had my cocoa yet."

"Please try and be quiet then."

"Sleep in the spare room Mum. I'll bunk in with Gran."

Margaret hesitated only a moment. "If you're sure."

Angie's grandmother waited until the door was shut. "Thank goodness, I won't have to listen to her snoring now." She smiled. "It'll be just like when you were little."

"I'll go and make your cocoa. Do you still have sugar in it?"

"Two please. Where's the changer thingy, I want to watch the headlines."

Angie changed the channel and handed her grandmother the remote control. They tutted over the latest news while they drank cocoa, and later giggled while trying to be quiet and not wake Angie's mother while getting ready for bed. It was the light-hearted tonic she needed. She lay with a smile on her face and took her grandmother's hand.

"I love you. I'm so pleased you came, Gran."

"And so you should be," Bridget joked. "Do you trust me?"

"Of course." Angie's response was instant.

"You feel things you can't explain, or realise you have a knowledge you couldn't possibly have, don't you?"

"Gran, I—"

"Answer the question. Or not. We can go to sleep if you'd prefer."

"How did you know?" Angie's voice was low.

"Because it's the curse the women in our family carry. Or most of them. Your mother says she doesn't have it, and accused me of making up stories when I asked her. Yours has come early."

"What do you mean? Early." Bridget chuckled at her. "Why are you laughing?"

"Because you didn't ask what, or for any detail. Early because it usually comes after you become a mother. I don't know why it's come early with you. Perhaps you are even more special."

Angie stared at the ceiling, she knew there was a darkening stain in the shape of a kidney above her. She couldn't see it in the dark, but she looked for it none the less as she processed her grandmother's words. Bridget Bearing was a normal lower middle class ex-school teacher. She had a cheeky sense of humour, was practical, down to earth and laid back. Unlike her daughter, Angie's mother, who was a little highly strung. So why were they in bed having such a conversation?

"What did your friend ask you to do earlier?" Bridget squeezed Angie's hand. "Don't worry I won't mention it to your mother."

"Or Ryan." Angie returned the squeeze.

"Or Ryan."

"She thinks I'm some kind of clairvoyant, and wants me to see if I can make contact with her dead partner."

"You won't be able to, not unless he comes to you, which might happen. I'm more interested in why she thinks you'll be able to."

"He is a she by the way. Karen thinks it because I started writing a story. A horrible story about a girl who was abducted twenty-odd years ago, and it's transpired some of it may be true. All coincidence, I'm sure, you know, because I already knew bits, and now I'm joining up dots that aren't really there."

"But she thinks differently."

"So it would seem."

"How does this girl make contact with you?"

"She doesn't. I sit and I write. Some details are as clear as day, like my own memories, other things are a sense of what was. Blurry if I try and remember them afterwards. It is weird, Gran. Sometimes I feel trapped. I know this girl is going to be murdered and I can do nothing to stop it or warn her."

"Because it's already happened. It's why it's a curse."

"Yes, if only I could go back in time and help her."

"Don't be ridiculous, Angie, back in time! Keep a level head girl."

"What? You have . . ." Unable to complete the sentence, Angie dissolved into laughter.

It wasn't long before her grandmother joined her. Once they'd calmed, they stayed silent for a while, considering what they had shared.

"Can I read it?"

"No."

"That was absolute, why? You've already told me about it."

"I know, but like I said it's horrible in places. I wouldn't want you to read it."

"Was she raped or something?" She searched for Angie's hand again and clasped it in her own. "I do know about sex, I have had two children."

"Possibly, I don't know, I haven't got that far yet, but he's a nasty piece of work, and yes, he uses sex."

"Let me read it."

"I'll tell you instead."

"No, I'd like to read it, because I think whatever you are experiencing is far greater than anything the rest of us have ever experienced."

"Rest of who? Are you a member of a club or something?"

Bridget hooted out a laugh. "Don't be daft. My sister, my mother, my grandmother. All gone now, it's only you and me left," she rested her hand on Angie's belly. "and her when she gets here. But I'll be long gone by the time she's had children."

"Okay, but I—"

"Are you two intending on getting any sleep at some stage tonight." Margaret burst into the room. "Giggling and laughing like schoolgirls."

"Sorry, Mum, my fault."

"She wants to go back in time." Bridget chuckled.

"Well she can do that tomorrow. Can we get some sleep please?"

"Yes, Mum. Sorry."

"Goodnight, dear." Bridget's voice revealed her amusement.

"Goodnight the pair of you."

Angie waited until her mother had closed the door. "I'll print it for you tomorrow, but you mustn't let Mum see it, under any circumstances."

"Do you think I'm stupid?"

A muffled, "Quiet" reached them, and Angie kissed her grandmother's cheek.

"'Night, Gran. Let's get some rest."

Angie lay awake long after her grandmother had rolled onto her side and begun to snore gently. Deep inside she'd known something odd was happening, and having accepted that, she'd assumed it was to do with the cottage. Weird but acceptable. What was totally unacceptable was the knowledge this might happen again in some way. She didn't want to live through anything similar in the future. She didn't want to bear witness. She had a hundred questions for her grandmother and she tried to get them into some sort of order.

After a fitful few hours Angie gave up on sleep and went to her laptop. She opened the Witness for Wendy file, and as was her habit read the last few paragraphs. She rested her fingers on the keyboard and waited. Nothing happened. Her pulse increased. Attempting to get things going, she typed a few opening words in the hope the rest would follow.

'The next morning . . .' Nothing.

'Wendy . . .' Nothing.

'Wendy loaded Tess . . .' Nothing.

Slamming the lid shut, she wondered if her newly found knowledge had somehow broken whatever link she had with Wendy. Unsure whether that would be a good or bad thing, she sighed, lifted the lid and started to work on The Village.

While she worked she printed off Witness for Wendy for her grandmother. By the time her mother appeared at seven-thirty, she had completed the work she had allocated for the day, which left her time to entertain her guests.

Closing the laptop she went to greet her mother. "Morning." She kissed her cheek. "Did you sleep well?"

"Eventually, yes." Margaret's eyes twinkled. "I was taken back in time, it was like you were having a sleepover with a friend."

"Ha. I'm sorry, it was lovely though. Kettle." Leading her mother through to the kitchen, Angie explained, "I forgot to shop, so breakfast will be basic. Porridge, toast and there are some yoghurts in the fridge. Once we've got breakfast out of the way I'll go to the supermarket and do a shop. Do you want to stay in, or eat out tonight?"

"I'm easy about tonight, but can I do the shopping? That way I can escape your grandmother for a few hours."

"Oh dear, are you two not getting on?"

"Oh yes, perfectly well, but every now and then it's nice just to be me. Doing whatever I'm doing."

Breakfast over, and after a fifteen-minute discussion, the three women decided on a menu for the rest of their stay. Angie found her mother a shopping bag, giving her directions to the supermarket as she walked her to her car. Angie looked up as thunder rumbled overhead.

"Park as close to the entrance as you can," Angie told her mother. "It looks like we're in for a storm." Walking back to the cottage, she wondered if it was the weather or a more sinister threat she was worried about.

Back inside, her grandmother held her hand out. "I heard the machine chugging. I'd like to read it now."

Lifting the document from the printer, Angie collected a pen and handed them over. "Make notes if you need to, although I can't explain much. I'm going to get on with some work. Let's talk when you've finished."

"Okay, I'm going upstairs, I read better in bed. I've made you a coffee, and before you ask, yes, it's decaf."

Laptop open and coffee on the coaster, Angie tapped her mouse wondering if she should try again. She clicked Witness for Wendy.

~23~

Tess curled into a ball at Wendy's feet, content to cuddle her human who was reading through the first scripts of The Village. Wendy was excited, apprehensive, and eager to start work. The meeting with the producer had gone well, and the other members of the production team she had met seemed like a great bunch. She particularly liked one of the scriptwriters, and had had a good laugh with the wardrobe team. The only cloud on her horizon, unless of course he turned up again, was the decision she had to make regarding the child she was carrying.

The words on the paper blurred, and her hand went to her stomach. It was still flat. Did she want to keep his child? If the father was anyone else but him she would, but he'd know, then he'd demand contact - whether he wanted it or not - she couldn't expose a child to him. She also had to consider this new job. If the series went down well this could be a job for years to come, and she liked that thought, perhaps the scriptwriters could dream up a story where Fran gets pregnant, then depending on whether they wanted a baby in the series, Fran could either keep it, or give it up for adoption. Letting her head fall back onto the sofa, Wendy closed her eyes and tried to clear her brain.

The opening episode was scheduled to air in June. Filming started at the beginning of the following month, with rehearsals every day up to that point. There was still some casting to be done, and the director the producer wanted, wasn't available, Wendy knew she had to get the first six episodes in the can, and then decide, that gave her about three weeks. Then would be soon enough, she wasn't two months pregnant yet.

She opened her eyes and looked at the script. Now able to concentrate, she made a little note here and there in case anyone asked her opinion, the time flew by, and it was almost dark when Tess jumped off the sofa and paced to the patio doors.

Wendy glanced at the clock. "Poor Tess. I'm a naughty mummy, it's hours since you've been out. Come on, then it's supper and bed." Opening the doors, she smiled as Tess bounded out and as was her habit, ran around the perimeter of the garden sniffing for intruders.

Wendy went back into the sitting room and switched on the table lamp, its light casting a warm glow around the room. Heading to the kitchen she filled the kettle. She found it had boiled and her drink was made before she realised Tess hadn't reappeared. Wendy set off in search of her, frowning in irritation to find the sitting room in darkness. Glancing at the lamp she prioritised her search for Tess over the search for a new bulb.

Her scream was smothered by his hand, and her knees buckled at the shock. She hadn't considered his presence. Having regained control of her legs she forced them straight, her body bucking against the hold of his arm now wrapped around her middle. Having no concern for her own safety she screamed for Tess. His palm turned it into an unrecognisable whine.

"Silly girl," he whispered in her ear. "Silly girl. You weren't ready for me. Did you think I'd give up so easily?" Tensing his fingers and increasing his grip on her face, he added, "If I take this hand away will you scream?" Wendy shook her head and he took her ear between his teeth before removing his hand, which he rested on her shoulder.

Wendy gasped in air, not caring if he bit her. Squinting she spotted Tess worrying something in the corner of the garden, oblivious to their presence. They stood, he behind her, one arm around her waist, the other on her shoulder and her ear clamped between his teeth for several minutes. Repulsed at the feel of his breath as he waited calmly for her to speak, she pulled her head to one side.

Releasing her ear, he licked her cheek. "What now, silly girl? Are you going to invite me in? I've been out here for ages waiting for the mutt to appear, I'm freezing and need warming up."

"Please, don't do this. It's over, I can't carry on as though nothing happened."

"Oh, but you can. I chose you, Wendy. Chose you out of hundreds of others. We were meant to be, and you shall be my wife."

Closing her eyes, Wendy's blew out slowly to keep herself calm, knowing she needed to pacify him.

"Speak to me, Wendy. I asked you a question. Don't be rude, I don't want to punish you."

"Why me? Why did you choose me?"

"Because you were good. A nice girl, someone I could trust and someone who would behave themselves. Except you didn't, did you?" He tutted. "You misbehaved, but I'm willing to overlook it, just this once, because I know it was the . . . whore," he spat the word as if it was causing a bad taste, "Jenny, who caused this blip."

Wendy stilled as she processed this. If he only wanted her because she was good, if he only wanted her because she behaved herself, what if she didn't? What would he do, if she told him she hadn't been good, that she had misbehaved? How would he react? She had to show him she was strong. She had to make herself ready to deal with whatever fall-out it caused. Squirming, she turned to face him, he lessened the grip to allow the movement. Hoping the fear didn't show, and glad he'd turned the lamp off, they stood in the shadow of the house.

"I need to think about this." She raised her hand cautiously and placed it on his chest. He allowed her to do so.

"What's there to think about? I won't let you go. I love you."

"That's what I need to think about. I can't see how you can love me, not if you want to do . . . things, with other people. I know Jenny wasn't lying. About the detail, possibly, but about the affair, no. She knew too much for that to be the case."

"Jenny had better hope I never see her again." He pushed his head forward so their noses touched. "I was wrong to choose Jenny, I should have realised it was too close to home."

Unable to stop herself, Wendy's laugh was grunted. "Oh, so it would have been okay if I didn't know? Is that what you're saying?"

"Of course. What you don't know can't hurt you, that saying is true. I promise if I feel the need to look elsewhere in the future you will never know about it. You won't be hurt, we'll both be happy. You know you love me, Wendy, why fight it. I'm making some serious money now. In fact, I shouldn't be here now, I have a big meeting in London tomorrow. But I had to put this right."

"Money isn't love."

"No, I'm well aware of that. But your love for me already exists, the money will be spent rewarding you for that love."

Wendy gave up any attempt at pretence. "I can't love someone who lies to me. I don't need money, money isn't any part of this."

"Ah, and we're back to good old daddy! Daddy bought my car, Daddy bought my cottage, Daddy will, Daddy won't." He tapped his forehead against hers. It didn't hurt but it was a warning. "Daddy can fuck off. You have me now. Daddy is surplus to requirements. How is he by the way?"

Wendy's blood ran cold. Was that a threat against her father?

"Children love their parents. It's natural. Parents love their children." She closed her eyes knowing she didn't love this baby enough. To be rid of him, she had to be rid of it. Her decision had been made and her tears flowed at the thought.

"I didn't love my parents, and they certainly didn't love me. It's not a given. But we're getting off . . . are you crying." He kissed her cheek gently and licked his lips. "Why cry? You don't need anything but me, I'll put up with your father if you both continue to behave, after all he won't be around for ever. Then you'll need me. I can give you such a good life, you'll want for nothing."

The vision of that life was almost too much for Wendy to bear. She readied herself, knowing what she had to do.

"I'm crying because I'm not good. I haven't behaved."

He laughed, but his arm tightened around her waist. She was ready. She had to say the words.

"Am I allowed to find pleasure elsewhere as long as you don't know about it?" His body tensed and she faltered and didn't complete what she had planned to say.

"Of course not. It would be wrong when you've given yourself to me."

Saying a silent prayer of thanks to his ex-wife for unknowingly stopping the wedding, Wendy pulled her head back. Seeing only the outline of his face, she asked, "So this would be a one-way arrangement?"

"Don't be silly, Wendy, this is how it's always been. A man has needs. He needs a home and a wife to love him, and if that love is not quite enough to satisfy his needs, then it is acceptable for him to find it elsewhere. I need nothing but your love."

"I need to think this through, will you go and allow me to do that?"

"I'm going early in the morning. London, remember? But yes, I'll allow you to go to bed alone for a few hours."

Needing to put an end to the situation, Wendy decided she was ready, and voiced the words she'd held back. "I've been seeing someone. I was asked out, and I liked them, so I agreed." Jerking her body away from him, she threw her head forward wincing at the sound of its contact with his nose, while lifting her knee forcefully into his crotch. It had the desired effect.

He fell to his knees with a groan, blood spurted from his nose. Finally free, Wendy darted into the house and slammed the first patio door. He was on his feet before she's completed the second one, and he lunged at the door. It banged on his outstretched hand, and he cursed. Terrified, Wendy turned and ran towards the hall, her hand was on the knob when he grabbed her hair and yanked it violently. Wendy's head snapped back and she lost her footing as he continued to pull her backwards. She landed on the floor of the hall at his feet. Instinctively, she curled into a foetal position.

"Naughty, naughty, Wendy." He sniffed and spat a bloody globule of phlegm at her. "Now you'll have to be brought into line. I did warn you. You have no one else to blame but yourself." He wiped his nose with the back of his sleeve. "Whose fault is this?"

"It's not mine. I never agreed to that life. You didn't give me that option. I don't love you, I couldn't love a man like you." She pulled her arms tighter to her head as he knelt next to her.

"I couldn't love a woman like you, Wendy. I misjudged you, you're a bad one. No fun, and disobedient. I've had a lucky escape. Don't you think?"

"Yes," Wendy agreed.

"Now you must apologise for being a lying, cheating whore."

Wendy bit her lip, would it end if she apologised? Would he go? She didn't move and with a sudden thrust with the flat of his hand he rolled her onto her back. She peered at him through her gap between her elbows.

"You have to apologise. I deserve more of course, and I won't leave until you do." He shifted round to sit on the stairs. "Who is it? This new man of yours. I know it's not someone on The Village, I asked, they said you were single, available. Imagine my horror, when I thought you were mine."

Wendy's arms fell away from her face. "At The Village? How did you know? I've not even started filming yet."

"I know lots of people, you know that." He smirked as he remembered the adventurous young thing he'd been with the night before, "I know who most of the cast are. I know who the producer is, so you see I didn't think you had any secrets, and then you tell me this. Tell me who it is, and I'll be gone. I don't want used goods."

Wendy didn't want to put anyone in danger. Was he asking so he could punish them too? She shook her head. "You wouldn't know him. Anyway, it was once. I doubt I'll see him again."

He nudged her with his foot. "Name."

Wendy closed her eyes. "Philip."

"And what does he do, this Phillip? Is he a lovie? Is he better than me in bed?"

"No, he's not an actor, I've not slept with him. One date!"

"Don't say it like that would be shocking. You're not the Wendy I thought you were. What does he do?"

"He's a builder. Now go, and I won't phone the police. Please." Rolling on to all fours she looked at him. "Please."

Silently, and with menace in his eyes, he looked at her for a long while. "What do you say to one for the road. You could stay right there."

His eyes darted to the door as the gate creaked. He'd hopped over it to avoid that. Wendy's head dropped between her arms in relief.

"Come on you bugger. Tess, this way."

Old Bill's voice could be heard approaching the door, and Wendy allowed herself to relax. It was a mistake, she was totally unprepared for the pain of his foot making contact with her belly. Collapsing, she curled into a ball, breathless.

He grabbed her face, lifting her head from the floor. "One word to anyone, and I'll be back. I promise you, I'll be back. Keep it shut, and you and Phillip can live happily ever after." Letting her go, he moved quickly and silently through the sitting room and out into the garden.

Bill knocked on the door, and she bit back her sobs. Gritting her teeth, she pushed herself to her feet. Panting out the pain, she put her hand on the latch and drew in a deep breath.

"Tess. You bad girl where have you been?" Kneeling with a groan, she pulled the dog close, Tess licked away the remains of the phlegm before Bill had time to notice. Remaining on her knees she apologised, "I'm sorry, Bill, she was in the garden, the bulb went, and she was gone."

"No harm done. When are they doing the fence?"

"By the end of the week. Do you want a cup of tea?" The last thing she wanted was for Bill to stay, but she needed to make sure he'd gone.

"No thanks, I'll be peeing all night if I do. Did you find a bulb?"

"A what . . . Oh, no. It's not a problem I'll wait until the morning now. I'm going to have an early night."

"Sleep tight then. She'll not need the garden, she did her business in the middle of my path. Bless her." He bent and patted Tess. "I'll be off then."

If he wondered why Wendy remained on her knees he made no reference to it. He pulled the door shut behind him, and Wendy listened for the creak of the gate being closed before jumping to her feet with a yelp and hurrying into the sitting room. Hitting the light switch, the room flooded with light and she blinked rapidly as she locked and bolted the patio doors, pulling the curtains closed. She then repeated the process on the kitchen door, and finally the front door. Setting the alarm, heavy legs carried her upstairs, a puppy training pad clutched in her hand.

"Tonight, Tess, this is your toilet area. There won't be any more wandering for you." Placing it in the corner of the room, she stripped off her clothes, each stretch causing her to grunt, before going to the bathroom to clean her teeth. Sitting on the toilet, she wiped away what was left of her makeup, silent tears aided her. Flushing the wipes away, she squeezed the toothpaste on her brush. That was when the first razor like pain hit her. The toothbrush clattered into the sink and the tube hit the floor. Unable to move, she gripped the basin for support and waited for the pain to pass. When it had she cleaned her teeth, and filled a glass with water. The second pain seemed more violent than the first, and she dropped to her knees placing the glass on the floor of the landing. The knowledge she was losing her child would in any other circumstances been devastating, but she was glad, and she welcomed the pain as punishment.

The agony eased and she pulled herself up on the doorframe. Looking down she saw the blood and went back into the bathroom.

"My baby is going down the toilet you bastard!" She screamed at the top of her voice, before the sobs took hold and she bawled as wave after wave of pain washed over her, and the toilet bowl turned red.

Tess came to find her, and unsure of the noise, lay on the threshold of the bathroom, her sad eyes watching Wendy's torment. She stayed for the two hours Wendy remained on the toilet. The pains became less frequent and Wendy, still sobbing, climbed into the bath and switched on the shower. With her wet hair clinging to her face she pulled on a robe and went to the bedroom. Her tears had stopped, but every now and then her body juddered and she gasped for breath. Retrieving the puppy pad she threw back the duvet and placed it in the bed. Then, hair still wet, and robe still on, she climbed into bed. Tess jumped up to join her and, her nose blocked, Wendy's laboured breaths filled the silence.

The next morning, Wendy was still losing blood, too much blood, and she knew she needed to go to hospital. She took another shower, pulled her hair into a ponytail, and called Bill. Telling him an emergency had come up, she asked him to look in on Tess, and she'd call him later. Assuring her he would prefer to have Tess with him, Wendy set off for the hospital. She was admitted immediately. The doctors confirmed she'd lost the baby and told her she would need a procedure to ensure she didn't develop an infection. She'd be staying overnight.

A shocked Wendy asked for a telephone. An auxiliary nurse wheeled one to the side of the bed. Her first call was to Bill and she arranged for him to have Tess, as always he assured her it wasn't a problem. Then she called the studio to explain she wouldn't make rehearsal that day as she'd had a minor accident and was in hospital. Brushing away their best wishes, she confirmed she would be in the next day.

The final call was to him. He sounded happy and carefree as he greeted his caller.

"It's me." Her tone was so cold he truly didn't recognise her voice.

"Me who?" There was laughter in his voice.

"Don't play games. Your footwork destroyed your child last night." She heard the gasp and continued, "You should have been more careful. There is a security camera connected to the burglar alarm, I now have a recording of you kicking the life of our child out of me."

"I didn't . . . that is . . . where are you?"

"It doesn't matter where I am. What matters is this, you will never come near me again. Ever. I have a written statement from Jenny about what you did to her, and I have a recording of what you did to me, and Bill saw you leave. I don't want the bother of a court case if I can avoid it, but I will go to the police if you ever come to my home again. Do you understand?"

"Are you blackmailing me?" He was back in control, and he sounded incredulous.

"No, warning you. Don't think I won't bring you down. I will. I'll go to the press as well as the police, let's see how far you get in this business then." She dropped the receiver back into the cradle as a nurse appeared, a porter hovered behind her.

"I'm going to give you a pre-med. Then Tim is going to take you to theatre." She watched the tear slide down Wendy's nose. "Are you sure you don't want me to call anyone."

"My father. He's on the form as my next of kin. But don't call him yet, wait until I'm back on the ward, and please don't tell him why I'm here. Tell him it was a woman's problem, and he won't ask any more questions. Too embarrassed." She managed a brief smile before watching the nurse inject a clear fluid into the cannula on the back of her hand.

"I understand. Now lay back and relax." The nurse fussed around the bed a little before summoning the porter. "And we're off."

As they left the room the phone rang. The nurse looked puzzled.

"Never heard it ring before. Two seconds." The porter rolled his eyes and waited while the nurse went to answer the phone. "Southmead Hospital, Nurse Brown speaking." She received no response, and staring at the receiver for a second, she shook her head. "Must be a fluke."

Wendy knew better.

An hour and a half later she was back in her room, and opened her eyes to a nurse patting her hand.

"All done." The nurse soothed leaning forward and dabbing Wendy's cheek with a tissue. "You've been crying in your sleep. I called your dad, and you were right he didn't want detail. He'll be here soon."

Wendy drew in a shuddering breath. "I must look a sight."

"You look fine, remarkably well considering. Bit blotchy around the eyes, but that will soon settle. I'll get you a cold compress." She placed Wendy's hand on the bed.

"No. Let me see. Can I get to the bathroom?"

"Too soon to be out of bed."

The nurse hurried back when Wendy threw back the sheet and sat up, and turned to allow her legs to hang over the side of the bed.

"Wait a minute let me help you."

Wendy was surprised to find, that other than feeling tired, everything worked, and she only felt a slight twinge when she walked. The nurse held her anyway.

Wendy splashed water onto her face and peered in the mirror. Her eyes were red. She splashed some more. Aided by the nurse, she returned to her bed, and allowed her to place a cold wet flannel across her eyes. It was soothing and Wendy drifted off. She awoke to the sound of her father's voice.

"You sleep my little girl. I'll be here when you wake up."

Opening her eyes, she remembered the flannel and pulled it away, smiling at her father.

"Hi, Dad, how are you?"

"Me? Worried sick, but more to the point—"

"I'm fine. I had a bit of an issue, all sorted now, my womb—"

"Don't worry about any of that. We just need to get you well."

"Dad, I'm fine. I can walk and talk, and could go home. The only reason they are keeping me in, is because I had a general anaesthetic. In fact, if you come with me I might be able to go home. Can you find the nurse for me?"

Although she had to stay another four hours, the hospital needed the bed, and on the promise she wouldn't be on her own, she was discharged.

Her father held her elbow, and they walked slowly to the lift. They were deep in discussion about Tess as they waited, and neither saw the bouquet of flowers being delivered to the reception desk, and they were already in the lift when the nurse realised they were for Wendy. Too late to catch them, the flowers were taken to the room of a lady with no family.

~24~

Angie pushed the laptop away and sighed. Glancing at the clock she knew her mother might return soon, and she went upstairs to see what her grandmother thought.

"And?" Angie smiled as Bridget held up a finger, and waited while she read the final few pages.

"You have to see this through, Angie." Bridget tidied the papers into a pile and held it towards Angie. "The bastard needs to be punished, and it looks as though you are the one to bring him to justice." Getting to her feet she tapped the manuscript. "Like this says, you are the witness for Wendy." Cocking her head, she studied Angie for a moment. "I think it's because you're pregnant."

"What is?"

"This is far more detailed than any of us have managed, that I know of anyway." She took hold of Angie's hand. "I've not had one for years, but I never had anything like this, only names or brief messages. Not the explanations to go with it. I think your connection was because of the house, but it's this detailed because of the baby. That's guess work, but it's what I think."

"But how can I do that? How can I bring someone to justice? I can imagine the conversation with the police. I know this sounds a bit loopy buuut . . ." Angie sighed. "She lost her baby by the way, she wasn't still pregnant when he took her."

"You've done more?" Patting Angie's hand, she hoped to comfort her. "That's good. You have to see this through. If you weren't capable you wouldn't have been chosen."

"When this is over, when I've had Junior—"

"Junioress," Bridget corrected.

"When I've had this baby, you and I are going to sit down, and you are going to tell me the history of this . . . this . . . *thing* you've kept secret from me."

"That will be nice, can't invite your mother, she still thinks we'd be taken to the nearest pond and dunked, or at the very least, thrown behind bars." Chuckling, Bridget put her hand on Angie's belly. "She's got it. You remember that, because you'll have to explain it."

"If Mum has never asked about it, how . . . Oh she's back, that's a conversation for another day." She put the manuscript in the dressing table drawer and called to her mother. "We're up here. I'm on my way."

When she got downstairs, Margaret had deposited two full shopping bags and was on her way back out for more.

"How much extra did you buy?" Angie followed her mother back to the car.

"I bought some bits to take home with me, but they'll need to go in the fridge. How did you damage your car?"

Angie stopped walking. "I didn't, why?" As she spoke she saw the huge gouge which ran from the front wing across the doors to the petrol cap. She was about to curse when she noticed something under the windscreen wiper. A sheet of paper had been folded and sealed in a sandwich bag. Shoving it in her pocket, she forced the concern from her voice, "I hadn't noticed it. Damn those vandals, that's going to cost me."

Margaret returned with another two bags, "How did you miss it?"

"No idea. I'd better phone the insurance company. Bastards."

"Language. Don't lower yourself to their standards."

"I'm sorry, Mum, but I think it's justified." Taking one of the bags from her mother, she teased her. "You've bought enough to feed an army. How long did you say you were staying?"

Her mother caught her arm. "Until this nonsense is finished. I can't have you dealing with this on your own in your condition. I've got a granddaughter to consider now."

"What nonsense?" Angie grinned and nudged her mother. "You believe Gran's prediction then?"

"She's right. And the nonsense with this Wendy girl. Poor thing."

Angie dropped the bag. "How do you know her name?"

"She told me to go and see Karen. I've no idea who Karen is, but I'm sure you can fill me in. Not a word to your grandmother though, I think she takes pleasure in believing I don't believe. And if you've broken the eggs, you'll be going out to get some more."

"Shit!" was all Angie could manage as she retrieved the bag.

"You did break them?" Margaret tutted.

"I don't know, I don't care. Bit shocked to find out I'm a member of a coven."

Slapping Angie's arm, Margaret huffed and walked away. "Nonsense! You see. That's why I don't encourage your grandmother."

Angie hurried after her. "But you'll tell her now? I can't have secret conversations with both of you, I'll forget who I've told what."

Margaret turned to look at her. "Secret conversations? What secret conversations?"

"About Wendy of course. Blimey, Mum, you do make things complicated sometimes."

"Your mother knows about Wendy?" Bridget stood in the kitchen doorway, hands on hips. "How does she know about Wendy?"

"Wendy spoke to her." Angie decided enough was enough. She was overwhelmed by what was happening to her, and what until today, had been a family secret. Hearing the growl of frustration from her mother, she announced, "End of conversations for ten minutes. I can't get my head around any of this. I'm going for a walk. You two can unpack the shopping, no talking about it, no recriminations. We are where we are and we have to get on with the task in hand. I need to work out how to do that." She looked from one to the other. "Can we do that? Because if this is going to blow up into some sort of row, you may as well go home, and I'll deal with it in my own way."

"There's no need for that. Don't overexcite yourself, think of the baby." Her mother stepped towards her.

"Who? The she-baby who will be able to talk to dead people?" Angie held her hands aloft. "Exactly. Now, for the baby's sake. Peace, calm, and a little acceptance will go a long way." She checked the time. "I'll be back by eleven-thirty." Grabbing a raincoat from the hook she pulled the door closed behind her.

Once out of the gate, Angie increased her pace and didn't stop until she had passed Bill's house. She then crossed the road to the bus stop, took a seat, and took the bag from her back pocket. Turning it around, she contemplated whether it would be better to drop it in the bin and not give him the pleasure of opening it. Curiosity won, and she opened the bag and withdrew the paper.

Move away bitch. You're not wanted here!

Angie grunted a laugh. He was trying to make her think it was the locals causing the problem. Guessing the typewritten sheet had only been handled with gloves, she still folded it carefully and returned it to the packet, he might have made a mistake, there might be fingerprints. Making the return journey at a slower pace, Angie decided to share his scare tactics with her mother and grandmother, and felt better for having made a decision. She found them sitting at the kitchen table waiting for her.

"Oh dear, this looks bad. I feel like I've been caught truanting from school."

"Sit down, we want to talk to you." Her mother pointed to the chair, and waited until Angie was settled. "When does Ryan get back?"

"Friday or Saturday, it depends on how soon they get what they want. Animals don't take direction in the same way humans are supposed to. Why?"

"Because we're staying until he's back, it might help bring this thing to a conclusion, if we Bearing women stick together. Especially as Wendy is now contacting me too."

Smiling, Angie reached into her back pocket. "Perfect, because I need your advice on something I believe is connected." Her hand slapped her forehead. "Two seconds." Jumping to her feet, she hurried to collect her laptop. When she returned, she logged in speaking quickly as she did so. "I've been receiving warnings, from him I think, which is why I wanted to speak to you, but I forgot about the camera. He might have been caught on camera."

"You know you're not making any sense, don't you? And what threats? You didn't mention any threats. Should we call the police?" Bridget got to her feet.

"You know about the rat, but I've also had a phone call, a note put in my bag at work, my car keyed, and this morning I found another note telling me to move away. It all started when I became Wendy's . . ." Angie frowned. "Wendy's witness. I've told the police about the other stuff . . . Shit. I hadn't thought the first note was about Wendy .... ." Her eyes widened. "But if it is . . ."

"Then you already know him!" Margaret closed her eyes and her chin dropped. Lifting her head, she looked at Angie, but spoke to her mother. "You're right, Mother, we should call the police. Now!"

"And tell them what? That we know he killed her, we don't know how, or where, but he's now threatening me?" Angie shook her head.

"Don't worry about that." Bridget waved her finger at the laptop. "Who knows you've been in touch with Wendy?"

"Only Karen, in any detail, although she may have spoken to Colin about it, Colin is our director. But she made a note about it on a script and Alan, our producer, read it out."

"To whom?"

"The meeting we were in. There were three men there, Alan, Colin and Harry Grayson."

"He's got a lovely voice, but I'm not keen on him in The Village," Margaret mused. When Bridget tutted, she added, "But they are all suspects, logic tells us it must be one of them, but not necessarily so, it could have been an innocent mention in front of the wrong person. We'll kick off with them though." She looked around the kitchen. "Pen and paper, we need to make notes."

Angie went to collect her note pad, she was glad to have them on board, but felt numb someone she knew, even Harry, whom she didn't much like, could have done the things she'd witnessed. She returned to the kitchen with a heavy heart.

Bridget got to her feet and pulled her into a hug. "I know this is horrible, but we will catch the bugger. Don't you worry, but we have to be sure, and we have to be careful. Now, take a seat and let's work through the evidence."

Margaret took the pad from Angie. "I'll do the writing, you two aren't detailed enough. She flipped to a blank page and headed it 'Wendy'. "What do we know about Wendy, age, date she disappeared etcetera."

"She disappeared in nineteen-ninety-four, she was twenty-five. She lived in this cottage." Angie placed her elbows on the table and cupped her face. "That's about it. In the reports I've found, there is no mention of a boyfriend or romantic interest past or present - at the time it was written of course. In fact, very little about her personally, it was centred around her connection to The Village. I haven't been to the library yet though, that may throw something else up."

"So, she'd be forty-eight now. A bit younger than me." Margaret noted this and looked at Angie. "Of the three men you mentioned, who would have been a similar age in ninety-four?"

"All of them, I suppose." Angie shrugged. "Colin is about sixty, so he'd have been older, but I sort of expected that. I don't know exactly how—"

"One at a time," Bridget interrupted. "We have to do them all anyway. What do you know about this Colin? Did he know her back then, do you know?"

"Yes, I'm sure he did. I think Karen mentioned he was around when they went to a concert . . . or did she say he wasn't?" She frowned. "Either way he was around, but would Wendy have worked with him if it was Colin? I bloody wouldn't have. I'd have told everyone exactly what he was like."

"But would you? It depends doesn't it." Bridget urged caution. "From what I read he manipulates, it's how he snares them in the first place, he might have—"

"Read what?" Margaret interrupted, she looked from one to the other. "Have I missed something?"

"I printed out my story for Gran," Angie explained.

"You're writing a story about it?" Margaret's expression laid bare her disapproval.

"No, but it's how I know. She doesn't talk to me like she did to you. I write what comes into my mind."

"I need to read it. Can I do that before we go any further? It might help me understand, like your grandmother does, it will help I'm sure."

"Of course. I'll go and get it, and I'll print the last chapter for you."

Margaret took the growing manuscript into the lounge. "Make some coffee, I'm a quick reader this won't take too long. Don't carry on without me, I might miss something."

"I need to read the last bit, the bit where she loses the baby."

"There was a baby?" Margaret's eyes widened. "Bastard! Come on Mother, we need to get this sorted."

Angie didn't even smile at her mother's use of bad language. A weight was bearing down on her shoulders, and she had an uncharacteristic need to cry. "I'll get on with some work while you two read it."

She went back to the kitchen and read the last chapter she'd printed.

~25~

Wendy watched the filming of the final scene of the day. It had been three weeks since she'd heard from him. Rehearsals had gone well and they were now recording. All six episodes would be in the can before they were aired, and depending on viewing numbers for the first two episodes, they would start on the weekly scripts if all was well. There was even talk about it becoming a twice-weekly soap. Most of the filming was done in and around Bristol, which meant on most days she could get home for Tess during the day. Bill was also pleased to have an ongoing involvement with Tess. On occasion, she even brought her to work. It depended who was around and how long she thought she'd be tied up filming.

Karen, one of the scriptwriters, had told her a new young hot-shot director had been appointed, although they were yet to meet him. Wendy hoped he was as nice as Freddie. Freddie had been diagnosed with osteoporosis and had decided to take early retirement and do as much as he could before the illness incapacitated him. The whole crew were a joy to work with. There was no bitching, no prima donnas, and they had a social evening at least once a week. This week it was to be a more organised affair. Marti Pellow was doing 'An Audience With' in the next studio, and the crew had been given tickets, Wendy was looking forward to it. Drinks in the bar beforehand, the show, and then a spot of people-watching with canapés after.

Freddie called it a day, and Wendy pulled her coat on, she bumped into Karen on her way out.

"Have you been shopping?" Karen touched the sleeve of Wendy's coat. "This is nice, and not the one you were wearing when you arrived."

"Yes, I grabbed half an hour earlier. I didn't have time to go home to Tess, so I invested in a warmer coat. My other one is in the rest room if you need it." Wendy offered as Karen had no coat on at all, and it was blowing a gale outside.

"Thanks, but I'll be fine. Louise, my flatmate, is picking me up, she'll be waiting outside. By the way, drinks on Tuesday next week. It's Jamie's birthday, he's invited everyone."

"Perfect. What's the dress code for the audience with thing? Should I bring a dress or something?"

"Absolutely, darling, they put the camera on the audience, you don't want to be caught wanting, not an up and coming actress like you. Oh, there she is. See you tomorrow."

The next day, Tess watched from her perch on the bed as Wendy selected several dresses which she tried on before rejecting them, eventually settling on a simple black number and a handful of brightly coloured bangles.

"Classic but stunning, don't you think?" Wendy ruffled Tess's head, and packed the dress into an overnight bag. "Mummy is going to be late tonight, so you'll be staying with Bill. Be a good girl." Tess's tail thumped the bed at the sound of Bill's name. Wendy pulled on her jeans. "Come on then, I need to go to the supermarket, we'll go for a walk first."

The word walk caused even more excitement and Tess bounded off the bed and downstairs. She'd done three laps of the house before Wendy had even pulled on her windcheater. "Calm down, puppy. You'll do yourself a damage." Lifting her jacket from the hook, Wendy caught hold of Tess. "I'll need something tidy to put on after if you're in this mood."

Tess sat peering out of the window, she saw his car pull away from across the road, keeping a reasonable distance behind. Wendy didn't, and when she parked in the far corner of the carpark she didn't notice the car slowing so as to be hidden behind a row of parked cars in front of hers. Letting Tess out, Wendy hurried to catch her as she flew through the gap in the fence. She didn't see him park several rows away and turn off his engine.

Walk over, Tess was towelled dry and given a treat. Wendy changed her boots and her jacket, and was in and out of the supermarket in fifteen minutes. Tess had been asleep and leapt to attention as the door opened.

"Home to Bill now, puppy, I've bought you something new to play with, so no more slipper chewing."

Wendy was looking forward to the day on set, and the entertainment afterwards. For the first time in weeks she had relaxed. Pulling out of the space, she headed for the exit, and indicated to join the traffic on the main road; as she pulled away she glanced in her mirror and her heart missed a beat. A car flashed her and allowed her to pull out into the stream of slow moving cars. When she next looked in her mirror she couldn't see him. If it was him. Once back on the quieter roads, her eyes continually darted to the rear-view mirror. She had relaxed only a little by the time she got home, she'd only seen one other vehicle and that had been towing a trailer. Back in the house she was still shaken, and she went to the kitchen and collected two knives. One was placed on her bedside cabinet, the other on the hall table. If he came back she'd be ready for him. Before she left, she checked her rape alarm was in her bag.

The rest of the day went smoothly. She was word perfect in all her scenes and managed to finish early enough to make herself look presentable for that evening. One of the makeup girls did something magical with her hair, and tiny wisps of curls gently framed her face as they fell from the topknot.

Receiving many compliments with a little embarrassment, and politely sidestepping unwanted attention, Wendy watched with amusement as her colleagues began to party. She was driving home, and not drinking, but it seemed the rest of the crew had other ideas, the alcohol was disappearing at an alarming rate. Freddie stepped up behind her.

"They do it so they'll laugh at the right moments, every joke told will seem hilarious." He laughed. "I'm not drinking either. Boring isn't it?"

"I don't much. But I love watching others have fun." Wendy smiled.

"Me too, nothing like people-watching, did you see the new Eastenders chap, he ... . . . ooh there's someone I want you to . . . Oh they're calling us through. I'll introduce you later."

Freddie had been right. The audience were perfectly in tune with those on the stage, they hooted their appreciation as each act was introduced, laughed at all the puns whether funny or not, and gave standing ovations to the few ballads. When the songs were more up-tempo they were on their feet and jigging about to the music. It was a good night, Wendy was fairly relaxed when Freddie took her elbow and guided her to the set which had been set aside for the after-show mingling.

"Quick now, there won't be much food, they've got what they wanted. They won't waste too much money on feeding the hordes after the event."

A plate of canapes in one hand, and a juice in the other, Wendy wandered to the edge of the crowd in search of a seat, she couldn't find one, so set her juice on the floor and ate while she watched the crowd move around, there were a lot of big names there, and it seemed everyone had someone they needed to talk to. She waved as Louise, Karen's flatmate appeared, and made a beeline for her.

"God, I hate these things. Loved the show, but you can't move for bumping into an ego or two. I've lost Karen, and Harry whatsit doesn't like taking no for an answer. I thought I'd have to knee him in the nuts before he'd accept I didn't want to go somewhere with him. Oh, there she is. She's beckoning, come on."

Wendy was about to follow when Freddie reappeared. "I'll miss all this, Wendy. I love the pomp and preening. I've spotted the chap I want you to meet, follow me."

Freddie was tall and slender, and manoeuvred easily through the crowd, Wendy followed blindly keeping as close to him as possible. He came to a stop next to the now empty buffet table.

"Wendy, meet Colin. Colin meet Wendy. Colin is going to be my replacement, and this is . . . no don't prompt me, I'll get there . . ." He squinted at the man who had been speaking to Colin. "Alan."

"There you are. I've been looking for you." Harry Grayson stepped into the group. He looked at the others. "I'm about to convince this lady to come out with me. I won't be long."

Wendy clasped her glass so tightly she thought it would break. Of course, she was bound to bump into him. Why had she believed she could spend the rest of her life avoiding it? The floor seemed to move beneath her feet.

Freddie placed his hand on her arm. "Are you all right, Wendy, my lovely? You look peculiar."

"I'm . . . I'm . . ."

"In need of some air, I think. It is warm in here, come on, the fire exit is open." Alan put his hand on her elbow. "I could do with some fresh air myself."

"No. I'm fine." Wendy shook his hand off, and sipped her drink, wondering how she could get away without making a total fool of herself. "A hot flush, that's all. I'm fine now."

Face it out, stand firm, do not be beaten, you can do this, she told herself silently.

"We've met before." Colin stepped forward. "How are you, Wendy?"

Wendy didn't have time to answer as Freddie clapped his hands.

"You know each other, how marvellous. That will make life easier, have you worked together before?"

"Oh, yes." Colin winked at Wendy.

"Is this going to be awkward?" Freddie grimaced. "Were you two an item?"

"Sorry, to butt in, but Wendy was about to accept my invitation to join me at a club. Weren't you?" Harry threw his arm around her shoulder.

Wendy's stare was cold as she looked at him. "No, I'm not." She shrugged his hand away.

Alan smiled. "I think the lady said no."

"Then the lady is foolish." Harry was smiling, but his voice told a different story.

"I doubt it." Colin stared at Harry. "I think that . . ."

"There you are." Karen pushed her way between Colin and Alan. "Sorry, chaps. But Freddie is needed. I'm stealing him." She glanced at Wendy. "Are you okay? You don't look it."

"No, not really. I'm going to go."

"Okay, see you soon. Drive carefully."

"Shall I walk you to your car?" Colin suggested with a smile. "You can tell me who that attractive young lady is."

"No! Sorry, I didn't mean to snap, I've got a banging headache."

"Are you sure you should drive?" Alan stepped forward and placed a hand on her shoulder. "I've got some aspirin in my jacket, if I can find it." He glanced over his shoulder.

Wendy threw her hands in the air. "No! Will you please all bugger off. I have a headache, I can walk to the car, and I can drive. Now please . . ." Swinging her arms in front of her, the three men stepped back. "Thank you. No offence, I'm . . . sorry." She looked into his eyes briefly, and they twinkled his amusement. "I have someone waiting for me at home."

The twinkle disappeared.

Lowering her gaze, she hoped it was warning enough for him not to follow her. She glanced at the other two, they looked amused. Turning away she walked into the crowd, hoping they didn't notice how much her legs were shaking.

~26~

"Shit. She knew all of them at that time." Angie closed her eyes. "Which one was it? Come on, you can do this now, who is he?"

"What's happened? Are you talking to yourself or Wendy?" Bridget placed a hand on Angie's shoulder.

"Both. She knew them all. She was confronted by him at a do, but although she let me know he was there, she didn't tell me which one. Why? *IF* she's communicating with me because she wants this sorted, why not show me? I don't understand." Angie slapped the table. "This is so bloody frustrating."

Bridget pointed at the laptop. "Print it. Your mother has nearly finished, I can tell, she's started crying."

Angie paced the kitchen as the two women finished reading the latest instalment.

"You need to keep writing." Margaret blew her nose. "We'll find a way to make this stick, I'm sure she'll show us how."

"It doesn't work like that, I can't . . . hang on, it's Ryan. He's somewhere with a signal." Angie paced into the hall. She listened to Ryan's excited report on managing to film some rare birds, and getting a shot of the chicks learning to fly.

". . . but we haven't got what we came for yet, that was a distraction that couldn't be missed. I might not be back until Sunday, we're back on the mountain later. We've got some labour and enough supplies. Everything is okay with you and the baby, isn't it? You seem distracted."

"Only because I have Mum and Gran watching me speak to you, and don't worry they've decided to stay until you're home."

"Great. That puts my mind at rest. Be good, love you, got to go."

Ryan had gone before Angie could respond, she looked at the others. "Not back until Sunday, at the earliest by the sound of it."

"Great. We can get on unhindered. Men don't understand, they get freaked out." Bridget refilled the kettle.

"I'm a little freaked out myself." Angie plonked herself back down at the table. "What now?"

Margaret tapped the pen on the table. "Now we get back to work. As you said, it wasn't clear from what you've written who he was. She didn't name him, and the interaction with all of them was negative."

"Who were we doing? Less chat, more action is needed. If our Angie is at risk the sooner we have something to take to the police the better." Bridget tapped the table.

"Colin." Margaret underlined his name. "He's about sixty, and we now know he knew Wendy before she died. We know she didn't respond well at their first meeting, and by what he said about Karen," she paused and pointed the pen at Angie, "we mustn't forget about her by the way. But his reaction tells us he was clearly a red-blooded male."

"Yes, and he did try it on with Karen, and they became close when she told him she was gay. She said he had a type, and it was common or working class or something like that. And, you're right, Mum, Karen also said he put it about a bit."

"Hmmm."

Angie leaned forward and smiled. Her mother had written Lothario, next to Colin's name.

"What about this Alan chap? How old is he, he was around at the time, but you didn't mention that when we were talking earlier?" Bridget was keen to move on.

"Because I didn't know. Alan is younger than Colin, I think, he certainly looks it." She gave a laugh, "But he's gay too, so I can't believe it's him."

"Oh. It complicates things a little, but he's still a suspect, stranger things have happened." Bridget moved the pad to face her. "Which brings us to Harry Grayson." She turned the pad back to Margaret.

"Yep. Good old Harry. I dislike him, and although he is also a *Lothario*," Angie winked at her mother, "I can't see him being brave enough. He doesn't strike me as brave."

"Let's get one thing straight," Margaret was waving the pen again, "he wasn't brave. He was a coward, a bully, anything but brave. In fact, he probably did this to those poor women because he was a coward. It gave him the feeling he was a real man. Also a suspect." She circled his name. "To summarise, all were around shortly before she disappeared, all were the right sort of age to be in a relationship with her." She studied Angie for a moment. "You obviously don't get on with Harry Grayson, but what about the other two? Have you had words, or anything bad happen with the others?"

Angie closed her eyes and recalled the incidents which could be relevant. She opened her eyes.

"All of them have been angry with me since I started writing about Wendy, and all told me to be careful, for one reason or another. That's what the first note said, the one someone at work had to have put in my bag. Harry was mad with me, he's always mad at me, but initially because I'd queried his intentions regarding a storyline he was behind, but Colin and Alan have been too. The first cross word I'd had with either of them occurred after they knew I was doing something concerned with Wendy. Both unnecessarily angry in my opinion. This isn't looking good, is it?"

"Well that depends, if, for instance, Alan was being overly nice to you, that would make me suspicious in its own right. Better we don't let our guard down against any of them." Bridget scratched her head. "We need a plan of action. If sitting you at the laptop won't help unless you get the urge, then we have to do some searching of our own. Shall we go to the library archive and see what we can dig up?"

"Good idea, let's get lunch and then go. First, I need to make a phone call. Where did I put the card?"

"Which card?" Margaret frowned, but Angie was already leaving the kitchen. "We'll get on with lunch, shall we?" she called after her.

Angie retrieved yesterday's trousers from the washing bin and retrieved the card. She checked the detail and her mouth fell open. She hurried back downstairs.

"This is the same refuge Wendy was recommended to use."

"After twenty-three years?" Margaret questioned. "It can't be."

"I promise you it is. I saw it twice, she was given it by both the lady in the street when he hit her, and the policewoman. I can't believe I didn't realise. I'm big on detail usually, this . . ." she held her hands up searching for the right word. ". . . bugger, I've even lost my vocabulary! This *thing*, is turning my brain to mush. It might explode if I get any more surprises to process this week."

"I know, I know, dear. Your first experience is usually simple, something you could brush off if you didn't want to deal with it." Margaret squeezed her daughters hand. "At least it was for me." She shot a sly glance at Bridget. "I'm not sure what your grandmother thinks."

"It's different for everyone, while I don't advocate shouting it from the rooftops, I think it could be counterproductive to try and keep it under wraps. Just because you don't want to deal with it, doesn't mean they won't contact you. Not dealing with it, or brushing it off would drive you mad . . . in my opinion."

"Let's agree to differ." Margaret offered. "At least we're all agreed we need to move this on as quickly as possible, and on that point, you were going to look at a camera. Don't know why, but we got a little sidetracked."

"You see? Mush!" Angie pulled the laptop forward and clicked away opening the recordings made by Ryan's cameras. "Ryan set some webcams up. I told him it was for wildlife, and to be fair I did see a fox I wouldn't have known about, but . . . okay here's the one which covers the front door." She pushed the laptop away to allow the others to watch the footage. "I'll speed it up a little. Shout if you see anything."

They called out in unison when the recording hit five-twenty-six. Angie hit the pause button and grimaced.

"I don't think we have much, that was there and gone in seconds. Mind you, I did tweak the camera to catch anyone approaching the front door, and this all happened around the car." She looked at Margaret. "Mum, write down "number" and ask me about it after, I might forget that too. Right, mister, let's see what we've got."

Although she kept her tone light, she was frightened. Even taking away the fact that a dead person was communicating with her, they were dealing with a murderer, maybe he'd killed before. Angie had already considered this as a reason for the frequently changing cars. Perhaps he was a serial killer. She wanted to be able to go to the police and say, "Here you go. Go and get him", but as that wasn't possible she needed to consider everyone's safety. Sighing she hit the play button.

"It's a lovely clear picture, in colour," Bridget commented. "Not one of those grey fuzzy things you see on Crimewatch, I never can understand why people bother with cameras if all you can see is a blob."

"Hush. Concentrate." Margaret rolled her eyes. "Although it's lucky you keep the porch light on."

Angie held her breath as something moved on the peripheral of the screen.

"A shadow," Margaret whispered unnecessarily. "He's coming to the door it's . . . Oh, quick what was that?"

"A flash of yellow? Just a flash of yellow. Damn it." Bridget leaned back in her chair.

"I think he spotted the camera." Angie replayed the thirty second clip again. "Yep, probably why he gouged the car, and left it under the windscreen. I . . . Fingerprints!"

"Where? On what?" Margaret tutted. "It won't help if you speak in riddles."

"The note was in a sandwich bag. Obviously to make sure it didn't get wet. But was that his original intention? Surely, he'd have used an envelope or nothing at all. You wouldn't choose a sandwich bag to put through a door. No, no, you wouldn't. That was an afterthought. Gloves for the note but where did he get the sandwich bag, and had he handled it before?"

"Good thinking, Angie. Well done. Let's call that nice young police woman, Helen." Margaret beamed at her daughter.

"No point. It's too soon. We still don't know what happened to Wendy. Even if they find out who left the note, what would happen? A slap on the wrist for being mean. We need more." Angie sighed. "I'm going to phone the lady at the refuge. Perhaps she'll remember something which may help. Or at least point us in the right direction."

"Is that why you told me to write number down?"

"Oh boy. No, it wasn't, but I'd forgotten again. I have the number from the bitch call. The policewoman told me not to call it. But in for a penny . . ."

Angie set her phone to withhold her number and tapped in the number of the call. She paused before she hit the ring button. "Absolute quiet. I'm going to put this on speaker so you can hear too, but I'm not going to speak until they have, if at all. Ready?"

The other two nodded and she hit the call button. The sound of ringing filled the kitchen.

"Good afternoon, BBC Bristol, how may I direct your call?"

"Which department is this please?"

"Main reception, which department do you want?"

"I'm not sure. I'll check and call back. Thank you." Angie dropped the phone onto the laptop. "Well that didn't help."

"No, but it's another thing dealt with. Call DS Clarke while we're checking things out." Bridget encouraged.

Retrieving her phone, Angie called the refuge. It was answered after only two rings. Hitting the speaker button, she placed the phone on the table.

"Hello."

"Hi, is that Mandy's Mission?"

"It is. How can I help you?"

"I'm hoping to speak to Sarah Clarke. Is she available?"

"Afraid not. Not back until late this afternoon, at the earliest. Can I take a message or help you?"

"Yes, please ask her to call me. Tell her I want to speak to her about Wendy Knight." Angie rattled off her name and number. Thanked the woman for her help and looked at her mother. "We'll have to wait. Am I imagining it, or did you say you were getting lunch earlier." She clasped her belly. "We are hungry."

"How hungry? Sandwich or shall I pop a lasagne in? It's already made, so won't take long." Margaret peered into the fridge.

"Is there garlic bread?" When her mother opened the fridge and held it up, Angie clapped. "Lasagne it is. I'll leave you two to it, and take this into the other room, I have to write some emails."

Angie sent the emails and clicked on the Wendy folder.

~27~

Wendy opened the door and released Tess's lead. Slamming it behind her, she slid the bolts into position, and glanced at the knife on the hall table. If he turned up she'd be ready for him. Walking through to the kitchen where she could hear Tess nosing her bowl across the tiles, she thought about contacting the police. It had been a while since she'd seen him, and although she considered she handled it well given the shock at coming face to face with him, she knew he'd not given up.

She was ready to take him on, she was even willing to use the knife - she thought - but should she at least alert someone to the possibility that he might hurt her, and have it recorded somewhere? The ringing of the phone interrupted her thoughts and she stood in the doorway looking at it, waiting for the answer machine to cut in. She heard the pips and the money drop, before Karen's voice called hello.

Wendy rushed to answer it. "Hi, Karen, sorry, I was feeding Tess."

"But you're okay? Freddie thought you seemed overwhelmed by male attention. I can relate to that." Karen laughed.

"Yes fine. Men are idiots when they have a drink in them. I didn't have the patience and needed to get back for Tess."

"That's okay then. Thought it best I check. If you're sure you're okay I'll leave you in peace. Louise has promised me supper in a nice little Greek restaurant."

"Go and have fun. Thanks for calling, see you tomorrow. Bye." As she hung up, he knocked on the front door and she lifted the knife. She could see his outline through the coloured glass. Remaining where she was, she called to him. "Please go away. Don't make a bad situation worse."

"I want to talk to you, and I refuse to do so through a closed door."

"Go away. I'm not going to talk to you."

"Wendy, I promise you I won't even step onto the doorstep. I know you have the camera, but I need to tell you something face to face."

"Go away."

"It was my baby too. I've cried tears over a child I'd lost before I even knew it was there. I forgive you. I love you."

Knuckles whitening on the handle of the knife, Wendy struggled to slide back the bolts before throwing the door open. She jabbed the knife forward and he jumped back a couple of feet, his hands held up in surrender.

"You didn't know because you didn't deserve to know. Are you telling me you wouldn't have kicked me if you did? What sort of man are you? Shall I tell you? You aren't a man, you are a fucking cowardly shit woman beater, now get out of my garden and out of my life, or I'm going public, I promise you that. I have the film, I have the hospital records, unfortunately I don't have our child as he was flushed down the fucking toilet."

Tears travelled unhindered, she wasn't prepared to risk losing concentration. "I know we will see each other, our world is small, but I don't want to talk to you, I don't want you to even look at me."

He stepped towards her and she jabbed the knife forward. It stopped inches away from his chest and halted his progress. She was surprised to see he was also crying and she sniffed, allowing herself to wipe her nose on the back of her hand.

"I love you. I always will. I would have loved our child. I know you won't accept that now, and as you request I won't ask you to take me back again, ever. But I would ask you to consider it, and if you ever change your mind you let me know. I'll always, always want you, Wendy."

"I won't."

"You might," he persisted.

She caught a glimmer of something in his eye. What was that? Amusement? Did he think this was a game? At that moment any feeling she had ever had for him turned to hatred. The kind of hatred that blurred your thought process, and she pushed the knife against his chest.

"I WILL NOT. Last warning, no more or I go to the police. I have Jenny, and I'll tell them to look for others. Your wife would be a start. I was never happy with what you told me there."

His head shook a little with the effort to control his temper. He leaned against the knife.

"I'm going. But be careful, Wendy. Very careful. I will ruin you if necessary." He looked at the knife. "You'd better be ready and willing if I ever have to come and find you." Turning away abruptly, the point of the blade caught his shirt and cut a small hole.

Wendy waited until the gate had shut before slamming and locking the door. Calling Tess, she set the alarm and went upstairs. Her skin crawled when she realised what she had nearly done to her life, and leaving Tess sleeping on the bed, she went to the bathroom. Stripping quickly, she turned the shower on full blast, wanting to wash thoughts of him away. As her skin turned red from the heat of the water she sank to her knees and wept.

True to his word he kept his distance, but Wendy was still unable to fully relax. She was losing weight, and not sleeping well, but determined not to let him control her life, she threw herself into her work. Popular amongst cast and crew alike, she started to rebuild a normal life.

~ ~ ~

Wendy removed the last of her makeup and stared in the mirror. They were going to the pub to celebrate yet another birthday, and she wasn't sure whether to replace the makeup she had removed with a more subtle version. Karen came into the dressing room.

"Great work today, Wendy. You make my words dance."

"Why thank you, kind lady. It's easy to be good when you have such wonderful material to work with."

"Oh, paaaleease." Louise appeared in the doorway. "You two are going to make me vomit in a minute and I'm not drunk yet." She rubbed her arms. "It's bloody freezing out there. I haven't thawed out yet. I thought I had a coat in the car."

"You'll need one." Wendy's reflection looked at Louise. "It's a fair old trek to the pub they've chosen for tonight's drunken fiasco." She got to her feet and walked to the rack behind the door. "Here try this on. I bought a new one, and haven't taken this home yet."

Louise put the red trench coat on. "I like this, if it's going spare . . . Don't you love a big button?" She fastened the large black buttons and tied the belt loosely at her waist.

"It's not. It simply hasn't made it home yet. Any money in the pockets is mine too," Wendy laughed as she pulled her other coat on. "Is it still raining?"

"Cats and dogs, they say the temperature will drop and it will freeze. It will be lethal. Glad I wore flat shoes." Louise looked pointedly at Karen's high heeled boots.

"I didn't know the weather would change, anyway it's not freezing yet. Grab the golf umbrella. They'll never miss it."

The three women huddled under the umbrella and, chatting and giggling, walked along the several streets to the pub as quickly as they could. They were so busy trying not to step on each other's toes, or place themselves outside the protection of the umbrella, they didn't hear him start the engine, and follow them to the pub.

He parked on the other side of the road. Patience had always been a virtue for him, he could wait.

It wasn't until Barry, one of the cameramen came in grumbling, that Wendy decided to leave.

"It's brass monkey weather out there. The rain has stopped but there's a bitter wind, and the windscreens on the cars have frozen already. Not even ten o'clock," he complained. "Landlord, another pint and I'd better have a whiskey chaser."

"Right. I'm making a move then." Karen announced. "We have to get a taxi and their driving is erratic enough without ice giving them a hand. I'll finish this with a ciggy and we'll be off, Louise."

"Perfect. I'm ready for bed." Louise yawned.

"I'll walk to the taxi rank with you." Wendy finished her drink.

"Bugger, last one." Karen held a cigarette in one hand, and crushed the empty box with the other.

Louise got to her feet. "I'll go. I'm not facing you in the morning before you've had a fag and a coffee." She looked across to the bar. "What time does the off licence around the corner close, Barry?"

"Ten." Barry looked at his watch. "You'd better get your skates on if you want to catch them."

Louise was already pulling on her borrowed coat. "Thanks. Going now." She turned to Karen and lowered her voice. "Only because I love you do I venture out into the cold, cold night. This means dinner is on you tomorrow." She gave Wendy the thumbs up. "Thanks for this." Pulling up the collar of the coat, she shivered. "I'd have died of frostbite."

Karen blew her a kiss. "Thank you. We'll be ready and waiting by the time you get back. Better make it two packs, might not get out tomorrow."

Louise set off, and Wendy buttoned her coat. "I wonder if we'll get snow?"

“It wasn't forecast, I like snow when it's Christmas and someone else is catering, and I don't have to go further than the garden to build a snowman. Other than that, not so much. We only end up with grey slush anyway.”

Waiting until Karen had emptied her glass, Wendy took them to the bar. “When was the last time you had a white Christmas? I can't remember any, ever.”

Stubbing out her cigarette, Karen rose to join her. “I must have had one.”

Calling out their goodbyes, the two women made their way out to await Louise's return. A taxi with its light on approached and Wendy flagged it down.

“Sorry, Karen, but she's not back yet. Am I being too cheeky?”

“Yes, but carry on. She won't be long.”

~28~

"What?" Bridget stood facing Angie. "You shouted."

"Did I?" Blinking back tears Angie looked at her grandmother. "I think he killed Louise. Karen's partner. She was wearing Wendy's coat."

"It must be why she told me to go and see her." Margaret had appeared next to her mother. "Don't you think, Mother? You know more about this than me."

"We're out of our depth, that's what I think." Bridget walked to the sofa and dropped onto it like she was exhausted. She looked at her daughter. "I don't know what to do, Margaret. I'd love to answer your question with my vast wisdom and knowledge, but I can't, I can't. This is way outside the sphere of anything I've ever experienced, Angie is something else."

She tried to smile at her granddaughter but failed miserably. "I don't know how to help you. You have to see this through, because you will anyway, you can't stop it. We'll have to deal with the end when you get there. But in the meantime, call the police and log the damage to the car and the note. We may need to catch him that way first."

"What if I go and see Angie's friend, Karen? Perhaps if I find out what Wendy wanted me to see, I might see him. That would help, not sure how at the moment, but it would help," Margaret suggested.

"Oh boy." Angie sniffed. "I'm so glad you two are involved or I'd be climbing the walls or booking myself into the nearest secure facility." Getting to her feet, she took hold of her mother's hand. "I'm not sure about Karen, I know it might help reveal him, but then what? Would you tell Karen if you found something out? If it does reveal which one it is, do we tell her, and how would she react? No, no, I can only see it making things more complicated."

"I can lie, tell her nothing happened. I'd remember the details, I always do . . ." Looking at her feet, Margaret cleared her throat, before turning to Bridget. "What do you think?"

To their surprise Bridget threw her hands in the air. "What am I? The bloody oracle? Did I not say I didn't know? I don't know, and I don't like Angie being in danger because of this curse. That's never happened before, well it has, but not like this. I'll tell you something . . ."

Angie's phone rang and she saw it was Colin calling. She held the phone towards her grandmother. "It's Colin."

"Then answer it, and act normal."

Angie didn't believe that would be possible, and she walked into the hall closing the door behind her.

"Hi, Colin, how are you? Did you get my emails?"

"I did, but events have overtaken us." He dismissed her question. "Can you come in?"

"Um, not sure. I have guests and we have plans." Angie's tone was hesitant. She didn't want to be alone with him. "Why, what's the emergency, can't I deal with it from home?"

"If you're entertaining, you can't work from home either, can you? What's the difference?" he snapped.

"Has something happened?"

"What like Grayson and Natalie having a punch up on set? Yes literally, he knocked her out . . . Okay, I'm exaggerating, but he knocked her down and now she's left in the middle of filming. Alan's had her agent on. She refuses to come back if Grayson is still involved, and she's suing him. Won't win, she hit him first. For fuck's sake, this is all I need. Alan wants a meeting now. Are you sure you can't come in? Gemma is God knows where, Alex is not picking up, and in any case Alan wants you here. We have to agree the best way forward."

"Will Harry be at the meeting?" Angie closed her eyes against the thought of having to sit and face all three of them.

"Don't be ridiculous. It's him or her. I know which I'd choose, but Alan may have different thoughts. He's already got the press office scanning twitter and facewhatsit for any mention. Half the bloody crew saw it."

"What about Karen?"

"I've asked her to come, yes. We can't have two dramatic departures so close together, might have to persuade her to stay on a while longer."

"I thought you were going too."

"I am. Today, the way this is going, but there's a job to be done. Are you coming in or not?"

"Give me an hour." Angie dropped the phone to the floor and gave a low moan. Her mother was with her in seconds.

"What now?"

"I have to go to work." Angie pressed the heel of her hands into her temples. "Unavoidable, and whatever the outcome with Wendy, I still have to earn a living."

"Would you like us to come with you?"

"Ha! I wish. No, I can just see myself explaining why I brought both my mother and grandmother to a meeting. But thanks for the offer."

"Couldn't we watch the filming, at least we'd be close."

"Filming has stopped for the day. I'll tell you what, come into town with me, and you can go to the central library and look at the archives. It's not far. You can drive, drop me off, and I'll call when I'm finished."

"A plan. At last. I'll tell your grandmother."

Angie took her phone upstairs with her. She dialled Karen and put it on speaker as she dressed. Karen used colourful language to confirm she would be there and Angie relaxed a little. She wouldn't be on her own. She then called Natalie, and left a message. She peered in the mirror, and grimaced before putting on a little makeup.

Her mother drove into town, and dropped her off outside the studio.

"We both have our phones on full blast, I don't care if we are in a library, promise you'll call if you need us. We should have a code word. Um, say . . . an Indian for dinner, and we'll know you're in trouble. Have you got that Mother?"

"Am I deaf now?" Bridget leaned forward and blew Angie a kiss. "Be careful."

Angie hurried into the building. She hadn't laughed when her mother suggested a code word. That wasn't good.

~ ~ ~

As Angie entered the room the silence was deafening. There were none of the usual cheery greetings. Alan gave a curt nod and Colin barely glanced up from his notepad, only Karen managed a half smile.

Angie pulled her shoulders back. "Sorry to keep you, I got here as quickly as I could, my mother was driving." She told them as though they were accustomed to her mother's careful attention to the speed limit.

"You're here now. Take a seat and I'll tell you where we are." Alan allowed his glasses to drop from his forehead, his pen poised.

Angie hadn't unbuttoned her coat when he began to speak.

"We have two options. Ditch Harry or ditch Natalie. Harry is refusing to fall on his sword or apologise, in fairness to him, since Colin called you we have watched the recording of the incident. They were having words, although neither will volunteer about what, and Natalie punched him in the face, Harry raised his hand and she stepped away losing her footing, and fell to the floor. He didn't make contact with her, and is demanding a copy of the tape so . . ." he glanced back at the pad "so, he holds a record of the truth."

"Would he have made contact if she hadn't stepped back? Why did she hit him?" Pulling her pad from her bag, Angie looked at Alan.

"No idea on both counts. Not relevant though, is it?" Alan snapped.

"I think it is. Natalie has never displayed a temper, unlike Harry, and I know they had words recently about her rejection of his unwanted advances." She paused to see Alan's reaction, he didn't even blink. "So, I think it's crucial. If one of them is to walk, it needs to be fair or this will run and run." Opening her pad, she placed her pen in the centrefold. "Oh, and are we even allowed to decide this? Isn't the top floor going to have an opinion?"

"Agreed." Colin linked his fingers.

"Of course. This is not a decision-making exercise. When I get out of that lift, I want answers to give them. I want to say if, in their ultimate wisdom, so and so is going, then this is the game plan, and this is how they will go. I need to confirm the current stories can and will be amended to cause as little delay to filming as possible, and the Corporation won't come out of it with egg on their face." Alan tutted. "Now that's clear, can we proceed."

"But, until we—" Her mouth snapped shut as Alan roared his interruption.

"For fuck sake woman. Do as you are told!"

"There is no need of that, Alan. Calm yourself for goodness sake. None of this is your fault." Karen's hands were on her hips. "I can't wait to be gone. Let's do a dual storyline with me and X flying over the cliff together." Allowing a smile, she glanced at Angie. "I can go over a cliff, can't I? You know I want no leeway to be able to return."

"It can be arranged." Returning Karen's smile, Angie made a note.

"Karen! I've told you. You can't go at the moment." It was Colin's turn to snap. "It would be ridiculous."

"I beg your pardon, but I believe I'm a grown woman able to do as I please. Don't you dare lecture me. I know you, like I, would prefer to go out on a high. But going is the most important factor for me. I'll be gone before Christmas." She held up her hand. "I love you, Colin, but even you can't keep me here a day longer than is necessary."

Frowning she turned her body to face him. "It makes no difference to you, why do you care if the idiot has turned things on its head. I'm sure there are going to be some waves, and the scripts will need rewriting, but as is the case with Alan, none of this is your doing, and you want out anyway."

Looking at Angie, she asked, "Tell me why they are like this." She waved her hand between the two men. "It's simply another blip, a pain in the whatsit, but a blip. In six months no one will even care, if of course it takes that long."

"I'm not sure why. Perhaps they could explain." Angie was watching the men closely, more to see if they appeared capable of murder, than worrying about the true reason for the meeting.

"Bollocks!" Colin leaned back in his chair and linked his fingers behind his head. "Bollocks to the lot of you. Go on then. You two decide. Karen and I are going, not that my departure seems to matter much," He pointed at Angie. "You can't stand Harry, and you, Alan," he moved his finger, "are smitten with the stupid bastard for some reason, best known to yourself. So, go on. Knock yourselves out."

Angie glanced at Alan as he sat motionless for a few moments, then without warning, he raised his fists above his head and brought them down with some force, and proceeded to thump the table repeatedly.

"Enough, enough, enough," he shouted. "I thought this room was filled with grownup professionals, but it appears I was wrong. Get out all of you. I'll go upstairs and see what they have to say." Lifting his hand, he wiped spittle from the corners of his mouth.

"Which is what you should have done in the beginning." Karen was shocked, she'd never seen the man in such a state, and whilst she was used to the occasional tantrum on set from the actors, she didn't expect it in this setting. As she got to her feet she wondered exactly how far his relationship with Harry had progressed.

"So, that's it. You get egg on your face and we've got to go through this all over again?" Colin also stood. Leaning forward, he challenged Alan, "Whatever they say we'll have to do this."

Colin was flushed and Angie blew out a silent whistle. "It might be better if we let the dust settle anyway," she suggested. Lifting her coat, she pushed her arms into the sleeves. "Perhaps it will look different tomorrow." Joining Karen at the door, she added, "I'll hang around for half an hour or so in case anything changes, but then I'll go home. But I'll give this some thought."

Karen pulled open the door for Angie to exit; the two men hadn't moved. "I'm glad you're staying for a while, I wanted to ask if you'd given any more thought to what I asked about Louise. Oh. You nearly gave me heart failure!" Stepping out of the room she bumped into Harry. He had a thick lip.

Although she should have known better, Angie asked, "Were you eavesdropping?"

"I was waiting to speak to Alan. I didn't want to miss him, not that it's anything to do with you."

"I think you should leave them alone for a while," Karen suggested. "There's nothing to be gained by attempting to sort this mess out now."

Harry looked from one to the other as though he was seeing them for the first time. "What is it with the women around here. Not one of them can keep her mouth shut, interfering bitches the lot of you."

Angie took Karen's arm, as the door to the meeting room opened. "I need to pop to the office, but I'll meet you in the restroom in fifteen minutes. We should leave them to it. Best to avoid having a slanging match in the corridor."

"Probably the only sensible thing you've ever uttered." Harry turned away.

~ ~ ~

Having handed her formal request for maternity leave into the office, Angie completed some other paperwork waiting for her and set off for the rest room. Pleased the lift was empty she took it to the ground floor, and started along, what the crew had labelled, the rat run. It was a tunnel connecting part of The Village set to the main building. Only it didn't quite connect, there was a gap of one hundred yards or so at the end, where if it was raining, a mad dash was made for the heavy metal door and sanctuary. There was no one about, which was hardly surprising given earlier events, most would have taken the opportunity to get an early finish. Shivering as she approached the end of the tunnel, she could see the wind had picked up as an empty bag was tossed around in the void.

She didn't hear him approach, his timing when he took her was perfect. A black bag was pulled over her head on her first step outside the tunnel, his right arm wrapped around her, finding a slot between her breasts and her pregnant belly, on her second. His left clamped her throat on her third. Directing her away from the set and to the left of the tunnel he propelled her forward. He uttered few words, but enough to make her comply.

"Speak and your baby dies. Scream and you do too." The words were delivered in a throaty hiss, as though the speaker had some form of impediment.

Disorientated, Angie lost her bearings and when they came to a halt and he told her to kneel she had no idea where they were. She dropped to her knees, ignoring the pain of the coarse gravel below them.

"Last chance, bitch. You will stop this nonsense now, do you understand?"

"I . . . I—"

He hit the back of her head with the heel of his wrist. "I said don't speak."

Angie nodded.

"That's better." He cleared his throat, the effort of the affectation causing him discomfort. "No more Wendy, no more Louise, no more anything. Ever. Understand?"

Nodding furiously, Angie let out a sob. Her only thoughts were for her unborn child.

"Lie down, face first," he demanded, and coughed a laugh as Angie struggled to follow his instruction. "I'm going now. Don't move for five minutes, or I'll find you, and I will kill you next time. Understand?"

Lifting her head from the ground, Angie nodded. Then gasped as his foot was placed on her head and pushed it back into the gravel, the bag offered little relief from the sharp fragments of stone.

"Don't move, Mother."

With a quick movement, the bag was removed and Angie heard his footsteps running away. Unable to move even if she wanted to, Angie sobbed quietly, it was only the ringing of her phone that broke her paralysis and with a groan she rolled onto her side. Ignoring the phone, she looked around. She was in a six-foot square void, formed by the tunnel on one side and several storage buildings. No windows, no one to see. How did he know it was there?

Getting to her feet, she wiped her face with her sleeve, and brushed herself down. Walking to the tunnel, she looked to the right along the storage unit. Seeing the red brick of the building which housed the set she stepped forward. Her phone rang again. It was Karen.

"Karen, can you meet me at the door please."

"Which door? The set? Are you okay, poppet, you sound odd?"

"Yes. I need you to take me home please."

"I'll be there in two minutes." Karen hung up, and Angie waited in view of the metal door for her to appear.

Karen let the heavy door bang shut and looked around, Angie appeared from the side of the tunnel, it was clear she was pretty shaken up.

Rushing forward, Karen pulled her into a hug. "Poppet, whatever happened? You look dreadful."

"Have you got your car?" Angie glanced around.

"Yes, it's parked around the back. Why?"

"Will you take me home please? Long story, I'll tell you on the way, but I need to get out of here now."

"Then we shall leave now." Karen linked their arms and led Angie into the tunnel. "You're shaking. Can you not give me a clue?"

"Not yet, I want to get as far away from here as possible. Did anyone else from the meeting appear on set? Colin, Alan or perhaps Harry?"

"Not that I saw, why?"

"Two minutes." They re-entered the main building and Angie increased her pace. "Shit there's Colin and Alan. Please act naturally, you can laugh when I've finished speaking, but please head for the exit."

Karen threw her head back and gave her trademark cackle. Looking at Angie, she smiled broadly. "I'm a little worried now."

"You need to be." Holding her face into the cool breeze as they left the building, Angie relaxed a little. "Which way?"

Karen led the way around the corner into Tyndalls Park Road. "Here we go."

Once they were headed towards the cottage, Angie relaxed. She texted her mother to say she'd finished early and taken a lift from Karen. They would meet them back at home.

Turning to Karen her smile was weak. "We know Wendy's abductor and Louise's murderer were one and the same person." She rubbed Karen's arm as she gasped. "I'm sorry, it wasn't an accident, she was wearing Wendy's coat, it was mistaken identity, but definitely not an accident."

"She was. It's one of the things I brought for you. That's what I wanted to speak to you about. But how did you . . . Oh." Karen fell silent as the truth came to her. "I knew you were special."

"I don't know about special. My grandmother calls it a curse. Oh Karen, it's such a long story, and I will fill in the blanks, but the person responsible is either, Harry, Colin or Alan." She waved her hand. "Don't ask. We need to be quick. Can you cast your mind back to the night you went to the Marti Pellow thing, think about Wendy and who she spoke to, did you see anything you now know might have been unusual?"

"It was such a long time ago." Karen shook her head. "I can't concentrate on that and drive, my mind is in overdrive."

"Okay, not a problem we can do this when we get back."

"One of those three. I can't believe it! If we'd written this into a script for The Village, we'd have been told to get a grip. Did you realise back there? Is that why you wanted me to take you home?"

"No, I found out this morning for certain. But whoever it is, attacked me too. He threatened the baby, and me. It left me in no doubt that if I don't give this up he will kill us." Her hand stroked her belly as she spoke. "But I'm not going to give up. I'm going to have the bastard. He killed Wendy's baby, but he won't get mine."

Karen pulled over and turned to face Angie. Concern increasing the lines around her eyes. "He attacked you? And Wendy had a baby? Are you okay? How did I not know?"

"I'm fine, he was rough. I'm not injured. Drive on and I'll tell you about Wendy." Angie waited until they were back on the road. "Wendy was pregnant, he kicked her in the stomach, and she was alone when she lost it." Angie's voice cracked and she coughed. "I'm sorry, Karen, I didn't want to drag you into this. It's nerve shredding, but you mentioned Louise in front of them all. I didn't know what to do for the best. He's started a campaign of fear against me with no proof I even know anything, and I guess if he knows you're talking about Louise you could also be in danger. It could be

Colin, you would have trusted him if he'd turned up on your doorstep, but until we know differently, it could be him."

"Stop speaking. I'm going to crash the car. I'm getting so angry I could smash someone's face in myself. Unbelievable."

Back at the cottage, Angie settled Karen on the sofa with a cup of tea and the manuscript, before calling her mother. It rang through to the answer service and Angie hung up, hoping it meant her mother was on the way home. She bolted the front door, and went back to be with Karen. Unable to concentrate on anything else, she watched Karen read. As Karen neared the end she was sniffing and blinking away tears, Angie went in search of tissues. When she returned Karen beckoned her to sit down. Taking a tissue from the box, she wiped her eyes and blew her nose before taking Angie's hand.

"I've remembered something. Reading about the night with Pellow, bits are coming back to me. I knew nothing of her seeing all three of them together, but Freddie did say she was acting oddly. That's why I called her, I also saw Harry have a minor altercation with Alan. I couldn't hear their exchange, but Harry suddenly flipped his hand as though dismissing Alan. Alan grabbed his shoulders and pinned him against the wall. He put his face close to Harry's and said something, no idea what, but then simply walked away. Don't you think that's strange?"

"Not with Harry, he seems to have that effect on most people. Why strange?"

"Because Alan clearly has designs on Harry. If looks could've killed back then, or perhaps if they were somewhere less public, who knows what would've happened. And now he makes puppy dog eyes at him. Perhaps it was something to do with Wendy."

"That's a bit of a jump, and we have to remember Alan is gay."

"Hmm." Karen shook her head. "Not exclusively apparently. He made a lewd comment about the runner to one of the cameramen, Clive, the nasty one that everyone avoids. He told Colin, when he questioned him, Alan laughed and told Clive he liked his bread buttered on both sides."

"Shit. I'd written him off almost. That changes things."

"If true. I wouldn't trust Clive as far as I could throw him. There is a chance he might be lying."

"This bloody thing gets more and . . . OH!" Angie gasped as someone hammered on the front door. "That scared me. Stay here."

Placing the security chain in place, Angie unbolted the door. She found her mother, grandmother and Colin on the doorstep.

Ignoring the others, Angie addressed Colin. "Hi, Colin, how can I help you?"

Colin frowned. "Are you not going to open the door?"

"Not at the moment, no. Why are you here?" If she wasn't trying to remain aloof, Angie would have rolled her eyes as the two women in front of Colin turned to look at him, her mother taking a step away.

"I wanted to make sure Karen was okay. I saw you ushering her out of the studio at quite a pace."

"Karen's fine. Thank you. Bye." Having no idea how get rid of him, Angie raised her hand and wiggled her fingers in a wave, hoping he would take the hint.

"May I speak to her?" Colin stepped closer to the doorstep and Bridget stepped in front of him.

"Hello, Colin. Bridget, Angie's grandmother." She held out a hand and Colin shook it. "My granddaughter clearly doesn't want you to go in, so you go off and I'm sure she'll ask Karen to call you."

"Why? Angie, what's going on? Why can't I speak to her?"

"Long story. Not now, please go Colin. I'll call you later I promise. Please don't make me call the police."

"You can call who you bloody like, I'm going nowhere until I've spoken to Karen."

"What's so urgent? Please, go, Colin. I can explain this, but not now." Pulling her phone from her pocket, Angie held it towards him. "Please, leave. I won't ask again."

"You've been acting up for days, Angie. Look at you now. Your mother and grandmother kept standing on the doorstep. Why won't you let them in? What have you done to Karen?"

"Done to?" Stepping away from the door, Angie tapped at the screen of her phone. She heard her mother gasp as Colin pushed her to one side and shoved his head in the gap of the door and the jamb, the chain straining against his weight.

"KAREN! KAREN! ARE YOU OKAY?" he shouted, only stopping when Karen appeared in the hall.

"Colin, please stop. What on earth has come over you?"

"Over me? Why are you locked up here?"

"I'm not locked up, you're locked out. Please do as Angie asks and leave us. We have some things we need to sort out." Cheeks flushed she took a step forward. "Why are you here?"

"I wanted to make sure you were okay. I'm sorry I cared."

"But why did you? What made you come here?"

"I won't fucking bother next time." Colin had already turned away and was marching along the path.

Once he'd cleared the path, Angie released the chain and ushered the women in, slamming the door and sliding the bolt home. She gave a scant introduction to Karen before running upstairs to see what Colin was doing. She was relieved to see he'd got into his car, and remained at her bedroom window until he'd driven out of view. Relaxing a little she went back to the others. She found them in the kitchen talking quietly. They fell silent as she entered.

"What?"

"Sit down, my love." Margaret pulled a chair out. "We need to speed things up. If that Colin, rude as he is, is nothing to do with it, you could be out of a job."

"And how do you intend doing that?" Dropping onto the chair, Angie closed her eyes. "I have explained I can't just make it happen. It either does or it doesn't."

"We know, but if your mother does what Karen wants, then it might give us more information. It might reveal who it is."

"Is it safe to do that?" Rubbing her hands over her face, Angie looked exhausted as she stared at the three women. "I don't want Mum to get involved if she doesn't need to. Perhaps I should take the laptop upstairs and wait."

"Is that what you want to do? Because it seems to me, like you need to sleep. Wendy and Louise are gone, but that baby needs her mummy to be healthy." Bridget put her arm around Angie's shoulder and kissed her forehead. "Another day or so won't make any difference. We're all here together, so no one can hurt us. Karen can stay too if she's worried about going home." She looked at Karen. "What do you think?"

"I think Angie needs some rest, and I need a cup of coffee with a dash of brandy. If you haven't got the brandy I'll settle for the coffee."

Smiling, Angie got to her feet. "If you're sure. I'll take the laptop in case."

"Good girl. I'll bring you some warm milk." Margaret was already walking to the fridge.

"I'm not six any more, Mum. A cup of tea will do nicely. Thank you."

Leaving them in the kitchen, Angie went to her bedroom. Slipping off her shoes, she lay fully clothed on the bed. She was drained of energy. Looking at the laptop now sitting on the bedside cabinet, she shook her head. "Later, Wendy."

In the kitchen, Bridget had taken command. "Margaret, make the drinks and take Angie's up to her. Karen get your keys, we're going to your car to get Louise's things. Once Angie is asleep, or otherwise occupied, we'll see if Louise wants to make contact." She put her finger to her lips. "Quietly does it, we don't want Angie back down here."

From the kitchen window, Margaret watched them hurry along the path. She stirred sugar into Angie's tea. Once they had returned with a large carrier bag, she carried the tea upstairs. As she entered the bedroom, Angie's mobile rang. She rolled her eyes as Angie answered, placed the mug on top of the laptop, and went back to join the others.

Angie got up and tiptoed to the door, closing it firmly. She had no idea what the call would throw up, but she needed sleep before she discussed it with anyone.

"Hello, Angie speaking."

"Hello, It's Sarah from the refuge, you left a message for me to call. How can I help?"

"Oh boy, where to start, umm—"

"Wherever it's easiest. Take your time."

Sarah Clarke's response was gentle and coaxing, Angie realised that Sarah probably thought Angie herself was in trouble. "I'm not a battered wife, if that's what you think. I'm looking to pick your brains."

"Okay, Helen told me that. She also told me you've been threatened. Is someone else intimidating you?"

"Oh dear, Sarah, please accept I don't need your help in that way. Shall I just spit it out?"

"Of course."

There it was again, the gently coaxing.

"Do you remember Wendy Knight."

"I do. Why?"

"Long story, too long for this phone call. Do you remember who her boyfriend was? You gave her your card, you knew something wasn't right." Angie was talking quickly. "That was a while before though, wasn't it? Were you involved in the investigation when she went missing? Were any possible suspects thrown up then? Did anyone try and contact Jenny? He had an ex-wife, goodness knows what happened to her, that's probably why he took her. I believe—"

"Can I stop you there." Sarah's voice was commanding. "May we go back a few steps please?"

"Yes, yes, of course. I'm sorry, it's just he frightened me today, and the sooner we can give the police something to work with—"

"Stop talking, take a breath and slow down, this isn't making any sense. What's your connection with Wendy?"

"I live in her house, I live in Applegate cottage. I'm so close, I know it's one of three, but—"

"Are you on medication, Angie?"

"Ha! No, I haven't been drinking either, I'm pregnant. I'm sorry, Sarah. Are you sitting down?" When Sarah said she was, Angie drew in a breath. "Do you believe in the afterlife?"

"Are you telling me that Wendy is haunting you?" Her disbelief was apparent.

"No, if only, then I could speak to her. She lets me write about her. I know she was gagged, bound ankle and wrist, and driven away from the carpark in a red car with black upholstery. I know she passed a church and a bridleway. But she won't go back there. It's all about before. About Jenny, that's what started it. I know about his ex-wife, the pub burning down, Tess. But now he knows I know, so I have to get a move on, because I don't know who he is, and he knows it's me. Do you see? It's why I need to know the name of her ex-boyfriend."

Angie paused for breath.

There was silence from Sarah as she scribbled down Angie's words and tried to make sense of them.

Angie thought she'd hung up. "Hello, are you still there?"

"Yes, I was thinking, look—"

"Thinking that I was stark raving mad, I'm sure. I do too. Look, Sarah, I don't want to drag you into this. It's bad enough I've got my mum and my gran involved, but if you do remember the boyfriend's name, that might make everyone a lot safer. Will you give me a call if you do?"

"Um, yes. It was a long time ago. I have to be honest with you. I do think you're . . . let's say emotional. But I'm intrigued. I worked this case and we had nothing. What names do you have, they might prompt my memory?"

Angie could tell from Sarah's tone that she was being humoured but she answered anyway. "Harry Grayson, Colin Anderson and Alan Ferris." Angie waited a beat. "Anything?"

"Possibly. They all sound familiar." The tone of her voice had changed, her interest was aroused, and she added, "Leave it with me,

I'm not on the force anymore, so I'd have to hunt through for my personal notes, and I'll make some calls. I'll get back to you if I find anything. You live in her cottage you say?" When Angie confirmed she did, Sarah wished her good luck and hung up.

Angie fell back on the bed and closed her eyes. She was asleep in minutes.

~ ~ ~

Downstairs in the living room, Margaret sat with the bag of Louise's belongings in front of her. She was nervous. In the past, she had avoided getting this involved, if she could, she ignored the messages which came to her.

She looked at her mother. "I'm not sure I can do this with other people here. Not that I know what *this* is, or will be."

Bridget smiled at her. "We'll leave you alone. We'll get dinner under way. There's no rush my love. Just handle the items in the bag and relax. If there's anything it will come to you. You can't force it, either it will or it won't."

Margaret unpacked the bag and lay the items in a line on the carpet. There were five in total. The coat Louise had borrowed from Wendy, a small gold locket, a well-used leather purse, a small rag doll and tee-shirt. Margaret scanned the objects, none of them meant anything to her, although she was aware of Karen dabbing her eyes. Drawing her shoulders back she gave a decisive nod.

"Are you ready?" Bridget spoke quietly.

"I am. You may leave now." Margaret's voice was charged with emotion, she looked back at the items as Bridget held out a hand to Karen.

"We won't come back in until you call us. This might not be quick. Took me two hours once."

Margaret ignored her. She was staring intently at the objects and wondering where and how to begin.

~29~

Wendy struggled to keep her knees as close to her face as she could; with her toes tucked in towards her backside, she forced her bound wrists towards her feet. She grunted with the effort on occasion, and then stilled in case he had heard, but he continued to sing along to whatever track was playing.

As she continued with her quest to be ready, she stared out of the rear window towards the sky, still holding on to the hope that any information she might gather would be useful. A shadow fell over the car and she realised they were going under a bridge. A red brick archway of a bridge, as they cleared it she noted the sign warning of a height limit.

Another grunt as she replayed the limited information about their journey over and over on a loop as she struggled on.

Church on the right, bridleway on the left, large mirror on the bend fixed to a stone wall, on the right. Red brick bridge, height restriction eleven foot six.

Every muscle in her body ached. Perspiration ran into her eyes and was blinked away to ensure she didn't miss anything. Her heart pounded and her head thumped. The tape stretched a little further, and her wrists now cradled the bottom of her feet, she realised her sensible shoes had to go if she were to succeed and she managed to drag them off by scraping the heels along the side of the car. She knew she was seconds away from succeeding, and then the car stopped. Trees.

He was speaking. To her? Wendy couldn't tell. Her ears were filled with the sound of her own heartbeat forcing the blood around her body at an alarming pace. She fought to regain control, dragging deep breaths in through flared nostrils. The mantra of the landmarks was replaced with: *Please calm down, please listen, please calm down.*

Eventually, she had calmed enough to hear a door slam. He was out of the car. Was he? What else could it be? Not caring if he heard her she screamed the last of her energy into the tape and forced her arms forward. She even laughed when they cleared her feet and the momentum sent them on a collision course with her forehead, such was her relief.

Wendy allowed her arms to relax before clawing at the edge of the tape running between her lip and her nose. Where was he? If he was out of the car, where had he gone? Managing to free her top lip by loosening the tape, she rolled onto her knees and lifted her head. The roaring returned to her ears. All she could see was trees.

Not true. There was a rough stone wall about two feet high, it was crumbling at one end. There was a litter bin. A litter bin? Did that mean they were in some form of carpark? If so, anyone could come. She turned full circle, there was nothing else to see. Had he locked the car? Could she get out?

Kneeling as best she could she shoved her head and shoulders between the back seat and the roof, silently cursing the headrests which impeded her movements. She saw a movement and froze. It was a dog. A dog would have a walker with it.

Move, move, move!

She slid head first onto the back seat, and wriggled until she was all the way through.

Release your feet, release your feet!

Raising her knees, her fingers found the edge of the tape and pulled. It was almost impossible to pull it around to the back of her ankles, and she cried out in agony as a cramp took hold of her thigh. But still she worked at it.

Hurry! Hurry! Hurry!

Finally, she pulled one ankle free of the other, she left the tape dangling from the leg of her jeans. She grabbed at the door handle, wondering which way to run, wondering where he was, and when he would return.

Release your hands, release your hands, release your hands.

That was her mistake. She'd been ready. Ready to open the door and run. To get out into the open and take her chance. Instead, she wasted valuable minutes attempting to remove the gag enough for her teeth to work on the binding around her wrists.

The car door was yanked open and he was there.

"Naughty, naughty, Wendy," He ducked down to peer at her. "This means you'll have to suffer a little more."

His head disappeared, and still working at the gag, Wendy scooted to the other side of the car, all the while watching his midriff. Groaning in disbelief, she saw his hands appear and unbuckle his belt, button almost ripped off, zip lowered. When his hands grabbed the waistband and pulled it down, Wendy forgot the gag and lunged for the door handle.

His head and shoulders appeared. Manic eyes locked onto hers before he lunged forward and punched her in the side of the head as he moved. Wendy's head hit the door frame with some force, and she was still dazed as he grabbed her legs and swung them forward, before pushing them apart and dropping his weight on her body. Her head now buried beneath his chest.

Although he hadn't removed her jeans, his body began a rhythmic thrusting causing the car to rock. Trapped beneath him, Wendy had no idea the dog, reunited with its walker, was now on a lead and approaching the car.

"Oh yes baby," he called with a groan. "Is it good? Is this what you want?"

Wendy screwed her eyes shut. He'd gone mad. How could he be enjoying that? Then he stopped, placing his hand across her throat he pushed himself up. Wendy thought she was going to die. But she was wrong. Not then, not in the car. The pain was excruciating, and barely conscious, she didn't catch his next words.

"Oi! Pervert, fuck off! Can't you see we're having a private moment?"

The walker, embarrassed, gave no response and hurried past, glancing only briefly at the bare backside visible through the opened door.

Pulling his hand from her throat, he dropped back on top of her. "That was close. Now you'll pay, my darling. You will pay." Wriggling down he kissed her forehead. "But I forgive you. I still love you."

Wendy grunted into the gag, and lifting his head away, he tutted. "I can't let you speak. You tell lies. First you tell me you love me - uh oh, not true. Then you insist I forced the whore barmaid to do stuff - uh oh, not true. Then you tell me you're going to see Bernice - uh oh, not true. How could it be? Here you are." He smiled at her. "You are going to die, Wendy. I won't let anyone else have you. But before you go, I'm going to make sure you have some happy memories to take away. Hold still."

Manoeuvring backwards, he got out of the car and pulled up his trousers. "Stay." He commanded as if she were a dog. He walked towards the back of the car and Wendy pulled at her gag again, but he was back within seconds. In one hand he held the picnic blanket and in the other a knife. The look of the knife alone caused Wendy to close her eyes against the evil and pain it promised. "Get out."

Wendy remained where she was. She'd missed yet another chance, she knew what was coming she wasn't going to make it easy for him.

Leaning into the car, he smiled. It was a genuine smile. "I know you're frightened. Roles reversed I'd be the same. The less fuss you make now the easer it will be."

To prove his point, he thrust the knife forward and drew it down her thigh. Wendy blinked at the three-inch rip in her jeans. He'd not cut her, how . . . and then the blood appeared.

"Now, what's it to be? Death by a thousand cuts, or quick and easy."

Wendy allowed the tears to flow as she shunted towards him. She swung her legs out of the car.

"Wait." He made her pause while he pulled the tape flapping from the leg of her jeans. "Stand up, mind your head." He saw no irony in his words.

Once out of the car, Wendy faced him, blank eyes ignored his smile.

"Hands out" came the next instruction, and Wendy held her arms in front of her. He draped the picnic blanket through the loop. "That's better, don't want any nosy parkers thinking you're doing this against your will . . . talking of which. Hold still."

The curved blade of the knife approached her face, Wendy twitched.

"Keep still," he snapped. "How can I kiss you with blood all over your face. I won't harm your face."

Still shaking, but holding her neck rigid the blade was drawn along the edge of her cheek, a little in front of her ear. With his other hand, he gently pulled back one corner, gripped it between his thumb and forefinger and yanked. It ripped away from her face leaving an angry red weal, it then tore clumps of hair out of her head as he yanked again. Rolling the tape into a ball against his thigh he rammed it in his pocket.

"Walk." The blade pointed towards the trees to their left.

"Please don't do this." Wendy's voice was gravelly and she worked her cheeks to create saliva.

"You left me no choice. Be quiet. I don't want to talk to you." The hand holding the knife pushed her forward. "Keep going until I tell you to stop."

Walking slowly, Wendy moved into the trees, her eyes darting right and left, looking for a chance. She was ready. No opportunities arose as she paced forward. Every few yards she would stumble, gasping as her foot was pierced by a sharp stone or twig. Be ready, be ready, be ready. She mouthed the silent words as she walked.

He also remained silent until he told her to stop. When she did, he pulled on the blanket and shook it out as best he could, allowing it to billow to the ground. "Lie down."

As Wendy bent her knees to obey, frantic eyes surveyed the perimeter of the area he'd chosen. She saw the spade first, leaning against a tree. A little to the left she saw a long pile of earth. She couldn't see it, but she knew on the other side would be her grave.

"BASTARD! HELP ME, HELP—"

His foot made contact with the side of her head and she slumped semi-conscious onto the blanket. Laying perfectly still, she kept her eyes shut until the buzzing in her ears receded a little. She made no movement when he sliced through the tape binding her wrists. Then there was silence. She opened her eyes and had to blink several times before she was able to focus. He had removed his clothes and was folding them into a neat pile at the base of a tree. The knife lay at the edge of the blanket an equal distance between them.

"I am ready, I have a chance, am I willing?" Her question was barely a whisper. "YES!"

Pushing herself up on one arm, she threw her body forward. Her fingers had grasped the handle of the knife before he'd fully turned back.

He took a step forward, as always he was magnificent in his nakedness. His eyes found hers. What was that? Fear? Yes, she saw fear!

Emboldened, Wendy scrambled to her knees. She saw his knees bend a little, caught the slight shift of weight onto the balls of his feet. He was going to rush her. Could she take him out before he disarmed her? He had the muscle to overpower her.

Realising what she had to do, Wendy smiled, she knew it would it confuse him.

Although his body was still taut and ready to spring, he cocked his head. "A smile? Do you think you've won, Wendy?"

"I'm willing."

"What?"

"Fuck you!" Wendy raised the knife to her throat. "I have the power to take away your pleasure."

The change was almost imperceptible, but she saw he'd changed his mind about rushing her as his muscles relaxed.

"I'll take no pleasure in losing you. I love you. And by the way, that potty mouth doesn't suit you."

"Fuck off! You don't know what love means. How many women have you hurt or worse, and taken pleasure from it?" she demanded, all the hate and loathing evident in her face. She pressed the blade against her skin. "Tell me."

"You wouldn't understand. They enjoyed it. They liked it." He smiled. "That's why I thought you were special, I knew you wouldn't. You weren't a whore willing to accept that shit for sexual pleasure. I thought you wanted to be loved."

"I did, I do." A calmness had come over Wendy. The hand holding the knife no longer shook, she had no more tears to cry. "If I was different, why am I here? Why is this knife at my throat, and why are you naked?"

Throwing his head back, he laughed. It was genuine amusement. He looked back at her, still smiling.

"Because you lied. Lied well too. I was fooled by you, Wendy. Taken in, hook, line and sinker. I'll never make the same mistake again. You're all whores. No love to give, only sex to offer . . . at any cost." His smile faded. "It's why you're here. I'm going to give you what you want. But you will pay the ultimate price."

"It's not what I want. I want a home, a man who loves me for me, one who doesn't go around picking up women for his own sick gratification. I want babies, I want to be secure in the love of my family. I want the fucking roses round the door. I don't want to be beaten, raped, damaged. I don't want to live in fear of the man who should protect me coming home. That's what I want." She sighed. "What do you want? Truly, from the bottom of your soul, what is it that you want?"

"Shut up," he snarled. "Shut your dirty, lying mouth. You could have had all those things but you threw them back in my face. So now we are here. My dreams, like yours, shattered." He blinked and his tears flowed. "And it was all your fault."

"Because I didn't want to be frightened of the man who claimed to love me?" Wendy shook her head. "You are unbelievable. How can you twist the truth like this? I could have loved you. I have had only you. I gave myself to you." Her laugh was bitter. "Look where it got me. Here on my knees, my grave waiting for me." Her eyes shot to the pile of earth. "How were you going to kill me?"

Her open questions, and the honesty of the situation caused him to falter. Wendy could see he was searching for the honest answers to her questions. His head seemed too heavy for his body, hanging between his shoulders, staring at the ground. Wendy took another chance and got to her feet. His head shot up, and she placed the blade back to her throat.

"It's too late, Wendy. We've come too far." He wiped away his final tear. "WHY DID YOU RUIN IT?" he shouted, his clenched fists raised above his head, and his face turning red with the effort of remaining where he was.

"Because you are a deluded, selfish, manipulating sadist."

Wendy was exhausted. Knowing she couldn't run fast enough to escape him, it became clear that one of them would die today. She didn't want to die, but she also knew she didn't have the courage or strength to attack him. What would he do to her if she tried and failed? But could she take her own life? She had the chance, with the knife pressed to her throat she was ready. But was she willing?

She shook her head, the movement causing the blade to slice her skin. Not enough to kill her, but enough to make her bleed. Her eyes had never left his and she saw the fear again as he watched the trickle of blood make its way to her collar bone.

"Will I take away your pleasure if I do it myself, or doesn't it matter if we poor, undeserving women are alive or dead?"

In the blink of an eye his fear turned to anger. "How dare you!" He roared the words as his body seemed to leave the ground and he flew at her.

Wendy's grip on the knife tightened.

~30~

Elbows on the corners of the laptop, Angie wept into her hands. Wendy didn't make it, and Angie hoped she didn't let him have the pleasure. Nor did she reveal who *he* was. Emotionally drained, even when her tears subsided, Angie remained motionless. Replaying different elements of Wendy's story through her mind. There were no clues. Nothing told her which one of the three men it was. After the scene he'd caused today, Colin was now vying with Harry for the chief suspect spot.

"Angie, are you awake?" Bridget tapped the bedroom door.

"Yes, yes." Getting to her feet, Angie blew her nose as her grandmother appeared. She attempted a smile. "I'm not sure he killed her, I hope he didn't. I think she killed herself to take away his pleasure."

"My poor baby." Bridget held out her arms, and pulled Angie into her embrace. She rocked slowly from side to side as Angie wept. "Let it out. She deserves our tears, our love," Bridget whispered.

"I know." Angie kissed her grandmother's cheek. "Now we have to catch him. We need to put an end to this. To him and his warped view of the world." Turning away from her grandmother, she headed for the bathroom. "I'll wash my face. Then we must get on. How are Mum and Karen?"

"That's what I came to tell you." Bridget leaned against the door jamb as Angie turned on the cold tap, and splashed the water onto her face. "Louise was knocked down deliberately. Your mother saw him smile as he accelerated. He called out, 'Goodbye Wendy', as the car hit her legs and she flew over the bonnet."

"She saw his face?" Angie had turned to face Bridget, and her tears found their way on to her shirt.

"No. Like you, it was a knowledge not an image. But at least we know, and when they catch the bastard it can be added to the charges."

Angie's hand flew to her mouth. "Does Karen know this? How is she?"

"Fuming. No tears, but he'd better hope that when we find out who he is, she doesn't get to him before the police do. She's pacing a hole in your carpet as we speak." Bridget glanced back towards the bedroom. "Did that throw anything new into the . . ."

A sharp rapping of the door knocker stopped her speaking, and she stepped to one side as Angie rushed past and ran downstairs.

"Be careful, Angie," she called as Angie reached the door before her mother.

Angie pressed her face against one of the glass panels and looked at the broad shoulders and neatly cut hair of Alan Ferris. "Shit!" She turned to face her mother. "It's Alan. What the hell is he doing here?" she whispered, and held up her hand to halt her grandmother's progress down the stairs.

"Only one way to find out. Keep quiet. In fact, go in with Karen, we don't want her out here." Waiting until Angie had entered the sitting room, she checked the chain and opened the door a few inches. She smiled as she greeted him. "Hello, how can I help?"

"Hello. I'm Alan, a work colleague of Angie's, is it possible to have a word?" He didn't return the smile, but frowned at the door chain. "Is everything all right?"

"Angie's indisposed I'm afraid. There's been a bit of bother, someone is threatening her. We're waiting for the police, they've told us not to let anyone in."

"Threatening Angie? Never. She's pregnant for goodness sake." He held his hand a little under the chain. "You must be her mum. She told us you were coming."

Margaret shook his hand, withdrawing it as soon as was polite. "I'll tell her you called. I'm sure she has your number."

"Is there anything I can do to help? I can't believe it, poor Angie. Does she know who's doing this?"

"She has an idea, as I say, we're awaiting the arrival of the police, but thank you for the offer."

"It's clear you're not going to let me in. But if it's all the same to you, I'll wait here until the police arrive. I'm fond of Angie, and my presence might deter whoever is threatening her if they come back. What exactly did you say they were doing?"

Huddled behind the sitting room door, Karen elbowed Angie. They'd listened to the exchange. "What's he playing at? He's either a genuinely sweet man, or it's him waiting to see if Margaret is lying," she whispered.

Angie merely nodded as she strained to hear her mother's reply.

"I didn't. I don't think they'll be coming back here tonight, but thank you for your kind offer." Margaret made a pretence of looking at her watch. "The police are due any minute." She heard the sound of a car, and she added, "Is it them?"

Alan turned to look, but the car drove straight past. "No. Are you sure I can't come in? I'd like to help."

"Let him in," Karen whispered. "There are four of us. He can't take us all on. He's not all wound up like Colin was."

"I don't think so. But this has gone on long enough." Angie went into the hall and stepped up behind Margaret. "Is everything okay, Mum?" She peeped through the gap. "Alan. What a surprise. I'm sorry, not a good time, as you can see. I'm not sure why you're here, but can we do this later? Via telephone would be the best option."

"Angie. Are you sure you're okay? Threats, in your condition? I wanted a private word if I may?"

"You may. But not now, we're waiting for the police to arrive."

"So your mother said. I hope they get here soon." Alan glanced over his shoulder. "Not here yet. I understand the security measures," he tapped the chain, "but, whatever your problem is, surely I can have a quick word?"

"No. It's a long story and I will tell you all about it, but now is not the time."

"Okay, but your paranoia is worrying me. I'll wait here for you until the police arrive."

"Paranoia? Meaning? Do you know what, forget it. Sit there all night, knock yourself out!" Angie slammed the door. "What is it with men? In here." She beckoned Margaret and Bridget into the sitting room and shut the door. "Gran has told me about what Mum saw."

She glanced at Karen. "I'm sorry, Karen. I've thought this back and forth and every which way about how to convince anyone that he killed her, although . . ." she flapped her hand, "another time, and the only thing I can come up with is finding the body. The problem is, getting out of the house if Alan is going to stay there until the police, who haven't been called, turn up."

"He'll get bored and go. How do you intend locating the body? Have you seen more clues?" Margaret looked at Bridget.

"Why are you looking at me? How would I know?" Bridget took a seat on the sofa next to Karen.

"I have, and it's not going to be easy, but we need a map of the area. An ordnance survey map would be best, we can work it out by the landmarks." She raised her eyebrows.

"Explain please." Margaret walked to the patio door and rattled it to make sure it was locked. "Better checked in case he comes around the back."

"I know the location of the supermarket, I know in fifteen minutes or thereabouts, the car had travelled past a church, some tall buildings, a bridleway, a bridge, several sets of traffic lights and ended up in a small carpark in a wooded area." She shook her head as Karen opened her mouth. "Now, I know the changes to the roads could have been huge since she was abducted, but he would have stuck to quiet roads. You don't drive through town with someone tied up in the back of your car, covered by nothing but a picnic blanket. That wasn't part of the game, it didn't excite him, he was relaxed when he was driving. Therefore . . ."

"If we find a map, we can try and plot the route," Karen finished the sentence for her. "Have you got a map?"

"No, but I have the internet and a printer."

"Splendid." Bridget got to her feet. "You get cracking, I'm making some sandwiches, there's not going to be time to cook." She went into the hall and peered through the glass panel. "He's sitting on the step. I hope he gets piles." She also hoped he'd heard her as she made her way to the kitchen, and Angie went upstairs to collect her laptop.

When Angie came down, her mother was waiting for her in the hall.

"I've decided I'm going to call the police. We are now on dangerous ground, and I would never forgive myself if something happened to you. We have a good chance of finding this grave, but what then? Dig the poor girl up, or try to convince the police to?"

Angie opened her mouth, but Margaret was determined to have her say and spoke over her. "The latter. So, I don't see why not tell them now. I doubt they will do much at first, and who can blame them, but, they will when we find out where she is buried."

Now she was wagging her finger. "Don't look at me like that, young lady, I have a granddaughter to consider now too. One of those three men has killed at least three people, Colin and Alan have acted strangely today, we only need Harry to turn up and we've had the hat-trick. Whoever it is, is very dangerous. I won't put you in any more danger than you already are." Her hand flew to her mouth. "Alan," she whispered, "is he still there?"

Angie rolled her eyes, and went to the door. She peered through the panel and couldn't see him. Shoving the laptop into her mother's hands, she checked the chain and opened the door. He wasn't there.

"Everyone can relax," she called. "He's gone."

Bridget came out of the kitchen carrying a large plate of sandwiches. "That's strange. I was watching the window, I didn't see him leave. Must have been when I was in the fridge. There's a tray of tea to be brought through."

Angie told the others to eat while she located the correct map. After much deliberation, mainly with herself, she printed off copies of her chosen map. Pulling the highlighter she'd picked up from her pocket, she pointed at the manuscript. "Mum, first chapter, tell me everything relating to the journey."

After several false starts and having printed several more maps the women agreed they had found the most likely journey. Their main issue was the woodland. It was a rural route, and there were several likely places once the other landmarks had been passed. Frustrated, Angie got to her feet.

"Only one way to test this. Karen you're driving."

"Okay. My car?" Karen slipped her feet back into her shoes.

"Nope, mine. I have a hatchback."

"What difference does that make, and why can't I drive?" Margaret got to her feet.

"Because you drive too slowly, and you won't concentrate. The hatchback because I have had the best idea yet. Get your coats on, I'll be two minutes." Angie left the women getting ready and went upstairs and returned with a pillow.

"Is your back playing up? Your mother gave me such trouble. Face presentation, her head was against my spine most of the time." Bridget slung the handle of her bag over her shoulder. "I'm ready."

"My back is fine. I'm going to take this journey the same way Wendy did. Minus the tape."

The others stilled, it was her mother who spoke first.

"Are you sure? It will be harrowing enough without that."

"I am. Get the manuscript, get the map, and unless it's necessary, let's keep the talking to a minimum. I need to concentrate."

Her mother collected the items and, as an afterthought, took the card for the women's refuge. They drove to the supermarket in silence. Once there, they assisted Angie in getting into the back of the car, and made sure she was comfortable, before taking their seats. Margaret sat in the passenger seat with the map, Bridget in the back with the manuscript.

"Everyone ready?" Karen looked around. "Then off we go."

Angie closed her eyes and as they left the supermarket her mind became Wendy's, she was feeling Wendy's emotions. She opened her eyes as her mother told Karen to take the next left. Staring at the sky, she knew they were going in the right direction.

"The church is coming up on the right," Angie called.

Bridget looked out of the front window. "You're right." She spoke quietly and patted Margaret's shoulder as her hand flew to her mouth. She dropped it as they passed the church. Her eyes searching the road ahead.

"Here comes the bridleway." Bridget spoke in unison with Angie.

"There's a right turn coming up, Mum," Angie called after a mile or so.

"But it's not on the map. On the map we marked straight ahead."

"The map is wrong. Wendy was sent off balance by a right turn any . . ."

Karen saw the small unmarked road, which cut across farmland. "Is this right, Angie?" she called.

Angie felt the same rocking sensation as Wendy had. "Yes. Not for long though, what can you see ahead?"

"Nothing. Fields and hedges, not even a barn. Hold on." Karen swerved to avoid a large pot hole. "Oh, wait. There's some sort of track on the brow."

"Left." Angie played the swaying of Wendy's body over in her mind. "Then it's straight on for a while."

Karen turned left and looked at the dirt track which led as far as she could see into the distance. "I think it will be a while too."

Margaret was tracing their journey on the map. "If I'm right, we'll come out by the bridge."

"Should be a bend with the mirror first." Bridget looked up from the manuscript.

Angie remained quiet, Wendy had almost moved her hands to the front of her body. Karen saw the signpost at the crossroads approaching. As they neared they saw the mirror.

"We have the mirror on the stone wall, and the signpost warns there is a height restriction." Bridget looked into the rear of the car.

"How are you doing?" Her heart nearly broke as she saw the tears making streaks across Angie's cheeks.

"I'm okay. Not long now. Tell me what you can see." Angie was expecting a running commentary but the other three women searched the road ahead for something more concrete. "We have to stop in a minute. Her shoes are off, her hands are almost free. What can you see?" Angie's voice was urgent, she couldn't do this again. Like Wendy, her head thumped and every muscle ached from an effort she'd not had to make. "Gran, Mum, Karen, talk to me."

"There's nothing here, love." Bridget twisted her body and took Angie's hand. "Sit up and look. Only the road and—"

"Stop the car," Angie called, "we've come too far. Far too far. She's gone."

Karen bumped the car onto a grass verge, and Margaret hurried around to the rear of the car to help Angie get out. As Angie stretched her aching muscles, she questioned the others, "There was no road or track off this main road? No signpost, wall, milestone, no nothing?" The three women shook their heads. "Then we've missed something."

Margaret walked back to her seat and lifted the map. "Perhaps it wasn't the bridge we thought it was."

"It was the bridge." Angie was definite.

Her mother handed her the map. "I've highlighted the journey we made in pink." Resting her head against Angie's arm, she traced it with her finger.

"But there's nothing there." Angie screwed the map into a ball. "And there was something."

"Twenty-odd years ago. Things change." Karen rubbed her brow. "What now?"

"Now you turn the car around and I'll walk back to the bridge. There will be something."

"I'm not letting you go anywhere on your own. I'll walk with you," Margaret announced.

"Gran, you go with Karen. Drive to the bridge and back again, Mum and I will walk. It's not far. I'm not giving up."

"I didn't think you would for one moment." Bridget cradled her granddaughter's face. "Good girl. Nearly there."

Angie patted her rear pocket. "I have my phone, if you find anything, call me." Taking her mother's hand, they had already started walking before Karen had turned the car. "It's here somewhere, Mum, I know it. We drove past it and she'd gone." She tapped the side of her head.

Her mother squeezed her hand, and they walked in silence. Zigzagging from right to left looking for signs of an old track or road amongst the trees and hedgerows skirting the road. They were almost half way back to the bridge when her mother stopped dead.

Angie turned to look at her. "What is it?"

"Hush!" Her mother's voice was harsh. She remained motionless, her eyes closed, her head bowed. Angie let her hand drop and remained where she was, rubbing her stomach while she watched her mother.

They remained there for several minutes. Angie could hear a car, and assumed Karen and her grandmother were on the way back. Without a word, her mother lifted her head, opened her eyes, and marched off to the left at a determined pace. She left the road, walked over the grass verge, and lifting a low branch ducked into the woodland.

Angie hurried after her. "Wait for me," she called as she untangled a twig from her hair.

"She's over here." Her mother answered without slowing. "It's urgent."

Angie followed her mother for a few more minutes until she stopped at the edge of a small clearing. Looking around, Angie could see the odd lump of concrete poking out of the ground, and then she saw the wall.

"This is where he parked." Whispering she walked to stand next to her mother. Lifting her hand, she pointed. "There's the wall, the bin should be . . ."

Angie swung her hand to the left, there was nothing but a clump of overgrown grass where the bin should have been. Walking forward she kicked at the clump of grass. Her foot made contact with a hidden rusting metal pole. "Here's the support for the bin. That means the grave should be over here." Arm outstretched, she turned to where the spade had been resting against the tree and her hands flew to her mouth, stifling a scream. "Oh my God. Mum, look."

A little behind the tree was the outstretched body of Harry Grayson. His eyes were open staring sightlessly into the branches above him. His arms were flung out to the sides, and near his right hand was a knife. Angie only glanced at the vicious gash which gaped open above the neck of his yellow sweater. She turned away and threw up.

“It's Harry.” She wiped her mouth with the back of her hand, grabbed her mother's arm as she attempted to walk forward. “No, don't. Now we have to call the police.”

“Call them. She's here. She wants me to go closer.”

Angie released her mother's arm and pulled her phone from her pocket, dialling the emergency services. Her phone bleeped, there was no signal. Turning to tell her mother, she saw her stoop down by Harry's feet and lift something from the ground. Swallowing back her fear, she went to join her.

“What have you found? We need to get back to the road, we need to call the police, there's no signal in here.”

Margaret's hands trembled as she unfolded the sheet of paper. In the same childish hand used for Angie's note, they read the simple message.

I'm sorry. I loved her.

“Wow. Perhaps guilt caught up with him.” Angie took her mother's hand. “Let's go. We'll call the police and we'll wait in the car. Gran will be worried.”

Margaret glanced back at Harry with a shudder. “Guilt or fear of exposure.”

~31~

"You're some sort of medium, then?" The detective balanced on the arm of the sofa looked sceptical.

"I don't know what am I. I'm sorry but I can't say this in any different way. I wrote what I thought would be a story, and found it to be true. I've since spoken to people who were around at the time." Angie pointed at Karen. "Karen being one of them, and they verified what I had already written was fact, not my imagination." She thumped the arms of her arm chair. "Stop asking me the same bloody questions. It won't change. You have the manuscript."

Detective Inspector Frank Tipper looked at the dog-eared pile of paper at his feet. "We do." He flipped back several pages in his notebook. "I'm going to recap ladies, and then I'll leave you in peace until the morning." A smile twitched and was gone.

"The body of Harry Grayson has been taken for post mortem, and it appears his throat was cut by his own hand. You believe the note," he tapped his pocket, and the plastic bag holding the note crackled, "was his admission of guilt to the murder of Wendy Knight who disappeared in nineteen-ninety-four. And you are suggesting we dig up the area beneath where his body was found and we will find the body of Wendy." He looked around the four women, as they agreed. "Ms Ellery is the only one of you who knew Wendy Knight at the time of her disappearance, and Mr Grayson was also known to her."

"I hope you're not suggesting Karen did it." Bridget straightened her back and glared at him.

"I'm simply trying to get my head around the fact you knew where to find a twenty-year-old grave." He raised his eyebrows. "If indeed there is a body there."

"Well you and me both. But it bloody happened. Will you just look, what's it going to cost to have a couple of blokes with shovels dig around. If we're wrong, arrest me for wasting police time. I would love to be wrong, but I was chosen to be her witness for a reason. That girl needs to be laid to rest." She looked at her grandmother. "Will she be okay now Harry is dead? Surely, it's what she wanted, isn't it, for him to pay for his crime?"

"You'll sleep peacefully tonight." Bridget smiled at her.

"I'm not so sure." Margaret shuddered. "I think they need to recover the poor thing, I'm not feeling peaceful, are you?"

DI Tipper rubbed his thumb and forefinger across his eyes. He had a body with its throat cut, a group of women claiming to be in touch with the dead and therefore possible witnesses to a murder in ninety-ninety-four, and the key witness was only eight at the time. He got to his feet.

"I have to go now, I'll come and see you in the morning." He stooped to get the manuscript. "Oh, and no talking to the press should they appear, it would be best if . . ." His phone rang and he checked the screen. "Excuse me, two minutes." Stepping out into the hall he pulled the door closed behind him.

"Oh shit," hissed Angie. "I didn't even think about the press. I don't want everyone knowing I'm part of a group of . . . weirdos."

"We are not weird. But it's true it will do us no good at all," Margaret agreed.

"I'm going to have to move again." Angie rubbed her stomach. "Sorry little one, but you don't get to sleep in the cot here."

"We must ask the police to be quiet about it. There's no need to release the detail of our involvement, we could have happened across the body while out . . ." Bridget fell silent as the detective put his head around the door.

"I'll be back in the morning. I need to go now, they did find remains at the site." His face was grim, but to his surprise the women smiled, and he shook his head in disbelief. "No press, no discussions with anyone. An officer will be coming to join you, I can't see any point in holding you all at the station. But no one leaves until we've spoken tomorrow, is that understood?"

"But Karen has no things with her. I have a fold-up bed but she'll need . . ."

"I have things in the car. I always keep a change of clothes ready to go, in case filming runs over and I haven't got time to get home." Karen smiled. "I'm happy to stay if you'll have me."

DI Tipper smiled. "That's that sorted. DC Bowden will be—"

"Oh, good. Helen is a nice girl." Margaret smiled.

"You know her?" DI Tipper stepped back into the room.

"She came about the rat. Angie told her about the notes and threats too, that's how we knew we had to find Wendy quickly - what?" Margaret looked puzzled as the detective tutted and placed the manuscript on the arm of the chair before pulling out his notebook.

"Just you." He pointed at Angie. "You didn't think this was relevant?"

"Connected, but Harry's dead, so we're no longer in danger." Angie raised her eyebrows. "Seemed pointless to waste your time."

"Shall I be the one who decides what's pointless? From the beginning and with as much detail as you can." He flipped open his notebook.

Angie told him about the threats and confrontations she'd experienced since she started writing Wendy's story. Explaining how they knew one of the three men was responsible, but only discovered it was Harry when they found his body on Wendy's grave.

"So," she concluded, "it's not an issue anymore. Although they were connected, Harry clearly realised we would find Wendy, and who knows perhaps there's some evidence there that would expose him? Or, perhaps he believed Wendy would show us who took her." She sighed. "Either way, he's gone and as a result so has the threat."

"Where can I find Ferris and Anderson?" Tipper looked at Angie over his glasses.

"Why?"

"Because they are now part of the investigation." His tone indicated that much should be obvious.

"But, then they have to be given the whole story, and I'd be grateful if our involvement didn't come out. We've done what was necessary for Wendy, I don't want people pointing and staring while I'm on set." Angie grimaced. "Or worse, keep getting asked to contact someone's dead relative."

"I can understand that, but the fact remains the interaction between you and Grayson may become relevant, and then I'll need to speak to them."

"You think I killed him?" Jumping to her feet, Angie stood arms akimbo in front of him.

"No, Miss, I don't. I think I've got to be able to explain all this somehow. The more information the better. How do I contact them?" His tone was sharp.

"Poppet, sit down. We've already had a bugger of a day, I'm sure they'll be discreet, if necessary." Karen pulled her phone from her bag. "I have no idea where Alan lives, but I have both their numbers and Colin's address. Are you ready?"

Ten minutes later, Tipper had gone and DC Helen Bowden sat at the kitchen table with the four women as they waited for their Chinese to be delivered. Angie got to her feet when Ryan called.

"I'm not telling him. Not yet." She wandered into the hall trying to keep her voice light. As she hung up, there was a knock at the door. A woman smiled at her and held out her hand.

"Sarah Clarke." She held up the tote bag she was carrying. "I've found some bits on the Wendy Knight case, and although I've yet to hear from my contact at the station, I thought I'd pop round and see if any of it helps." She studied Angie carefully.

"You've also come to see exactly how crazy I am. I can tell. Well, join the queue it's only going to get longer. Old Bill is the only . . ." She hit her forehead with the flat of her hand. "Bugger. He doesn't know." Angie pulled her coat from the hook. "I have to go and see a neighbour. He'd want to know we've found her." She paused as Sarah looked mystified. "You don't know either." She pointed towards the kitchen. "I won't be long. Go on through, they will bring you up to speed."

Angie buttoned her coat against the wind as the first splats of rain fell. Pulling up her hood, she held it under her chin to stop the wind from blowing it down. A brief warmth flushed through her body, and puzzled, she paused. It was what had happened when they were nearing the grave. Was Wendy back? Suddenly, the heavens opened, and ignoring the thought, she put her head into the wind and hurried towards Old Bill's home, wishing she had his telephone number.

~32~

Sarah Clarke greeted her old colleague, Helen Bowden, and introduced herself to the other women.

Margaret got to her feet to make her a drink. "Take a seat. Tea, coffee or there is wine, not much to celebrate, but at least he's gone."

"Would you bring me up to date please. Angie mentioned you'd found Wendy's body. Is that true?"

"It is." Helen Bowden confirmed. "No offence, ladies, I can't get my head around how, but once they'd removed the body, they started digging as suggested, and they found human remains. No confirmation on anything other than that though. It might not be Wendy, but these ladies are convinced it is."

"Moved what body?" Sarah frowned and rummaging into her bag, stacked several notebooks on the table.

Helen eyed them. "Shouldn't they be in evidence?"

"No, the official ones are. These are the notes I made once the case was put on the back burner. I carried on poking about in my spare time for her father." She placed her hand on the stack of notebooks. "Only for a couple of weeks, but it was the right thing to do." Her eyes challenged Helen. "I doubt anyone would care now. What body?"

"Harry Grayson, ex-pop star, Kelvin from The Village, it seems he went to her grave and killed himself." Helen looked around the group. "The media are going to have a field day once this gets out, and if they find out about . . ." Unsure what to say she flipped her finger between Margaret and Bridget.

Sarah Clarke frowned and sat at the table lifting the top notebook. "Nothing I ever came across linked Wendy with Grayson. I met all the main suspects and he wasn't one of them." She flipped through several pages. "Damn. Where is it?"

"What?" Helen leaned forward.

"You look worried. There is no need to be worried dear. It's all over bar the shouting." Margaret placed the mug next to her and patted her shoulder.

"I don't think so. I recognised Harry Grayson's name when Angie mentioned it, not because it was part of the investigation, but because my sister had a crush on him. If he had been involved in any way there's no way I would have forgotten. I . . ." Sarah fell silent as she read through her notes, shaking her head and flipping pages rapidly. "Here it is."

"What?" Bridget knew bad news was coming.

Sarah flattened the notebook on the table. "As Angie suggested on the phone, Wendy's father wanted her ex-boyfriend brought in for questioning. He was. But, not only was he not in Bristol that day, but he didn't want us to stop looking for her either. He kept badgering the DCI. And I quote, '*I did so much damage to that poor girl, because I was a coward, I did love her, but I knew deep down it couldn't work*."

"That's not what Angie says. He was kidding himself that she'd want such a life. He couldn't understand why Wendy thought differently."

"He was kidding himself for years, it was Wendy loving him and he her, that he realised . . ." Sarah Clarke turned to look into the hall. Someone was hammering on the door. Margaret hurried to answer it.

"Ladies," Tipper marched into the kitchen. "We're going to have to find you somewhere else to stay. I'm sure there's nothing to worry about, but better safe than sorry."

Bridget was on her feet. "What isn't a worry?"

"Grayson was murdered. He couldn't have made that wound himself. He also has sticky residue around his wrists. He was bound before being killed I'm told. And if that's the—"

"Hush!" Margaret pushed past him and grabbed Sarah's hand. "Who was it? What was his name?"

"Alan Ferris."

Karen threw her hands into the air. "But Alan is gay."

"That's what I was going to tell you. He finished his relationship with Wendy because he was gay. He'd been in denial. He said something like, I thought if I found a nice girl to settle with, I'd change."

Bridget marched into the hall. "I'm going to call Angie. She needs to know. Karen get the car, we'll go and pick her up."

"Pick her up from where? I told you all to stay here." Tipper turned to Helen Bowden his anger apparent. "You let her go out? Which part of my instruction didn't you understand?"

"You can sack her later. Angie's not answering her mobile." Bridget waved her own phone at him. She looked at Margaret. "Do we even know where Bill lives?"

"Down the road. Middle cottage of a rank of three apparently. I'll go, my car's outside. I can't believe he's still alive? You lot stay put. Bowden!"

Helen Bowden jumped to her feet and followed him out.

"He read it." Margaret murmured and stood on the doorstep watching his lights disappear down the road.

"Can I read it?" Sarah Clarke came to stand behind her.

"The police took it. But Wendy's boyfriend was absolutely not gay. It is not why they split up. Although, if he was, he tried to get over it by bullying, intimidation and the abuse of women." Margaret shivered as the wind picked up. "Perhaps it's why he was such a bastard. Ask Angie to print you a copy when she gets back."

"That's what her father said, but he definitely had a boyfriend when we caught up with him, we had no evidence against him, and it appeared he had no motive."

"Did anyone contact Jenny? She would have put you right. What a clever manoeuvre." Bridget shook her head. "I can't wait to hear what Angie thinks."

"We didn't contact Jenny as far as I know. I tried, but the number I had for her was a shared house. She didn't leave a forwarding address." Sarah sounded defeated and Margaret turned to her.

"Did you bother to find out what his ex-wife had to say?"

"He'd been married?" Sarah shook her head. "We didn't know that either."

"You didn't know much it seems." Karen pushed open the door to the sitting room. "I'm going in here. What a smart little shit Alan Ferris was. He must have been feeling so smug until he realised what was going on with Angie. I think it's my fault too, I left a note about it on the script." She sighed as she slumped on the couch. "At least they can get the bastard now."

Margaret stepped out onto the doorstep and looked down the road. "Where are they?"

~33~

Concentrating on not losing her footing in the dark, and battling to keep her hood up in the wind, Angie neither heard nor saw the car on the opposite side of the road. It pulled off the drive of one of the new town houses, and followed her.

Alan Ferris smiled. The houses would begin to peter out in a moment, then she'd be exposed. He had no idea where she was going at this time of night, but he was glad to be on the move. It was time to silence the bitch once and for all. The car purred along quietly and slowly. The houses on the left stopped, he knew there were a couple more on the right, and then nothing for half a mile or so. That's where he'd get her.

Without looking, Angie stepped out into the road, and although he was nowhere near close enough to hit her, he stopped dead, frowning. The frown became a snarl when he watched her head for one of the houses on the right. He'd thought she was going for a walk.

"Shit!" he cursed and accelerated as the door opened and Angie stepped in. He drove past without a sideways glance and turned the car around half a mile or so further down, then turning around, he drove back to the house Angie had entered. He pulled over a little way past the row of houses, ensuring Angie would have to walk towards him. Adjusting the rear-view mirror, he settled back with a sigh.

Angie stayed only ten minutes; having delivered the news to a tearful Bill, she promised to go back and see him the next day. Bracing herself against the wind, she headed back up the road, wondering whether to tell Ryan about the latest turn of events when he called, or if it would be best to wait until he returned home. She was surprised when the passenger door of a car opened and her name was called. Placing her hand on the top of the door, she ducked down to look in.

"Alan. Have you come back? Sorry about earlier, I can tell all now, although you won't believe me, so brace yourself. Come back to the cottage."

"Sounds intriguing. Jump in, it'll be quicker and warmer." Alan smiled.

"Thanks, glad the rain has stopped. To say it's been a day and a half, is an understatement." Angie clicked her seatbelt into position. "I'm knackered, shocked and—"

"Shut up, bitch"

Alan's fist connected with the side of Angie's head, with as much force as he could muster. Angie's neck made a sickening cracking noise, and her head collided with the window. Still dazed, he'd already taped her wrists together when she started screaming.

"I said, shut up!" Tearing a strip of tape free with his teeth, he pinned her head back against the headrest by pressing his left forearm across her throat, and slapped the tape over her mouth with his free hand. Dropping the tape into the footwell, he accelerated away.

Angie drew air in through her nostrils, and experienced the same sensation of panic as Wendy had, when tears began to well. When she swallowed she could taste the blood from the wound made in her lip when he'd hit her into the window. As the car sped past her cottage she could see DI Tipper standing on the doorstep. She screamed her frustration into the tape as Alan laughed.

"Who's that? Not the husband, so I'm assuming the police have finally turned up. Poor old Harry. Did you see him? Did you see what you made me do to him?" He turned to face her. "ANSWER ME!"

Angie cowered as he bellowed at her. She nodded frantically and a smile played around his lips.

"He cried you know. Even Wendy didn't cry, bless her, she was so brave, she surprised me."

Angie grunted into the tape.

"I might take it off later. Not sure you have anything to say that I want to hear. But you'll pay for wrecking my life. I've spent years, fucking years, pretending to be a shirt-lifter. Fending off unwanted advances, making passes at men who I know will reject them, humiliating myself. But it worked. I can go out of town when I want some real fun," he wiped his nose with the back of his hand, "now you've ruined it. You've smashed my life to pieces, and I'm going to make you pay."

Angie realised he was crying. She grunted into the tape. Blood was rushing around her body so fast she could barely concentrate on his words. She felt faint and her nostrils flared as she tried to draw in a deep breath.

"Pack it in. You sound ridiculous. You are an intelligent and apparently psychic young woman, you know it's a waste of energy. Wendy realised that I'm sure." Banging the steering wheel with the flat of his hand, he turned his head to look at her. "Why didn't you listen? Why do you fucking women never listen? Now I'm going to do something that will live with me forever. I don't want to kill that life inside you. But what choice do I have?"

Nausea hit hard and Angie gagged. Her mouth filled with saliva and bile which she tried to swallow. She began to choke. She swung her arms wildly as the liquid forced its way down her nose. The horn blaring as Alan swerved onto the wrong side of the road didn't reach her as panic took hold. Her body was jolted back against the door as he corrected the car's position and he ground to a halt on a grass verge.

"You feeble bitch. Don't you throw up in here." His movements were swift and accurate. Turning swiftly in his seat and lunging forwards, he placed his left hand on her shoulder. With his right, he released the seatbelt, opened the door and yanked the tape from her mouth as he shoved her upper body out of the car.

Coughing, spitting and spluttering into the wet grass, her feet still hooked over the door frame, Angie gasped for air. Running around to the passenger side of the car, Alan grabbed her by coat lapels and yanked her forwards. Scrambling to get onto her knees to protect the baby from more trauma, Angie struggled against him. Pushing her feet against the car she surged forward, flipping her body onto her back as she did so. Alan lost his grip, and pulling his foot back, tried to kick her, he missed which left him off balance.

"*Be ready, be willing, take your chance.*" Wendy's mantra was on repeat in her mind. To stop it, she shouted, "Okay. Enough. I won't scream, I'll do what you want, just leave the gag off. If I'm going to die, at least let me have some dignity for God's sake. Like you did with Wendy."

Having regained his balance, Alan was moving forward to hit her again, he stopped dead, his head inclined.

"I'm curious about that." From his pocket he pulled a knife, pressing the catch with his thumb, the blade flicked out, and he pointed it at her. "Let's have a little chat. But make no mistake, the first, second and third cut will be to your belly. Only when I see the baby will I start on you." He smiled. "Agreed?"

"Of course. What do you want to know?"

Angie was panting in time with her heart beat. Still on her back she felt the wet grass soaking her jeans, and knew she was willing to do whatever it took to save her baby, but she had no chance to take, even though she was ready. Unsure how long they had been out of the car, she was sure no one had driven past them as yet, if someone did she needed to be ready. How could she be ready flat on her back behind a car?

Alan took a step closer and stood looking down at her.

There it was. That glint of amusement despite the seriousness of the situation. She closed her eyes and there he was looking at Wendy. Unlike Wendy she didn't react.

"Open your eyes." He dropped onto his haunches and rested the blade on her belly. "If I can see your eyes, I can see if you're telling the truth."

Angie obeyed. "I won't lie. What would be the point? Will you let me sit up?" Flinching as several heavy raindrops hit her face, she added, "Please, Alan. Surely that's not too much to ask."

Pushing himself upright, Alan transferred the knife to his left hand, and grabbing the tape which still bound her wrists, he pulled her to her feet. Angie was amazed her legs held her weight. Thunder sounded overhead, and the rain became heavier, Alan grabbed her arm and pushed her against the car.

"Keep still, don't want any accidents." After a hesitant start, he flicked the knife up the outside edge of her sleeve, it cut through the fabric like a paperknife through an envelope. "And perfectly still." He cautioned as he reached the shoulder and used a sawing action to cut through to her neck. "Good girl." He watched as the front of her coat flapped down to her knees. Moving quickly to the other side he repeated the action, and with one quick tug removed her coat. "You didn't think I'd let you take that mud in there? Get in and fasten the seatbelt. Move it!"

Angie glanced around the car as she fastened her seatbelt, at that moment the only way she could think of stopping the car would be to try and grab the handbrake, steering wheel, or gear stick. Any of which could cause damage to her, and more importantly the baby.

Slamming his door and brushing rain from his face he stared at her for a moment. "Any funny stuff and I'll push you out again. Next time the car will be moving, we're going for a ride."

"I'm not stupid, Alan. I know you mean what you say."

The car increased in speed and his laugh was hollow. "Oh yes, tell all. How is she contacting you? What lies has she been telling?"

"I don't know. I sit at the laptop and I type. The scenes appear in my mind and I type what I see." Hearing the tremor in her voice, Angie coughed. "I didn't even realise it was real . . . or Wendy's version of real of course," she added quickly. "I thought it was my imagination."

"Interesting. I suppose she chose you because of the cottage. I hate it by the way, I considered torching that too, but thought it would be too obvious. I . . ."

"Why aren't you surprised? This has freaked me out, even when it was just a possibility. Even my husband poo-pooed it, or thought I was losing my marbles, as have I at some points. So, why aren't you surprised?"

It was Angie who was surprised, when he clenched his fist and flicking his hand hard towards her, punched her in the chest.

"Don't interrupt me again. Final warning. Understood?"

"Sorry." Looking into her lap, Angie added, "It won't happen again."

"Is the correct answer!"

Angie watched his hands relax on the wheel.

"And as a reward, I'll answer your question." He drew in a breath and glanced at her. "First, east or west?"

Looking out through the windscreen Angie realised they were approaching the motorway. Wendy would have known that, Wendy knew to take notice. Angie knew she had to up her game. "Does it matter?"

"Nope. Thought you might like to choose though. I call west. I know some nice little haunts down in Somerset, Devon too, come to that." He barked a laugh. "Talking of haunt, that's how I knew. The bitch has been haunting me."

Angie turned her shoulders towards him, all thoughts of watching for landmarks forgotten. "How?"

"By being there," he waved his hand back and forth over the steering wheel, "by being here." He gripped his forehead. "There have been occasions when I thought the bitch would drive me mad."

The man thought he was normal. There was little Angie could say to that that wouldn't earn her a punch or a slap. "She doesn't speak to you either then?"

"No. Too spiteful for it to be that straightforward. She's messing with us. You and me both. How much easier would it have been for us if she'd simply entered into dialogue? But no, too easy, let's make them suffer. Well I did suffer, for years. Didn't you have a million questions? Don't answer that, of course you did. Well so did I." He hit the indicator and floored the accelerator and the car flew past a queue of lorries. "Let's open her up. She drives like a dream." Wendy forgotten for a moment, he stroked the steering wheel.

Angie looked at the signposts and an idea sprang to mind. Here was her chance. She knew there were cameras all the way along the second crossing. Lifting her taped hands, she pointed at a signpost.

"The second Severn crossing. You had a conversation with a very nervous Jenny about that. Just after you asked her if she was after a threesome, do you remember?"

"Fuck." He laughed. "You really do know. Funny thing that. I liked Jenny, really liked her, not marriage material, of course, but she too disappointed me come the end."

"She liked you too. You were simply too physical for her, and then of course she found she really liked Wendy. I've never been over this bridge, crossed the old one a couple of times years ago, but never this one. Have you?"

Hoping the desperation in her voice didn't sound as clear to him as it did her, Angie read that the exit for the bridge was now only half a mile away. Her feet tapped against the flawless carpet as the countdown began for the exit. They stilled when he hit the indicator and crossed two lanes to join the road for the bridge.

He glanced at her. "Call me soft, but one last wish and what have you."

"I don't think you're soft, you're . . ."

Unable to concentrate, when her phone began vibrating in her back pocket, Angie was unable to complete the sentence, and her mouth opened and shut as she tried to focus. Her grandmother had called while she was at Bill's and she'd set it to silence, knowing she would soon be heading home.

"Finish the sentence. I'm intrigued to know what you think I am."

"I . . . I, was going to say misguided, but I think - from what Wendy has communicated of course - that you tried too hard. You put too much pressure on yourself, and as a result on those you cared about." She turned her head to look at him. "Am I wrong? Did I misinterpret what I saw?"

"That depends on what you saw? Tell me. Looks like we'll be here for a while, bad idea this, Angie. I shouldn't have listened to you."

Angie caught the edge in his voice. Exactly as Wendy had, and knew she had to appease him to stop the bubbling anger overflowing into the car. A van blared a horn as Alan cut across three lanes of traffic to join the shortest queue for the toll. Angie flinched as he thumped the steering wheel again.

"No bloody change. Angie, Angie, Angie. You really have made a bad choice." He swivelled in his seat. "How do you turn around? Or have you got some money in those baggy trousers of yours?"

"Nothing. Sorry. I thought you had to pay the other way. I thought it was pay to get out of Wales, not to get in." She scanned the row of kiosks. "You can pay by card. Have you got any cards on you?"

"Good thinking. I do have a card." He grinned at her, and she saw the tension lines at the bridge of his nose disappear. Shifting in his seat, he slid a slender business card holder from his back pocket, and pulled out a credit card. "I suppose I shouldn't use this. They'll be able to trace it, but too late for you of course."

Lifting her taped hands to bang her forehead, Angie groaned. "We don't need to do this. You don't need to do this. They don't know about you. I didn't know about you until you took me. Everyone thinks it's Harry." She stared at the roof of the car. "We can sort something out. Please God, tell me we can sort something out."

"God? You don't strike me as the religious type. Anyway, too late for him, he's not going to be able to save you."

"I promise you, on my child's life, I won't tell anyone about this, about any of it. If we talk this through we can come up with a plan. No one knows, no one needs to know. I promise. Alan, think about it, I got into your car willingly, I had no clue you were involved. No one knows you took me, we can come up with a plan, and go home."

The car was now stationary and Alan rested his head on his hands, which gripped the steering wheel, and he laughed. It was genuine amusement.

"I'm not stupid," he managed to sputter. "You've been through all this, and you expect me to believe that." The laughter stopped abruptly, he turned his head to face her, and cold eyes pinned her to her seat. "Every fucking woman I have ever known has lied to me. They all paid, in one way or another. But you take the prize, Angie, you take the fucking gold medal. I know you are desperate, but did you seriously think I'd believe that?"

"I never set out to do this. It wasn't in my control." The first sob escaped. "I should be thinking about becoming a mother, having a family, not chasing ghosts, and now . . . now . . . this! I don't care what happens to you, my only concern is for my child." Her chin hit her chest and she sobbed quietly as the car inched closer to the kiosk.

"Stop crying, it's irritating. I can see that Wendy put you in this predicament, and I'm sorry, I really am, but as a wise man once said, we are where we are."

Sniffing, Angie turned in her seat to face him. "So, you kill me and my baby. What then? Suicide? Go on the run? WHAT?" She bit back the insult that was to follow.

"Not sure." His shrug was casual, they could have been discussing where to go shopping. "On the one hand, I could get rid of you and go back and face it out, I've done that before. Or I could go with you, I'm so fed up with this life. Pretending to be a feeble, stereotypical gay pushover is hard work. My acting skills are ten times better than those idiots we have to work with every day." Blowing out a frustrated breath, he snapped, "You have only yourself to blame. If—"

Unable to keep her temper any longer, Angie linked her fingers and punched him as hard as she could in the arm. With her wrists taped, and in her sitting position, it had little effect, other than to surprise him, and his amused eyes watched her rant.

"I didn't have any control! You know that, you stupid sadistic bastard. I have no idea how your brain is wired, but you must see that. What is it you want? Control? Superiority? Why did you do it? Why did you fucking kill her instead of moving on? It was a step too far, look at the lives you ruined - for what? So she wouldn't shag anyone else? There are thousands of other women who would have taken you on. Flaws and all, happy to let you have your *fun*," she spat the word at him. "But no, no, you had to have her? WHY? Did your mother not love you enough? Were you teased at school?"

She ranted on, and with her phone vibrating in her back pocket, she saw there was only one more car in front of them before they reached the kiosk and the attendant who might hear her plea for help.

She saw her chance, she was ready and she was willing. Her heart thundered in her chest as she saw his fist clench. Angie was ready for that too, and she threw her body towards the door as his arm flicked towards her. It was a glancing blow to her shoulder.

"Shut up. Do you want to know about my mother? Do you want to know what it was like being brought up by a whore? Not in the traditional sense of course, she didn't pick men up off the street, no she married a supposedly decent man when I was four. She let him and his friends humiliate her. I watched. She enjoyed it. I ran away eight times by the time I was ten, but she wouldn't leave him." He glanced at the green light and released the brake. "Keep your mouth shut."

Lifting the knife from between his legs with his left hand he flicked out the blade, and held it by the side of his leg. With his right, he held the card through the gap at the top of the window.

"I hope you've got heating in there. Sorry about the card," he called to the attendant cheerily.

"Bloody freezing even with the heating." The attendant held the card machine towards him.

"You do it. Two-one-two one. I trust you." Alan smiled his charming smile.

Lunging forward, Angie put her hands on the one he had holding the knife, and headbutted the side of his face. Screaming for help at the top of her lungs as she did so. She knew it was risky but didn't know when she'd get another chance. Pulling her head back to do it again, he pulled his hand free, leaving the knife where it was, and pushed the flat of his hand into her face.

Her voice didn't travel far, it was whisked away by the cross wind, and lost on the attendant concentrating on punching in the pin number. He did glance down, but assumed it was the radio and went back to tearing off the receipt. Alan didn't know that, he was watching Angie. To be free and clear all he had to do was take the card from the attendant's outstretched hand. But he didn't, he panicked, for only the second time in his adult life, he panicked and made the wrong decision.

Hitting the accelerator hard, the rubber burned and the wheels spun as the car sped forward. The barrier smashed into the windscreen and a cobweb of cracks appeared on the passenger side. The barrier didn't snap as it does in films, but the force at which the car hit it caused it to bend. The rear end of the car skidded to one side as the front ground to a halt. Alan put the car into reverse, aware that the attendant was already on the phone. The car shot back smashing into the front of the car in the queue behind. Changing gear, Alan floored the accelerator. This time the barrier relented and the car shot into the traffic. Seven booths dispensing cars that drove towards the three lanes on the bridge, all seeking their slot. Alan ignored them and kept the accelerator on flat to the floor.

Clasping her belly between her elbows, Angie leaned forward. Believing a crash was imminent she tried to protect her baby.

"See what you've done. You stupid bitch! Why do none of you do as you're told?" he screamed as he swerved around a delivery van and looked at the vehicles dotted along the bridge ahead.

"You did this, you selfish, self-centred bastard. You took her, you took me. You told me you were going to kill my baby, and then me, I . . ." Angie caught the flicker of the blue police light up ahead. She also remembered the knife, now resting along his thigh, and within her grasp. She needed to distract him. "The police. You need to stop now."

"Stop? We're going all the way, Wendy, all the way."

Focused on the road ahead, and the second police vehicle now reversing across the bridge towards them, he didn't notice Angie twist towards him and lift her arms across her belly.

"I'm not Wendy, I'm Angie." Wanting to keep him talking, she looked from the knife to the handbrake, not knowing which would serve her better. She only had one chance. Settling for the knife, she opened her fingers.

"Wendy is dead. You killed her. I don't want to die too, Alan. Stop the car, the police are here."

"I didn't kill her. I was going to, but I changed my mind. I was going to humiliate her, leave her there in the woods naked. She . . ." Glancing in the rear-view mirror, he snorted a laugh. "This is going to be quite a party, Wendy. Everyone's coming out to play."

Not bothering to look, or correct him, her arms flew out and her fingers grabbed the knife. The shock of the loud crack as his elbow found her nose delayed the pain long enough for her to pull herself back into her seat. The blade sliced into the skin of three fingers as she manoeuvred the hilt of the knife between her clenched hands. Jabbing it towards him she pierced his bicep.

"STOP THE FUCKING CAR!" She pulled the knife out, and thrust it forwards again, higher this time.

"Once more, Wendy, and I will kill you," he warned.

"Take your best shot, you sick bastard. I'm not playing this game anymore." To her utter surprise, the car skidded to a halt and he released his seatbelt, turning to face her.

"That's what you said last time, and look what . . ." His head inclined and he frowned, realising she wasn't Wendy.

Angie saw the flicker of fear as his eyes darted left and right, the swirling blue lights closing in. “Give it up, Alan. There's no need for anyone else to die.”

“I didn't kill her. She did it. You know that, she must have told you that?”

“No. I saw you tape her up, bundle her into your car, drive to those woods and pull the knife. I saw you strip naked, for what? Sex or lack of evidence? And I saw her take her chance and pick up the knife. She held it to her throat watching you prepare to rush her. Even if that knife was in her hand at the time, you killed her. Just like you intended killing me.”

“No, I didn't. When I realised I would lose her, that having her alive was better than her not existing, I surrendered. I got dressed, I turned my back and started walking to the car.” Closing his eyes, he smiled. “I thought she might try to kill me. I would have let her.” His eyes opened and he looked at her. “No lying, nothing to lose. I'd given in, I thought she had defeated me. I was wrong. There was no sound of her feet coming towards me, nothing. I assumed she had run off in the opposite direction, when I reached the car, curiosity got the best of me, and I turned back. Wendy was kneeling in the centre of the blanket, her head slumped on her chest.” His tears were now flowing freely, he sniffed and ran his hand across his face.

Angie was aware of shouting outside the car, but her eyes remained glued on Alan, she wasn't going to relax and give him a chance. “I want to get out of the car now. I don't want to hurt you anymore than I already have.” Her voice husky with emotion, she coughed and tasted the blood from her injured nose. “Will you let me get out of the car?”

“Of course, but first I need you to know the truth. I didn't kill her, I loved her, and I held her until she passed. My heart was broken and my life since has been shit. Which I'm guessing you believe I deserve, and you may be right. She was so brave. Not one tear, no complaints, the light simply left her.” He gulped a sob.

“Did she cut her throat like she threatened?”

“No. She cut her wrists, so it took much longer than it should have. Her throat was the best option.” His head jerked to look out of the windscreen as the light from a torch shone into the car. He held up his hands, so the policeman could see he was unarmed. “Wait one moment,” he shouted, and turned back to Angie, his hands remaining where the policeman could see them. “It's time, isn't it?”

Angie nodded. “It's time. Yes.”

His movement was so swift, so unexpected, Angie didn't even have time to shout. Grasping her hands between his own, he tilted the blade and dropped his full weight on it. The blade was so sharp there was little resistance, and after a second Angie's hands were warmed by the flow of blood. Opening her mouth, she screamed, and didn't stop until the police officers ran forward and opened the doors.

“Get this bastard off me. NOW!”

The policeman threw his hat to the floor and ducking into the car grabbed Alan Ferris by the shoulders. “Come on, sir. Enough is enough.” Pulling Alan backwards caused the knife to slice a little more flesh, although it wasn't until Alan hit the ground, that he saw the blood. He shouted for an ambulance, and ducked back into the car. “Hold on, Pete, she's got a knife,” he called to his colleague. Then he saw the taped wrists, the swollen belly, and the state of Angie's face. “Oh.”

“Let me through.” DI Tipper ran towards the car. He didn't see Alan Ferris bleeding onto the tarmac, and he shouldered the officer on the passenger side of the car out of the way. “Angie, are you okay?”

Angie didn't cry, not then, she turned to face him. “I can't release the seatbelt.” It didn't sound like her voice and she shivered. “I'm cold. He cut my coat off.”

“I'll buy you a new one.” Tipper could now see the knife and the blood covering Angie's hands and lower body. “I'll get that knife out of the way first.” Rummaging in his pocket he found a handkerchief. Loosening Angie's fingers, he managed to grasp the handle and slowly remove the knife. He disappeared for a few moments. “Get me an evidence bag. NOW!”

One of the officers held out a bag, and collected the knife. Tipper returned to Angie. “Excuse me.” He apologised as his body pressed against hers and he searched for the release button. He lifted the belt away from her before holding out his hand. “Come on, let's get you home.”

“Is he dead?” she asked as he removed his jacket and slung it around her shoulders.

“I hope so. My car's this way.”

Having settled Angie in his car with Helen Bowden, he went to speak to the officers from the response cars. Giving them a brief resume of events, he concluded, “So, I don't care how far over the bridge we are, this is my case, dead or alive, he comes back to Bristol."

~34~

Bridget and Margaret rushed forward as Tipper helped Angie from the car.

"The blood, are you hurt?" Margaret called frantically, before ignoring it and pulling her daughter into a hug.

"No, I'm not." She held up her hand. "Few cut fingers. I need a stiff drink and a cigarette, but as they're not allowed, I'll settle for a cup of tea and a shower."

"Good girl." Bridget leaned across Margaret and kissed her granddaughter on the forehead. "It's over my lovely, brave girl."

"I know." Angie returned her smile. Once out of the car, a calmness had descended, the shock and fear were gone, only a feeling of disgust lingered. "I need to shower first."

They had reached the hall, and Tipper was the last to enter. He held out a large evidence bag. "All your clothes in there please. We'll talk later." He looked at Bowden. "Make the tea. I need to take this." He pulled the ringing phone from his pocket, but before answering he looked at Margaret. "She wouldn't go to the hospital, you might want to get a doctor to check her over."

Angie ignored them all, and taking the bag went to the bathroom, bolting the door behind her. She dropped each item of clothing into the bag, and switched on the shower. Dried blood covered her hands and her stomach, his blood. Stepping into the flow of water she scrubbed first her hands, then her belly, then every inch of her body before sitting with her back against the bath, the water pounding her head. Then she cried. Silent sobs racked her body as she said goodbye to Wendy. It didn't take long, but when she opened the bathroom door, she laughed as Margaret and Bridget jumped to attention.

"I'm fine. I promise. You don't have to follow me around."

"You were a long time." Margaret was defensive. "We've called the doctor."

"Thank you, there was no need." Angie walked to her bedroom, they followed closely. "Are you going to watch me dress too?"

There was a lightness to her voice and Bridget relaxed. "She's gone?" she queried.

"Oh yes. Everything is over." She saw the silent exchange, and demanded, "What?"

"He didn't die. He's in intensive care, but not yet dead." Bridget took her hand. "I'm sorry."

"It doesn't matter. The police have got him, Wendy has gone, and can be buried." She pressed her hands against her belly. "This one is fine, and kicking like crazy, and I'm looking forward to some boring normality." She pulled open a drawer. "Are you really going to watch? No."

"We've both seen you naked on numerous occasions." Her mother stepped forward and kissed her cheek. "But point taken, we'll wait outside."

"Downstairs." Angie rolled her eyes, and ushered the women out.

Once they'd gone she dressed, and sitting on the bed, she processed this new information.

She'd known Wendy was content the minute Alan Ferris's body hit the tarmac on the bridge. Her body had felt light, and her mind blank for a moment. There were no more questions, no urgency to gather information. But what if he lived? Would they know how Wendy died? Because although he was the cause of her death, it wasn't by his hand, would they know that? He'd killed Harry, though, so one way or another he'd be going to prison for a long time. She hoped that was enough. Pulling the brush through her hair, she decided she'd keep the final revelation to herself. No one need know that Wendy had killed herself, if forensics didn't discover that, then she was happy to carry that secret. It was the least she could do. If he was convicted of Wendy's murder she could live with that.

~ ~ ~

Ryan wiggled his finger and his daughter grasped it firmly. He glanced at Angie. "She's beautiful, perfect in fact." His gaze returned to his daughter. "We need a name."

"I know, to all of that." Angie smiled. It hadn't been a difficult birth, her labour was only four and a half hours, but she certainly hadn't popped her baby out. She was tired and she wanted to sleep. "I'm too tired to decide on a name. I hope they let me out today, she's fine, I'm fine, but I can't sleep in this bed, I need to come home."

"Everything is ready for you. Your mother called, she'll be here by lunchtime, she has to pick Bridget up on the way."

"They're both coming? Where will they sleep?"

"I didn't like to ask, didn't want her to think she wasn't welcome. Don't worry, we'll sort something out." He glanced at his watch, and placed his daughter back in the plastic crib next to the bed. "I have to go now. This meeting will take two hours, three tops, and I'll be back."

"Good luck. Don't rush, I need some sleep, and Mum and Gran are coming."

The door closed, and Angie lay on her side and smiled at her daughter, before drifting off. Sleep came almost instantly, she slept for an hour before the baby demanded her next feed. As she lifted her from the crib there was a tap at the door and her grandmother appeared. She hurried across to the bed and lifted the crying baby into her arms. The child fell silent.

"Hello, Lily. I'm so pleased to meet you." Bridget kissed the forehead of her great granddaughter.

"Lily? Why did she stop crying? Are you a witch?" Angie laughed and got back into bed. "She needs feeding, pass her back, you can have her in a moment."

"Just wind. Look at her eyelids." Bridget held the baby higher, and sniffed. "Actually, not wind, a little more than that I think. Shall I do it?"

"Do what?" Margaret bustled into the room carrying a large, expensive looking shopping bag. She placed it on the bed. "A few bits for Lily? What were you going to do, Mother? Let me see her."

"Lily? Why are . . . Oh hello."

DI Tipper stepped into the room, but hovered near the doorway. "Congratulations', your husband said you'd be here."

"You've spoken to Ryan?" Angie frowned and tried to focus on Tipper, and ignore the giggling going on at the end of the bed, as the two women changed the nappy. "What do you want? Sorry that sounded rude. How can I help you?"

"Ferris is dead. Two days ago, I knew you were in labour so thought I'd leave you in peace. That means no trial, you'll be pleased to hear. Quite a lot of cases closed."

"How? What cases?"

"Hanged. Cowardly bastard killed himself. Anyway it's done, he's history. As to the cases, Wendy and Harry of course, Gary

Williamson, Ferris did set fire to the pub. The hit and run, Louise Jones, your friend's flatmate, and last but not least he confessed to killing his first wife, Bernice Ferris. She wouldn't sign the divorce papers on demand and he lost his temper."

"He did kill her then? He really was mad."

"Yep. The chaps up north have spoken to her sister. When Bernice got back from Vegas, she realised it wasn't going to work, and despite agreeing to give it a go, she called it a day and got beaten for her troubles. Later she met someone she wanted to marry and chased him to finalise things; he refused out of spite. When she disappeared several years later, no one connected it to him. Her body hasn't been found, although he gave a location, the search didn't come to anything. We're also looking into his frequent change of car. I've got a couple of men looking into missing or murdered women around the time he changed them." Tipper pulled up a chair, and held out his arms. "May I?"

Bridget placed the baby in the crook of his arm. "Do you like babies, Detective Inspector Tipper?"

"Love 'em. We've got three. Our youngest is five now." He looked at Angie. "Here's something that will surprise you, although he admitted killing both Bernice and Grayson he refused to admit to killing Wendy. He said she'd killed herself. The body was too decomposed to show one way or another. I wonder why he wouldn't confess to killing her?"

"I think in his own perverted way he actually loved her." Angie grimaced. "I don't care though. All over now."

"The remains are being released for burial. So, yes, nearly all over."

"Can you let us have the details. We'd like to attend." Margaret smiled as he cooed at the baby.

He glanced at her and nodded.

No one spoke for several minutes. The three women exchanged glances, was he going to stay all afternoon?

"I need a cup of tea. Can I get you anything Inspector?" Margaret decided to check.

"No thank you. I need to get going, but before I go . . . and I have to confess I can't believe I'm saying this . . ."

Bridget smiled. "Spit it out, Detective. You've waited long enough."

"What?" demanded Angie. "What's he going to say? How do you know, do you read minds now?"

"Angie, he's come to visit you with news he could have delivered by telephone, and having delivered the news, he's hanging around cuddling Lily. He has something else to say, I would have thought that obvious, no mind reading involved."

"Her name is not Lily. Inspector, what is it?" Angie's tiredness was making her grumpy.

"There was a girl, sixteen. Mandy Jenson, she went missing five years ago. She'd been jogging on the downs, but disappeared without a trace. We stopped working on it after two years, the file remains open though, I wondered if you might like to see her things."

"NO." Angie and Margaret spoke in unison, but Bridget smiled.

"I will." She tutted at the others. "I'm not long for this world Inspector, I've got what, three, five, ten years? I'd like to do something useful if I can."

The baby started to cry, and Bridget took her from him and passed her to Angie. "Lily needs feeding. Time to go Inspector, I have your number I'll give you a call tomorrow."

Looking around the faces of the three women, Tipper knew now wasn't the time. It appeared he'd put a domestic on to brew. He smiled at Angie. "Lily is beautiful. Congratulations once again. Bye all." He hurried from the room.

~ ~ ~

It was a warm July afternoon when, after a short service, Wendy Knight was finally laid to rest.

The congregation was small, Colin stood with his arm around Karen, and on the opposite side, Sarah Clarke stood with DI Tipper, Angie, Margaret and Bridget. Wendy's uncle, Tom Knight, was the only living relative and looked almost as frail as Bill. Their wheelchairs were positioned next to each other ready for the committal.

"So, sad. But as the vicar said, she's at peace now." Margaret took hold of Angie's hand. "We'd better go and rescue Ryan. Lily was quite ratty this morning . . . what has taken your attention?"

"Jenny." Angie pointed at the smart middle-aged woman hurrying towards them. "I don't know how I know, I just do."

Jenny reached the grave as the vicar laid Wendy to rest. She dropped a red rose on to the coffin, and then smiled at Bill, whose handkerchief reappeared and he dabbed his eyes. When the ceremony ended Jenny went across to him and knelt beside him, and his arthritic hand stroked her cheek.

"Come on. Time to go, she doesn't know us from Adam, let's leave them to it." Angie turned away, linking arms with her mother. "Gran?"

"I'll see you at the car. I need a word with the inspector."

"What's she up to, Mum?"

"I have no idea. I'm not asking. If I don't ask I don't have to get involved."

Angie glanced back at her grandmother who was deep in conversation with DI Tipper. Sarah Clarke went to join them.

"I hope it's that easy, Mum. I really do."

AUTHOR'S NOTE

Thank you for reading Witness for Wendy. I hope you enjoyed reading this story as much as I enjoyed writing it. If you did, I'd be grateful if you would be kind enough to leave a review, or contact me with your thoughts and any comments. Constructive reviews are invaluable to authors. If you would rather contact me personally the details are below.

If you would like to read more about the Bearing women, An Unexpected Giftis the next in the series.

ABOUT THE AUTHOR

Having worked in the property industry for most of my adult life, latterly at a senior level, I finally escaped in 2010. I now work as a consultant for several independent agencies, but I dedicate the bulk of my time to writing and, of course, reading, although there are still not enough hours in the day.

I began writing quite by chance when a friend commented, "They wouldn't believe it if you wrote it down!" So I did. I enjoyed the plotting and scheming, creating the characters, and watching them develop with the story. I kept on writing, and Meredith and Hodge arrived. In 2017 the Bearing women took hold of my imagination, and the Bearing Witness series was created. I should confess at this point that although I have the basic outline when I start a new story, it never develops the way I expect, and I rarely know 'who did it' myself until I've nearly finished.

I am married with two children, two German Shepherds and a Bichon Frise, and we live in Bristol, UK.

I can be contacted here, and would love to hear from you:

Website: http://mkturnerbooks.co.uk/
Twitter: @MarciaKimTurner
https://www.facebook.com/M-K-Turner-1888785704701831/

Printed in Poland
by Amazon Fulfillment
Poland Sp. z o.o., Wrocław